Clementine Lane

Eoghan Brunkard

First published in 2021

By

Clementine Lane Publishing

Dublin

Republic of Ireland

ISBN 9-798713022-79-2

Cover design by Gary Nolan & Fionnuala Halpin

Text edited, designed, and set by Coinlea Services.

With Thanks to

Seán O' Maoldomhnaigh

Shane Murtagh

Contact

ClementineLanePublishing@gmail.com

Dedicated to my loving fiancée, Emma, who always pushes me forward. To my parents, Tom and Betty, who gave me, among many other things, my sense of humour, and to a friend, who thought I should have left well enough alone, Shivan.

Contents

Prologue

A SMALL CROW GLIDES PAST THE SPIRES OF ST LUKE'S CHURCH and over the freshly built and somewhat oddly placed apartments that sit beside the small, dingy Cartigan's pub on McDonagh Street. It is here that he enters Clementine Lane in the south inner city of Dublin. The lane, positioned just outside the famous Liberties (an ancient manufacturing centre of the city), is imprisoned on all sides by these new apartments that have sprung up with hidden speed. Filled with "foreigners" (defined as anyone not from Clementine Lane), these titans are slowly gentrifying the area, like moss covering bark. The lane itself is long and narrow, layered with each new generation's attempt to accommodate more and more inhabitants into the city.

At its mouth, standing in two matching rows, are Victorian red brick artisan cottages, two bedrooms upstairs, kitchen cum dining room downstairs, all that was necessary for the small family, though a liberal lust mixed with a conservative Catholicism meant they usually housed a large one. Slowly moving along, the lane widens to facilitate eight rows of high rise three-storied flats from the 1930s. The flats have recently been provided with large security gates, meant for the protection of those who dwell within. Truthfully, these measures really only serve to increase the already existing siege mentality of their occupants. Between these flat complexes lies a basketball court with no hoops and a playground that is perpetually locked to the public. An amenity that the locals cannot be trusted with.

Past these, there is a row of housing built during the roar

of the Celtic Tiger; these are smaller and worse built than their Victorian counterparts but as social housing their price was right. At the street's widest stands a beautiful deconsecrated red brick chapel and accompanying former nunnery dating from 1869. A beautiful cherry blossom sits outside this building, which in April fills the dreary urban landscape with pink petals. However, it is barren now as the New Year is well and truly baptised. Beside this beautiful memory of the past lies in state a concrete warehouse built in the 1980s and now abandoned; it is outside this building where the story must begin.

Arthur Gallagher stood watching from the other side of the street as two council workers fixed a sign to the warehouse gate. It must have been a heavy sign, though admittedly it did not look so: one A4 sized piece of paper, sandwiched firmly between two pieces of Perspex glass. Nonetheless, its weight must have been considerable, as it needed two workers to complete the task.

Arthur simply stared on through his dark framed Morecambe glasses. The quickly darkening evening painted black all around him as he stood still under a streetlamp, which was slowly buzzing to life. The two council workers must have felt that the evening was approaching too; the sign was only cable tied once to the gate before both men decided to call it a night. The second cable tie would have to be accommodated in the morning, when more time could be afforded to such an intricate process. Perhaps the whole morning; who were they kidding? Of course, the whole morning! The two luminously clad men slowly walked back to their van and pulled out of the lane, leaving the sign flapping in the gentle breeze.

As the van passed, Arthur crossed the street into the darkness, his gelled white hair the only thing visible. He moved, surprisingly quickly for a man of his years, to the warehouse gate and studied the new addition. "Oh dear," he whispered to himself.

"Howaya, Arthur?"

The voice behind made the old man jump just a little. He

quickly composed himself and placed his right hand over his left, as was his wont, to hide the mild Parkinson's shake.

"Eh… hello Terry," he said.

"What has you out in the cold staring at gates? Not even nice gates, not gates like the Brandenburg Gate or the Dublin Castle Gate, just shitty warehouse gates?" local historian/taxi driver Terry Walsh continued, with a smile plastered across his small square face.

The old man simply pointed to the sign. "Get the word out, Terry, there will need to be a meeting."

As Terry stood beside Arthur, studying the sign and cursing under his breath, both men were oblivious to a mild groaning coming from beyond the gate. Somewhere, in that abandoned warehouse, something lived, if barely, or maybe not at all, but whatever it was, it groaned.

1.

A Parochial Affair

IT WAS MONDAY MORNING. THREE DAYS HAD PASSED SINCE THAT odious sign had been placed on the warehouse gate, with its foreboding news. It remained hanging limply by one cable tie.

Terry was talking to Marion and Mick Ryan. The former was on her way to work in the local crèche; the latter, unemployed and by his own choices unemployable, felt like an early morning constitutional, and why not? Though admittedly, he probably should have worn a coat over his beloved and perpetually donned Liverpool jersey, as he was feeling a little cold.

"So you'll be there? It'll be on in the old chapel, the padre was good enough to give us the use of it tonight. We need the numbers, folks, we need the numbers, if we're to have a chance against those muck savages in the Council." Terry spoke intently.

"We'll be there." Marion was formidable enough to speak for both herself and her husband. Mick nodded in solemn agreement; it was important to his dignity that he gave an assent, even if he had no real choice in the matter.

Marion continued, "Now don't you go losing the head, Terry, and start shitting on about historic Dublin being ruined. I'm only saying, calm heads will have to prevail, slowly, slowly catch a monkey. Keep it together." The amply sized lady waddled slowly on with her taller, thinner, fitter, though less useful, husband in tow.

Morning turned into afternoon, and as is both tradition and scientific necessity, afternoon gave way to evening. It was time for the meeting and for calm heads to prevail.

***

"It's a fucking disgrace, the same fucking story, always the same fucking crap," Marion announced with authority, though truthfully she wasn't entirely sure if it was the same story; she didn't read the notice of planning. She never did.

Nonetheless, the agitated small group of neighbours sat in silent agreement. They knew Marion Ryan well, and even though they also knew she was easily annoyed and usually ill-informed, her sentiments sat cosily with their own and her anger was reassuring.

"Those arseholes in the Council never give a damn about what they build here, we're a dumping ground," she continued.

This cliché was surprisingly true, she was correct. Since the early '90s, this part of the inner city was a dumping ground. The Council felt that rehabilitation centres, wet shelters and homeless hostels should be situated near the most likely place where people would utilise them. This problematic logic of heaping social problems on areas rife with social problems seemingly escaped these public servants, or perhaps they just wanted to get through their working day the same as everyone else, without incident, without thought.

The purple-haired Marion abruptly sat down, causing her chair to creak. It was already unfair that it was expected to carry this weight, but the sudden movement really just seemed like rubbing it in.

"Thanks Marion, but eh… could you watch the language, some folks brought their kids here, please." Arthur was chairing the meeting. He seemed an obvious choice, a well-spoken gentleman and elder of the area, well regarded by all. Marion's harsh language offended him, as it would have his parents.

The children were a useful excuse, but they weren't listening and heard none of it. They were busy leaning awkwardly on their chairs, one trying to get his feet to touch the ground, the other staring blankly at her phone.

Arthur was afraid of Marion; most people were. What she lacked in informed opinion, she made up for in force of will and general loudness.

The old Convent Chapel was dim and dark in the evening light. The lights never reached high enough to the beams and so they turned the floor into a lit stage. The choir balcony and windows were enveloped in a rich blackness which, even if one focused on it, was impenetrable, a perfect place for others to observe the community meeting in anonymity. Presumably, there was no one there now… presumably. At least, there was not meant to be. Ethereal or real, the only visible thing occupying that space was the unremitting dark. The worn magnolia walls that surrounded the small group of neighbours were decorated in white pages with crudely crayon-drawn pictures of Santa. It was mid-January now but the youth project that occupied the Chapel's time during the daylight hours preferred seasonal art and it would be a while yet to St Valentine's Day.

"I'm a Clementine lad, as you all know, all me life, and I know all you donkeys, and yous know me, I say it as I see it, I'm not afraid to tell the truth when it has to be told. If they load the area with more of these rehab houses, the kids won't be able to play, we'll be terrified that a junkie will have a go or try to sell shite to the kids." Mick Ryan's bass-leavened voice had told several lies in that sentence. He did not tell things as he saw them. He feared confrontation, a trait learned from his 22 years of marriage to Marion. His primary concern was not the children; he barely cared for his own. No, Mick was following unspoken instruction.

Marion was upset for the children. Mick was, therefore, upset for the children.

Shane and Phyllis Farrell's children (they should really be referred to by their names, Sienna and Joe, as, after all, they are people too) were getting bored. Joe was no longer stretching to touch the floor, particularly since Phyllis had become more mindful of his behaviour, and Sienna's phone battery had long since beeped its last. Besides, they had more important affairs to attend to. The two had found a way into the neighbouring abandoned warehouse the previous night and were anxious to get back to explore it. The warehouse was the location under the residents' present scrutiny. It was planned to be felled for a state of the art, if there were such an art, drug rehabilitation residential centre. While the adults gathered to discuss its fate, the two children knew of other news about the building. Other children from the area had recently started to tell stories of groans emanating from the abandoned property. For Sienna, the mystery was becoming too much. The meeting continued.

"While I understand the anger of people here, it is always important to remember that what people are calling 'junkies' are in fact human beings," Fr Matthew began. "We must remember not to lose sight of the human in the addiction." This contemplative, grey-haired, heavily bearded man in his 60s was relishing giving this sermon. He rarely had an audience these days and he meant to take full advantage of it. "We do owe an obligation to these people. They are products of a broken, individualistic society, caught in a cycle of indifference by their fellow human. While the centre is not ideal, indeed, it's not community led and it's being run by some private company, the fact is that these people need treatment." Fr Matthew was sincere in these words, and he liked the fact that he was sincere in these words. The group was respectfully quiet for a moment. The moment of quiet was an advance payment to now ignore the content of his contribution.

Terry Walsh stood up with a sense of drama and urgency.

"There are twenty-three of us here (*there were actually twenty-four*) and there's a good few who couldn't make it. We need to get ourselves together and say to the Council 'no actually, you're not building this here, you bunch of culchie arseholes, this is ancient Dublin, with a rich culture and people, and we won't kowtow to you and your thick culchie ideas, go back to your hedge school!'" He had become increasingly stirred up by the other comments and now wanted to deliver his own O'Connell-style speech which he had been practising earlier in the shower. Seemingly, now was not the time for calm heads to prevail.

He continued, "The fact is, unless you stand up to these people, they'll run riot on ye. We've got the numbers here, we should march on the Council, placards, banners, get the local papers involved, the lot, it's the only thing they understand, they're dopes, absolute, fucking, dopes." Terry's cheeks bullied his lips together in such a fashion that every word he spoke popped with saliva-covered pressure.

Arthur shuddered.

Terry had hit the right note and the meeting had begun to circle into a pit of darkening anger. In succession, speakers voiced similar disdain for local governance, people outside the pale, and the human-like "junkies." The others gathered similarly bemoaned their fear for the future of their children and where they were meant to play. How the (locked up and never used) playground would become a war zone, strewn with heroin-dripping shrapnel. The little group became increasingly emboldened. The initially meek among them swelled with nervous energy to suddenly take the floor and spurt their piece, to be reassured by the others present that they had said the right thing. Truly this was local democracy in action.

Nonetheless, the repetitive comments had become howling like wolves and were producing little by the way of practical dividends. The next step was as murky as it had been when the group started to fill the room. Arthur knew this. He was also tired;

he had wanted the meeting to conclude for some time now and this increasing anger would only serve to lengthen the braking time. Though he recognised Terry as a pseudo intellectual, Arthur saw an opportunity to bring the group back into focus using his words. "Just to bring it back to what I believe Terry said, perhaps we could think on what next steps we should take, to remonstrate our disapproval to the Council. I know Terry spoke of a protest but perhaps it would be wiser to write a letter first? Let them know how we feel and, eh… maybe see how they respond?"

Initially the little group was dismissive but they could see that this was probably the most logical next step, even if they still felt that placing the city planner's head on the Ha'penny Bridge was its most natural conclusion.

"Then it's agreed, I'll draft a letter and one of the lads here can do it up on the computer fella. Well thanks for coming, folks, let's see how they respond and take it from there." Arthur deliberately phrased this as a statement. He, like the children, was bored of debate.

As Arthur marched at a quick pace towards the door, the other locals chatted amongst themselves. Some discussed which pub they would go to; others were inquiring about their neighbour's relatives. The lights of the hall were gradually extinguished. Finally, the last of the little group had left the old chapel and darkness reclaimed the stage. The outside yellow streetlights garishly shone through the dark blue and crimson stained glass, casting a tobacco-influenced variant of the original colours on the floor. There, after a few moments of charged silence, the balcony planks gradually creaked as slow steps moved towards the spiral staircase. A form scarcely distinguishable from the darkness made their way down the stairs. The unseen twenty-fourth had not entered with the group, the group were not aware that they were there. But there they were.

2.

Sides Of A Coin

16th January 2018 (Tuesday)

CONOR MAGUIRE WAS STANDING AT THE TRAM STOP AT ST JAMES'S Hospital. The ponytailed 34-year-old was tired. The damp Tuesday morning did nothing to lift his spirits or wake him from his drossiness. Across the road, he could see Mick, in a Liverpool jersey (wasn't it too cold for just a jersey?), loudly laughing while leaning against Terry's taxi, which was parked. Both men seemed able to stand around laughing with no particular place to be, how was this possible? How could these men support themselves doing nothing? While Conor had to wait there, on what would be no doubt a packed tram that would ferry him to the financial district and his glass cage.

His titian eyebrows narrowed as he thought of these men as his neighbours. The resentment boiled within him. He had to work hard for his apartment on McDonagh Street, though hard work was no longer enough to gain such necessities. A helpful bursary from his father was also required. Unlike these two men, who were gifted a home either by the state or dead relatives, he assumed. Parasite classes, he thought. Conor liked this phrase. It made him feel witty, like the acerbic wit of Oscar Wilde, though truthfully, it had none of Wilde's understanding of society, or his empathy.

Of course, this assumption was wrong. Terry worked nights. People tended not to use taxis too frequently in the mornings; it was an expensive way to travel. While Mick owed his keep neither to the state nor to a dead relative, but to Marion, who was very much a living relative. Both men lived in social housing, this was true, but to be fair, neither had a father who could provide a helpful bursary for a nice apartment either.

The tram came to a gradual stop and Conor boarded, finding himself sandwiched against the window and two teenagers whom he vaguely recognised from the Clementine Lane flats. They acknowledged his presence with a stare that made him uncomfortable. He turned to face the tram window and swayed gently as the tram resumed its course. The teenagers began to converse behind him, their proximity forcing him to be a listener of their conversation.

The first teenager began, "I'm not joking! She told her boss she had dysentery. I think she thought it was the same as diarrhoea. Now that would be grand and all, if it wasn't for the fact that she works in a crèche, so they got the health authority out thinking there was some kind of fucking outbreak. Next day, she goes to work and there's a load of lads in hazmat suits, who told her to shit into a jar."

"Your sister is some dopey cunt, Johnno," laughed the second teenager.

"Don't call my sister a cunt, you spa," the first teenager snarled in reply.

The tone now was noticeably different and it made Conor, once again, uncomfortable. He hated the tram. He checked his phone for messages. There were none; his digital friends, formerly his real ones, must all be in work by now and there was nothing from his parents. As the city passed his window view, he thought about his oncoming day. Eight hours of being belittled by superiors whose intelligence compared meekly with his own awaited him. Well, he thought their intelligence compared meekly anyway, and that thought comforted him.

***

As Conor's tram snaked across the city with him held captive to more stories of the teenager named Johnno and his sister's apparent dopiness, the middle-aged Frank Cantwell was dancing around his kitchen in apartment 3B, McDonagh Street, while making something resembling coffee. The radio blared full blast and filled the audaciously orange-painted room with early 90s pop music, to which the grey haired, pot-bellied man now danced.

Eventually, he sauntered out of the kitchen, past his bedroom where a full-size election poster of himself sat frozen in time above his bed, and into his living room. It was a large white room, where no pictures of family hung but rather framed posters of the great authors of modernity. There was Kafka, Joyce, Dostoyevsky, all famously inaccessible; not that Frank would know, he never read them, fuck that.

Frank turned on the television and started to watch a recorded episode of a reality TV show, which seemed to pit famous sport stars' wives against each other on a desert island setting. These rich spouses were materially satisfied and had little financial need to participate in such degrading shows, but the attention was nice, even if it was at times bad attention. Perhaps that was what was missing in their lives. Who wouldn't eat a plate of spiders for a little attention?

Frank loudly guffawed at the sight of these attention-starved women falling about in mud as some challenge no doubt required them to, his laugh tinged with a hint of rural Ulster. At that moment, his mobile started to hum on his coffee table. Placing it cautiously to his ear, he answered, "Hello, Frank Cantwell, PR man extraordinaire," in a voice more sophisticated than the previous laugh would have indicated.

A voice at the other end was barely audible in the large room/

museum to inaccessible authors.

Frank spoke again. "They're putting what? Where?!"

***

Time had travelled on, and Conor's working day had come to an end. Conor had heard the buzzer but was content to ignore it. It was 6.20 p.m. He had gotten the rather packed tram from the professional and impersonal financial centre at 5.50 p.m. It had been a long ride for him; one of the parasite classes had tried to chat with him the whole ride over. An old man who was clearly drugged and on his way to Tallaght, Conor incorrectly summarised. He actually was drunk and on his way to St James's Hospital. Nonetheless, Conor alighted at the same stop and walked briskly to his apartment before the man could slowly raise himself to see his cancer-ridden brother.

Conor placed his microwavable pasta in the oven (it tasted better that way) and turned on the news. He didn't listen to it but the background noise was company. He started to peruse the various textual conversations on his phone that had been posted during his work-imposed absence, between his friends whom he rarely saw. The actual potential company at his buzzer was unwelcome. This meant the effort of listening and talking, something he felt he had done enough of today, though truthfully he had hidden rather successfully in his cubicle, in the large communal office.

The buzzer kept ringing. It seemed clear there would be no peace. This day was not done with him.

"Hello, yeah, can I help you?" He had hoped they had gone.

"Hi ya, Conor, yeah, I saw you head in there, it's Frank by the way, can I come up? Big news, big and pretty shitty news, Conor."

This was an annoying conundrum; though openly cordial, Conor found Frank Cantwell incessantly boring, always rattling on about some property management committee that was of little interest to him. That said, he was curious about the forthcoming shitty news. "Of course, Frank, of course you can come up." There was nothing guaranteed about this invitation; Conor's curiosity was simply piqued.

"Just make yourself a space there, Frank."

Frank moved the jacket, laying it awkwardly on the couch to one side, and awaited hospitalities that were not forthcoming; offering tea seemed antiquated to Conor. After a period of silence, Frank began. "As you know, Conor, I am the chairman of the property management committee—"

"Chair*person*, can't be having that, Frank," Conor interrupted, thinking himself clever.

"Oh, you're dead right, chairperson. Anyway, we received word that Clementine Lane Residents' Association met last night over a new proposed planning permission at the top of the lane, adjoining ourselves. A new junkie hotel, Conor, the Ritz for those off their tits." Frank was undeniably camp but even in this more open time Frank preferred to keep his business to himself, assuming there was any business to keep.

"Are you sure they read the planning right? It can be hard to read as it's usually in small print and... when you're pissed and illiterate." Conor smirked to himself.

"Now, that's not on, they are our neighbours, ordinary decent hard-working people, and we're all in this together, time to rally." Frank believed the exact same things as Conor; he set up the property management committee despite being invited to the Clementine Lane Residents' Association meetings on several occasions. He too loathed the locals from the neighbouring street. He saw them as coarse and uncultured even if he himself was, well, coarse and uncultured. Nonetheless, he wanted to be cultured, even if high culture bored him; he wanted to be sophisticated, as if to continually rebel against his father's simplistic Catholic Monaghan farming roots. The truth was Frank, like Conor, was a snob but he liked his own persona too much to be seen for what he was, so his views, like his sexuality, were suppressed.

"So what's the plan? Banners and placards outside the Council, an interview with the local paper maybe? Or are we writing letters to our local councillors? The good ones now, not the ones with the outline of Ireland in their crest, dirty nationalists or the Trots' red fist, no, not them, but you know, the ones who fight for the rainbow flag and the economy. Like your gang, Frank." Conor felt aggrieved for being scolded earlier and wanted to remind Frank of his unsuccessful run for Labour in the local elections.

The older man stared sharply at Conor, initially wounded, but anger quickly began to pour into the holes of self-pity. His eyes widened, his smile carved into either cheek, and his teeth shone bright white.

"Had I been elected this would certainly not be happening now. Had Labour controlled the Council, this service would be located where it was needed to be, not where it is now. Somewhere, where there was real deprivation, and people in that terrible situation could find the help which they needed. But I wasn't elected, and Labour doesn't have the majority of the Council, do they? The Shinners and the Trots rule the roost, as was voted for by the people of the area, and aren't we grateful?"

This reply was manic; it was also nonsense. NIMBYism was apolitical, any party was happy to engage in it, but the smile was nearly to the eye and the younger ponytailed office employee was uncomfortable. Frank cooled, his smile returned to something more human and he continued, "So I guess we really have to band together. Let's start with a letter maybe and a petition. I'll talk to that elderly gentleman, Arthur, and see if we can liaise on something. Will you sign?"

Conor nodded. Despite his earlier sarcasm, he hadn't a better idea and that microwavable pasta must be cooked by now.

3.

Maturing Children and Immature Parents

17th January 2018 (Wednesday)

KIDS ARE BASTARDS. IT'S A WIDELY KNOWN FACT BUT LITTLE stated, because you know you can't tell them they're bastards, otherwise they become whiney or more bastard-like. Both are equally annoying. Their problem is that they are young and as such haven't failed enough to be considerate to the failures of others. They are also, at least in the case of good parenting, the centre of other people's worlds, and have no concept that they are actually one of billions and not that special.

Sienna Farrell was a 14-year-old with brown hair that parted like curtains over each eye with the rest in a bobbin at the back. She looked like a sharp wind would break her; a lanky thing, to be sure, she was tall for her age. Her face was thin and pale, with a pointed chin and a narrow nose and perfectly oval brown eyes. What was taken from Sienna in weight was awarded to her rotund 9-year-old brother, Joe, who sported blond hair with a duck-tail quiff. His eyes were constantly narrowed, squinting, as though strong light perpetually shone on them or he was cross about something that no one else would ever know about.

The two, like others of their age, had the freedom of the lanes and flats up until the night time. For children travelling past in cars, this seemed like an amazing luxury. These inner-city kids were free. There was some truth in this. While these car children went home after their Sunday trip to Glendalough to a healthy meal and family time in front of the telly, the inner-city children were still out on adventures.

Of course, the other side of the coin meant no trips to Glendalough, no healthy dinners, little family time and the same dirty lanes quickly became dull. Though not this night; this night Sienna and Joe were heading to the abandoned warehouse. They were told not to by their mother Phyllis, out of sincere fear of needles, broken glass, junkies, the bric-a-brac, human or otherwise, that occupy abandoned places.

What the children were doing was dangerous. To gain access to the warehouse involved pivoting oneself onto a pillar, crawling across its capstone, beside rusted barbed wire, avoiding the serrated, alluvium shards that waited patiently on top of the gate and lowering oneself down. Then there was the warehouse itself. Entry meant crawling through a space between the splintered wood of the rear door, now broken in two, and the concrete.

The warehouse used to contain mattresses, in what for many adults was a recent enough memory. Of course, that is the problem of "recent enough memories"; they are deceptive. The warehouse was closed for over a decade, by this stage. Time seems to speed up as we age. The mattresses, in the main, were gone from the premises. Now the only thing that was soft which dwelled there were the rats, and presumably, the source of the groaning, that newly acquired mystery to the warehouse that was commented on by the children of the street, as they walked between flat complexes. Something was in there and it was alive, if not for long. Phyllis was right to warn her two children about the warehouse. It was dark, trash laden, cold, and dangerous; but then, kids are bastards.

Sienna went first. Climbing the gate pillar, crawling on its capstone, and gently lowering herself down presented little problems; she was an aerobics champion. Disinterested with the local senior youth project, who were likewise disinterested with her, Sienna would pursue anything involving dancing or aerobics. That meant hard work to youth workers who preferred kids who sat on game systems or played pool, while they could place bets on their phones. The volunteers from a different age shuddered in the shadows at the professional class youth workers' modern and contagious sense of professional indifference.

Sienna didn't mind, she was not a naturally social teenager. In fact, it often provoked anxiety in her and she was more interested in the physical exertion of acrobatics and dancing (these days done sans partner). She had joined other clubs specific to her ability, an ability which had now led her safely onto the warehouse grounds. Joe was less graceful. One attempt to jump high onto the pillar provoked gravity to mockingly remind him of his size. His next attempt to pivot between the wall and the pillar returned the same results. Sienna had worked for her grace, Joe had not, what's fair is fair. The third attempt gashed his arm on the granite pillar; gravity was irritated now.

Joe was sobbing. "Look! Look at me arm, it's wrecked."

"It's not, relax would ye? Just wait for us here, I'll go on have a look, don't go home, just stay there." Sienna was firm with her instructions and Joe was partially relieved. He was never keen on the warehouse expedition and only participated because of loneliness and a sense of male duty. She turned and walked towards the warehouse. Over her shoulder stood a charmingly small round figure rubbing his eye; in front of her, a large grey concrete building, yellow lit and of course, the home of the groans.

***

Shane and Phyllis Farrell were good people. Not spectacular, normal, and considerate of their neighbours. Neither was educated past their Inter-cert, but for each of their families to get them that far was a new brick on the road forward. Indeed, both were committed to getting their own children past their Leaving Cert, another new brick albeit ridiculously out of pace with the rest of the knowledge economy.

Formal education may have helped, but they were naturally ordained intelligent people. In some ways, its absence allowed them to be humble. They were both capable of self-analysis and could clearly see what was happening around them, without a cumbersome ideological group membership that often impedes a graduate's sense of self or society.

Shane was a thin man, too thin, shaved head with dark red stubs still fighting to emerge. His skull was easily observed, and his skin looked like a tanner had worked it. Phyllis was curvaceous, not fat, attractive, with blonde hair brought up like a geisha; she was tanned too, but it looked a lot better on her. Her eyes were brown with long dark eyelashes jealously guarding them; her sizable bust and thin legs made her top heavy, completing a somewhat traditionalist view of attractiveness.

The two had married young, and admittedly, privately regretted it. Children followed, copper fastening their situation and its privately held regretfulness. They felt that, in their race to maturity, they had missed out on youth. Those places that could have been seen, opportunities that could have been seized and their possible true loves. This was human nature. It was also nonsense; had their relationship ended before Sienna's birth, there still would have been regret, real regret. They would have known the exact metrics of what was lost, the other person. They were together, they did love each other, and, for the most part they were happy.

While elsewhere Sienna was making her way into the warehouse, as Joe was looking crossly on with tears in his eyes, their absence was not felt here. Phyllis and Shane were good people and raised their children with interest, but they also raised them as they were raised.

"You're messing! Go on, stop, would ya!"

"I'm honestly not messing, I went into the labour activation place and I was sent into this guy, who's there to advise me on how to get a job. So I sit down thinking he might do the usual routine of CV and letter of interest and all that. This chap comes in, somewhat wide eyed and sits in front of me." Shane exaggeratedly walked towards Phyllis and squatted down in front of her, much to her laughter.

"Then he looks down at his file on me, which I would say is an epic read, and he says 'Ah yes, yes I've seen this yarn before.' Eventually, he looks up and says, 'Listen. I want to give you a bit of advice because you broadly remind me of me, actually not broadly, considering you're a bit thinner than me'." In act of imitation, Shane loudly guffawed to replicate the public servant's laugh.

"So my rotund friend continued, 'I was unemployed for five years, no hope, not a bit of confidence, they sent me in here, put me in front of some public servant, like they have sent you to me. That fella says to me, 'Now I am going to help you with your CV,' and I said 'No you won't, pal, you'll give me a job right here and right now,' and they did, they gave me a job right here! Like that."

Phyllis started giggling again. "He didn't say that! Shane, ya spa!"

"He did! So I said to him, 'You know, they should give everyone a job in the employment advice department, and then there wouldn't be anyone on the dole!' I annoyed him with this extension of his logic and he said, 'You can't have that! Only those who can hack a man's day of labour like yourself and meself.' Honest to God! As if that barrel ever lifted anything more than a pint."

Phyllis could not contain her giddiness and broke down laughing again. After a short while she stopped. "So, any news on a job or are you going to live on me wage for the rest of your life?" Phyllis was still smiling but she wanted an answer just the same.

"There's labour work going in the building of those hotels and student places. We have more student places now than colleges, all to end up in jobs down the employment advice!" Shane humorously if vaguely answered.

His answer, though non-specific, was no attempt at deception. The truth was he had travelled to four building sites in the area after his mandatory visit to the labour. They were hiring all right but even labourers, these days, needed more than his junior cycle maths. Experience in building was not as highly valued as knowing functions or probability, he mockingly noted to himself. He had never felt so insecure or unsure of his own prospects but Phyllis was not to know.

"Worst comes to worst, I'll go down to Frank and show him these lovely cheeks. D'ya wants that, Frankie? Tis good but it'll cost ya, pal." Shane returned to humour when he felt threatened.

"Love yourself much? Frank has better taste than going on with some ginger nut," Phyllis teased.

"Right then, I'll give my bottom cherry to Terry, historian, man of the people, protector of antiquity and yes, all-round aggressive simpleton." Shane had risen in stature as he was speaking. "Georgian Dublin was our birth right, the lowly intellectuals from the country have destroyed our cultural treasures with their jealousy and their brutalism."

Shane's "Terry" impression was more caricature than imitation, though perhaps he was a little harsh. Terry was many things, but simple was not one of them.

Phyllis began laughing again. "If anyone heard us, they'd say we're a right pair of pricks!"

She lay on the couch in their small sitting room, with her hands at her eyes, rubbing the merriment away. Shane had stealthily moved to hover over her in her moment of temporary blindness.

She opened her eyes, to see him peering directly into her eyes. The mood was altogether suddenly different, the laughter was gone, only a shared stare, a moment of anticipation, delicate; too quick and the moment would be contrived, too long and the laughter would return. Shane gently pressed his lips to hers and after a moment of tongue in other's cheek, they quietly climbed the small staircase to their bedroom, occupied by a bed (too big) and TV (too small). The door closed.

Time passed. There is no point in recounting the specifics. The lack of eloquence in such matters, much like kids being bastards, is another great unspoken truth. The arts, music, sculpture, the brush, even the written word, seldom recount intimacy with its clumsy, beautiful reality. It is always seen as something grand. Orchestrated and planned to the subtlest movement. It's usually a little messier, wilder, and at times funnier than what is illustrated in the great epics. They momentarily forgot their financial woes and nagging regrets. It was beautiful, if short lived.

Phyllis awoke suddenly to a familiar whine.

"Ma!"

For a moment she thought she had imagined it, but then the call was repeated.

"Maaaa!"

Shane didn't rise. His energy was depleted. He had long since learned to sleep through this signal for attention. Phyllis walked to the window and gently pushed the veil to one side, briefly spying all four feet of Joe standing outside. She looked at the alarm clock in the corner of the room. In neon form, it flashed twenty-five minutes past eleven. Joe was outside! Joe was still up! Phyllis opened the front door with anger. "What are you doing out at this fucking time?!"

Joe sobbing and a little unsure, stood looking at her. Eventually he replied, "Sienna, she's missing."

4.

Moans and Groans

17th January 2018 (Wednesday)

GARDA PAUL GIBBONS WAS PLAYING WITH THE LID OF HIS CUP OF coffee, sitting in an unmarked car outside their local gangster célèbre's house. He wasn't there to catch this fallen soul in some brilliant sting, he wasn't there to observe his movements, or foil some drug exchange; Gibbons was there to protect the gangster from a potential hit. They had no intelligence that such an event was planned in the short term. Or even in the midterm, but there had been other hits between the gangs over the last few years, and it was getting rather embarrassing, so the top brass had issued protection for the gangsters célèbre, like they were former ministers or Taoisigh. Perhaps some of them were. Gibbons didn't mind; this meant overtime.

His two-up-two-down was very expensive and needed a lot of work. A former social housing unit, it was built to be given to its former occupier as a home and as a human right but was sold to Gibbons as an asset. He needed overtime. In a strange way, he and the local gangster célèbre very much relied on each other, partners in crime. The locals didn't mind either; since that unmarked cop car had arrived (complete with two Garda inside, subtly in uniform), crime had fallen in the estate. Who knew? Garda presence was directly correlated with less crime. Certainly, a positive for that area. Not so good for those who needed the Garda presence elsewhere though, like Clementine Lane.

Garda Paul Gibbons was tall, he had to be, it was a requirement when he joined the force. Dark haired, pale, with a little red in the cheeks, otherwise as though painted in chalk. He was of a big build, another requirement. Nearing 40, but a bachelor, Gibbons was fair minded, but black and white. He felt sorry for the young, but experience had taught him to be mindful of the adults of his watch. Sadly, this was qualitative experience instead of quantitative. The majority of the area were good people but human memory loves the spectacular, and there were a few spectacularly bad people there too. A native of Tipperary, a small and rural place, he found the city already intimidated him. These bad experiences were scorched easily onto an otherwise innocent mind. He was at this moment very, very bored.

"Stop fiddling with that. You're doing my head in," Garda Aoife Quinlan said sharply. The attractive Garda was visibly annoyed, not that Gibbons noticed; he tended to miss out on these things.

"Sooo bored, go in there and ask him to make us a cup of tea there would ye? I'm gasping," Gibbons whined.

"There's some still in the flask," she replied jadedly.

"I want his tea though, drug tea is the best, I'm told, made with the finest blend of filthy lucre, in gold rimmed cups and with bad boy milk, made from diamond cows." Gibbons was mildly ranting.

"How goes the refurbishments, Paul? When's the housewarming?" Quinlan wanted to order the conversation into something that made some sense.

"Between the gouger electricians and the gouger carpenters, I'll barely have enough for the gouger property tax," Gibbons replied as his eyes narrowed; he could now see the local gangster célèbre, who was standing at his front room window. The crime boss was stark naked, displaying a large hairy belly, amongst other things. In his left hand was a cup of tea, while his right hand was formed into the familiar gesture of "up yours" aimed directly at Gibbons. The local gangster célèbre was cheerfully smiling, Gibbons was not.

"Ignore him, Paul. Remember the overtime," Quinlan helpfully advised.

"Fucking gouger, I should go over there and smash his face in with my torch," Gibbons replied, once again returning to playing with his lid.

Of course, he wouldn't, but his pride had been hurt by this smiling, naked and now swaying purveyor of opiates. He needed to vent his woes in a way that would allow his ego to continue to function. Quinlan did not believe him either. She knew Gibbons well, and knew his sense of fairness would preclude him from such harsh acts. It was one of the things that she liked about him, and she liked a few things about him.

"Units 3 and 4 to Clementine Lane, Missing Person Report, Patrol Officer to replace Watch," suddenly cracked from the car radio.

"Lovely, a bit of action." As the Garda car pulled away, Garda Gibbons was sincerely pleased. If nothing else, the view would certainly improve.

***

The warehouse was cold. Actually, that's an understatement. It was dark too. Considering these two adjectives "cold" and "dark", we can add "abandoned" with the noun "warehouse" to get one more adjective: "scary". It would have been scary to an adult, never mind a 14-year-old, who was now just trying to cautiously make out what she was seeing. What was she seeing? The almost complete darkness was disorientating.

Sienna's peripheral vision was awash with yellows and blues that disappeared when her pupils trained on them, a memory of the streetlights outside. Then there it was. A very faint low groan. Though it was low in volume, the otherwise completely silent warehouse allowed it to be heard well enough. Sienna stopped. Her intrepidness deserted her; now she was afraid... but is it fair to only see things from her perspective? Is she the protagonist, considering she is the intruder? After all, the source of the groans had experiences, before this teenager disturbed their disturbance. Perhaps it would be helpful to see things from their view, and to do that we will first need to talk about Mr Freddie Taft and Mr Brendan Freeman.

Freddie Taft was a messer growing up. In a different time, a phrenologist wouldn't have predicted it, as he was fated with an elongated head, shaved at the sides and topped, with a blond fringe, just visible on the horizon of his forehead. Like all fads it was popular in the past, and only popular there. Freddie's face was punctuated with freckles, rather like a slice of pork, onion and tomato roll, which accentuated his paleness. It looked greasy to touch. His eyes, made dark by long eyelashes, and barely visible as they were always half closed giving the impression that he was under heavy sedation. Most identifiable of all of Freddie's features was a permanent half grin, which did nothing to bestow confidence.

He was the child who would deliberately provoke the teacher's ire for the amusement of his class. Though, truth be told, after the first five minutes the class would bore of his antics and in some cases actually want to be taught, by way of distraction from Freddie. Taft was also the first to achieve anything on the road to adulthood. The first to have pubic hair, the first to become erect, the first to have a wet dream and of course, not forgetting the first to have his period (he abandoned this point discreetly upon further research). Naturally, when he reached each milestone he'd tell his classmates, often with proof. Stained underwear from an alleged wet dream (smelling suspiciously like Jeyes fluid), a cluft of hair apparently from his crotch (it looked a lot like cat's fur) and so on.

Freddie, perhaps unsurprisingly (though presumptuously on the part of the reader) was not gifted academically. A combination of not paying attention in class owing to the heavy burden he felt to be its entertainer, and not caring at home because nobody watched him and he wasn't going to police himself, Freddie's mind never progressed. He did have cunning though, and knew that it wouldn't do to continuously fail. His lifestyle was better unobserved. The enterprising Taft befriended an academically gifted and mannerly boy named Brendan Freeman.

Brendan had remarkable grey eyes. They always looked intently worried; it did not help that he rarely smiled and spoke without confidence. He seemed always concerned, even at that young age. He walked with his arms perpetually folded. A little thinner but a little taller than Freddie, his nervous and thoughtful countenance contrasted heavily with Freddie's narrow eyed half dopey perpetual grin.

Brendan became Freddie's glance card. The Oracle of Jamestown Road was constantly beseeched for answers by the little annoying prick of Clementine Lane. They moved through the years of primary and secondary school hiding Freddie's inability to retain anything at all. Professional indifference made such subterfuge surprisingly easy for two children to achieve.

There was something undeniably charming about this couple of friends. They were polar opposites. One loud, boyish, a thing that would wither without the group cheering it on, the other quiet, bookish, who hated too much company, as the constantly missed social cues both embarrassed and drained him. While there may have been a touch of undeniable cynicism in the beginning of this relationship, there was no doubt, after a time, they were real friends.

Freddie and Brendan's families contrasted too but perhaps that, also, was unsurprising (though still presumptuous, mind). Brendan's mother was a homemaker who spent time helping

Brendan with his homework, particularly languages and history, to which they both had natural aptitudes. Brendan's father was a small-built man from Antrim. A Freeman from unfree Ballymena, he often joked in the pub so people knew he was from the right side of the tracks. He earned a good wage collecting the TV licence fee for the national broadcaster. A modern Zacchaeus. Well he would be, if anyone acknowledged him at their door, which to be fair, they didn't. He loved his children and always brought them to Glendalough on Sundays. Their family of five (Brendan had two younger brothers) lived in a nice redbrick in Inchicore with space and modest but real comfort.

The Taft family maintained that they could trace their roots in Clementine Lane back to the 17th century, which was interesting, as the area was under water as a basin for the city back then and wouldn't become drained and built up till the 1830s. They lived in no ancestral home either, but a flat that the then Taoiseach, Dev, awarded their grandmother after the Trade War. In this small flat lived six, two boys and a daughter, all younger than Freddie. Freddie's father worked as a lorry driver and was away for long periods, to support the family. His mother, while her own parents juggled her offspring, worked in a video rental shop (no one sang songs about this particular occupation's fall to progress).

When his father, Mr Taft, was in the house, he oscillated from joviality of Jupiterian quality to moments of extreme anger, also, regrettably, of Jupiterian quality. This hot and cold relationship created a constant tension in the house when he was present. Amateur psychologists might argue that his father's unstable and violent nature drove Taft Jr's need for attention and acceptance, but this would be giving too much credit to what was essentially a monster. Freddie's mother smoked heavily and read Barbara Cartland books by the kilo. She was not disinterested in her kids, she was just tired. Freddie, who with the help of Brendan could easily hide his underperformance at school from teachers, could easily hide it from his parents here. Nobody was watching.

The years, of course, passed, and brevity in this story is required as we must be cognisant of Sienna who is still patiently waiting in the cold, mostly abandoned warehouse for the reader to catch up. The awkward phase of secondary school moved quickly for both as Brendan achieved and Freddie survived on his scraps to pass, sometimes fail, when even plagiary was too much effort. At this time, of course, young people are introduced to alcohol, relationships and other evils.

The unsupervised and enterprising Freddie grew in popularity, taking advantage of his parents' absences from the home as he hosted parties and drinking sessions. The difference between the two concepts was academic as both meant sitting in, watching TV with cans, while Freddie's siblings were piled in their small, shared quarters. Brendan was sometimes present, when his misled parents allowed, but other times not, when work towards relevant life-changing exams was required. Habits grew harder, as temperance and moderation, unfortunately, come later than access and experience. Eventually, Freddie hardly arrived into school at all. Though still friendly with his old friend Brendan, he was very much moving in different circles, which was both sad and life at the same time. They would see each other less and less. Brendan would continue towards university and its promises. Freddie would not.

***

Sienna was still. She could make out the broken forms of abandoned conveyor belts, long since put to perpetual sleep. The groan was there and gone, intermittent but fixed in position. It was not intimidating. After a while it seemed more pathetic. She was no longer afraid; she was sure it was human. Kindness was a Farrell trait. Sienna would not pass by the sounds of suffering; besides, the story would be much better if she had the conclusion to the mystery.

She slowly clambered over boxes and pallets that cracked under her meagre weight. She moved across old cellophane wrapping, which popped. The groans stopped. They knew something was approaching. Sienna, undeterred, passed the large conveyor belt with its opened jaw and turned around a large column. All the obstacles that had inhibited her view upon entering the warehouse were now defeated and there was an expanse of floor in front of her. She could now see all.

Her eyes were immediately fixed on her quest's goal. There, on the floor, a stained tattered green mat. Beside it, a plastic two-litre bottle of cider, with some reflected gold near the bottom. Finally, a form lightly moving in the dark, a man. The darkness made his clothes hard to discern. As she moved slowly towards him, he began to sit up. The smell of alcohol mixed with piss was nauseating. Sienna's eyes slowly drew to his face, a shaggy reddish beard, but what was immediately striking was his powerful, if worried, grey eyes. He looked up, and said, under visible pressure from an unseen ailment, "How are ye, sweetie? My name, my name is Brendan."

5.

A Life Story

"SHOULD I CALL SOMEONE FOR YOU? LIKE YOU'D HAVE TO GIVE me your phone, but I'll make the call. I think I should make the call, I'm the adult, yeah I should, it'll look bad otherwise. I lose my phone on a periodic basis, always seems to be ringing when I'm not there. Do you want me to ring someone?"

Sienna did not address the question but instead simply stared, still not sure what to make of the dishevelled heap that was now interrogating her.

"Not a talker? I wasn't a talker either for a long time, long time, but sure the things that I've seen, experienced, I could speak volumes now. Ever been to counselling? Or… or rehab? Course you haven't, what am I saying? Full of lunatics, nut jobs, I can always spot the ones that are going to overdose, that's experience, and reading people, but no one ever listens. I'm a piss-stained Cassandra."

Brendan's eyes lowered to the floor, his briefly remembered reality sobering him.

"I've a cousin called Cassandra," Sienna ventured. Empathy rose within her as she stared into the sadness plainly presented in those grey eyes. "She lives in Clondalkin with her fella, she brags a lot about everything. My ma thinks she's a stuck-up trollop."

"Clondalkin? Impressive." Brendan's eyes remained fixed on the floor. "Lots to brag about there. What's your name? I'm not calling you sweetie all the time, it sounds deviant."

"Sienna," the teenager replied.

"Sienna? You must be very down to earth." He smiled to himself; he delighted in his intellectual humour, particularly if the riddle was lost on others, which it was. Sienna simply thought he was mental. Brendan winced. He writhed on the green mat and closed his eyes, emitting a soft groan.

"You all right?" A troubled concern lit Sienna's face.

He looked at her. For a moment to look at either pair of eyes, it was unclear who exactly felt sorry for whom. "Nah, Sienna, when a person is lying on a soiled mat, unable to move, pissed, mildly suicidal, talking to a teenage girl that they are not a hundred per cent sure is really there and feeling sharp digging pains in their side that are probably a late sign of cirrhosis, they are not all right. They're probably a bit worse for the wear." In fairness to Brendan, this observation was well made.

Sienna thought for a minute. Not all that was just said had been processed by the refinery of her young mind. It was still undergoing construction, though she was still sure that her first approximation of "mental" was not a bad diagnosis. Nonetheless, she detected tones of anger; she interpreted them as having been born in the present and that she had somehow been the cause. She was wrong, however; they were tones of bitterness and they were quite mature now.

"Do you want me to go then?" Sienna was climbing on the conveyor belt beside the self-pitying pile.

Brendan briefly looked up at her. "No, turns out being on your own is incredibly boring." He leaned back on a pillar that was keeping him in an upright position and coughed. Small molecules of phlegm, made visible only by the outside streetlight, flew from his mouth to the floor.

He lifted the cider to his lips and drank greedily. It streamed into many tributaries across his bearded chin. His gulp moved his neck like a pre-industrial age wooden machination. Then it was empty. He belched and, quickly turning to his side, vomited. Almost immediately, the pungent smell filled the void between the two of them and made Sienna heave with disgust. He spat the last gums of vomit as his face rose. He was careful not to make eye contact with the teenager, as if her gaze would freeze him in stone, perpetually held in that pathetic position.

"That's knacker," she eventually said.

"Yep, it's not great," he gasped ashamedly.

She was now sitting on conveyor belt beside him. Up on the sheathed roof above, rain began to dabble. It was surprising how quickly it occupied the silence of the warehouse. A few drops at first, but then momentum began to gather. Eventually it was pelting.

"How did you end up like this anyway?" Sienna's question was more about the immediate. Specifically, she wanted to know what drew this wreck to the warehouse, but for Brendan it was an opportunity for a counselling session, which he would gladly accept.

"You sure you don't want me to call someone? Well, OK." Briefly ignoring her question, he uncomfortably shifted to another angle, suggesting his bum was all but numb.

"It's a funny one that, I guess not that funny. I have been asked that a lot in my life too. I've an answer already pre-prepared like a job interview. College is where it started."

Immediately, Sienna's eyes rose to the ceiling, as she realised her question was misinterpreted. The drunk had not noticed.

"I was constantly told there would be a path, an order to life, like levels in a game, study in school, you'll go to college, study in college, you'll get a great job, a house, and the family and wife, they'd just magic themselves in between somewhere." Brendan belched; his eyes widened for a minute then returned to their semi-closed state of poisoned inebriation. "When I first went to university, I was studying Arts. I went with what I loved… history, instead of what I needed, which was anything that wasn't an Arts subject. I could have been a pigeon fancier, hanging out with all the sexy pigeons, and I would have made a better fist of it."

Sienna giggled a little, which made Brendan smile. It was nice to be appreciated.

"I was nervous, kind of hated anything new, always anxious, afraid to talk to people. I kind of depended on others to make an effort with me. I said to myself when I first started 'just talk to the first person you meet', which I did, and we became friends soon after. He introduced me to his little circle of friends and we would have a pint once a week together debating, discussing, laughing at the eccentric weirdos colleges are just teeming with. And that's how it started. I never really drank before then, maybe just the odd occasion."

"I've had vodka before, it's foul," Sienna interjected.

"Good, stick with that thought," Brendan replied. "After a while, the group grew, and people studied different subjects, met at different times. I loved my new freedom, I loved that my parents couldn't control me here and I could do what I liked. I could retell stories from any period of my life and people would laugh and it would all be new. Stories would be exaggerated or the emphasis was deliberately misplaced to allow me to come out as the smart one, or sophisticated one, who knew the score, even though truthfully it was usually a friend of mine who was the real star back when I was young. His life stories I appropriated."

Sienna began to listen intently. She was warming to his eccentric mannerisms and the way his eyes would open wide with recall. "So you were a little spoofer then?"

"Something like that." The drunk smiled.

"With all the new friends, I suddenly found myself drinking very regularly. I began to lose track of coursework, but I always crammed for exams and they carried the lion share of the grade. I would be there enough to know what was happening. You know, you think being hungover would stop you drinking, but instead you could force through it, you were going to feel shite anyway. So I would keep saying to myself 'well, I'm not getting anything done today because I'm bolloxed, I might as well have one, but less than last night, just to take the edge of it.' Then I'd wake up the next day hungover again and the cycle would continue on and on." Brendan waved his hand in a circular motion with a simple gesture to demonstrate the inextricably complicated concept of infinity.

The rain continued to pelt on the roof above them, and in the dark, the barely visible form continued. "The scales tipped when I realised that I was drinking the majority of the days in the week. I lied to my parents and came home late after 'study'." Brendan sloppily formed quotation marks with his hands before they lazily fell to his side. "I gave them no trouble as a child and I was clever about hiding my drunkenness. I'm drunk right now and you would still think you're talking to an erudite young gentleman."

Sienna assumed "erudite" meant "smelling of vomit and piss" and nodded her head with agreement, much to Brendan's pleasure.

"Time went on, and I graduated. With honours no less, and alcohol, I had graduated with a fucking love of alcohol. Sorry, I shouldn't be cursing like that."

Sienna was nonplussed by the cursing and the apology.

Brendan continued, "I assumed work would be waiting for me, why should getting a job be hard to an honours graduate? This was simply the next level. Except the game had changed. The economy had collapsed and there were lots of little Arts graduate shites like me but employers didn't want people who thought they could do something. They wanted people who had done something. My parents could never countenance a retail or pub job for their graduate son, it had to be a 'good job'. They felt similarly about trades, which was also nonsense, when I think of my classmates from school who were now electricians and plumbers, and were also on happy salaries. Now they didn't know shit about the de Medicis or have a fucking clue about the religious wars in Europe. They did know how to build things though. Apparently, that's more useful. Who knew? By this stage, I was beginning to become lazy in my subterfuge. Boredom had brought me to the pub more and more often and my parents began to realise my problem. I was depressed and no longer cared about what anyone thought of me. Perhaps, I had been depressed for a long time and didn't realise it." Brendan stopped for a moment, caught in a moment of reflection, and then continued. "That was when the rows began.

"Eventually, I ended up in a low paid admin job to a private company with 'Solutions' in its title, though what it fucking solved I still don't know." Brendan had forgotten about his self-imposed prohibition on cursing. "I found the awkward social interactions in the office with people I didn't know hard to deal with. So I would pop into the pub on a now daily basis, it gave me something to look forward to, when you're depressed, some little stable comfort is your grasp on life… ah fuck!" The ginger bearded man's invisible pain stabbed again. He changed the angle that he was sitting in and began a fresh round of coughing.

"Of course, my friends had their own jobs and partners now. Plus they had become aware of my excess. I'm sure those little cunts had their Masonic meetings in secret, piously asking 'what are we going to do with poor Brendan?' Either way, they weren't coming out anymore. I could put up with their 'concern' but if they weren't coming out, they were useless to me. I was now drinking increasingly on my own."

Sienna sat swaying her legs on the conveyor belt, looking at her shoes. She could feel the coldness of the machine she was resting on rising through her limbs.

"I couldn't concentrate on anything. I had killed my brain. When I was fired, which looking back was inevitable, I got into a huge row with my parents, which was also inevitable. Things were said, I reminded them how easy they had it growing up with their council house and straightforward jobs, which to be fair wasn't actually true, but when you say things with enough conviction, veracity seems unnecessary. I walked out of the house and I haven't seen them since."

"You just walked out? God imagine, the face on your dad!" Sienna thought of her own father.

"I have no idea how he looked. The last time I saw him, I was hammered." Brendan's hands were shaking. It sounded like the rain was trying desperately to break through that roof. He groaned again, sitting up and beginning to rock gently back and forth while rubbing his side.

For the first time Sienna could see his face more clearly as he rocked into the street light, shining through the window. His face was mostly covered by that stained ginger beard, but he had a round red face with sad grey eyes that looked very considerate and focused. Brendan's head wore a dirty helmet of red hair. There was no denying that this man was Irish; if not that, then maybe a Viking. A morose, depressed, stinking Viking who was having some kind of crisis, thinking of a life spent chasing poor monks up towers.

"So college made you into an alco? I'm sure me da would love to see me talking to you."

Brendan looked uncomfortable; something in his eyes suggested that he wanted to say more about his past, maybe even to correct her, but her summation was an accurate reflection of what he had said, and so he let the comment stand.

"I don't think me ma is that interested in anything I have to say either." The teenager's eyes now focused on the concrete floor. "She ignores more or less everything I say."

"I wouldn't hold it against her. Teenagers are designed to be ignored. It's all that drama, emotion and near psychotic levels of self-obsession. Most adults ignore them," Brendan replied.

"Me da doesn't, you don't."

The man who was clearly in his late 30s smiled. "I am a teenager."

Eventually, she passed her judgment. "You should stop drinking and go back to your family."

"It's not that easy, Sienna." He launched his appeal.

"Eh it is yeah, no matter how much I annoy me da, we get over it, you just have to say sorry to him, make him feel bad about it." The appeal was rejected.

"I don't think you know how hard…"

"Then get them to help you, did you ever ask them for help?" Sienna interrupted.

The morose would-be Viking sat there silently for a period. It was clear the conversation was still continuing inside his mind. At length he said, "Nah, they'd look at me and judge me. The old man had nothing but disgust for me in the end. I was an unforgivable failure to him. 'We gave you everything, Brendan.' 'It was worse for us, Brendan.' 'Look at the fucking state of you, Brendan.'"

"Oh yeah, he sounds like the worst da ever alright…" Sienna interjected.

"Well, maybe not the worst, I knew someone with a worse father," Brendan absently replied without realising Sienna's obvious sarcasm.

"How worse do you think it's going to be for you than this?!" Sienna had a rather straightforward logic that was hard for Brendan to ignore. He stopped rocking.

"You're a sharp one just the same, aren't you?" he smiled.

Sienna was pleased. Nobody really said she was sharp and meant it as a positive. Usually she was described as "cute" followed by a less flattering word.

"To be honest, sometimes I think about it, then I get positive about ringing them, then I get drunk and forget the whole thought, being drunk is life's fast forward button."

"So how long have you been living in this warehouse?" Sienna still wanted to know and hoped a direct question would spare any further digressions.

"I came here a week ago. I was cold. I venture out in the evenings to get me bits but the pain is making that harder."

"You steal them, you mean." Sienna was a little judgemental.

"No, not necessarily, I do get some money," Brendan said in mock hurt, knowing full well that he hadn't claimed the welfare in some time. His begging takings were also slim. He felt that people were less generous to the man on the street when they could give a subscription to a staff-heavy charity. It did give people the bragging rights that they wanted, whilst allowing the further virtue of being able to say that they would not support a habit. His habit was very poorly disguised, to be fair. Still though, he blamed their piousness for his thirst. This same piousness did also ease his thinking about re-appropriating some necessities, sans compensation.

Brendan was anxious to move the discussion along. "I remember when this place was teeming with life. Me and my old friend Freddie used to sneak in here at night, when it was closed, and lie on the mattresses smoking. Proper pair of little pricks." The drunk's head began to slump a little; a sad smile of a man reminiscing better times became apparent. "Me and Taft had a few adventures around here." The recollecting seemed to turn sour as some other memory tried to force its way through uninvited, and his smile momentarily left him while his brow lowered. He cleared his throat and continued. "A lot of history on this lane."

Sienna began to observe beads of sweat forming on the ginger bearded man's forehead. "There is nothing interesting about this area," she dejectedly replied.

"Weird things live in old places, Sienna…" Brendan attempted to appear mysterious but, ultimately, achieved the look of one demented. "Ever been to the neighbouring chapel? That is a weird place…"

"No, it's not, it's boring," the teenager quickly retorted, remembering that over-long meeting from a few nights ago.

"You don't know its story, then?" Brendan raised one eyebrow.

"What story?"

"The chapel has its own sad tale and its own secret."

"Which is?" Sienna was growing impatient.

"That maybe not all supernatural stories are shite talk." Brendan coughed but still managed to hold a lofty gaze. "I know what I'm on about, I saw it. I remember it perfectly too."

"Is this going to be another story about why your auld fella was a prick to you?" Sienna was sardonic.

Brendan ignored her and continued. "Me and Freddie decided to try and break into the chapel one night. I, being the cautious one and a good deal smarter… at least then, reminded him that this area sleeps with one ear opened and every flat-balcony mouth would have descended on us if they heard a break in. We were still arguing about when he decided to break in anyway…" Brendan shifted on his mat, trying in vain to make himself more comfortable. "The place was so dark… it was impossible to see… we made our way through it as best we could."

Sienna leaned in; this story was beginning to captivate her.

"After a while, we couldn't really move any further, when there was this… this sound of movement. We were not in there alone. The two of us stopped dead in our tracks and turned around… And… I guess not everything you hear is fantasy."

Brendan's eyes lost focus as he coughed again and spat onto the floor.

"What are you on about? Like a ghost or something?" The teenager never thought it possible that something as exotic as the supernatural would bother to occupy the insufferably banal Clementine Lane.

"You don't have to believe me, but if a drunk who was waist deep in his own vomit in an abandoned warehouse told me he was seeing supernatural apparitions, I'd believe him. But I am the trusting type." Brendan chuckled to himself, then he winced. He really shouldn't have laughed, he thought.

"What did you see?" For a moment Sienna ignored the obvious discomfort her company was in and, indeed, how quickly he seemed to be deteriorating. Brendan was presumptive. The teenager did not know any story about that chapel. He looked at her a moment, the smile ran from his face, that terrible memory from before seemed to be returning. Finally, he turned to speak....

BANG!

Rising above the clatter of rain, the noise filled the warehouse. It startled both conversationalists. Silence, momentarily, returned as both looked at each other and then louder than before...

BANG!

It was coming from where the broken back door was situated. A strong country voice yelled "SIENNA? SIENNA FARRELL?!" followed by a lower mutter, "Where the fuck do these people come up with these fucking names?! Sounds like a fucking car!"

6.

An Argument, An Arrest Then An Ambulance

17th January 2018 (Wednesday)

"Look, Mrs Farrell, there is no need to shout, your daughter is probably still in there now." The rain was pelting on Garda Gibbons' hat so hard that it was bouncing back on to Phyllis Farrell's scowling face. A small crowd had gathered at their doors, while under a purple brolly stood Frank, who was on his way home when the fracas between Gibbons and Phyllis suddenly burst from private conversation to public knowledge with each rising decibel.

"She is only fourteen! She could have stood on something or fallen off one of the machines. What's wrong with ya?! My poor little thing!" Phyllis pleaded.

"Why can't I go in there?!" Shane roared. His body was tensed and his face was bludgeoning red.

"The building is unsafe, it is structurally unsound, just relax, I need to get permission from my sergeant for entry." Pointing out the building that Phyllis's daughter was currently housed in was structurally unsound was something of a tactical error on Gibbons' part.

"Structurally unsound? Jesus Christ! What are you doing here talking on the walkie talkie, you fucking plonker! Get in there and get her out then," she bellowed at him.

Gibbons stared at her. He wanted to be intimidating; he was, however, intimidated and he quickly looked away.

"Officer, I understand you're following your protocol but I really think it would be in the interests of everyone if you waived your rules and got in there and helped the child." Frank decided to join the conversation.

"Please step back, sir."

Frank duly did. Gibbons felt empowered that someone still listened to him.

Garda Quinlan had returned from the warehouse, informing Gibbons that there was a back way in.

"Will you fucking get in there and help poor little Sienna, oh me heart! Me heart! Phyllis! She's always been like a granddaughter to me." The rain had screwed down Marion's dyed purple hair to her head. She was genuinely concerned; however, her heart was fine. Despite only a decade and some change between them, Marion and Phyllis's relationship imitated a mother and daughter. This closeness served them both well, particularly when Marion found her own family with Mick wanting.

Phyllis somewhat aggressively appealed to the rigid officer. "It'll be pitch black in there, she could trip over something, stop being a fucking sap and go in there." To her annoyance, he merely looked away, as if lost in thought.

The truth was none of the people of Clementine Lane had a spectacularly good relationship with the guards. That, of course, was very much a two-way street. Most had a family member or knew someone who was arrested by the guards. Sometimes over small things, sometimes over larger things; either way, that person captured by the force was always described as "misunderstood" or "treated harshly", "a good person caught in a bad situation." This thinking wasn't always strictly wrong; it wasn't always right, either. The arrest procedure itself was always retold amongst the locals in the most undignifying terms, which is fair enough; arrests are seldom dignified. It was also true that many people in the area were engaged in some level of fraud, be it Revenue or Welfare, against the State. Official Authority frightened them for many reasons. Talking to guards, social workers, even teachers, was considered a betrayal of the Provisional Republic of Clementine Lane. It was also true that the residents would never call the guards when there was a genuine problem in the area.

For their part, the guards saw Clementine Lane as hostile and never really policed it. Even if cooperation had been forthcoming, the guards had already written off these people anyway. There were mock accents and piss taking in the station. A Marxist might say they were engaging in classist humour but that would ignore the simple fact that most guards were near equally as poor as those they mocked. In the end, both had reason to distrust the other and both did.

Gibbons was not happy that he was being observed by so many and he knew from experience it wouldn't be long before dozens of interrogatory camera phone lights would be focused solely on him. Like a cold war film, "the guard who stayed out in the cold." When that happened, things would quickly escalate. He foresaw an injured girl reported on the news, her would-be saviour parrying with locals outside over his inaction. Videos would soon be streaming across the internet of an officer condemning the mother and father of a child that was in clear and present danger. So what if he followed protocol then? His higher ups always presented a head to Madame Media's Guillotine. Either that or feed her their own.

"Culchie assholes! If it was one of your own, you'd be in like a shot." The voice was invisible to the two guards. Terry had withdrawn from the flat balcony as soon as he had yelled it.

Tensions were rising. People were getting irritable standing out in that rainy night. Gibbons was secretly loathing the people who surrounded him. If they had looked after their own children, as his parents had looked after him, he wouldn't be here. No articulate argument from a statistician, sociologist or psychologist could allow him to think this negligence was acceptable. He could not understand why someone would allow their 14-year-old daughter out on a lane in the middle of a rainy night. He could not see the world through these people's eyes, any more than they could see it through his…

Phyllis was crying bitterly into Marion's shoulder. While he disapproved of a lot, he knew her fear was real, and it pained him. He looked at her small redbrick. In the upper window, in pyjamas that looked like Victorian wallpaper, sat a little boy, looking down. He looked so cross. Was everyone here angry? The little boy was also crying. Gibbons grimaced. He turned to his colleague who awaited instruction. "We'll head around so, we can't leave her in there."

The two entered their car and drove up to just outside the warehouse gates. A small retinue followed on foot. The gold light of the street lamps briefly illuminated the torrents of rain plummeting from the night's sky. Shane, on his own, led the group in front, followed by Marion and Phyllis, both covered by a purple umbrella, held over them by a selfless and now soaking Frank, who for the first time in a long time genuinely felt sorry for someone. The balcony mouths followed behind. Their role was to be vultures of the word, harbingers of sorrow, gossipers. For them an event could not be missed, especially one with the potential for tragedy.

Quinlan stayed on the street side of the gate to ensure that there would be no intruders from the group that now waited outside. Gibbons was not young enough to make his entrance seem graceful but he was strong enough to pull himself over. He landed awkwardly, his right leg nearly skidding in the dark wet muck. His clothes were soaking and the left knee on his trousers was now ripped. He mused that perhaps boredom inside a car, awaiting an assassination attempt that was never coming, was better than real action. The soaking, grubby guard quickly crossed the outside of the warehouse and reached the broken rear door. He knocked heavily on the door and then a second time. After hearing no response to his calls, Gibbons became slightly more alarmed. Needing this new anxiety to quickly subside, he ploughed through the door and entered the pitch-black symposium of Brendan and Sienna.

After several minutes of ineffectually waving his torch around, the guard began to systematically look down every corner and aisle of the cold, dark and damp warehouse. The noise of the rain was beating hard on the roof and, though whoever was in the building would be in no doubt of his presence, Gibbons didn't feel confident to shout out the young girl's name again. At length, he happened on the two, who both silently stared back at him. Both fell quiet when they first heard his voice; an instinctual distrust, or perhaps they simply did not want his interruption into their conversation. The guard now pointed his torch at them and was regarding the situation.

"Sienna, come here, away from that gouger!" Gibbons spoke with clear disdain.

"I never gouged anything in my life that I recall, officer." Brendan was not impressed by the guard's presence.

Sienna walked over to the guard. She had been brought up to respect authority by her parents, who fifteen minutes earlier had berated this very guard to whom she was now acquiescing.

Gibbons stood almost perfectly still; his only movement was to mechanically move the torch to Brendan's face. The unfortunate man squinted in the sudden sharpness of the white glow.

Sensing loosely withheld anger burning through the guard as he stared at the articulate heap, Sienna spoke softly. She knew how to be manipulative when needs must. "Don't hurt him, he's sound, he tried to call someone for me, I think he might need an ambulance." Sienna did have a fondness for the man lying on the ground; he respected her. For what it was worth, Brendan liked her too; she respected him. That respect was absent from both their lives for some time, if it was ever there.

"He's a gouger and what he'll be getting will be a mat in a cell, which is still too good for him." The guard was not well disposed to people who smelt of alcohol. This man was up to something – or worse, he was up to nothing, when other people had to be up to something. The guard thought to himself that he had to work hard for his small house and accompanying modest bachelor life; why did anyone think that they didn't? He was incapable of realising this vagrant's life was far from desirable and was filled with too much self-reflection, self-loathing and the smells of vomit and piss.

"Your mat is probably cleaner than mine, to be fair, officer." Brendan smiled but then quickly groaned and pathetically tried to move himself up on his cold concrete pillar.

"Look at this gouger, you must think we're all a shower of yahoos. 'Oh, I'm so sick, so I am, poor me!' I'm not a bloody thick!" a completely focused Gibbons snarled.

Brendan was silent. He was sitting upright. A fear washed over his face and the little beads of sweat on his forehead had amassed in a glossy finish. The warehouse was Baltic, not a place for sweat to naturally occur. The guard was unobservant to his bounty's obvious worsening condition.

"Now stand up."

I don't think he can, he's getting sick all night." Sienna interceded once again, feeling rising tension.

"You fucking disgrace!" Gibbons momentarily forgot the young girl's presence and immediately regretted his harsh language in front of her. Still Brendan stayed silent and his gaze became less focused. His head was beginning to loll as though Lilliputians had attached several ropes to it to tie him down.

Gibbons leaned in and grabbed Brendan by the side to bring him to his feet. Immediately the drunk yelped, and a belch of blood and vile leapt from his mouth landing on his chin. Gibbons quickly lowered him. His face turned to undisguised shock. After a second of confusion he spoke into the box emitting crackles from his shoulder. "We need an ambulance, Clementine Lane, the eh… the eh… what's this address? The warehouse, come to the warehouse. Come quickly!"

The guard had lost his confidence and anger. Brendan's grey eyes were open fully, they were beautiful, redness sieged them from all sides. He was not looking in any direction and he was heaving again with laboured breathing. Tears escaped Sienna's face.

***

A crow flew over the little redbricks. The glow of the streetlamps was his guide in the darkness and the rain, as he swiftly made his way back to his nest for the night. The crow had misjudged the malevolence of the clouds when he had flown out earlier and he was now resentful of the rain, which poured heavily on his feathers. The little bird climbed high to assail the towering blocks of flats and, to his pleasure, descended with the wind at his back down towards the little steeple atop of the chapel. Hovering in a circular motion, he eventually majestically landed as he had done countless times before on his little nest, which was cleverly positioned in the corner of a ledge just in front of the chapel's beautiful stained glass windows. He would have protection from the wind and rain now. It was cosy.

To the little bird's annoyance, there was constant, garish, blue, flashing against his wall. Understandably irate, the little crow approached the edge of the ledge and he looked down on an ambulance. Two brightly dressed humans were carefully loading a red headed one into the back of the vehicle. He was not moving, with his head to one side. Looking at this non-moving human was a large male in a blue jacket drinking from a cup, while a smaller female, also in blue, spoke into her shoulder. Down from them, there was a small group assembled under multiple umbrellas, their voices raised in chatter. The topics ranged from "What could the junkie have done?", "Why did he keep her there on her own in that place?", "What was he planning?" The conversation changed to talk about the new development and how "Something must be done or the next time we might not be so lucky." One bald male human in a grey fleece nodded with the others in full agreement, simply muttering, "It's a disgrace, what are we going to do about the drugs… eh?"

Finally, the bird gazed away from the group, to where a male with red stubbed hair stood. He was holding the shoulders of a little female as tight as he could, as the little female looked on at the stretcher, crying.

7.
Who Am I?

12th January 2018 (Friday)

Name: Sienna Farrell
Title: Who Am I?
Date: 11th of January 2018
Subject: English

I am writing this essay for Mrs Grimes English class, on the subject of who am I? My name is Sienna Farrell, my ~~ma~~ **mother** named me when I was born in the Coombe Hospital in 2004. I have brown hair and am 5 feet and 6 inches tall. I am quite thin, but my old aerobics coach says that helps me with my balance. I have reddish brown eyebrows, but they are faint, and a thin nose.

I have a brother named Joe, he is 4 years and 8 months younger than me. Joe has a problem with his eyesight and he has to squint to see things. It makes him look like he is always ~~pissed off~~ **very cross**. In fairness, he is not usually ~~pissed off~~ **very cross**. I love ~~me~~ *(Sienna you know that is bad English and it appears a lot, the word is 'my')* brother, though sometimes he is very annoying, especially when he tells on me to my *(better)* ma for being out late, or not bringing him to the shops. He used to ~~piss~~ **pee** himself a lot when he was younger, but he has stopped that now and we are very proud of him. He has problems saying big words and the doctor thinks he has a cleft pallet, I haven't a clue what that is but I do think he is ~~a little slow~~ *still learning.* I love him anyway. He loves playing football with his team in St. Michael's Primary school. I think his friends are ~~little spas~~ *enthusiastic,* they laugh at everything even if it doesn't make any sense. There is a big age gap between us and sometimes that makes it difficult, as I only have one brother, and I sometimes get lonely at home. The smell off him sometimes makes me think he ~~shits himself~~ *breaks wind now and again.*

We share a room because our house is too small, which is hard, as I have to wait till ma dresses him to change into ~~me~~ *my* clothes. My ma says it's the best the Council can do. We have been waiting for a new house for 5 years. My da says they have stopped building them to push the prices and rents up, he says the government can get bigger loans because of the ~~GDB~~ *GDP,* ~~I haven't a clue what he does be on about~~ *I am unsure as to what this means.* Ma says our position in the list has only moved up 64 places and we have 2330 to go. She thinks they are a ~~pack of cunts~~ *(Sienna that language is unacceptable and I am sure your mother did not say anything like it! - Mrs Grimes).*

My da's name is Shane. He is very strong and has a shaved, red head. He used to work on the building sites in town. He loved working there, he had lots of friends and he would come home laughing. He does not work in town anymore and he seems a little sadder. He only hangs around with our neighbours now, because he does not see his friends that much. He says a lot of them went abroad for work. I do not think he is fond of a lot our neighbours as much as his old friends. He always says they are a ~~bit thick and full of their own shite~~ *uninformed and arrogant.*

My da drinks with our neighbour, Terry, I think he likes him, even if he does slag him a lot. He thinks Marion's ~~fella~~ *partner,* Mick, ~~is a sponger,~~ *does not pay his way* and thinks he'll go blind, constantly looking at that gambling machine. Me *'my'* and 'me' are not interchangeable da says Mick never did anything for his kids and he is like his own father, ~~a waster~~, *otherwise preoccupied.* My da also says Marion is a ~~big mouthed yob and part of the rentacrowd lot~~ *outspoken with strongly held personal beliefs.* He goes out every morning looking for work and every Thursday to the welfare office. He ~~hates the welfare~~ *does not think the people in the welfare office treat him fairly.* He thinks they look down on him and treat him like he is stupid. Plus, they always push him along. They never are patient with anyone.

My ma's name is Phyllis. She is short with blonde hair. She works very hard as the manager of the local crèche. She also volunteers in the senior citizen's club. She says someone has to look after the cranky ~~bastards~~ *old people,* because a lot of them have no one. My ma tells people she is 37 but she ~~I think I heard my da say she was 42.~~ Her best friend is Marion, she says she is in her 40s but my ma always says that Marion was old enough to be her mother.

Marion keeps changing the dye in her hair. It was red at Christmas and last September, when I started second year, it was a weird blue, now it is purple. Marion gives out a lot about the neighbours and says they are all mouths but she tells my ma everything about what happens in the flats. They never talk about him though, that bald man whose forever in that manky grey fleece, and his two mates. I told ~~me ma~~ *my mam* about them, like its obvious what they're at but she just ignores me and tells me to go out and play, which was ~~a fucking joke~~ *unfortunate* because it was raining.

Ma sometimes drinks with Marion in Cartigan's but she does not like her friend Leanne, ~~who she says has yo-yo knickers.~~ *(Sienna you really need to stop being a tattle tale. You said you didn't like it when your brother did it to you, you should remember that when you are talking about others).* Like I get that it must be hard for my ma but like it's hard for all of us, she takes it out on my da, which is crap. He just looks depressed. I hate it when she says she should never have married him. I know she doesn't mean it but it's ~~a shite~~ *bad* thing to say to someone. My ma gets cranky a lot and, sometimes, she seems really tired. It makes me feel, I don't know, guilty.

My ma does not like her job anymore. She loves the people she works with but she says the government is continually coming up with more rules and that she doesn't know how to fill in half the forms. She says she is doing more work but they won't give her any more money. She thinks the government is deliberately trying to stop funding for the crèche because they do not want to spend tax money on poor people. ~~She says they send middle class whores to judge her who probably took the boat to have their career and she, a mother of 14 years apparently, is not meant to know anything about child minding.~~ *Sienna refer to my last comment, adult conversations are private and should not be repeated.* My ma says she wanted to open her own ~~custom~~ *bespoke* soap shop and be in business but says her credit rating is too low for a loan and the banks won't touch her. Sometimes she gives out that she has to keep the job, because my da is not working. He usually, just leaves the house when that happens.

I think living on the lane can be very boring. It's just a tiny stretch of road with houses on it and we aren't really allowed go anywhere else. The boys on the road act like a load of ~~thicks~~ *thick headed people.* They think Clementine Lane is something special and if any of the lads from other lanes come onto it they have a massive ~~scrap~~ *fight.* It's ~~fucking~~ *(this language is not acceptable and I will have to talk to your mother about it)* stupid, ~~bleeding saps~~ *(this is a creative writing exercise Sienna, you should not write as you speak).* I don't like being on the lane too late because that's when the junkies come out to score. ~~They're eyes do be popping out of their head looking at you~~ *it is clear that they are under the influence of narcotics*, it's unnerving.

My folks recently found out about a ~~junkie centre~~ *rehabilitative clinic* opening on the lane and they are taking me to a meeting next Monday, because they think I should be involved in the community. What's the point in that? They won't listen to me, most people don't, I have been telling them there are dealers in the flats for ages now. They just ignore me. Everyone here knows everyone's business, so how is it that the dealers get ignored? They're always there. It gets too much sometimes, when your ma just shuts you off before you can say anything. My da does listen, he told me to stay away from the flats but that's not realistic, is it? They are on our road, I can't avoid them. Some of the kids I know live there. They are frightened too but they don't say it. Everyone wears their own mask and pretends that they are stronger than they are *(good Sienna)*.

I suppose you could say Christy, Darren, Stephanie and Tanya are ~~me~~ *my* mates.

When I go out with them, we mostly sit outside the basketball court. ~~There does be nothing~~ *There is nothing* to do. In a lot of ways, they have had it harder than me, ~~Darren says he was fiddled by his da's mate and sometimes Stephanie is very quiet, because her da smacks her ma~~ *(Sienna I don't want to see anymore hear/say in your work!)*.

I think they think I'm a bit of a weirdo because I love exploring and seeing new things. I don't really care about what others do. I want to do stuff myself! They don't want to go anywhere. Their world starts and ends in this lane. I watch the travel shows with my da and I think I would love to go to places like Egypt or Turkey but none of them have been further than Courtown or Lanzarote and they like it that way. It feels sometimes like I am in cage.

I wonder sometimes if I could be a professional acrobat or even a writer and just travel the world but the reality is I can't even leave the street I'm on, and who would read my ~~crap~~ *work (that would be me, Sienna)* anyway? Maybe I am a weirdo but I don't think nothing will change for any us. We will be like our own parents. We were born here, we will work in some government paid-for project here and eventually, we will die here *(Sienna please spare us the drama! Your life isn't that bad, think of the children in Syria!).*

I think a lot of people from outside here see us as at the bottom anyway. The ~~posh pricks~~ *(I will be speaking to Mrs Farrell about the use of the language in this piece, Sienna it is off the charts!)* in the apartments do anyway. It's obvious when they walk the long way around to avoid going down the lane. They run into their little boxes and close the door. They're never in Cartigan's and they're always just passing through. And the yuppie cafes never let me or anyone I know my age in. There is this ~~spa~~ *person,* who lives in one of them with long hair tied back, Conor I think his name is, ~~he always does be~~ *he is* laughing at us. He thinks he's so smart, my ma just tells me to ignore him but ~~fuck him~~ *(Honestly Sienna! Who do you think you are writing this for?!),* he moved into my area! He shouldn't be laughing at us!

The question of this essay is who am I? How am I meant to answer that anyway? People usually answer that question with what they do, who am I? I'm a doctor, I'm a vet, or I'm an electrician. But I do nothing, am I nothing? *(Sienna do not start a sentence with 'but').* They also answer that question by saying where they are from. Who am I? I'm a Frenchman. I could say I am from Clementine Lane but I do not feel like I am the same as anyone else from Clementine Lane. I'm not like Marion or Terry or ~~me~~ *my* ma or Mr Dempsey or Mr Cartigan. I don't even feel like Tanya, Stephanie, or Darren or the ~~little scrote~~ teenagers that pick fights up in the flats. So that doesn't answer the question either.

I know who I would like to be, I would like to be someone that people respected and clapped for. When I won that aerobic competition in Liverpool, I loved how the crowd went ecstatic *(good Sienna, good use of language)*. I want to be respected and I know that is earned, but let's face it everyone looks down on us and it doesn't really matter if we try hard or not, we will still be looked down on. In this way, Clementine Lane does define me, and all of us, it is who we are because practically, it is all people will ever see. No matter what else we do. So maybe it is enough to say, I am from Clementine Lane after all. We may all be different here, but wherever else we go, we will always be seen as the same. Who am I? I am Sienna Farrell from Clementine Lane.

Sienna this work is littered with foul language and poor phrasing, you are holding yourself back by speaking like someone who sat her entire life on the side of a street. You have been schooled to this point and it is inexcusable to use language like this in an academic project. Your use of hear/say and exaggeration is disconcerting and has no place in creative writing. I will be speaking to your mother on Thursday morning regarding this assignment. You are better than this Sienna. I can see language use here that if further refined can see you sit at Higher level. It truly is up to you.

Mrs Grimes

33%

It is adults who teach children to lie.

8.

The Chats

IT WAS A BEAUTIFUL CLEAR FEBRUARY MORNING, COLD AND FRESH. The leaves were still wet from the memory of rain the night before but the sky was optimistic for the new day, and why not be optimistic? It was Friday. Nestled among the modern social housing was a crèche, managed by Phyllis Farrell, while Marion, a room leader who never stayed in her room, accompanied her everywhere as she did her rounds. The last of the buggies delivering their "one in the world" cargo was being dropped off, as parents busily disappeared to face their own working day, while the rearing of their child was left to another. The weight of the invisible wealthy, whose profit-seeking ways drive down wages, has removed so many from their most basic of human duties. The age of the nation of cuckoos had long since begun.

The sun shone brightly through the large kitchen window over the sink. Directly across from the window, at a table, sat Phyllis, Marion and a number of other ladies busy taking their tea break and gossiping away.

"Your Billy has the Downs, doesn't he, Joanne?"

A woman at the table politely nodded an affirmative.

"Poor little thing, he's too beautiful for this world," Marion mused, while gripping her scalding thin bone china mug in both hands, a feat that always amazed the others; what were those hands made of?

Phyllis interjected, "He's probably a lot more able for this world than you, Marion. My cousin has Downs and she'd buy and sell you. You'd give her a tenner, then later that day you'd hear 'ah Phyllis, where's me pressie?'"

The other women chuckled.

"Ah, she's only massive really, never was any trouble for my aunt." Phyllis was crunching on a chocolate digestive.

"They don't know their own strength. My son works in one of those handicap centres and he got a box off one of them and it shattered his nose," one of the older women volunteered.

The mother of the child with Down Syndrome looked into her cup and Phyllis could sense her discomfort. As was her natural ability, she discreetly changed the topic, without any of the other women noticing it.

"Sienna is beginning to chat again after what happened. Well, to her father, anyway." The other women looked at Phyllis with concern. "She says he didn't touch her and that he was a lovely guy, she wants to visit him in hospital for fuck sake!"

"Ah your Sienna has a big heart like you, she probably feels sorry for the louse," Marion theorised.

"She asked me if the chapel was haunted the other day, I said 'yeah by my shitty memories going to that youth project.' Little weirdo, I don't know where she comes up with the stuff." Phyllis, much like her daughter, also thought Clementine Lane was too banal a place to be haunted.

"Wonder where she heard that?" Marion seemed suddenly interested.

"Probably off that alco bastard, he probably was spouting all sorts of crap."

Marion, this time, didn't rush to agree with Phyllis and instead thought for a moment. Eventually, she said, "You know Mr Gallagher?" Arthur Gallagher's outward but quiet dignity had earned him the sincere use of the title "Mr" among the residents of Clementine Lane; such formality was distinctly unusual. "Mr Gallagher told me a story about that place when I was collecting some of mine from it, years ago."

The kettle boiled and Phyllis got up and shielded her eyes from the sun rays intruding in through the window. As she poured some more hot cups of tea, just outside the door a baby was crying, while another woman was cooing unsuccessfully to mollify her. Marion looked at Phyllis as the other women stared at her to start her story. Ghost stories were always popular. Phyllis after placing a fresh cup in front of her subordinates, sat down.

***

While Arthur Gallagher's name was being mentioned in the crèche, a couple of hundred metres away the man himself was struggling, valiantly, to open a café front door. The spring on the door was determined not to let the old man in. Eventually, Frank arrived and forced the door open. Both men sat down to a table together, though admittedly Arthur was confused and uncomfortable. He was sitting on a school chair. Why would a café give him a school chair to sit on? Wasn't the point of cafés to be comfortable? How was this progress?

Frank sat easily and ordered some form of coffee that was more milk than coffee and more foam than milk. Arthur ordered a tea. The men knew little about the other. They were both well reared and always curtsied when passing. Both could spare the morning; Frank worked in PR and was his own boss, Arthur retired probably when Frank was still in college. It was here though that the similarities ended.

"Lovely to see you, Arthur." Frank was not from Clementine Lane. Their customs were not his own, there would be no "Mr" here.

"Hello, Frank, how are you anyway?"

"Good, good. Well, there's no point in dancing around the bush, it's too early for me and not good for your hips."

Arthur was once again confused by this comment, but his eyes looked intent on understanding. The main road was busy outside. Cars were chugging along into the city centre, intermittingly stopping at the multiple traffic lights, while the cyclists, darting in between them, ignored such regulations.

"Did the Council respond to your letter?" Frank continued.

"They did, Frank, it was most reassuring. They said that the facility would house people far into their recovery and every effort would be made by the service provider to ensure that their users would respect the area and its residents. Much like the previous letter we got from the Council when the wet centre across the road opened." Arthur pointed to two drunks arguing on a traffic island, just in view of the café's large windows. "Or the homeless shelter two years before, which doesn't seem to shelter so much as provide a new door space for them to sleep in and inhale from their pipes, ehh… or what have you. Most reassuring."

Frank genuinely smiled at the old man's cynicism.

"Well it seems to me that a protest march has to be organised, to kick them up the bum. Why not get your crowd together and I'll get the property management company involved and we can all meet in the chapel, make posters, get the community spirit aroused." The pot-bellied man stirred his coffee.

"It's a shame that only negativity can bring the community together these days, Frank. There was a time people met up for sale of works, bake sales, church festivals. The community has no centre anymore," Arthur solemnly reflected.

It took everything that Frank had to control his involuntary shudder at this reminiscing. That Ireland he wanted dead, all of it; the maidens should be prevented from dancing at the crossroads, at gun point if necessary. Nonetheless, he smiled at Arthur, an ability he had learned when on electoral campaign. "I'm sure we'll get the numbers, Arthur, particularly after what happened to that poor Farrell girl a couple of weeks back. People were horrified, horrified. What could that dreg of human life have done to her? There's a movement building here, Arthur."

"I'll ask Fr Matthew to read out a notice at Sunday mass," Arthur added. Frank once again smiled politely.

***

Shane was walking down the street. He had begun to hate his marches through the city during the morning hours. He hated watching all the people to-ing and fro-ing. He presumed all had been bequeathed a duty, a responsibility, anything, it meant something to somebody. Nobody gave him a responsibility, nobody trusted him with a duty. The responsibility he had, to feed his family, he was failing miserably to accomplish. He doubted his own abilities, and his worth. The pedestrians ignored the traffic lights and frantically travelled across the road as if by osmosis. They had to be in hurry to get somewhere, he surmised. His job hunt was, unsurprisingly, unproductive and he was preparing his answers for Phyllis, later. Leaving the professionally dressed Dame Street and crossing High Street for the more casually dressed Thomas Street, Shane was not far from home.

As he walked, lost in his own thoughts, a long shadow emerged over him.

"How are ya, Shane?"

"Grand, Mick, and yourself?"

"Not too bad, not too bad."

Phyllis may have had a daughter/mother relationship with Marion Ryan, but her husband had no such regard for Mick Ryan. Shane had worked long and hard all his life to support his family. This momentary loss in employment was eating him alive with shame. By contrast, Mick never performed the march into town in search of work. Not once. Sure he had jobs when he was a teen and his father made him. Sure he was involved in employment in labour activation schemes, when the social welfare made him. Sure he would take employment when Marion made him; but inevitably, he would quit when the employer was being "unreasonable." His definition of "unreasonable" would have made Arthur Scargill blush. After a while, even the dogged Marion gave up trying to keep him in employment. This was Mick's skill, surviving without doing anything. He would have been a right-wing party's poster boy. Shane tried to hide his low opinion of him. Then for one awful moment, he wondered if that's how others regarded himself, now. The thought further depressed him.

"I'm just after putting a flutter on Stalin's Boy in the 5.15, bit of a controversial name for a horse just the same, eh?" Mick continued.

"Yeah I guess it's a weird one all right," Shane replied, half listening, still wondering had he become the replica of this tall gaunt waste of space.

"Listen, Marion was telling us that your little Sienna is only beginning to talk again. I'm sorry, Shane, that's not an easy one."

"Ah she started talking a few days ago, we took it as shock, we still have her out of school, she wants to visit your man in hospital. I don't know what to make of it. She was never exactly outgoing, usually have to push her out the door. I think she is genuinely concerned for him. Like, everyone is describing him as some kind of axe murderer, but when I looked down at that stretcher all I saw was a man in his 30s struggling to breathe. I kind of felt sorry for him myself." Shane was sincere in these words.

"You shouldn't, Shane, he's a fucking low life! Who knows what he could have done?!" Mick interjected. Piousness is a useful deflection for those with little to be pious about.

"Considering he could barely breathe, I doubt he could do much now, Mick. Who knows how these people end up that way. It's like a modern leprosy, nobody wants to remember they were somebody's bambino once; they are sick, and therefore, they have to go," Shane reflected.

"Hitler was a baby once too, Shane." Mick thought he was clever with this comment but to the younger man it just confirmed that this man was incapable of considering anyone's situation but his own.

Shane wanted this conversation to end. "Any luck on the job front, Mick?" It was ultimately, a self-destructive comment, as he would no doubt ask the same, but Shane wanted to shame Mick, even for a moment.

"Nah, Shane, sure you know yourself, there's no work for a real man these days. What about yourself?" He did not even flinch, dammit; a lapse in judgement, he was amazed and disgusted that Mick did not feel shame.

"No, Mick, none." The ginger-stubbed Shane looked at the pavement.

"Chin up champ, you'll get there." Mick walked on after squeezing Shane's shoulder. Well, that backfired.

***

Marion had already begun. No one dared interrupt her. She had habit of voicing her opinions and commenting on the plot as she was telling stories, which could make them infuriatingly long-winded. Her audience's curiosity had been piqued; they wanted to know the old chapel's secrets with as little filler as possible. Naturally, they were going to get some filler.

"Well, going back to when the chapel had nuns, and there were no gluaisteáins, only the auld horse and trap men, and all this place was like the top of the road, with the little Victorian cottages. I think the Brits were still here too. There was a family called 'Barnes'. Now I think that's a planter name, Mick says it's Norse, but sure look six of one and half dozen of the other, but I guess I shouldn't be too hard, sure we're meant to be at peace now, but then they're still in the north just the same and until that changes, feck them." Her listeners waited patiently.

"There were seven in the Barnes family, the two parents, the father's widowed mother and four daughters. As many of them as there were and as tiny as those houses are, sorry, Phyllis, but they are small."

Phyllis fidgeted with her cup, while quietly thinking that Marion's flat was no bigger than her humble redbrick.

"They lived in relative comfort. Do you know what I mean? It was the time of the tenements, when people were stacked on top of each other. Now the youngest was a girl called Emily, she had a birthmark on forehead like the Russian fella." The younger women present were oblivious to this reference to former General Secretary Gorbachev.

"Now there was something of a hidden scandal about Emily, which indirectly brought about a rather tragic end to the story, in that chapel. You see, Emily's mother was not her actual mother. Things were done different in those days, the story of her parentage was a bit messed up…"

The door suddenly flew open, scaring the women assembled. "Phyllis, little Stacey is after whacking her head off the fire extinguisher, she's gushing."

Phyllis leapt from the table. Naturally Marion followed. Break was over, the story would have to wait. How annoying.

9.

The Father, The Son, and The Holy Ghost

2nd February 2018 (Friday)

A s THE LADIES IN THE SMALL CLEMENTINE LANE CRÈCHE WERE returning to work, to reattach pieces of an overzealous three year old, no further on in their ghost story, it was still only eleven hours into the day and some four miles towards the northeast of the city, Conor was furiously typing. The February morning sun was curious and it gazed into the glass hive where Conor was consumed with his paperwork. Conor was reliving his already long morning in his thoughts while absently staring at the screen. Neither truly at work nor in himself, but something of an android amongst a collective of androids linked to their computers, working or secretly on social media, physically in the room, their personas diluted across the globe.

Conor had been awake since 7.15 a.m. He started his day with a brief shower, and a trip on the tram from his local stop, across the city in the dark, to his office cubicle. After a quick cup of coffee, he was called into a meeting with his manager, that twenty-something, fresh with a degree, little tyrant. The man had little experience but knew the terms "synergy," "big data" and "going forward," which sufficiently impressed his interviewers. The meeting was rather short and to the point. Through the manager's own fault, deadlines had amassed without due delegation, which led to Conor's orders to write the report he was currently writing in a daze.

Conor was not that different from his manager. He, too, had a degree, though not as advanced. His parents were in a position to push him further and to help with the mortgage of his little apartment. An émigré of Dublin South East, he was also capable with buzzwords, but at his age and experience he recognised them for what they were. The letters printed with fury onto his screen, but his thoughts were elsewhere. "They haven't rang yet, that can't be good, fuck this cunt and his fucking report! Poser, doesn't know his arse from his elbow. This is complete bollox. This could have been done two months ago when I flagged it but no, the little shit had to play Napoleon, 'it can wait, Conor.' It can't fucking wait now can it? Talked down to in a meeting by a fucking child." There was six years between Conor and his manager. "Why hasn't she rang me yet?"

"Fair play, Conor, you're grappling with it well. Listen, sorry about the short notice, but it can't be helped, these things just appear, sure the TOIL is yours anyway." The manager said these words with a mouth full of raspberry doughnut, as he passed the cubicle. Conor half grinned and grunted.

He stopped typing and momentarily rubbed his face, his hands still firm against his cheeks as he read the screen. "This will need to be refined a lot... she said 11, it's nearly half, when is she going to fucking ring?!" Suddenly, his mobile rang. The low grade recording of "Ride of the Valkyries" was a much laughed at joke between Conor and his mother.

"Hi Mum."

"Conor, I'm sorry, we're only getting out now." The fragile voice on the other end barely mumbled. "The consultant, the consultant said he has two months max, they're no longer trying the chemo." Silence answered this message as the blood raced to Conor's face, followed by an ache in his throat as he struggled to breathe.

"Conor?" a now tearful voice queried.

There was a forced cough then a reply. "I need to get some stuff at home, and then I'll head over, Mum. I'll see you in a few." This was a small lie told for the sake of mercy; what Conor needed was time. There were precious amounts of it in his apartment. He picked up his jacket and without saying a word to his manager, who was now chatting aimlessly with a similarly aged woman who wanted desperately to return to her work, Conor left the hive.

**

Fr Matthew was smoking out the side door of the church. Delores, the sacristan, was morally opposed to smoking. She saw it as suicidal and an affront to God, but for Fr Matthew it was a break from the tedium. His last parish in Coolock was a lot busier than Clementine Lane. In that church there were christenings, first communions, weddings, the lighter side of the circle of life; here all there seemed to be were funerals. None of the family rites seemed to be honoured in this area, only the necessary ones. The residents were respectful, and a lot were spiritual in their way, but not in his church. There were no lambs in his flock, though the grannies and granddads that sparsely decorated his Sunday masses were loyal.

The newcomers to the area, the apartment dwellers, were much the same as the younger locals. If anything, they were a good deal less spiritual. Most of the time, he and Delores haunted their holy castle together alone. Fr Matthew enjoyed his cigarette as he spied all the different people going to their lunch. He alighted from the side door and headed to the local newsagents; one of the alcoholics had bummed his last cigarette. He walked past a homeless man sleeping awkwardly in his church door. The man was clearly under the influence of some narcotic, and two little brown bottles were firmly in his hands as he slept. Fr Matthew had been putting off talking to the man, feeling extreme guilt over asking him to move, but pragmatically he knew that church attendance was low enough without having a vagrant impeding access.

Fr Matthew was a holy man. Indeed, he was something of learned theologian, a thinker. He was also a kind, compassionate person, and person of the people. While all this was true, there was no denying it, he was staring at the woman in front's arse while waiting in the shop queue. His age had loosened discretion. So far he had gotten away with it unnoticed, but he was being careless. There would rightfully be trouble if he was caught; though these days that kind of priest did not make national news and people would probably be more forgiving of him, due to the actions of others in his vocation. It was a gift given by relativism. He was relatively a good priest. Fr Matthew knew what the laity thought of his vocation. He had noted that no one trusted him to be alone with their children, even though he strongly believed paedophile priests were sent by Satan to destroy the one true church. But nowadays, priests were relatively untrustworthy as a whole. Relativism giveth and relativism taketh away.

"It is always important to consider the situation of those who are deprived. We must fight for them, as St Michael fought Lucifer. We must abandon our wealth and walk with them like Christ did before us."

"Thomas, you are the only one who really cares. There is fire in those eyes that would shame the wealthy."

Fr. Thomas Matthew was daydreaming of sermonizing to the attractive woman in front of him. It was pleasant and it made him feel more powerful than the stark reality of his actual life. In his mind, he was also far nobler than he was currently being in reality. The Fr Thomas in his daydream would not be staring at his audience member's arse as he uttered his impassioned words. As with us all, we imagine ourselves better than the rather uninspiring truth.

Escaping his daydreams and returning to reality, he saw that young man from the apartments walk across the shop windows with tears streaming down his face. Truthfully, he found the man arrogant, sneery and cold, as every young man from his generation and class seemed to be these days. Perhaps then it was the shock of seeing this young man openly weeping that made the priest quickly purchase his fags and leave the shop to follow.

"Conor, isn't it?"

"Not now please, Father, not now." The young man walked on and the priest pursued.

"Now seems like the best time, Conor."

"Please just leave me be."

"I will of course, it's just you're a tall young fella and I can't reach the switch on the boiler. The caretaker ran off with my steps. Delores is freezing, poor old thing."

Conor felt a surge of guilt; his own dying father would not approve of ignoring such a plea for clemency from an old man. Besides, that old sacristan Delores did remind him of his mother. "All right, yeah, I'll knock it on for you but then I have to go."

"Thanks, Conor, you're marvellous." Fr Matthew walked briskly ahead of Conor. Having reached the church door faster, facilitating enough time to successfully hide his step ladder, a now visibly breathless Fr Matthew welcomed Conor in.

After pulling a pew out of the church into the parish centre, so he would have something to stand on, Conor managed to switch the boiler on. He was bringing the pew back when Fr Matthew walked in with two rather dilute milky teas in each hand. They did not have time to brew correctly, but the priest knew an anchor was required to keep his guest in the harbour.

"Thank you so much, Conor, here, here, sit down a second."

This time Conor did not decline. He was feeling increasingly drained. Even the mild exertion of moving the pew had tired him, more than it usually would have.

"They train us in the seminary at counselling, you know? Do you know what? Having served in as many communities as I have,

I always thought it was fucking useless." The priest saw cursing as vulgar behaviour, but he hoped his usage might help build rapport with the quiet ponytailed young man looking gloomily into his mug.

Conor did not respond to this opening gambit.

"Sorry about the mug, I think it's from a Kit Kat Easter egg. We only get castoffs here."

"Father, I'm not a religious man…"

"Well that is a pity. In better times I could have had you stoned for that. Of course, these days it's fashionable, both not believing and getting stoned!"

Conor was distant and now a little confused. Fr Matthew thought he was making a rock music reference. He now felt that he had said too much on something he knew far too little.

"Thanks for the tea, I best be going." Conor rose to leave.

"You're not the type to cry over any old thing," the priest suddenly blurted out, with a hint of desperation.

Conor stopped and looked sternly, though truthfully his red eyes betrayed his fragility. "It's none of your business."

"Certainly isn't, certainly isn't, but I've lost people on me too, I know that pressure, I know the disorientation."

Conor became angry. "I haven't lost anyone!"

"You are about to, Conor, I may be a nosy priest but I am also an old man, I seen this all before. Those eyes tell me what I need to know."

Conor rubbed his face with his hands. He was still standing near the door that separated the church from the outside world, the sacred from the profane. "My father has terminal cancer, he'll be dead in two months. There is nothing else to say about it, he's not going somewhere else, he's not going to live forever in paradise. That is nonsense. We know how the universe came into being. We know how the earth was formed. There was no magical wizard in the clouds, casting spells. My father, the man who taught me everything, the man who brought me to Leinster matches, the man who brought me for a pint after my first break up, who helped me buy my home, will be buried in a pitch black box, with six feet of earth placed on top of him, and he will decompose."

Conor had not realised that he was weeping as he was speaking. Eventually, the meaning of his words hit him and he broke down, sobbing.

The priest rose and walked briskly to him and placed his arms around Conor's shoulders and held him. Fr Matthew was satisfied, not at this rebuff of his most sincerely held beliefs, but that the man now crying heavily on his shoulder was finally talking honestly. "That's okay, that's what is needed, Conor, that's all right, let it all out."

The 30-something cynic now resembled a child losing all braking power on his emotions, as the tears continued to stream. They sat down and Fr Matthew began to question Conor about his father's conversation with him, after his first break up. They both laughed when Conor related that his father, with a pint in hand proclaimed that, "the back of one was the face of another." This coming from a man who was only ever with one woman in his entire life! They spoke for an hour, before a much more composed and able, though still hurting, Conor thanked him and made his way to Stillorgan. There he would joke with his sick father and look resilient to his suffering mother.

Fr Matthew thanked God for helping him with his role, by a quick prayer, and went to the side door for a smoke. In a role now often disgraced by the behaviour of deviants and the mentally deranged, here stood a good priest, even if he did stare at women's bottoms.

10.

An Antagonist

2nd February 2018 (Friday)

IT WAS NOW 2.40 P.M. IN THE AFTERNOON ON THAT BEAUTIFUL February Friday. Sienna had not been to school since meeting Brendan two weeks ago, or the "incident" as her parents had termed it. Her concern for him had not waned in the intervening period. The scene of him being stretchered out, barely conscious, constantly replayed in her mind. Phyllis was deeply worried that Sienna was holding back on what happened in the warehouse. After all, it couldn't have been just a conversation about some addict's life story. Why had Sienna cried so much when that dishevelled mess was placed in the ambulance that night? That question may seem like it has an obvious answer but the truth was her mother was right. Unfortunately, Sienna had already seen people in that state carried out of flats, onto waiting stretchers; sadly, more than a few times. Phyllis felt that Sienna could do with a break. Perhaps, she was right about this, too. Sienna, since starting secondary, had increasingly frequent moments of anxiety. A year in and this situation had not abated.

The truth was for some time she had been struggling with something that she could not put her finger on. This was something that had dogged her and made her environment seem hostile, even different. This was something she was unable to express or articulate to anyone. It was depression. Nonetheless, at two weeks of absence, even Sienna felt her over-protective mother was taking the piss. If this continued, she would surely become the newest member of social worker kids' gang, that sad collection of children whose drug-addled parents' inconsistency had meant sparing, unhelpful visits from social workers that achieved little other than to make them the topic of neighbours' gossip.

For Sienna, her now-complete imprisonment in the house had become quite intolerable, which was one of the reasons why she was now not in it. Instead, she had taken to periodically walking down to the chapel and climbing the bins around its side. From this vantage point she could stare in through the stained glass windows. Often she was shooed away by the youth workers inside, who could not understand this young teenager's obsession with the place. Why wasn't she in school or, if not there, drinking cans somewhere? Her purpose there was known only to her. Those small utterances from Brendan had created so much curiosity. She wanted desperately to see what he had seen, almost as much as he seemed to want to un-see it.

Standing awkwardly atop two olive green bins, she was peering in through the windows at those fatigued youth workers limply trying to calm the hyper-charged youngsters running around within. These were the younger children, not yet tired despite their short day at school.

Sienna once again scanned the old chapel with her eyes. She had not yet discovered anything remarkable about the building in the two weeks since her investigation began. The chapel did look old, no doubt about that, and its choir balcony did appear forbidding, but she couldn't help but see it as just another repurposed community building. Complete with the same anti-racism posters on the wall, now accompanied by LGBT ones declaring that it's OK to be different. It is unlikely that the children who used the project understood this statement. They were not yet sexualised and had another few years in front of them before that revelation would bring them into a new world of choices. It also had the same computer game machines, which were a couple of models behind the present one. The same mutilated dolls that looked like they saw action on Omaha Beach. Sienna just could not see the extraordinary, in this rather ordinary building.

"What did they kick you out for? Oh wait, better question, why do you want to get back in?" The voice came from behind her. It was oddly familiar, a Dublin accent yes, but a different Dublin, a Dublin with trees and spaces with bistros and clean wood panelled bars. Sienna turned around. She was unsure of the grey-suited man with sallow skin and black hair. Nonetheless, she decided to be brazen.

"Who are you?"

"I'm an adult, so show me a little more respect than that, if you wouldn't mind," he said with an empty grin. She climbed down from the bins and stood eye to his neck. He regarded her for a moment. "Don't worry, I won't tell your mammy that you were skipping school, you little rascal."

"I'm not skipping school, me ma is keeping me out because she thinks I'm in shock."

"Sure she is, you little fibber." He chuckled to himself. Respect was a one-way street, it would seem. The man's eyes moved to the chapel. "What a majestic building. So much history…" Once again, he lowered them to Sienna. "What's your name, darling?"

"Sienna."

"What a beautiful name. I'm Eamon." He placed his hand out to be shaken, to which she obliged, albeit reticently. "You've probably seen me on the telly. I'm the guy on the news who's usually arguing with the Government stooge for *people* such as yourself."

At 14, Sienna was still aware of the implication of this putdown and was quickly putting two and two together. "You're the drug addict guy?"

"I'm the man who helps those in addiction, yes," he half chuckled.

"I don't do drugs. You're not helping me," she sternly replied.

The well-dressed man smiled and turned his back to the chapel; he was now facing the warehouse. "I love the frankness of the people here. You're dead right, Sienna, but I am going to help those you probably know. When we tear down this awful warehouse, I will be helping your friends."

The teenager resented this comment. She did not have friends with addiction. She barely had friends. "Me ma thinks you're a self-righteous, well-paid wanker, who doesn't live in the areas where your centres are and pretends to be one of the people while living miles away from them."

The man's eyes darkened but the smile shone as bright. "Well, we all have our opinions, uninformed or not, but you can tell your mother from me I would gladly do my job for whatever she gets herself, because that's what I was raised to believe, to help the community."

"But you don't though, do you?"

The man in the grey suit was still pondering if this last question was referring to his wage being the same as the girl's mother or whether he helped the community, when Terry came marching by.

"Sienna, how are ya, love?"

Sienna saw an opportunity. "Hi ya Terry! I'm talking to the drug rehab guy."

Terry was nearly past the chapel when he turned on his heel, back towards the teenager and the now only half smiling Eamon. Hawkins was a wealthy man and had a natural apprehension of people he perceived to be of the working classes. To him, they had energy and an earnest honesty that, frankly, frightened him.

"Ah yeah? Lovely to meet you Mr…?" Terry's smile was dripping with insincerity.

"Hawkins, Eamon Hawkins." The hand was produced again but this time Terry would not indulge.

"Can you tell me, sir, why you're hell bent on destroying ancient Dublin? Just a simple question if you don't mind."

Sienna smiled. Terry was a lot of things, predictable chief among them.

"Now you have me at a little bit of a disadvantage, as far as I know the warehouse wasn't built by the Vikings. That, my friend, is the wonderful pragmatic brutalism of the 1980s." Eamon beamed.

"I am fully aware that is not from the Early Christian Ireland period. I am the local historian around these parts and it's the function I was referring to, which I imagine you may have figured. You see, pal, this area has become a dumping ground. The good people living here have to put up with sanctimonious do-gooders from outside the area, dropping the poor unfortunate wrecks of human life on their doorstep. These same do-gooders then go on TV and radio and act as if they have carried Christ from the cross, while drawing a six-figure sum. Can I ask you, where do you live?"

Eamon had begun to prepare his answer for this question when Terry first started to speak. "Ah sure, I think you have me wrong, I'm only from down the road, my grandparents were from this area, well one of them was, I'm not so different from yourself." It was astonishing how his accent sanded off the varnish so quickly, into something similar to Terry's coarseness.

Terry persisted. "Where are *you* from, pal?" The "pal" in this sentence dislodged some saliva, which flew aimlessly to the ground.

"Em, Dalkey."

"Dalkey? Very nice. Do they have many drug rehabilitation centres in Dalkey?"

"Well, we have our share of social housing." Eamon was no longer smiling.

"Really? Do you think that social housing is the same as a drug rehabilitation centre? That is very interesting, I thought I lived in a home, but it turns out I have been living in a drug rehabilitation centre this past 40 years. Fascinating." Terry was now livid; his mock revelation aside, every "t" sound that sentence produced had been hammered out of his tongue, as the anger took him.

It is odd though, in a story about the indifference of society to people living in areas of social deprivation, to make a man who is trying to build a drug rehabilitation centre its antagonist. It seems rather unforgiving to those in such desperate circumstances dependent on such services, that they be made the pariahs, by extension. But Eamon Hawkins is the antagonist, and has always been the antagonist through every century of human endeavour. He was the civilizing emperor, the soul-saving punitive parish priest, the pious liberal, the one who used the face of angels to push his own personal advancement. History has given birth, countless times, to that one person who took moral authority for their own personal use. In essence, the man was a bollox. Even Terry could be right now and again; the fates had shown sympathy to him this day.

"Now Terry, may I call you Terry?"

Terry was too annoyed to answer and simply stared on.

Hawkins continued. "Terry, nobody likes the nuisance of dealing with people in addiction, I get that, but these people are in trouble and they need our help. This site is perfect for us to help people get back on their feet. I have to talk to people like you a lot when I build one of these centres and I understand, I really do, but we have got to work together to help the vulnerable."

Terry was unaffected by this attempt at appealing to his compassion. "The fact is, Mr Hawkins, you don't live here, you don't even live near one of these centres. The fact is, Mr Hawkins, you're no councillor, no priest, no nurse, you're management, you don't work with the addicts. The fact is, Mr Hawkins, this rehab centre could have been placed in the middle of a beautiful meadow looking out at the sea, near where you live, for a few extra bob and the folks inside would be able to relax and recover.

The fact is, Mr Hawkins, you probably can't afford to build a place like that, because of the wages you're creaming off the top. Instead, you build it here, beside a youth project, in an area where any of those lads could simply walk out the door and into a dealer in a neighbouring street."

Hawkins had begun to step back.

Terry continued. "You don't give a bollox, you think you can talk down to the ordinary people here because you're some blow-in, used to talking in front of a camera or with politicians, and we're just simple-minded fuckers you can patronise. There are children who will see people trying to recover, dealers will flood the area to feed a new batch of customers and the poor bastards will have temptation screaming at them from the other side of the fucking door. Fact is, Mr Hawkins, my brother Gerard died 7 years ago because in one of your centres they pushed him on to methadone. A drug he didn't need nor want but one of your staff thought he should have, and he went from having a joint of heroin once or twice, to a full-blown addict, who would go on to overdose on that fucking poison."

Sienna's eyes opened wide. Terry had never spoken about his family or the death of his brother. People assumed his opposition was purely based on some preservation argument, which itself didn't make much sense, as time had already repainted Clementine Lane several different colours by now.

"I'm sorry to hear that, Terry, truly I am, but if one of my staff recommended that dose, then I have to assume they did so for a reason. Quality of care is central to what I believe and what our organisation believes in. Look, I'll be happy for one of my staff to allay all your concerns about the centre, through our customer service line, but unfortunately, I must be moving on. I have a meeting. It was lovely talking to you both. Oh! Could you take this little girl back to her home, I think she is skipping school. Very important is school, little one, very important." With these words, Eamon briskly sidestepped Terry, who was still recovering from his own personal admission and at the same time wondering why a drug rehabilitation centre would have a "customer" service line.

Sienna had realised that today's investigation was over. A sapphire blue Rover drove past both of them. Eamon Hawkins was gone for now.

Terry came to his senses, and looked at the girl. "Come on, Sienna, I'll walk you back up. How are you now, sweetie? Are you over your little shock?" Terry looked visibly more shaken than the skinny 14-year-old walking beside him.

"I was never shocked, Terry, everyone just overreacted. Brendan was decent. You never told me about your brother?"

"No one wants to talk about a brother on drugs, Sienna. Ah he was good like, he was actually a lot nicer than me, just got caught up in the mix."

"I'm sorry, Terry." Sienna meant these words. She could see tears in his eyes.

"Thanks, sweetie."

Sienna thought for a moment. Terry was a local historian, of sorts. Maybe he knew about the chapel. "Did you ever hear about the chapel being haunted, Terry?"

"The Barnes girl story, yeah, it's amazing that no one round here remembers their history, it's a good story."

"Will you tell us it?"

"All right. I'll get you orange. I could do with a pint." Today's investigation was not over after all.

***

The kids were slowly saying goodbye to their individual room leaders, as their little clunky bodies waddled along the narrow crèche hall, which was now a chicane of buggies. The crèche would stay open for another hour or two, but only with a handful of toddlers. Most of the staff could go, there wouldn't be much need to stay. Little Stacey Daly had an adult plaster more or less covering her forehead. The small cut that the fire extinguisher had imparted her with was already mending fast. She had terrified the crèche women, who had seriously begun to suspect a concussion, but it turned out the little wagon was deliberately crossing her eyes every time they looked at her, and quietly giggling to herself. Kids are bastards. The little freckled and plastered ginger nut was covered in an anorak that was far too big for her, and, after careful and diplomatic explanation by Phyllis, the mother relaxed and had withdrawn her original claim that she would sue.

The quiet part of the day had begun, but the part time staff had not all left for home. Gathered once again in the kitchen, Marion was summoned to resume her story. With most of the toddlers asleep, she re-joined the morning's company. She sat down with a scalding bone china cup of tea in her hands and began.

11.

The Barnes Tale

2nd February 2018 (Friday)

CARTIGAN'S WAS A SMALL PUB ON McDONAGH STREET. IT WAS nestled among the new apartments that were home to Frank and Conor and other professionals new to the area. It faced Fr Matthew's church, St Luke's, which was still complete with a homeless man in its main entrance. At the end of the road was freedom from the warren that is the Liberties and its environs.

The pub was built in the 1960s. Its three stories were covered in brilliant white, with dark blue edging that suggested a maritime theme, though it was situated some two miles from the docks. The bar was tiny, covered in replicas of the Proclamation of the Provisional Republic, bodhrans and sketched drawings of Wolfe Tone, Emmet, Connolly right up to Sands. Each generation was venerated.

It was now 3.30 p.m. and though it was still bright outside, the light within the pub was dim. Venetian blinds had taken away the lion's share of the sun's radiance. The main source of light in this small dark bar emanated from the poker machine, sitting in what was a former channel for a dumb waiter. ABBA's anthem about the Mexican revolutionary "Fernando" was playing quietly in the background. Three grizzled men sat at the bar staring into their pints without saying a word. Two electricians who had skived off work early for pints were laughing loudly. A bald man in a grey fleece anxiously stared at his phone. Eventually he rose from his stool and made for the exit. For the briefest of moments he grimly met Sienna's gaze, forcing her to look away.

As only a stone's throw away, Marion had begun to enlighten Phyllis and her staff in the crèche on the very same topic of the chapel's haunted past, Terry had just returned to Sienna, a Guinness in one hand with a yellow cream top head (just how the pint was in Cartigan's) and a Fanta, alive with fizz and audible from the sound of the clinking semi-submerged ice. When he sat down he looked at Sienna and said, "So you want to know about Emily Barnes?"

Emily Barnes was born in or around 1904. She was the daughter of Sean and Doreen Barnes. She lived with her three sisters, her parents and her father's widowed mother, Hannah, in one of the little redbrick Victorian cottages in which Sienna herself now resided. Her father worked in one of the local abattoirs, which were as numerous in Dublin's inner city as the distillers and breweries at that time. It was physically hard work that, unfortunately, contributed negatively to the smells of the city, but it was consistent and reasonably paid. The Barnes family were comfortable. A testament to this comfort was the small number that resided within her home. Though they still had their challenges; Hannah's mind had absconded by way of dementia some years back. The harsh realities of living in those post famine years had slowly knocked it loose in search of less harsh skies.

Noticeably, there was a sizable age gap between Emily and her eldest sister, Theresa, who was 15 years Emily's senior. Matters were made stranger by the fact that Theresa was also sent away from the area around the time of Emily's conception, to help her childless uncle and aunt with their farm in north county Dublin. That was according to her father, anyway.

"Well, you probably grasped the first bit of shite about her story."

"What was that, Terry?" Sienna asked eagerly.

"She was the eldest sister's daughter. Theresa's parents pretended to be Emily's mother and father to spare the family a scandal. Of course, that still meant that some dirt bird impregnated Theresa when she was only 15, sad as that is," Terry reflected.

"That's awful." Sienna had no idea that the story would get so dark so quickly.

Emily may have had an unusual or even mysterious conception, but her birth was standard enough, save for one little birthmark on her forehead. It resembled a snapdragon whose mouth perpetually gaped towards Emily's nose. Much like the perennial, Emily came into this world in a mild spring. The locals knew the child was not of Mr and Mrs Barnes. News flowed through those small intertwined lanes like blood from arteries to capillaries.

"But you know, Sienna, people were decent back then, at least in this area, they got on with it, no one passed comment." Terry was nostalgic for a past he never knew. He was also wrong. People always talk. It is the majority's natural condition to talk of others and spread news, and the minority who don't, to nobly listen. While there was rumour and indeed, insinuation, the locals still did not know the full truth of her story. Emily was no more to know the specific story of her origins than the neighbours, and her grandmother Doreen became her mother rather seamlessly. An unusually intelligent girl, the precocious Emily read people brilliantly.

"Of course, such a job would have been easier back then, Sienna. People were more honest, you know? They were straight forward salt of the earth Dubs." Terry's eyes beamed with pride. He had quite recovered from his earlier altercation with Eamon Hawkins. He took a gigantic sup of his Guinness, felling the pint in half, as the reddish darkness glowed like an ominous soul trapped in a glass prison.

One related story of her cunning was how she secured her first job at the age of 12 years. She paid the local general provisions store a visit and spoke to the shopkeeper, a man called Casey. Knowing that Casey was an Irish Citizen Army man, who did his best to provide for those out of work during the Lockout and had a genuine heart for the people of the community, Emily in her saddest tones related the story of poor Jimmy Doolan, an otherwise likeable young man who was finding his jarvey work increasingly demanding on his health. The breweries had increased their demand for barley but had not increased his wage and he was required to take on a second horse even though he could scarcely afford the first. Jimmy, who lost both parents to typhoid at an early age, was finding it hard to feed his horses. The poor man would face destitution if he could not maintain those beasts of burden in their work to and from the canal and the breweries. At this time, he was feeding them at cost to his own meals.

Naturally, Casey scowled at those Protestant brewery owners and their thirst for profit on the poor working man's expense and he resolved to help in any way he could. He discreetly put away bags of apples for Jimmy with a third taken off the rate. Emily of course, reminded the man that Jimmy Doolan was proud and he wouldn't accept charity so easily and that the arrangement needed to be kept between themselves. Mr Casey readily agreed. His reward was knowing he was playing his part, whether it was publicly known or not. The unconsecrated marriage of Catholicism with socialism, peculiar to Ireland at that time, was ripe for the exploitation of this formidable manipulator.

After the reduction was secured, she headed to the hapless jarvey who was already a little drunk and said she would like a job getting his horse feed for him. He liked the girl and said he would give her what he could, and sure, it would do no harm. Emily said nothing about the new rate of apples; after all, that was to be her wage. Of course, the lie that created her profit did have elements of truth. Jimmy Doolan was not the wealthiest man and he often skipped meals, but perhaps that was more to do with his addiction to the brewery's product than their Protestant Ethic. And his parents may have died of typhoid; who knew? After all, many people did. It was possible, if not definitive, in Emily's mind.

Now there was a nun from Galway called Sister Sheila, she was one of the Sisters who ran and lived in the Chapel Convent. She was only in her late 30s and was well liked. She was an attractive nun if a little short; the kids used to enjoy laughing at the many tiny steps she would have to take to keep in line with the other penguins.

Sheila took a direct interest in the children of the area. Young enough herself to be less austere and more approachable than her sisters, she taught literacy through detectives and penny dreadfuls, rather than the more obscure language of the Bible. The truth was, though a committed Catholic, Sheila envied the mothers. Maybe even she was a little irritated at their indifference to the gifts they were given when she was cajoled into marrying Christ.

Sister Sheila was very fond of Emily. She loved her intelligence and her maturity. There was also a genuine sympathy for the girl. You see, Emily frequently was on her own, too clever for her peers who bored her easily with their silly un-enterprising games, and too young for any adult to take seriously. Too much of an age gap between her and her siblings who were courting and soon would leave the house, leaving her to live with her aging, adoptive mother and Hannah, whose dementia had, sadly, brought about increasingly violent rantings. She was on her own.

Aside from her little earner providing Jimmy with horse feed, she spent her time with Sister Sheila or watching the increasingly frequent movement of the mix-matched uniforms of the Irish Volunteers, as they marched to and from Cork Street. Sister Sheila would often take Emily for walks around the area. They would feed the pigs that were present in the many little allotments along the lanes of the Liberties. To the nun, Emily could talk freely and exercise her mind. In return, the nun would ask that she pray with her in the chapel, for relief from these increasingly troubled times. Though, truthfully, saving Emily's soul was not the nun's main objective but her company, to save the nun from her own loneliness. They were very close.

"Because she was her real ma!" Sienna spoke for the first time in a while, her Fanta nearly drained. The interruption momentarily dislodged Terry's thoughts.

"What are you on about? No, her ma was her eldest sister, Theresa. You know, Sienna, this isn't Hercules Peroite, or whatever his name is, sometimes things are what they are. In real life, the drama is seldom the twist in the story, it's the thing that was obvious from the very beginning, always present, that grows with mounting pressure. This isn't some fiction, it's history, and sadly, in history 15-year-old girls sometimes get impregnated by unscrupulous assholes and are left up the duff, with no one but family. There is no great unseen narrator telling a great interwoven story." Terry finished his pint and made for the bar to look for something similar, while the great unseen narrator felt somewhat aggrieved by his character's insolence.

Sienna took out her phone and saw two missed calls from her father. She texted him her location.

Terry swiftly returned to his warm stool. The bar was unchanged from when they had entered. Perhaps the electricians were a little louder, but otherwise it was still quiet, as to be expected for Friday, during the daylight hours.

Once settled, Terry began again.

The times grew more turbulent and marches more frequent; things were quickly changing in the city. Despite increasingly worried calls from the Castle, John Bull's stare fixated on France and he could not see what Ireland was planning. Britain's present indifference to the island was seen optimistically by a large amount of the city's population. They mistakenly felt that an abusive relationship of centuries was about to mend, like some broken delusional housewife. A small cabal realised the reprieve would be short-lived and sought to sever the union while Britain was not paying attention. On Monday of the 24th of April all things would change utterly.

Three days after Emily's 13th birthday, she could hear a distant cacophony of bangs. They seemed miles away; they were one and a half in actuality. The Rising had begun. It must seem strange now but the people in Clementine Lane still went about their business as best they could in those early hours, as if the various rebel occupations and British Army barricades were a passing inconvenience, like road works or the Council fixing sewerage pipes. The fighting surrounded all sides of Clementine Lane. Solitary sniping fire was followed by the loud roar of Lewis machines guns, occasional screams of anguish or glass shattering. It was beginning to dawn on the residents of the area this was no passing trifle, but history turning the page to a new chapter.

During those dark but few days, the Barneses, like other families on the Lane, stayed huddled in their house with little by the way of provisions and a lot by the way of uncertainty. The bitter smell of smoke filled the air and a shroud descended on the city. Dublin was being beaten for its insolence and boldness. There would be a terrible price to pay for this stand for dignity.

As the nuns gathered in the small chapel to continue their vigil for an end to hostilities, Emily sat with her family over the precious amounts of food they had left. Hannah, the dotty and senile elder of the house, stared at Emily over the meal. She ate nothing, just stared. A fool's grin slowly took over her face. It was not her fault, of course. Finally, after the others had finished their meagre crumbs and black tea, she croaked, "The little snapdragon has her mother's eyes." Theresa and her parents suddenly looked up, but it was too late. "You have Theresa's eyes, snapdragon."

Emily smiled at first. "No, Nanny, Theresa isn't my ma, she's me sister." Thinking no more of it, she felt sorry for her poor soft grandmother.

"They always tell me you're the cute one and yet, for all your cuteness, you haven't figured it out yet? Poor, poor snapdragon, sister's mammy and mammy is gran-mammy, too old for new sprogs like you." Hannah began to giggle to herself.

Emily said nothing for a moment. She looked around the silent table and could see that Theresa was staring at the table, with her hands around her forehead. She stared at Theresa, then her glance darted to her supposed parents, but they just stared back in silence. Fatigue and fear had dumbed their powers to conceal.

Emily's eyes widened, and what would have been curable in a little time became insurmountable in the intimate claustrophobic immediacy of the present. She pushed herself from the table and stood up, knocking her chair to the floor. She ran to the door, opened it to the sound of intermittent cracking gunfire in the distance and ran to the one place – or more importantly, the one person – she could turn to, Sister Sheila.

Her "father" chased after her but the sight of a man running on to that deserted street drew fire from the soldiers in their nests. He was forced to duck into doorways, while the determined Emily kept running with tears welling in her eyes and blurring her vision. The outline of the chapel came into view and with it a black figure, running towards her.

The nuns had been aroused by the intense gunfire and were discreetly peering out the window, when Sheila saw her Emily come into view. She broke through the huddled, black swaddle of women and pounded through the Chapel door, into the smoke-filled daylight and the fray.

∗∗∗

In what could be considered immaculate timing, the story was hitting a similar conclusion in the crèche, much to the collective interest of those present in the small crèche kitchen.

"Ah Jaysus, I know where this is going, Emily is going to get shot, for fuck's sake, I should have known better than to have asked you, Marion, you're a right miserable fucker by times." It wasn't Marion's fault Phyllis was upset. She had spent a long time listening to this story and began to see shades of her Sienna in the birthmarked girl from a century ago.

"Ah the poor thing, who was her father anyway? You never said that part. Are his relatives still living here?" another woman piped in, perhaps hoping old stories could bring new gossip.

Marion was mid swallow of a fresh cup of tea and could not yet respond.

***

While Marion was still managing to swallow the remainder of her tea in the crèche, Terry had made it to the end of his own rendition in Cartigan's.

"You see, Sienna, that's who your ghost is meant to be, that poor girl." Terry seemed satisfied that he had done the story justice. Truthfully, for all his talk of being an historian, he quite enjoyed the idea of being known as a storyteller better than an academic. With this temperament in mind, he delivered his epilogue. "They pulled the nun's body into the chapel and said prayers over it, while the gunfire roared on the streets outside and the little girl screamed as her adopted father and an elderly nun tried to comfort her. She was covered in her third mother's blood, not the mother who birthed her, not the mother who fed her, no, but the mother who wrapped her habit around her as the bullets pierced her back. Sister Sheila, your ghost."

"Starting her early, Terry?" Shane stood in the Cartigan's doorway.

"We had a run-in with our new neighbour, the rehab fucker, and Sienna wanted to know about the history of the chapel," Terry replied as he headed for the bar.

"You've nothing better to be doing then annoying the

neighbours about ghost stories, told to you by homeless alcoholics? G'wan home, your ma will be coming in the door and will want to get the dinner on. Here, I'll get this, Terry, thanks for watching her."

The two men stood at the bar, as Sienna got up to leave. She was still processing the story. Two things were clear: she would get inside of that chapel, and she would visit Brendan in hospital. She must know what he saw.

12.

Little Brown Bottles

2nd February 2018 (Friday)

As a crisp, cold, clear night enveloped the streets outside, that long Friday in February was drawing to a close in Cartigan's. Terry and Shane were happily drunk at the bar. They may not have left with Sienna, but their sobriety was not long after her. Despite their different personalities, their shared childhood found the universal tongue of memory. Naturally enough, their reminiscing had turned into a game of "which teacher was a prick, and which teacher was a fiddler prick." Sadly, Shane was feeling somewhat unattractive, in part due to Terry's seemingly unending knowledge of the fiddlers.

Fr Matthew was drinking a pint with Arthur and Frank in the corner, the former by arrangement, the latter by coincidence. Frank had intended to meet a friend there, by way of illustrating his down-to-earth, working-class connections, though this visit to Cartigan's was his first in nearly a year. Unfortunately, his friend cancelled but the text arrived after Frank had ordered a glass of wine. He was grateful to Arthur for inviting him to their table. Even if it was with an old man and a priest, it certainly seemed to him less threatening than some of the other options.

Marion was holding court in the centre of the pub with two women from the crèche, both in their early 50s, both peers of hers and without child-raising responsibilities, ideal drinking companions. At one side of her was Leanne, thin, sallow skinned with dark brown hair and a face that had been aged by smoking. The winkles ran across her forehead line, like waves of sand on a desert mound. She was loud and coarse. In her own mind, she was the comedian from the rare auld times, but the other girls in the crèche largely just found her annoying. To the other side of Marion was Hope, a Nigerian woman, who despite living in the area for 17 years was still having Irish culture explained to her by well-meaning colleagues. She was stout, bigger than Marion, her black hair sophisticatedly styled like Jackie Kennedy. She wore dark purple lipstick and her eyes were always wide in perpetual disbelief. More reserved than the other two, she was a pensive but friendly lady, whose quietness hid not only intelligence but a secret longing, not for home but for family.

Mick came in, as was expected, to sit in front of his poker machine, but upon seeing Marion immediately walked over and told her not to worry about the dinner, to which she answered that she wasn't. He left as quickly as he came in.

Under the television sat Hugh, a man in his late 50s, arms folded, with eyes that were every bit as narrow as Hope's were wide. Hugh was known in the area for being in the old IRA. Now not the old, old IRA, just the old IRA. Apparently he didn't accept the Good Friday Agreement initially either, so for a time he joined the new IRA, now not the new, new IRA just the new IRA. Periodically, he liked to get up and show the pub how he was trained to march. Marching is very important to a clandestine urban guerrilla warfare paramilitary group, he often loudly pointed out from the bar.

The pub was now well lit up and was noisy. More electricians joined the two from earlier in the day. They were drinking some Belgian beer in small medicinal-sized brown bottles. Vinnie, the landlord, was protected by the growing rowdiness by a semi hexagonal wood-finished bar. The thin, hunched barman stared at his customers from above his glasses as he poured. He usually engaged his customers in mild conversation, often stating his disdain for politicians, commenting on the cold weather or asking after X. Vincent Cartigan's small talk was older than the dusty old steins that adorned the shelf behind him. Pop music from the 80s played in the background. The overly dramatic ballads would largely go ignored, but their absence would suggest finishing time and so even on a subconscious level they were always listened to.

"Another pint of something similar, Vinnie, that's the lad." Vincent Cartigan was older than Hugh by two years.

"Ah very good, Hugh, very good, it's bitter out, isn't it? Fierce bitter."

"That it is, Vinnie, that it is." Hugh's vocal style was heavy in gravitas. After all he wasn't just a bus driver, he was a former Volunteer.

"I hear Terry had an encounter with Mr Hawkins. Well, I tell you, if his shop brings the dealers back into the Lane, I will have to make it known to the higher ups. Community first, and as we know, there are people who will protect the locals if the Garda don't." Hugh looked around furtively. "We shan't be having that problem investing itself here again, shall we? We shall not." He handed the exact, correct change to Vinnie.

"It's the politicians, Hugh, they don't care, they don't care about the small folk, they don't, not an iota, am I right?" Vinnie peered into Hugh's eyes over his glasses.

"All I'll say is, politicians or no, any dealer who comes onto my street should first write a letter to his widow, am I right?" Hugh half smiled at his own tough man rhetoric.

"Oh there's the man now, there's the man." Vinnie laughed in response.

Two doors down from Hugh Dempsey's flat on the second row of Clementine Lane Flats lived two men who had been dealing crack for nigh on two years now. Hugh was unaware, despite the frequent comings and goings of dishevelled and broken human beings passing his door, on their way to score. It's just as well, as if he did know, and rang his link to the IRA supreme command, he may have been told to keep fucking quiet as they were the supplier to his neighbours. Unbeknown to Hugh, his "link" to supreme command were not the most recent incarnation of the near mystical Oglaigh na hEireann, whose legitimacy was derived from the 1919 First Dáil, either. Nope, they were just some happy-go-lucky drug dealers, who thought it funny posing as a republican splinter group to hide some revolvers in some 50-something-year-old idiot's house. Can you believe that they even got him to march up and down? Well, they did. And they were right, it was funny.

"Would you fuck off, you'd put a tenner on and that would be your lot, ye windy prick!"

"Don't tell me what I'd put on a horse, ye squeaky little geebag, bringing your ma's fat fanny to Burger King costs me a few bob. I have to play big for those magic nights out." The electricians' banter was still kind of good natured, though that could change.

"Hear this one now, would ya listen to her, as if butter wouldn't melt! If one of those young fathers from the crèche came knocking on your door, Mick would be sent to the pub and you be in and out, in and out!" Leanne loudly cackled before coughing up half a lung; the other lung was hanging on for dear life. Neither Marion nor Hope was particularly impressed by this coarseness.

"No, I wouldn't, Leanne. I'm not a dishwasher like you, with yoyo knickers." That wasn't true, to be fair, either. Leanne preferred a can to a man any day of the week, and her knickers to be rigidly in place.

"Your ghost story was very good today, Marion. Life can be very sad," Hope reflected.

"Ah it is what it is, ghost stories are often a load of old bollox anyway, aren't they?" Marion was delighted her story was well received but was gracious too.

Hope thought for a moment then asked, "You are not a believer, Marion?"

"She's a believer in a bit of young mickey, am I right?" The crèche women were right, Leanne was annoying.

"I do believe, now I haven't been to mass for a while, but I do believe. I got me angels protecting me. I think me brother and folks are watching me from up there. I suppose people laugh at me for that, I'm not so clever or whatever, but life is hard and it can be lonely, so they can have their cleverness, I rather have me faith, it's made me strong. Sure, who knows in the end?"

Hope nodded in agreement before taking a small swallow of her white wine.

"Fuck the dead nun, I'm stuck with two living ones tonight, ah I'm only slagging, Hope... you know, having a laugh, that's what 'slagging' means."

"Yes, I know, thanks, Leanne."

"Get your hands off me, you gay cunt!" One apprentice electrician shoved his older companion, who had been leaning into his ear singing to the radio while seductively curling his hair.

Frank was uneasy watching the electricians, but then he returned to the conversation.

"Look, guys, I get it, but if not here then where? The problem has to be faced up to and dealt with and we're engaging in 'Not In My Back Yard' behaviour. You were a councillor, Frank, you must know that this kind of thing always finds complaints when it is proposed but it doesn't change brass tax, it's needed."

Frank glared at that worn, heavily bearded face but the padre's mistake was genuine.

"I only ran for councillor, Matthew, but the locals needed someone more interested in moaning than doing and I didn't get in. Anyway, no one is saying that there shouldn't be services, of course there should. It's about placing them in the right areas and not beside crèches. I'm a member of Connolly's party, the people's party."

"Except when you are needed to be a nappy for O'Duffy's party, eh Frank?" Yes, it was an unusually aggressive tone from Arthur, but then Frank did not address the priest by his prefix "Father" and as a lifelong Fianna Fáiler Arthur hated both Labour and Fine Gael. To him, God and the Country had been affronted and, well, he was also a little drunk.

"Do you want it there, Arthur? Am I wrong?" Frank was aggrieved.

"No, you're not, as it happens, the area can never hope to move forward if every do-gooder sends its problems to it. We're an easy target because the majority don't vote and that's the truth of it," Arthur reflected. He placed his pint down with a mild wobble in his left hand.

"Look, I will facilitate the community's will, use the chapel, speak at mass but I will not speak out against it myself, it's not a Christian position," Fr Matthew conceded. He could see the wind changing, and he didn't want his flock to dwindle further because he was playing at being pious.

"The Church seldom holds the Christian position these days, Matthew." Both Arthur and Fr Matthew turned to Frank who regretted this comment and quickly made light of it. "Sure look, of course we would argue politics and religion, look at the two of us, a politician and a priest."

Fr Matthew laughed to allow the lightening of the mood.

"Would-be politician," Arthur muttered.

"I fucking mean it, Dave, calm the fuck down, calm right the fuck down."

"Or you'll do what, friend? Or you'll do what?" The electricians' table had become covered in little brown bottles of beer.

"Lads, if you can't hold it, there's a crèche around the corner but I'm not serving you anymore. Now love, what can I get you?" Vinnie had become aware of the increased volume.

"I'd ride that one." Leanne was staring at the boisterous table.

"Fuck off, Leanne, you were in your 30s when he was born.

God, there's a thought, you probably changed his fucking nappies! Ye old bitch! Besides, I wouldn't go out with a sparks, their work's too temperamental," Marion stated with authority.

"Could be worse, could be like your Mick and be too temperamental for work!" Leanne had avenged herself well; Marion was visibly annoyed. It's funny, they were friends, but they really enjoyed irritating each other, two curmudgeons.

"Hello ladies." Frank was on his way to the bar, to buy a peace offering for his needed ally, Arthur.

"How are ya, Frank?" Marion smiled. They had lived beside each other for some time, but it was only that rainy night on the way to the warehouse that they, finally, introduced themselves.

"Oh look, here's the ladies' man." Leanne didn't care for the intrusion.

"How are you getting on, Marion, how's Phyllis and her daughter?"

"Ah they're fine, they're fine." Marion nodded. She was still grateful for his umbrella that night.

"Here, are you not trying to get a three-way going with the priest and the fucker who forgot he was dead?" Leanne snarled. The other women looked on in shock.

"I much prefer your company, Ms 'every fag loves a hag'." With that, Frank turned to the bar and walked off, content for his one-liner and genuinely missing the company of the table he originated from.

"Ah for fuck's sake, he's gone and called the guards!" The electricians went for the entrance, as the blue flashing light beamed through the Venetian slats of the bar. Hugh stood up like a meerkat and fear flushed his face white. The Volunteer ran out the fire exit, skidding on the door mat and showing his ample arse as he did so. Shane and Terry looked at Vinnie for answers, but he was as bewildered as they were.

The door opened wide and in walked Garda Gibbons. He stood and surveyed the room. Gougers, he thought, drunken gougers, the lot of them. The Tipperary Javert looked grim. What he was searching for was still unclear. Finally, he settled on Arthur and approached the elderly man, as the bar stared on in silence. "Fr Matthew, I presume?"

"Eh, no that would be this gentleman here." Arthur gestured towards the priest, who was not in a dog collar. It seemed unseemly to him to wear one in a public house.

"Oh no, not Delores, not my poor Delores." The priest was terrified of the news that Death's luminous yellow messenger would deliver. Suddenly, he thought of all her nagging and how much it filled the silence of the church.

"No, no. I'm sure she's fine, but unfortunately, we got a call thirty minutes ago, there's an addict outside your church door. We believe he expired some two hours ago. We were hoping you could name him."

"Oh no, ah God no." The priest sat for a moment as the Garda patiently waited.

"I never asked his name, you know? I would give him cigarettes and the odd sandwich, but he never was really much of a talker. To be honest, when I saw him with the little brown bottles, I assumed he was on something. I was afraid of the poor soul," the priest said with a deep shame.

"No, the bottles appear to be some form of medication. Looking at his teeth, we've summarised crack cocaine was his drug of choice. We believe it was an overdose of the same."

"Looking at the teeth?! He's not a fucking dog!" Terry shouted from the bar.

Gibbons became aware of the bar's silence and turned around. "Yes, of course, yes, I'm sure."

Aware that his choice of words was harsh, the Garda knew it was time to go. Though he felt a little aggrieved, he had genuinely felt sadness when he first discovered the cold body outside. He even went as far as to grab the blanket his mother gave him for Christmas from his car to cover the man, and say a prayer over the body.

Gibbons walked out the door.

The priest looked broken. "If he was in a centre, Arthur."

"I know, Father." Arthur's gaze shared sympathy with the ashamed priest.

The women returned to a low murmur about how they always passed the man by and that he was usually polite, and how more had to be done to deal with the drugs situation. Terry, now emotional with drink and the feeling of repeated history, began to tell Shane about his brother, the second time he spoke of the man that day.

Frank had observed all and was thinking something different. He ordered a whiskey, which he swallowed without appreciating its value. He could see something else on the horizon. A man dying in a church doorway, on a cold night, was political capital. The political parties would make hay in his demise, when none of them did anything for him in his life. The media would be here soon. This would frame the debate. A chance of a political career was in the offering. Would he remain loyal to the locals? Would he take the party line and support the centre? Choices had to be made and quickly.

The ambulance came for the remains. The little side street was awash with blue for most of the dark hours of the night. For an early February Friday, it was a long day. It had started with such optimism.

13.

Oh, What A Circus!

THE SUN OF THE PREVIOUS DAY WAS LONG GONE AND AN ALL-encompassing, banal, grey sky was releasing a blanket of tiny droplets on the people of Dublin. Though not thick rain, its consistency had completely covered the bright grey pavements and coloured them almost a dark paper bag brown. At 12 p.m., the dullness of the sky was as bright as could be hoped for the remainder of the day. The cars were more audible than usual, as they swished and swashed on the moist roads. The short and narrow side street, filled with the isolated autonomous apartment blocks and now several news vans, looked smaller than usual. At one end of the street a radio man was interviewing people smoking outside Cartigan's pub. Down the street outside the church stood a cameraman, angling nervously with his machine, aiming it at an increasingly irate, short, well-dressed man in his mid 40s.

"My bollox is turning blue, get that fucking thing in the right place and count me in." The camera was steadied. Donal McGlynn stared dead-eyed and suitably grim. "Three, two and go." The cameraman's hand gestured slowly, and gracefully guided the reporter to begin.

"I am standing outside St Luke's Roman Catholic Church, near the mouth of Dublin's Liberties area, where in the early hours of this morning the body of a homeless man was found dead, from an apparent drug overdose. The Garda have identified the deceased as a Mr Peter Williams. The 28-year-old was originally from Drumcondra and has been living rough for the past several years. He was interviewed by this very station at Christmas time, just under two months ago. In that interview, Mr Williams spoke about the need for clean emergency accommodation and how it was his genuine belief that his own problems with addiction could have been addressed if such accommodation was more readily available." The vignette of the interview with the now dead man played, while the short, tanned and dark-haired Donal played mindlessly with his microphone.

"You're back in two, one and…"

"The news of the man's death has been seized by the opposition parties in Kildare Street. Many TDs have argued that the government has persistently failed to address rising addiction problems, as well as homelessness, in the capital. Sinn Féin is currently calling for a vote of no confidence in the Minister for Health. Their colleagues on the opposition benches, Fianna Fáil, who support the minority government, have dismissed Sinn Féin's proposal and are advocating the establishment of a committee to further identify what additional services are needed. Earlier this morning, I spoke to the Labour Leader Michael Norton, who had this to say." A new vignette played.

While waiting for the clip to end, Donal looked at a group of teenagers who were looking at him while resting on the handlebars of their bikes across the road. "Fuck off, ya little Johnny rippers! Nobody wants to see your little spotty fuck faces on TV!" The teenagers were actually shocked. Jason the cameraman wasn't; he knew the difference between onscreen Donal and real Donal.

"You're back in two, one…"

"The people of this community, so long troubled with

addiction, are deeply affected by this young man's passing. A rehabilitative centre with residential units is planned for the area, though there have been objections from some quarters in the community, who feel that more services of this type will bring further anti-social problems. I will be covering this issue over the course of the week through a series of vignette interviews with residents of the area, as well as other interested stakeholders. Until my next instalment, Nuala, back to you.

"Are we done?" the short-tempered journalist asked. The camera man nodded in the affirmative.

"What a fucking shambles, the Shinners try to embarrass the Fáilers, who support the Gaelers to keep the Shinners out even though they allegedly hate the Gaelers and have more in common with the Shinners. Somewhere in the background Labour tries to seem like they are relevant outside of the numpty posh Dublin East Arts degree fuckhead crowd. Ultimately, he's just a fucking junkie cunt who every single one of them would have passed to the other side of the fucking street to avoid, and the pricks send me here for the fucking week to talk to a load of pissed welfare fucktards in a no doubt vain attempt to make it pertinent. It's a fucking agenda, Jason, either the top brass want to topple the government or they want to topple me!"

Jason simply ignored this foul-mouthed rant from Donal as he gradually wrapped camera wires around his arm.

A man crossed the street in a newly purchased, silver, glossy suit with a salmon pink shirt and a paisley patterned tie. The shirt popped against the dark grey themed day, though it did nothing to conceal his pot belly. His grey hair was neatly jelled back, and he walked briskly towards the reporter, who was looking for his cigarettes in his pocket.

"Hello, Mr McGlynn. That was an excellently presented report. I was actually just watching you out my window and on my TV at the same time, I was in total Donal vision!" Frank awkwardly laughed while the unfazed reporter continued his search. "Anyway, my name is Frank Cantwell, I'm something of a community leader in these parts and I was wondering if I could have a word?"

"Yeah, sound." Donal wasn't really paying attention and was more interested in trying to get his near-wasted Bic lighter to ignite his cigarette.

Frank was a little taken back by the reporter's flatness but continued. "Well, I would know the people around here very well and I wouldn't mind speaking in one of your vignettes about the need to help these poor unfortunates."

"I hear Ulster from that voice, not a local?" Donal's eyes peered up from the semi lit cigarette.

"No, actually I'm originally from Monaghan."

"A very urbane part of Monaghan, it would seem. Let me guess, you're pursuing a political career?" His narrow eyes maintained their stare at Frank.

"No, no, I just want to express the opinion of the area as eruditely as possible. I want the locals to be fairly represented." Frank was beginning to blush.

"Right, so politician then. Monaghan? Hmm… Fianna Fáil would have been my first guess for a border county man in a suit, but they want this to go away as it makes them look like dickless wankers against the government. Sinn Féin would be my next guess, but you really aren't the type. I know they've come up in the world but you're not a sprog, and when you were, the Shinners probably would have had you shitting yourself. Nah, you're a Labour man. 'Erudite' is not Shinner or a Fáiler word, it's a Labour liberal word if ever I heard it. Not a Labour working class word either, daddy must have had a big farm and must have been quite disappointed that his son ditched the blueshirt for the rose. Fair enough, make my life easier, give me a list of people who won't say 'fuck' or 'cunt' when I have a mike on them. I want a granny, some young couple shitting on about kids, I'll get the padre myself and none of your posh pals either. I want people from here. Do that for me and I'll give you a 2-minute slot. Deal?"

Frank had turned the colour of his shirt. He was feeling indignant at Donal's surprising candour and his implications about his insincere sincerity. His temper cooled though, as the reporter still stared at him awaiting a response and he realised he had his interview. "Great, I know just who to ask, they're wonderful people, so full of colour."

"Like your shirt then, sound. Well, you get on that for me and ring this number." Donal offered a card and then walked towards the van. A still visibly shaken Frank crossed back across the road as Donal muttered to himself, "Pompous prick."

As the van pulled away up the street, Hugh was standing outside Cartigan's pub talking to a piece of fluff on a stick beside Terry. Both men were ridiculously hung over but had felt that a pint might remedy their previous night's poisoning. And it was poisoning. Vinnie Cartigan was a good man, but he must have left those pipes for a long time without cleaning. For it was evident that you could have eleven pints and you might be a little tired but these men had headaches, which was clearly the landlord's fault. The radio interviewer pointing the stick at them was gently asking them of their pedigree in the area.

In what was a long and utterly unenlightening segment, the two waxed lyrical about Dublin in the rare auld times and reminisced about the area before the drug and homeless problem. Men were only drinkers then and drink doesn't harm you like drugs. The conversation changed to the drinking limit and how unforgiving the government was when a man could easily be able to drive after four pints, just as sure as he wouldn't have a headache after eleven (provided the pipes were clean of course).

On the main street, a broadsheet journalist was looking at the church from its front and the shadows of the brewery behind. As he observed the street, he began watching a couple aged by heroin, though they were probably just in their 40s, shouting at each other outside the newsagents. He began to pen a piece, which he titled "Forgotten Pieces." He was even imagining the picture of a jigsaw with some pieces removed that would sit above his name. The article began, "How can we call ourselves a society, a complete picture? Surely there are pieces missing, uncared for..." and so it went on. When he was done, a homeless man asked him for some change. The journalist politely told him to fuck off, as he boarded his bus back into the city centre.

***

"We just want people to understand that we are good people too. We're trying to raise families around this problem the same as anyone else. Everyone thinks you should just dump society's problems here, because this is where the flats are, and all the people are on drugs. We're the same as anyone else, everyone is afraid of these services when it's right beside them, but the media demonise you like you're a heartless monster! I'm only saying we have enough of our own problems without importing everyone else's!" Marion was speaking outside the crèche the following day, in the first of Donal's vignettes, standing beside Hope at the reporter's behest; he felt the latter's ethnicity showed new Dublin, though he did not interview her.

It was Sunday and the crèche was closed but he felt it would emphasise her points and background. Two thoughts ran through his mind. "The Monaghan prick did well with this one," and "She has some rack for a granny."

The camera swung back to Donal as he gave his closing comments. "The voice of a caring woman who has given her all to the community, Marion Ryan voicing the fears of local parents and indeed, a community that feels abandoned by the State. A counterpoint to politicians and NGOs, a simple message: with more services, there is a need for more careful planning and an end to social dumping. Back to you, Grainne."

"We're clear."

"Thanks Jason. Mrs Ryan, I just want to say thank you so much for that interview, you were wonderful." Donal had a remarkable ability to show respect to those he felt could cause him problems. He would never speak to this obviously outspoken lady as he would to Frank. She wasn't playing the same game and he had no leverage over her. He knew that. He also knew she could be on the phone to his employer, if he did say more than his prayers. Truthfully, he also kind of liked her; he believed her when she spoke.

"Ah thanks, it's terrible about the young fella but you can't let them fuck all the world's problems on ya." It was also remarkable how quickly Marion could change her dialect when no longer in a formal setting.

Donal began walking down the lane to his next interview, a Mr and Mrs Shane and Phyllis Farrell. It would be filmed today and shown on tomorrow's bulletin. The reporter was admittedly looking forward to this interview. According to his cameraman, Jason, who had already met the couple, Mrs Farrell was very much the stunner. "It's gas, I always thought that hipster cunt was gay," Donal thought to himself.

From the opposite end of the street, Sienna was returning to the path after stepping onto the road to avoid a bald man in a grey fleece, and his two friends. They had been loudly laughing and had not noticed her. She briefly scowled at them. The teenager was on her way to the chapel. The ever-enterprising Sienna had acquired the keys to the premises from a youth worker. She had convincingly lied to her about dropping off leftover food from the crèche on behalf of her mother.

Sienna stopped when she had reached Donal. The abruptness of her movement caught him a little off guard. "Are you the news guy heading to me ma and da?"

"Probably, I take it you're a Farrell?"

"Yeah… are you guys going to be shite-ing on about that poor junkie?"

"My job is to be shite-ing on about things. In fact, people seem to like it when I shite on about things, particularly junkies."

Expecting a rebuke for her own bad language, Sienna smiled at Donal's response.

"Not one for being on TV yourself? It would be a good shot with a local teenager in the frame. I tried to get a few outside the crèche just now, but for some reason they became somewhat abusive when I asked." Donal had genuinely forgotten his comments to the teenagers on bikes, from the previous day. Frankly, he forgot about them the moment after he attacked them. Today their leader told him to go fuck himself when he asked for them to be in the shot. He didn't care about that too much, either. But the memory of that young fella's face, when Donal told him that he would soon be doing a report on his mother's record-breaking attempt of gurgling the most semen at one time – naturally, not all from the same man – still was making the reporter beam from cheek to cheek.

"Nah, you're grand, I'm going ghost hunting." Sienna smiled back.

"Ah I was beginning to like you and now you sound like you might be a bit simple. What the fuck do you mean, ghost hunting?" Donal was still smiling.

Sienna's brow furrowed but she still liked being spoken to like an adult. The frankness was refreshing. She stood for a second and then decided to tell this foul mouthed, well-dressed man the story that had occupied her own thoughts these last few weeks. About how she sneaked into the warehouse, her long conversation with Brendan, how everyone treated her like a child and him like a molester and, of course, their conversation about the happenings in the chapel.

Donal stood in silence. For all his quick retorts, and his well-known anger, he was a fantastic listener. It may have kept him in a job, considering his otherwise less recommending traits. The teenager went into detail about her dislike for Mr Eamon Hawkins and then the story of the Barnes family that Terry related to her.

When she was finished, Donal was still processing all that was said. Tales of the supernatural were immediately filtered out, as were tragic stories of Ireland during the revolutionary period. However, there was another addict who could be interviewed, living, though maybe not for long. His story sounded perfect, if the chap in question was every bit as pathetic as the girl made him sound. The interview could be the heart-warming piece he needed. It could be the perfect snap of this time, forever replayed in anthologies of this period.

Donal continued his analysis; then there was the presence of Hawkins. Donal hated Eamon Hawkins. Some years ago, Donal had run a story on the man and his centres. There were financial irregularities, unqualified staff, unhygienic conditions, third world digs for those who needed first world care. These centres seemed to thrive on cutting corners to maximise profits. Of course, Hawkins did not take such affronts sitting down and he fired back with a libel case. The stakes were too high, and the broadcaster pulled their leash on McGlynn. He would spend the next two years, demoted, as the midlands correspondent at farm festivals. Donal hated farm festivals. Too many memories of being roughly pulled up on to some large tractor by some farmer with a Hapsburg chin. Donal saw opportunity; there was room to settle scores. He could cause a bit of hardship for Mr Hawkins. There was potential in this story after all.

He smiled at the teenager. "We should go to see Brendan, you and I." After depositing a card into her thin hand, he continued on his way to her parents; she on hers, to the chapel.

***

"Hi Siobhan, it's me, Frank, guess what? It's time to get the old band back together!"

Silence greeted Frank on the other end of the phone. It

was a Sunday morning but, to be fair to Siobhan, she acutely remembered her time as his campaign manager. The times she had to scold him for snapping and being condescending to the electorate. The times he shouted at her because the posters made him look both fat and, well, past his prime. The time he made her cry on the count night, when he called her a stupid bitch, and called into question her qualifications in politics from Trinity. After all, how qualified could she be if she could not get a man as likeable and friendly as Frank Cantwell elected?

She wasn't too keen on the electorate either, to be honest. They tended to be hostile and self-serving. All those complaints of recent welfare cuts flashed through her head, as they sat in rooms with high definition TVs. How dare they? There were definitely some republican dissidents about as well; she remembered feeling like she was being shadowed in the flats. Some even chose to be anti-choice! The bastards. Then there were the Catholics, hadn't they done enough damage? They should crawl into a hole and die. No, the electorate were reactionary. Racist. Bigoted. Opinionated. People (who were not liberal) did not deserve a vote if they could not think clearly. To her, and, strangely, to a lot of other folk, that was liberalism.

Eventually, she spoke. "Hello Frank, I heard you were in touch with head office. They're pleased that you're getting some airtime. However, I don't know why you need me, the Council elections won't be for another three years and to be honest, I thought you had given up on politics?"

"Forget Council elections, Siobhan, if enough is made of this we can force Fianna Fáil to drop their support for the government. It will be a general election, Siobhan!" Frank seemed manic on the phone. "And I'll be at ground zero, the one who forced them!"

"Frank, I honestly can't see this getting the legs you think it will, the Shinners will try, Fianna Fáil will ignore them, and the media will forget. Two weeks max. And then it's back to regular viewing."

"You've got it wrong, Siobhan. Come round to mine. We're going to make history."

He hung up. So did she. Siobhan would go round; in fairness to her, she was always polite.

14.

Are You There?

4th February 2018 (Sunday)

"A RE YOU THERE?" BRENDAN HAD BEEN PRESSING THE BELL for a nurse for some time and now felt that it would be simply better to just shout.

"Mr Freeman?" The nurse appeared in the doorway.

"Have you anything to read?" he asked. Brendan smiled. He knew that nurse didn't particularly like him. She did not appear to be a snob; maybe it was a ginger thing.

"Is that all that's troubling you? I'll see what we can do for his lordship." The nurse left the doorway. Two hours had passed from when he made his request before she returned with an assortment of well-thumbed women's magazines, proving what Brendan suspected: she was not fond of him. Still she was right, he hadn't much to be troubled about just now. Two weeks ago, he thought he would die and, to be fair to him, he nearly did. Untreated pneumonia combined with a kidney infection would kill most people. If that girl, Sienna, hadn't shown up and brought the world with her, he would have expired in that warehouse, like a rat. Now he was being fed and in a warm bed. Sure, soon it would be time to go, but that was tomorrow's problem. He was dying for a drink but he wasn't dying, and that was good. The absence of alcohol was lifting his spirits too. He began to peruse the gossip rags thrown on his legs. To anyone looking at him it looked as if he was reading. He wasn't though, he was thinking.

He had been in hospital for two weeks now. The first week had been eventful, as nurses worked steadily to turn Brendan into something more android than human. Breathing apparatuses, thin tubes protruding from his hands, he had become gradually entombed in a web of medical devices, as he struggled to breathe. He could still remember the beeps informing him that his roommates in intensive care were still alive. The fear that haunted him that at any moment any one of them might ring in a long sustain.

As Brendan battled for life, he vaguely remembered the regular temperature takings, hand baths and blood lettings. It seemed medieval, but every day someone was draining him for something. Of course, the memory of the visits from the beautiful nurses was more vivid. Filipino, African, Irish, they were all wonderful, except the male nurse, who was rough and less attractive to a man of Brendan's disposition. They all seemed genuinely concerned about this ginger vagrant's survival.

For Brendan, it was nice to feel cared for. It brought back memories long since buried by bitterness. Of course, this attention could not last forever. In fact, it was favourable that it did not! Medical practitioners lavish their attentions on the dying to seduce them back to life. As much as Brendan enjoyed the nurses' company, it relieved him when they began to visit less and less. Once he was stable, they became just a face at the door, with none of the intimate intensity of before, like a lover who had become bored and was still considering how best to say it was over.

As he healed, they moved him from the ICU to his present ward with six beds. He liked it there. It was cosy and well lit by the sun, from the windows at its southern end. All the beds were occupied, of course; there was no such thing as a free bed these days. Brendan did not mind that either, he enjoyed their company.

He liked watching the two elderly gentlemen with dementia having the same conversation every day as if for the first time. They also stole each other's belongings while the other slept, often telling a watchful Brendan that they were just taking back what was theirs. After all, "the fella in the next bed was gone a little soft."

Then there was the young chap beside his bed, who never lifted his head from his digital tablet, watching the lush green pitch of a never ending soccer match somewhere. At the window end lay a chatty, middle-aged man talking across the ward to a young man who seemed like he just wanted to sleep. No one really talked to Brendan, and that suited him fine, he just wanted to read and to think. He certainly had time to think.

He thought about the shame he felt that first night he came through those large, flapping hospital doors. Bounced from the ambulance into the A & E, the bright lights confused and frightened him, accustomed as he had become to the dark. He remembered the triage nurse staring into his eyes. Brendan did know how to read people, and what he read was a professional closing his thoughts into a cold analytical dead stare. He knew the nurse was disgusted by him. The dirt, the smell, the aged, cracked skin of a young late 30s man, aged by his own indifference and self loathing. Time had stopped for Brendan, but to everyone else he was already rotting.

He remembered the comments of disdain from those waiting to be treated, a chorus of damning hisses and tuts. "There's another one, straight in, we're here 5 hours, 6 hours, 8 hours and they go straight in for taking something. It's a fucking joke!" The professionals in the hospital did not judge Brendan but he began to judge himself, that long night in and out of consciousness, hearing the passers-by, as parents moved their children away from his gurney with protective instinct, as others commented on his appearance and smell. He was waiting for a bed in intensive care, but to him he felt like he was waiting for a vet.

Yet there was hope now. The alcoholic's sores were healing,

his cough less frequent and violent, the aches were lifting and he felt and smelt clean. It was a long time since Brendan felt so – so human. In the beginning of his life as a societal stray, he had ventured into emergency accommodation hostels for fear of the street. Not long after, he was on the street for the first time, for fear of the hostels. Of course, he tried rehab, not out of commitment to reform (he felt people reformed out of coercion or fear, it enabled him not to be troubled by the thought) but out of desire to come out of the cold. Even for this purpose, he found it unsuitable for his needs. Those shabbily decorated large rooms, usually in priest houses, were depressing, and the company, narcissistic whingers, he thought without irony. To be fair, the smell of alcohol off him would ensure that his participation was always short lived. He was a contagion, a dangerous temptation to others. The door would be promptly shown.

Brendan had been out in the cold for a long time; his hospital bed in his small ward was comfortable and he had forgotten comfortable. In his forced sobriety, he had watched his fellow patients visited by loving parents, caring daughters and sons, playful siblings; his cynicism about the idea of the family waned. As he stared at the vacant look on the celebrities' faces plastered on the magazines the nurse had brought him, he began to think about his conversation with that girl in the warehouse. She had that annoying, immature, straightforward logic, just do this and this will happen. A real adult would have made it so much more complicated, with due regard to emotions, and given him far more room to argue. He felt her simplicity was not a sign of a lack of intelligence, it was the contrary. Could he just ring his father? What was the worst that could happen? His father was judgemental, yes, harsh, maybe, but he was no Mr Taft either, his oldest friend's violent and changeable patriarch; for a moment, Brendan shuddered thinking of that man. An unpleasant memory began to return once more, only for Brendan to shut it out again. No, in his heart Brendan knew his own father was, fundamentally, a good man. There was definitely hope now.

***

"Are you there?" Eamon Hawkins put his head around the sacristy door. The priest had his robes wrapped around his head and was clumsily staggering back trying to free himself.

Fr Matthew was irritated by the intrusion. He was looking forward to his post mass smoke. It was one of his many rituals.

A muffled, polyester-wrapped voice replied, "Yes, can I help you?"

"Sorry, Father, hate to intrude on you mid disrobing, lovely mass by the way."

Fr Matthew had seen the silver-suited man come in halfway through his sermon. Poor show, he thought, a proper parish pump politician would have arrived at the beginning. "Hello, Eamon, isn't it? I recognise you from the TV. Come to sell me on the rehabilitation centre, I presume?" The priest finally managed to remove his robe.

Fr Matthew continued. "You're wasting your time, you know? For one thing, I actually agree with you. Young people on drugs should be in treatment and not on the street and we all should do what we can. Nonetheless, I am allowing those who wish to protest to use the church's properties for their events anyway. My beliefs aside, the church cannot argue against helping people finding redemption but I also must be practical and the majority of my parishioners are, well, not fond of the idea of another rehabilitation centre in their area."

"Ah come on now, Father, when has the church shied away from taking a controversial stance? Is it not your whole raison d'être? Is it too much to ask you to remind your flock of their religion? Or has the Christian ethos changed from helping those who are most disadvantaged?"

Fr Matthew moved across the room carrying his robe, staring

absent-mindedly in front of him. He disliked when non-believers used the beliefs of others to further their agenda. "I'm not a spokesman for anyone but the Lord, Mr Hawkins. If people have fears about their community becoming a dumping ground, it is for you to assure them that your service is well run, not me. This area has enough scars left from people with good intentions."

"Well of course, it is your church and if you're not willing to help me or those who genuinely are in need…"

The priest turned his eyes to the sky. "Please, Mr Hawkins, let's call a spade a spade here, you're not some benign charity. You're a private outfit, who was contracted by a right-wing government to provide public services without public servant salaries. Spare me the downtrodden sermon. This is a problem in community service provision since its inception. No government really believes it's needed, because the ones who need it don't vote; in other words, governments don't need it. So they fudge the job by sending profiteers like you in, who, I'm sure, have lowered the standards to make a bottom line. This is business to you, this is expansion."

Hawkins folded his arms. "Do you not make a living on the needs of the vulnerable, Father?"

The priest placed his robes pristinely in a neat rectangle drawer and closed it swiftly. "The church pays me to live. I don't profit, I survive. You pontificate on TV about the marginalised fringes of society, what would you know of it? We've seen the news programmes, wonderfully reminding us you make the same money as a CEO of a car manufacturer! The people who work in the community here, the ones who take care of children, teach the young and counsel the addicts, they are not some professional class paid to care, they simply care."

Fr Matthew glared at Hawkins who was, surprisingly, still smiling. "Nice speech, maybe a little slanderous but overall not a bad performance." He walked past the priest and looked into a full length mirror. "Of course, the poor or, to use your phrase, 'the community' are always nobler when they do something, aren't they? We're both selling something to those in need, Father. Of course, the difference is my services work. Ah well, I'll have to find another way to reach the..." Eamon looked straight into the priest eyes, "...dozen or so people of your flock." The silver-suited man turned his back to the mirror and made his way to the door.

"'When you give to the needy, sound no trumpet before you, as the hypocrites do in the synagogues and in the streets, that they may be praised by others. Truly, I say to you, they have received their reward'." Fr Matthew loved the verse when annoyed.

Eamon stopped and turned. "Progress is impossible without change, and those who cannot change their minds cannot change anything. Kind of the church in a nutshell, eh, Father?" He continued out the door.

The priest needed that smoke.

***

"Are you there?" Sienna stood in the empty chapel. She awaited a response, but the chapel provided none. It was deathly silent. Now that her parents were distracted by Donal McGlynn's somewhat disingenuous questions, she would finally have time to explore this repurposed temple. "Are you there?" she inquired again, the first time she felt unsure, afraid of hearing the affirmative, "yes, I am." Now, however, she was beginning to feel silly.

The chapel was dark, dreary; it was an overcast morning. She slowly closed the front door behind her and entered the main chamber. Along the side stood brass candle holders percolated with dark stains, a dust-covered pulpit and old statues of saints, painted hot chocolate brown or breakfast tea yellow, with a perpetual sorrow plastered on their faces.

The youth project's presence was made visible on the wall, decorated as it was with mostly red crayon-hewn love hearts, pre-emptive of Valentine's Day and owing to the youth workers' lack of imagination. Each of these tattered pieces of paper, with their rudimentary and culturally understood representation of the heart, foretold something about the future of its colourer. There was the heart coloured red, pristinely between the lines, a feat made more impressive considering the imprecise nature of worn crayon nubs. Certainly, this child will grow up to be painfully anal about the smallest detail. They will probably spend great amounts of time writing on social media about the correct use of "their, there and they're." Then there was the page where the crayon seemed everywhere but the heart. An outside thinker, they'll end up in an office, heavily resenting management for their lack of imagination. Of course, there was the heart that was not red at all. These little ones will be surefooted, they won't be told what to think, and will be obnoxious in bar debates about politics; they'll also usually be wrong. Finally, there was the solitary heart where the crayon was dug deeply into the paper, almost ripping it, with a silent, unrestrained, psychotic concentration. These charming children will grow into adults with large, if intense smiles perpetually adorning their faces, until that one bad day...

Sienna walked slowly down the chapel, past the hot-drink-coloured saints, past the Rorschach hearts, past the hand-me-down TV with hand-me-down Playstation 2 and the tub full of broken action figures that looked to be veterans of some highly unforgiving war.

She climbed the stairs to the choir balcony, a black metal spiral that looked like it had been pushed through the upper wooden floor by a giant wine corkscrew. Light though she undoubtedly was, each one of Sienna's steps created a heavy din on the metal steps, as she ascended to the upper floor.

Upon reaching the balcony, she stepped towards the wooden partition and looked into the main nave of the chapel and out towards the former altar. Beside her were dust-covered pews, left there in storage, never to be used again. Behind her, two long stained glass panes, a mixture of purple and red, stared menacingly into the small of her back. She could see all the chapel now and it was disappointingly empty. So much for ghost hunting.

She slowly trudged back down the stairs and decided to open the side door that led into the old convent where the nuns once lived. It had long since been appropriated by the Council for social housing, a gift from the state, who had in turn received it as payment for the orders' past indiscretions elsewhere.

Sienna knew the chances of the door being unlocked were slim and even if it was, all she was likely to see was a long hallway with the small numbered cells now depressingly homes. Nonetheless, she would take advantage of her freedom of the premises. When her mother found out about her deception of the youth workers, it was doubtful there would be opportunity to carry out this investigation again. It was more likely she would get a telling off, and her mother would send her back to school to stop her being a nuisance about the place. She reached the door, placed her hand on the handle and twisted. Locked, damn. A dejected teenager sighed heavily and made for the door that she had first entered.

Her investigation was over; there were no ghosts, just boring reality. As she walked back down through the chapel, rubbing her finger along the dusty statues on her way to the main entrance, something felt different. A tension slowly built where her spine met her neck, causing a jolt of energy that spasmed fluidly across her body. She shivered. She felt eyes on her, nature's most basic instinct.

Sienna stopped and stood still. The silence seemed like it was growing in intensity, all around her. It could not be one of the residents of the convent, she would have heard the door unlock. There was no one else in the chapel. She had clearly seen all that could be seen from the choir balcony. Sienna's arms were perfectly by her side as she stared directly into the altar space and those beautiful large stained glass windows. Stapled to the floor, unable to move, terrified to turn around, Sienna's breathing had slowed down and was now audible.

"Are you there?"

The question was met with silence. This silence was different, heavier, charged with expectancy. Sienna did not dare move. All those yellow-stained windows along the sides of the building seemed to be looking directly at her. Every horror movie motif played in her head. The imagination can be such a cruel, evil thing. She imagined a skeletonised apparition behind her, wearing a habit. She imagined this demonic bride of Christ with gaping eye sockets piercing into the back of her head with a stare absent of all emotions.

Then there was nothing, there was no response. The density drifted, became lighter, her mind simply playing tricks; relieved, Sienna took a long breath.

"Yes, child."

It was so faint as to hardly be audible, but it seemed so definite. The voice emanated behind her. Sienna's eyes rose suddenly to the wooden beamed ceiling and she slumped into a small pile on the floor.

15.

Hospital Visits

"WHAT WAS HIS NAME AGAIN, SIENNA?"

"Freeman, Brendan Freeman, da."

"Yeah, I am looking for a Brendan Freeman, what ward is he in?"

It was true that Shane had misgivings. The kind of misgivings a father would have about bringing his daughter to visit an alcoholic vagrant in his late 30s, whom she befriended in an abandoned warehouse, on her own. One would suppose these were legitimate misgivings. All that said, Shane was a soft enough soul. He had noticed a change in his daughter, and while he was ignorant of her supernatural investigation, he felt that seeing the young man somewhat recovered and looking better could lift some of the obvious preoccupation from her mind. Shane may have questioned his worth as a provider, but as a father he took pride in the fact that he was second to none. Nonetheless, he swore Sienna to secrecy. If Phyllis found out, he'd get his arse handed to him, but she was collecting Joe from school and what she did not know wouldn't hurt her – or more importantly, him.

It is true, the last time we saw Sienna she was in a neat little heap, unconscious, on the Chapel floor. That was Sunday, and this is now Monday. Perhaps something happened in between when

Sienna awoke and now, and perhaps again, it was important, but other things are important too. Think of poor Brendan, without visitors for over two weeks; he's important too. Don't worry, we will revisit the neat little heap on the chapel floor, but for now let's see how Brendan is doing.

"Okay, Sienna, I just had a chat with the nurse and she tells me your friend Brendan has mostly recovered, so he's off all the machines and they're just observing him. All the same, we're not staying here all day. For one thing, he's been through the wars and will probably get tired and for a more important thing, if your ma finds out I brought you here, my life won't be worth living. If you see anyone you know in here, just say you're with your da, and he's applying for a porter's job." Shane was a gifted pugilist in his youth, with a wiry frame that allowed for swift movement and a sharp brain that facilitated quick judgement. There wasn't a man in the area that was not at least partially aware of his ability and duly respectful. Not a man. Phyllis of course, was not a man. Despite her warm, charming demeanour, when she was suitably annoyed, she could shake Shane right to his foundations. Kangaroos and men punch, a painful experience but ultimately short lived. Women on the other hand, have greater recall and persistence and bore at minds with a prolonged mental attack. They are by far the deadlier of the species.

Father and daughter walked into the vanilla labyrinth, their only guide a painted red strip on the wall to guide them to St Cillian's ward and to Brendan, who was busy thumbing women's magazines and wondering if he had cellulite. Well, he was, that is, until the nurse told him to put his blankets back over himself, pointing out rather accurately that no one wanted to see his chicken legs. Thankfully, he was fully covered when Sienna and her father entered the ward.

Sienna ran over to the bed containing a now smiling Brendan. "Here you go!" She dropped a plastic bag on his lap, filled with monkey nuts and bananas. Irish people bring food that they would not usually eat to the sick in hospital, in an effort to coax them back to the outside world. Monkey nuts are solely bought on this island for this exact purpose. The tradition goes back to the ancient Gaels. Recently, archaeologists have discovered monkey nut shells outside ancient apothecary sites in county Offaly. Sienna also brought pre-flattened 7-up, a lemon and lime fizzy drink that, once decarbonised, takes on the mystical properties of curing all diseases up to and including Ebola. Capless 7-up bottles have also been found in ancient druid burial sites around Antrim.

Immediately, Brendan's face lit up. During their brief first encounter he took a shine to the girl, and truth, be told, he really was not expecting visitors and had gradually become somewhat lonely. "Well now, hello, Sienna, how are you?"

"I'm grand! How's things with ya? Everybody thought you'd kidnapped me! Fuckin dopes."

"Sienna, language!"

This sharp intrusion drew Brendan's eyes to the ward entrance, where a rather serious looking ginger-stubbled man stood awkwardly in the doorway, periodically moving in and out to facilitate other visitors and nurses.

"Is this your father?" Brendan said more formally as he moved himself up in the bed.

"How's it going? My name's Shane."

"Hello, I'm Brendan. Listen. I just want to say, I didn't know your daughter was coming into that warehouse, I was just getting in out of the weather and there she was and…"

"Listen mate, it's grand, Sienna told us the score, you're grand. I don't think you're a nonce, relax." Funnily, this sentence served to make Brendan slightly more uneasy, though it was sincerely not Shane's intention.

Sienna was already bored of listening to the two of them. "So what did the doctor say? You got AIDS or something?"

"Kidney infection and pneumonia, according to her. If you

didn't happen upon me I'd be dead. That wouldn't be great, to be honest. You saved my life." Brendan smiled at the teenager.

Sienna saving Brendan's life was very much incidental but Shane was still very proud to hear these words. "She's a good kid, is our Sienna."

"Well, I would have been done without her," repeated Brendan, trying to rid himself of the obvious awkwardness of this meeting.

"So you're on the mend?" Sienna continued.

"I am, yeah. I feel a bit renewed all over, to be honest. I haven't smoked or drank in two weeks. I've been to AA meetings where I wasn't that successful. There's no point in lying, I'd love a drink, but I am comfortable." He appropriately nodded. There was a truth in this, he was comfortable and optimistic. There was a little deception too. He really, really wanted a drink and that morning he had smoked his 66th cigarette since arriving in the hospital. Nonetheless, the long journey to the entrance and coldness outside did lessen the hold tobacco had over him. It was a slight exaggeration more than a malicious deception. Truthfully, he just wanted approval for his imposed rehabilitation. "I was actually thinking about what you said. A lot. I was thinking of ringing my folks. Letting them know how I am. What's the worst that could happen?"

"Ah you should, they're probably worried sick about ya." While Sienna was delighted to hear her advice had not only been listened to but in fact may even be acted on, it was not really her purpose for being there. She was still barely a teenager and, as with most of her demographic, their world comes first. Her true purpose was delicate. Shane didn't know that she had gone to chapel. If he found out that Sienna used her mother's name in a lie to get into the premises there would be negative repercussions. Yet she had to find out what Brendan knew about this nun. She must continue the conversation as banally as she could, until her father zoned out.

"So will ya ring them?"

"Yeah, I was thinking I might, I'm nearly here three weeks, granted I was dying for a bit of it, but I don't think I can pull that trick again to extend my stay."

"Do you want to use my phone?" Sienna helpfully offered.

"Ah no, you're grand." Brendan became immediately nervous. Plans are easier than actions and he was not yet ready to make that phone call. "I just need to get myself into the right mind for that conversation. That isn't something you can just do on a whim. It has to be planned." "Planned" in this instance meant procrastinated. Ironically, alcohol would have facilitated him making the action much sooner, but then, the action probably would not have worked out as well.

Sienna was distracted, discreetly eying her father, waiting for his attention to wane. "They found another homeless guy dead around the corner from where we found you."

Brendan was mildly annoyed at Sienna's lazy categorisation. Self-deprecating as he could be, it was different when others did it; then they were like his father. For her part, she meant nothing by it, she was simply pushing the conversation along until her father settled. "Yeah, I saw it on the news in here. It's just another bleeding-heart story that no doubt everyone will jump on but ultimately, do nothing about. Anyway, the world won't miss Peter."

"You knew him?" Shane came in from the doorway.

"Our paths crossed a few times, he wasn't a pleasant guy, lot of problems," Brendan replied letting out a low yawn. "Not every tapper is as honest as me."

"You're an honest tapper, are you?" Shane smiled.

"Someone has to keep the noble institution alive as it was intended." Brendan grinned back.

Shane sat down the far end of the bed. He looked at Brendan's young neighbour, the young man with a digital green glow across his face. Shane was curious at what match was on that early in the day. He enquired as to who was playing. The young man replied Ghana vs. Egypt. Shane raised his eyebrow.

Sienna pressed on with her dreary mission into the fine art of banal conversation. "Are you getting on with the rest of your ward?"

"They're oddly therapeutic in their set ways," replied Brendan as he sifted through his bag of monkey nuts and bananas hoping to find some human food. "There were two auldfellas here with dementia. Constantly bickering with each other. One was released this morning and now the other doesn't know what to do with himself. It was kind of sweet when they were here together."

Shane anxiously looked at his watch. Phyllis and the perpetually cross Joe would not be too long from home now. Finally, he was suitably content that the conversation was innocent enough and picked up a copy of *Woman's Way*. He had not long started to read it when he began to wonder if men could get cellulite.

Sienna saw her cue. Her father was lost in his own world and now was the time to turn the conversation. "Here, Brendan, remember you were telling me about the chapel, you know, about what you and your mate saw?"

"I don't remember a lot of that conversation, to be fair. I was hammered and slowly coming off my mortal coil."

Sienna stared at him and continued, "Do you remember telling me about the two of you seeing something?"

Brendan looked at Shane, who seemed engrossed in the magazine. "I hope you haven't been telling people that?" Clean Brendan felt shame a lot easier than warehouse Brendan, to be sure.

"No, I haven't, you just never told me what you actually saw," Sienna persisted.

Brendan again looked at Shane, who was now checking his thigh. He lowered his voice and continued. "All right, well, myself and Taft heard steps inside the place. It took a while for our eyes to focus."

"What did you see?" An eager Sienna was now fully tuned in to the conversation.

"Well, you have to remember the chapel wasn't a youth project then, I think the Order still had it but were basically just using it for storage. There were statues and boxes of things. The place was littered with crap. When our eyes finally took in the whole mess, we realised that we had been looking at her the whole time."

"Who?!"

"Hold onto your guns will ya? Let me finish. She was just standing there. She might as well have been one of the statues, she was the right height. It was a nun. You see there is a story…"

"Sister Sheila…" Sienna interjected.

"You know the Emily Barnes story?"

"A neighbour told me it. Did she say anything to you?" Sienna's eyes were lit with expectation.

"She said…" (He leaned in for dramatic effect). "She said…. you're some prick, Brendan, for lying to that young one." Suddenly, a sharp grin shot across Brendan's face.

Sienna looked confused. "What?"

"There was no ghost, I was messing with ya. I just wanted you to change the subject from my misappropriation of goods from the local newsagents and, well, I was drunk… which, weirdly, doesn't bring out the best in me." Brendan returned to rooting in the bag. He was becoming increasingly annoyed at the complete absence of chocolate in it.

Sienna was visibly upset. "No, you're wrong, there is!"

"I based it on that old folk tale that was going around the area at the time. These days, you'd probably see it on a Facebook page called 'Dublin's Rare Auld Times' or 'Wasn't Dublin great when we were all getting raped and had no money'." Brendan smirked, then looked a little guilty when he noticed Sienna was not returning his smile. "Look, I'm sorry, I didn't think you'd take me seriously, it was just a bit of fun. Sienna, there are no ghosts, the whole story is made up. I mean, birthmarked girls are a bit of common horror trope, d'ya not think?"

Sienna persisted. "No… you don't get it… there actually is!

Please, I thought you'd listen to me, I know something."

Brendan looked sympathetic; in his heart, he knew that all he was going to hear was some teenager's overactive imagination, but he liked the teenager in question, and so he humoured her. "Alright, alright… I'm listening!"

Sienna leaned in, which admittedly half startled Brendan who was still preoccupied trying to find something useable in her gift bag. She said in a very low voice, "I need to tell you something."

Rather annoyingly, and in a familiar trend, their discussion stopped there, as Donal McGlynn, complete with chocolates, stepped into the ward. "Well, if it isn't the Farrell family, hello, how are ye?" Donal beamed.

Shane roused from his transfixion with his horoscope, which he was suspicious was actually just Spandau Ballet lyrics and not, as advertised, a precognition based on celestial alignments. Sienna immediately turned, annoyed at the intrusion, while Brendan's mouth formed a perfect "o" as he was in mid contemplation of what Sienna had just said. Now he had questions; now he would have to wait.

"Lovely to meet ye all here. How's the patient? My name is Donal McGlynn, I'm a reporter for…"

"I know who you are, why are you here?" Brendan asked.

"I was just wondering if we could do an interview with you on what it is like being an addict on the streets of Dublin and what your views are on the residential rehabilitative centre planned for Clementine Lane?"

"Well, I'm sure it's a great idea but I don't know anything about it and to be honest…"

Brendan was interrupted before he could finish the sentence.

"Sound, yeah, I hear ye, but nonetheless, I think you could give a really powerful insight into what it's like to be an actual homeless person on the streets of Dublin. People want to know. Brendan, isn't it?" McGlynn smiled.

Shane rose from the bed. "Sienna, come on, we're going, your ma's probably coming in the door now."

"But Da!"

"Come on! Let's get going!"

"Fine, Da." Sienna wished Brendan good luck, Shane nodded respectfully to both men. Father and daughter left the ward while a slightly bewildered Brendan waved half heartedly at them, as Donal pulled up a chair beside him.

After a smooth negotiation by the informed and a signed consent from the ignorant, the reporter briefly explained what would be expected. Donal and Brendan removed to a smaller room, where Jason stood with a camera already set up. They sat down and at Donal's prompting Brendan began the story of his life up to that point. All the while, a frequently nodding Donal asked questions. Importantly, in this recantation of his life Brendan was not talking to a teenage girl but a reporter who was on the hunt for a piece. McGlynn wanted emotion. He could edit this vignette as he wanted, but Brendan's new found optimism was ruining the preconceived narrative in his mind. Gradually, the reporter began to pull at the story, returning to painful pressure points. "Can I ask you if you ever sought meaningful rehabilitation before now?"

"No, but it was because…" Brendan began to feel weak. The camera's unrelenting stare began to weigh on his mind.

The narrative he had constructed of a forceful father was not the real truth. In his weaker moments, he realised that in between the fights there was a very worried man looking at his son who seemed committed to a slow self destruction. It was not a complete lie either, his father was disappointed in him. How could he not be? Their son was always so academically gifted and now he threw it all away for no discernible reason. Of course, addiction requires only access.

"Did your father ever argue with you over your drinking?"

"Yeah, but it was more than that…"

Over the years, Brendan had successfully ridden himself of

his father's perspective and instead instructed his memory to only retain the incessant arguments between them. It justified him. It made him the victim, and not the perpetrator. With it, Brendan was free to find comfort where he sought; in his case, alcohol. He was free to steal to survive because he had been wronged, and he was merely doing what he could in an evil world. He was free to believe he was still an intelligent man, whose life was made harsh by the disease of addiction and an unforgiving father.

"Do you think it was fair to your family what you put them through?"

"Well, no, but…"

Despite his abilities for introspection, and to be periodically honest with others about his own past, deep down in his mind he kept his narrative. It was not true, and in his weaker moments he knew it was not true, but it was what he needed to be true. Brendan knew there were other demons living in his past. Doors he kept firmly shut. Doors marked "Taft".

"Have you ever been involved in criminality?" This truth was being brilliantly unravelled by Donal, in his attempt of gaining a televised breakdown. For Brendan, the constant reminding of his spectacular failures was slowly ebbing away at his truth.

"Brendan, we spoke to the doctors and they related to us that you were in a bad way when you came here. What do you think your parents would think if they saw you when you first arrived here two weeks ago?"

"Ehh…"

Memory was duplicitous; she had saved those painful moments of his father crying. She had not discarded Brendan's empathy for him, only hidden it. Unsurprisingly, the professional broke the vulnerable patient and soon Brendan was inconsolably crying, as the reporter offered him tissues with a sympathetic half smile. When they had left with a "well done, Brendan, that was great," the alcoholic returned to his bed, sullen, raped for the world's consumption. He laid there, his confessions replaying in his mind. He resolved there would be no phone call. He was a moron for thinking that his parents would talk to him again. Why would they? He remembered the last time he saw his old friend Freddie Taft. A memory he continuously tried to suffocate. He remembered that he was a monster.

16.

Politics

7th February 2018 (Wednesday)

IT WAS THE FIRST WEDNESDAY OF FEBRUARY, THREE DAYS ON FROM Sienna's trip into the chapel. That tale's conclusion is sure to be riveting, maybe even world changing, or it could be a damp squib. Either way, it is not the focus of this chapter. Time has moved on. Don't worry, it will move back, just, perhaps frustratingly, not right now.

Donal McGlynn stood outside Clementine Lane Flat Complex. While it was true that there was evidently a grand stretch in the evenings, at five o'clock the night was beginning to claim the sky. The freshness of the day was yielding to the coolness of the night, and Donal was beginning to see his breath. "Jason, did 'university challenged' say when he was going to be here?"

The cameraman shrugged.

"Sweet suffering Jaysus, I do this little shit a favour and I'm kept waiting," Donal continued.

Frank Cantwell turned the corner onto Clementine Lane, flanked by a tired looking Siobhan carrying a pile of hastily made leaflets explaining why the area needed the new rehabilitation service; a picture of the late Peter Williams adorned the back, taken when he was still on time, and on the front, Frank Cantwell, with cheery grin, silver hair gelled back and a large Cheshire smile.

The picture of Frank was very much the reverse of Dorian Gray's portrait; events moved too quickly for him to get an update in photo form; He didn't mind; less crows' feet, less flab.

Frank smiled at the reporter. "Good evening, Mr McGlynn, brisk enough for you?"

"Nice suit, Mr Cantwell, perfect metaphor for Labour, a guy dressed in Hugo Boss standing outside a flat complex, while the locals look on wondering who the fuck he is." Frank looked momentarily aghast at the reporter's sarky comments.

Siobhan shook the reporter's hand, to break the awkward silence. "Hi, my name is Siobhan. I am Frank's campaign manager."

Donal lightly shook it, then turned to face the camera. "Maybe you should be the reporter, Ms, I wasn't aware there was an election to campaign for."

"Three, two and…"

"I'm here with local community activist Frank Cantwell. Mr Cantwell has the unusual distinction of being a local resident actually in favour of the rehabilitation residential centre planned for Clementine Lane. Frank, can you give me your reasons for supporting what is, locally at least, a controversial proposal?"

Frank looked into the camera lenses.

***

It was 10.40 a.m. that same Wednesday when Frank had answered the phone to his party leader Michael Norton.

"Hello, Michael."

"Frank, are you well? Great to see you're alive and kicking. Well done for bringing this poor man's demise into the public eye."

"Oh, it's a terrible thing, Michael, that poor man, every day I would be out to him with a sandwich from the local shop and a cup of tea, and people had the cheek to give out about this rehabilitation centre. They were actually calling it 'the Ritz for those off their tits,' I ask you!" Even Frank felt a little shameful referring to his own comment and attributing the ownership to his neighbours; nonetheless, he was anxious for the leader to know he was onside.

"Well, you know how people are, and Dubliners are great at rhyming slang, to be fair, must be the cockney barracks blood in them." Norton, the Cork native, chuckled. "Sure anyway, we need you to really push this, Frank, get out there, make as much of it is as you can, lots of stories of the poor chap, really humanise him. The people hate a homeless death, reminds them that the safety net isn't that strong, when they look at their own mortgage repayments. It makes them feel guilty that they put a government so indifferent in power. It reminds them of social justice and that their society really isn't that sophisticated. Even Fianna Fáil are getting embarrassed, this is the fourth one this year, it's only February! Jaysus, there'll be none left to go into the centre at this rate! Add to that the 'rehabilitation from addiction' element and the centre becomes a big win for the people looking in." Norton's folksy style was a big hit with the voters in Cork South but perhaps wasn't appropriate for this conversation.

The leader continued. "Frank, you create enough steam, keep it in the news and we'll make of it what we can. We'll try and force Fianna Fáil to pull their support, get us back on an election footing. An opportunity for the Party to get back in and help people like Paul Williams."

"Peter."

"I'm sorry, what was that, Frank?"

"Oh, the poor so and so, he was named Peter Williams."

"Of course, of course." The professional politician on the other end of the phone affected an air of concern.

"Michael, Siobhan was saying that maybe it wouldn't be wise for me to get behind this. The centre is very unpopular here and they do, to be fair, have a lot of them already. She thinks that if

I was to run again, and I was the sole politician in support of this project, that I would be singled out and it would hurt my chances." It was Frank's turn to sound concerned. He sounded more genuine, too.

"Frank, those people in Clementine Lane don't vote. Even if you were banging up and down the halls of the Council with them, they still wouldn't vote for you. To be honest, and I'm sure you can understand it, they can be very narrow-minded folk and they need the right people to lead them. It's not their fault, but they have limited schooling and can be prone to missing the bigger picture. You are a leader, right, Frank? Representatives need to be leaders, the vanguard, not the led, that's how it works. You'll get your votes from the educated apartment dwellers, away from the flats. Those people are professionals, they are open minded, not the type to succumb to prejudice. Plus they actually vote, which as you can imagine helps a little, Frank." Michael chuckled again before concluding, "Don't worry, we have strategists for this kind of thing!"

"I understand you completely, Michael. Sure the ones who do vote around here are with the Shinners! Bloody populists, how is that democracy? You're right, I have to be a community leader here. So what do you want me to say?"

***

"Well Donal, I actually live in apartments across from where the late Mr Williams slept rough, in the hallway of a local Roman Catholic Church." Frank was one of the few people in the state who referred to this religion with the prefix "Roman". It was a personal statement to ensure his separatism from it was known.

He continued, "I knew him quite well. I would sit with him now and again, giving him blankets in weather like today, when the poor man would be near frozen. Naturally, I provided food and warm tea, when possible. He was a very articulate man, loved his Hurling, he used to joke with me that Dublin for the double was only around the corner. Such a sweet, sweet man. He was in a state of shock at this government's indifference to the people in his plight, he really couldn't understand it." Peter Williams spoke two words to Frank Cantwell during his stay in the church doorway: "please sir…" before he was immediately cut off with "no, sorry." Peter Williams didn't care for Hurling either, he preferred heroin. When he was younger he supported Chelsea because his brother did, though he had more or less forgotten that at the time of his death.

"So you can see, Donal, that if there was a service here which dealt with people in Peter's situation, the outcome might have been different and that poor man might still be alive." Frank looked to the ground sorrowfully speaking these words.

McGlynn grimaced. He was disgusted by the disingenuousness of Frank's opening gambit. In addition, he was providing his nemesis, Eamon Hawkins, with free publicity. Time to make things harder. "It sounds like you had quite the relationship with Mr Williams. Can I ask you, why do you think that Mr Williams had not approached some of the other rehabilitative centres in the city?"

Frank stared blankly, but recovered. "I think we will never know the mind of someone in such desperate circumstances, the poor man. What I do want to say is we should organise a town hall meeting, so everybody can come together and discuss the project."

"And on that very topic, I understand you have canvassed the locals in support of the new centre. What has been the feeling on the doorstep?"

The mike, once again, was turned to Frank.

***

It was 12.35 p.m. that Wednesday afternoon when Frank Cantwell had finished berating Siobhan, his campaign manager, for arriving late from the printers with the new leaflets. The canvassing was meant to be well under way by now. He marched, with a spring in his step, to the first of the neat little redbrick cottages which open onto Clementine Lane.

"Try and smile, Siobhan." Frank rapped lightly on the door. "Good afternoon, I'm Frank Cantwell, a local representative, and I want to talk about the need for the new rehabilitative residential centre."

"Fuck off." The door slammed.

Frank's shocked face made Siobhan smile. "Well… thank you for taking the time to talk to us, we appreciate your concern," Frank continued, as if the door had not been slammed. The closed door was a more attentive audience, to be fair.

Frank turned to the next house, and rapped lightly. "Hi, I'm…"

"You're that chap who's always in that Zen café place on the Street?" A tall man had opened the door and cut Frank off mid-sentence.

"Why yes, I have frequented that café."

"Is it all that vegan crap or do they do any normal food?"

"Well, I'm sure they have other items if walnut salad isn't your bag." Frank smiled.

"It's fuckin mad expensive though, isn't it? I was looking at the menu the other day and a coffee was 6 euro, for fuck sake. Mad, isn't it?"

"Well, I'm sure the coffee in the local shop is just as good and… anyway I was wondering if I could get your support for the new rehabilitative residential centre for the lane, particularly, considering the recent demise of Mr Williams, I think…"

"Ah no way, mate, we've enough head bangers around here. G'luck." The door closed.

"Well, the local newsagents will benefit from our efforts if no one else will," Frank fumed, as he marched to the next door. A small frail old woman in a coat answered.

"Oh, have we caught you on your way out?"

"Well, unless I'm about to drop dead! Come in and let me close that door, it's freezing!"

Siobhan and Frank thanked the seanbhean for her hospitality and entered into a small sitting room, populated by pictures of the Sacred Heart, old photos and doily-laden furniture.

"You'll have a cup of tea?"

"No thank you, we've a lot of people to visit today and…"

The old lady had already floated into the small kitchen as Frank was speaking. Five minutes later she rattled back into the sitting room, carrying a tea service on a tray filled with biscuits. Siobhan eagerly grabbed a biscuit, having missed breakfast in her rush to get the flyers printed.

"So, Mrs…?"

"Bridie, everyone knows me as Bridie."

"Well, Bridie, thank you for the lovely tea and biscuits, I just want to talk to you about the residential rehabilitative centre planned for the top of the lane."

"My Martin is always talking about those poor addicts, God bless 'em and their mothers, isn't it terrible?" The old lady thoughtfully looked at the pair.

Frank's eyes momentarily lit up. Finally, someone sympathetic!

"It is, it is, well, you must have heard about poor Mr Williams?" Frank inquired.

The old lady was taking a bite out of a coconut cream and ignored Frank's question. "My Martin is always trying to help the less fortunate though, that's him. He worked in Bristol, in one of those shipping yards. There was one chap there who couldn't read and every day my Martin would spend his breakfast hour teaching the poor boy, just the way he is. A very kind man, some people are just selfless."

Frank looked at Siobhan wondering if the lady had heard him. She was very old after all, past the summit of her powers and on the descent back down.

A new tact was required; maybe bringing Martin into the subject at hand would help. "Your Martin sounds lovely, Bridie. We can do with a man like him in my party." Frank smiled.

"Oh, Martin isn't a man for a politics, never has the time, always working. God bless 'em."

"Bridie, about the centre…"

"Of course, he always has time for a pint does Martin, the little fecker." She laughed as crumbs jumped from her mouth onto the worn carpet. The two guests politely laughed.

"Well, don't we all, Bridie, don't we all. Of course, it's when we overindulge that the problem arises, am I right? So, Bridie, what we are proposing is the establishment of a service that can cater for people with addiction problems, a warm secure place where they'll be treated with dignity and respect."

"Of course, my Martin would always know when to come home, he doted on me, even with a few jars." At this Bridie picked up a photo, neatly framed, the man, ageless now, behind the pane. He was dressed fashionably, for the late 1960s.

Siobhan now connected the dots, while Frank continued to try and push his newly found cause. She smiled at the old lady. "Bridie, where's Martin now?"

"Somewhere better love, somewhere much better."

***

"Well that was a waste of half an hour, the mad old biddy."

"Leave her alone, Frank, some people never get over loss."

"Oh do shut up, Siobhan."

The two had this conversation while waving and smiling at the old lady in the coat now standing behind her window. Frank was reticent about the next house, Phyllis and Shane's home. Ever since Sienna's experiences with the homeless man in the warehouse, Phyllis's feelings, at least, were clear on the new centre. He knocked; thankfully, there was no response.

By 4.15 p.m., both Siobhan and Frank had become somewhat jaded. Somewhere between the nasty fuck offs and the polite fuck offs. Somewhere between being deliberately held up by supporters of rival parties and accidently held up by those who just wanted a chat. Somewhere between being admonished for the government's unforgiving cuts to welfare, and the rise of the tax on cigarettes, despite being from a non-government party. Somewhere between being chased by dogs and shouted at by drunks. Frank and Siobhan had lost their sparkle.

They slowly climbed the second floor of St Clementine Flats. The orange lights slowly buzzed to life as the evening crept in, casting an eerie and isolating glow on the narrow pathway. Worryingly, it also illuminated a new problem. At the end of the balcony, a gang of teenagers loitered. Their laughing was alarmingly loud for both of the fatigued evangelists. What became more alarming was the sudden cessation of their laughing as the teenagers spied the two well-dressed canvassers on their balcony. Frank and Siobhan may as well have been pale Swedes in an Ottoman coffee house, they were that different and that foreign.

"Here, look at these spas, Johnno, your ma and da are here for ya!" The group of four had an accumulative age of 68, two in tracksuit jackets, zipped to the upper lip, one in a raincoat with a hood over his cap, and the fourth in just a Barcelona jersey trying not to look frozen, but still shivering uncontrollably. They were outside his mother's flat. He refused to do the common sense thing and go in to get his jacket. He thought it would make him look weak. In fairness to the others, they just thought he was thick.

"Don't acknowledge them, Siobhan, we'll just go down the other end," Frank whispered.

Siobhan did not need to be told twice. As they proceeded down the north end of the balcony, all the time being berated by the teenagers at the southern end, they received the same mixture of nasty fuck offs and polite fuck offs as had been their day.

When they returned to the stairwell, the two did not feel brave enough to continue down where the teenage hyenas sat in wait. Instead, they proceeded up to the next level. This was, of course, a tactical error. The teenagers, who felt aggrieved that their quarry had tried to cheat them, followed them onto the upper storey. Siobhan and Frank now found themselves cornered, with no way of passing the group of not well meaning youths.

"Here, why aren't you asking us what we think of the centre? I think it's a great idea to have a drug centre on me doorstep. I won't have to be tracing down to the Dolphin's Barn for me drugs." The rest of group sniggered. Of course, the teenager who made this comment never had anything stronger than a cigarette, which caused him to cough for fifteen minutes. As weak as individually each of the group were, the lies they told each other collectively made them strong. Those same lies would also serve to influence them in pursuits that once again, individually, they would never countenance. That was their danger.

"Hi ya, lads, look, we just want to talk to your folks about possible changes to the area and as you know, your folks do have a right to know, so just let us get on with it, thanks." Frank tried his best to be firm, though truthfully, he was feeling very intimidated. He believed this group of young people were capable of anything; perhaps they were. Strangers by definition are an unknown quantity. Despite living around the corner from them, he could not recognise a single face. They knew him though, they were observant and he was distinct. He had breached unspoken rules entering their complex. This was against convention, they were permitted to walk past his apartment block, never in them, and he was intruding where he did not belong.

"Here bud, who's your tailor, I wanna see if he can hook me up? It must have cost you a fair few?" One of the teenagers looked directly at Frank.

Frank took this to mean an attempt at theft was being planned. In his mind's eye, he felt his economic circumstances were being evaluated. Frank chivalrously stood in front of Siobhan, which truthfully surprised both of them.

"Ah look at the action hero standing in front of his missus."

"Would you stop, he is a bender," interjected another, making one of the other members of the gang somewhat uncomfortable, struggling as he was with his own sexuality.

Siobhan stood out from behind Frank and glaringly said, "Oh fuck off, you little shits. We're not in some Roddy Doyle fucking book!" The group were momentarily quiet. They were actually too young to know Mr Doyle's work.

"See you, ye dopey cunt, you shut your mouth," the jersey-wearing youth shouted, agitated as he was due to the slowly dropping temperature. He had taken several steps towards them, which elevated the threat, as now the others felt compelled to do the same. Group think was horribly mutually reinforcing. His aggression terrified both Frank and Siobhan, who were now looking to see if there were any lights on in the windows of the flats. There were not, but as we know these two will survive; after all, Frank has an interview to give in less than a half an hour.

Steps rang through the stairwell, as the four teenagers turned around and slowly saw the broad outline of Garda Gibbons and the smaller, but similarly broad, outline of Garda Quinlan come into view. "OK ye little gougers, break it up and fuck off home," Gibbons snarled.

"We are home," one of the braver ones said, though his courage immediately diminished after uttering it.

"You don't sleep on a balcony. Now fuck off home, and leave these people alone, come on, scram!" Gibbons bellowed.

The group of four shuffled off back down the stairwell. It was amazing how quickly they turned from possible criminals back into almost children.

"You folks OK?"

"We're grand, thanks," Siobhan said though Frank looked a little shaken.

"Maybe if you're canvassing around here again, you might want to dress down a bit," Gibbons advised after regarding the two.

Frank came back to his senses. "Oh, I have an interview at 5 p.m. for the news, it's pre-recorded for the six o'clock bulletin."

Gibbons looked at him. "Good for you."

"Do you have any opinions on the new drug rehabilitation centre, Garda?" Frank beamed a smile at Gibbons.

"Do you know those Filipino death squads who do it for the drug dealers?"

"Yes... I believe I do..."

"Neat idea." Gibbons grinned and turned his back to the would-be politician.

Gibbons and Quinlan descended the stairs with Frank and Siobhan hot on their heels. Local retired Volunteer commandant Hugh turned onto the stairwell and, upon seeing the procession led by the aluminous clad Praetorian guards, quickly alighted in favour of the dark street.

Frank and Siobhan had only a few small houses left to visit, which they dutifully did. As they knocked on the last door, the warm light greeted them on the step, as it opened. "Hi ya, my name is Frank Cantwell and I would just like to briefly talk to you about the new residential rehabilitative centre and its importance for the area."

"Would you ever fuck off!"

***

"...And on the very topic, I understand you have canvassed the locals in support of the new centre. What has been the feeling on the doorstep?"

"I'd say mixed, Donal, a lot of positive feedback and a lot of interesting points that were well made. Definitely, going forward, we've learned a lot today and we will take it all on aboard." Frank smiled best when he was lying.

17.

Better the Devil You Know

7th February 2018 (Wednesday)

CONOR MAGUIRE ADJUSTED HIMSELF ON THE BUS SEAT. NARROW though he was, he always found public transport seats too small for his frame. He was deep in thought, thinking of his father, how shrunken he had become, and even though he was bald for most of Conor's life, the absence of the little edge of grey hair around his ears from the months of chemotherapy still disturbed Conor. They had lunch together. Well, Conor ate a sandwich with him while his father spoke mindlessly about their neighbour complaining about Ginger, his father's aging spaniel, barking all through the night. The spaniel had not left his father's side for some time. The species had senses long understood by humans, if not by science. Conor took out his phone and scrolled through his social life. There were messages of sympathy sure, but his friends so far had not made their presence known in the material world.

Nearly six days had passed since he received that life changing phone call in his office hive. Once again he scanned the group on his phone for new messages. There were none. In fact, the conversation had gone quite dead. It's not that they were uncaring. They had established another digital group sans him to discuss the matter. In a way that was the problem. Their social life was digitised and they were left unsure and unaware in the unplugged world. Theories on the best approach to aid Conor were being fiercely debated at length, in another digital room, leaving him alone in his one; and he was alone.

When he was with his father, it took the full concentration of his powers to overcome the irrepressible anxiety welling within him. He could not expect relief from his mother. For all his faults, he cared too much for her to allow her insight into his own pain. He was midway home now. A new routine was quickly establishing itself. A shower, a coffee, maybe some toast, then the bus to the tram and the tram to his father and back again. Conor was determined to spend as much time as he could with his father; for once, work was not a priority.

He waited patiently for the bus to start. The wait did not irritate him as it once would have done. Now he wanted everything to slow down. The present can never be made the permanent but in times where the future is so terrifying, that is exactly what we all attempt to do. Conor thought about visiting Fr Matthew. It was the last time he had laughed with sincerity, the day he was told his father was going to die. The thought made him smirk, laughing the day you hear your father was dying. We already know we are going to die. How was this different? Is it the further information of "when" that is so destructive?

Even when the cancer diagnosis had come in a year ago, Conor never seriously countenanced death and what it meant. He enjoyed too much feeling smarter than religious people who worshipped the ridiculous and impossible, even though his parents were among them. Of course, Conor reasoned that they had simply been brainwashed by the statue-touchers and paedophiles. This thought gave him pride at his own immunity.

Now he was caught in the unbreakable stare of Anubis. One who meant so much to him was facing an eternity of non existence. All his father's jokes, kindness, love, wisdom, to be wiped clean from the face of the earth. Is this what he believed in? What comfort was in this knowledge? Even the thought made him feel like he was losing grip on the world around him. Can someone simply "cease"?

He did not realise it, but he was weeping. He also did not realise that the drunk from three weeks before had stumbled onto the bus. Lost in his own thoughts, he did not overhear the argument the old man had with the bus driver over an incomplete fare. The alcoholic shuffled along the gangway, momentarily swaying when the bus started to pull off. Conor only became aware of the man's presence when he roughly landed beside him on the adjacent free seat. The smell of stale alcohol overwhelmed him but he was so caught up in the great metaphysical debate in his mind that he did not really recognise the man now smiling at him.

"How are ye, young fella?"

"Hi, em hello." Conor pulled his jacket into his side to facilitate his companion and then returned to staring out at the cold, grey Wednesday afternoon. Watching the people moving to and fro, he thought how happy they must be not to have his problems. He mused how different the city, so familiar to him for years, had become in just a few short days.

"It's bitter out there, isn't it? Oh be the hokey!" This casual and friendly beginning to a conversation was ignored. "Ah cheer up pal, it's not that bad!" the alcoholic continued.

"Is it not? And how do you know that?! How do you fucking know it's not that bad exactly? You're just some drunk!" Conor was surprised at himself. The quick swell of anger so thoroughly possessed him when he was forced from his thoughts back into the real world. This was the second time in only a few short days that he had lost his temper with another person. First, when he shouted at Fr Matthew; now, at some vagrant who just said hello. Conor saw himself as sophisticated. This loss of control was not the persona he had created for himself. Sure, he was condescending, snide, sarcastic, but never angry, that was for the working class who couldn't keep their business amongst themselves.

The old drunk did not seem offended. He stared ahead of him and placed one tobacco-stained hand on the handle on the seat in front of him. "Ah son, it's never all right, it's never all bad either. We get into our little routines and look at the news and say 'how terrible it is for them', never realising that our turn is just around the corner."

"Our little routines? What routine do you have?" Conor tersely replied.

"You don't need to have a big job to have a routine, son. Anyway, they're important, they keep the reality that one day it will be us on the chopping block away from the auld noggin," he said while pointing to his own head that was partially covered by a dirty grey-haired combover. "Survival instincts, pal. If we realised what suffering was coming, we'd stop and die on the side of the road. Clever is the auld brain." The old man produced a small glass bottle and strained to uncap it, politely offering Conor a drink and after Conor's quick hand gesture to demonstrate his refusal, the old man took a large gulp. "I love the bus! Even when I was a kid," he confided to Conor with a smile.

The man's warmth distilled guilt in Conor, who now felt distinct shame for his early brashness. He now remembered the old man from that tram trip, only three weeks ago, yet it felt like it was years ago, in someone else's life. Then, the old man was an old drunk, just another sponger, another obstacle in a life where work occupied too much time and the comfort and security of home too little. Now that he needed time to slow, Conor was inclined to listen. He needed company, too. The old drunk's reply had a general wisdom, as well. It was also delivered with a dignity that Conor did not believe a man smelling of vodka, cigarettes and possibly piss, yes definitely piss, could deliver. "I'm a little short with people at the moment. I'm just working through something." It's amazing how an apology is not an apology without that small two syllable word. That word contains a magical value not yet quantified.

The old man turned his gaze, though not his head, towards Conor. "What's wrong with you, pal?"

Usually, the "parasite classes" would only have Conor's contempt, though today his mind was less rigid, and less formed. "I've recently found out that my father is dying." Annoyingly for Conor, he had started to weep again.

"Oh, that's terrible, pal. Oh, that's terrible."

"Yeah, it is."

"I remember when my father passed. He was such a good sturdy man, I never thought time would fell him and yet it did, as it will me and my brother who I'm now visiting."

"Is your brother sick?" Conor turned to the old man as he spoke these words.

"Ha I'd say so, the fucking cancer is on the dessert course with him, the poor bastard." The old man drank another gulp and wiped the tiny wild grey hairs that nestled above his upper lip.

"I am sorry to hear about your brother. My father has cancer too," the young pony-tailed man sympathised.

"It's what gets most folk in the end, that or heart disease, at least it isn't hunger, eh? Maybe we're lucky. In past times we'd just call it 'old age,' though me brother is only 68, God love 'em."

"God has nothing to do with it, it's just chance." Conor's brow furrowed and he resumed staring out of the window. The old man said nothing for only a few seconds but it was enough time to provoke Conor to continue. "How can you be the most compassionate being and then ordain that certain people will rot away with cancer?" Conor's eyes concentrated.

"Sure didn't he nail his only son to a tree? You can't stay here, son, that's the point, it's someone else's turn when someone dies. God knows all things, you don't, all this is a trial." The old man lifted his arms high. One came worryingly close to Conor's personal space.

Two young teenagers sitting in front of them turned around to look at him. "Howaye loves?" he beamed at them. They quickly turned around and returned to their phones.

Non fazed by the teenagers' disgust, the old man continued. "Heaven isn't heaven just because God made it so, son, heaven is heaven because the people who chose to go there were decent down here during their trial. It's the people that make it bliss, not the clouds or cherubs."

"What about the people down here who suffered more, eh? Do you people ever flesh out your ideas? What about the people of Syria? Or some person who was raped as a child? Not a very fair trial." Conor was hurting.

"Maybe their judgement is easier, son. Who knows? As you say yourself, I am just some drunk on a bus in a Dublin. What do I know?" The drunk rubbed his brow. "Though I do know something is better than nothing and if you are believing in nothing then you're definitely missing out on something!"

"Yeah, well, maybe so." Conor felt an increasing need to apologise to the old man. A lifetime of shooting people down with sarcasm and believing in his own superiority had rendered him quite useless at atonement. The bus turned around Christ Church and onto High Street. "I'm sorry for being so dismissive the first time you tried to talk to me, there a while back. I know you were just being friendly and I am sorry for calling you a drunk, that was unnecessarily aggressive of me. It's actually very comforting in a weird way, this conversation, I'm just all over the place."

"What first time? We meet before?" The revelation that the drunk did not remember him from three weeks before ebbed a little in Conor's mind; maybe he was initially right to think little of him. Surely, this man did not stay long enough in reality to warrant respect. "Nah, I remember ya, I just thought you were an ignorant little shit, reminding me that I was being an annoying little shit." The old man laughed and Conor actually grinned.

"These days it's hard for folks to sympathise with a stranger, especially if they look like they need sympathy. I couldn't blame ya. Well you know me now, anyway." The old man, who had long since stopped offering Conor the bottle, took another sharp swig.

"Excuse me do you mind putting your bottle away, my 7-year-old is with me." A woman sitting behind them spoke into the old man's ear. The 7-year-old was unaware, busy as she was putting her mouth against the dirty bus window.

"Of course, miss, sorry miss." The old man returned the glass bottle to his inside pocket and sighed. He leaned into Conor. "People have gotten very self righteous these days. Wishing to be a victim, I think. In the old days, people were victims trying hard to pretend they were not." The smell from his breath, acetone, Conor knew from his mother; this old man was a diabetic. Its sharpness, mixed with the vodka, was quite the cocktail on the senses.

Conor returned to looking out the window. After a while he turned to the old man. "Do you have anyone other than your brother?"

"Nope, that's it then, just me, just me." The old man's gaze returned to the front of the bus.

The bus was passing the Guinness Brewery. It briefly stopped outside the white gates. Two Americans, laden with bum bags, alighted. The bus moved off again.

"Son, do your best to reach out to others and find comfort where you can, the world has become a very lonely place. I feel sorry for the lads and lasses these days. All the free college made you too smart for church and too health conscious for the pub. Truth is, you lot need both more than we did, locked in your small office cubicles and your neighbourless apartments. You don't got no one to talk to or mind the kids in an emergency. The world has put you on your own. You need to get back in the stream, young salmon, get back into the school." The old man rose rather unsteadily to his feet. "Community and family are far more important than wealth and status, pal."

Conor rose too. They were now at the bus stop just outside his apartment and not far from the hospital. When he got off the bus, he shook the old man's hand and wished him well. The old man farted. Smiled and walked on.

Conor decided not to return to his quiet apartment just yet and instead go for a ramble. It was cold out but it was fresh and his mind was energised with the conversation with the pissed, stained sage. He looked at his phone; the symposium on how to deal with his future bereavement was still ongoing. The group where he had left his terrible news was still frozen with the last "I am so sorry to hear that Conor" message that he had received that morning.

Conor looked at the traffic island where two drunks were laughing loudly, while a third pissed on a local monument, in full view of all outgoing and ingoing traffic. Usually, his mind would utter "scum" with a deep-seated resentment. Now he pondered if they were just lonely men and how they had fallen so far and if they had anyone left. He circled his block and turned the corner on to Clementine Lane. In the distance he could see a smartly dressed Frank being told rather loudly to fuck off, with an attractive woman next to him.

Shane Farrell stood at the door to his house smoking. On seeing Frank, he stubbed his cigarette, walked back indoors and closed his front door.

Down the lane, Conor could see Hope, Leanne and Marion chatting away with cups of tea outside the crèche.

Eventually, he had returned to his own street. Outside Cartigan's stood Terry and Mick with half-drunk pints in their hands. Both men were silent, observing the world around them.

Terry looked directly at Conor. "Is your name Conor?"

The long haired 30-something was a little surprised. "Eh yeah, yes it is," he replied.

Terry continued, "Fr Matt told me about your da, I'm very

sorry to hear that, son. That fucking cancer is fucking awful thing."

"Eh, thank you."

"Sorry, I know it's none of my business, son, word travels though, especially if Fr Matt's involved. Never go to confession to him is all I'm saying."

"I won't." Conor politely nodded.

"I'll say one thing for the dirty cunt, he's no peado. I caught him staring at your one Carol's arse the other day in the shop. Good thing she didn't cop it, she would have cut the fucker," Terry said with a smile.

Mick started laughing at Terry's observation.

"Could you imagine it? 'Oh I am very sorry Ms, I was lost in thought thinking of Paul's letter to the Corinthians." Terry's impression was rough, to be fair, but it made both Mick and Conor laugh.

Mick lowered the remainder of his glass and turned to Conor. "Here, young fella, come in and we get you a pint. Take a little load off ya for a while, and fuck it, you can get us one back if you're feeling guilty about it. Terry may be a prick but sure when you get to know him he's not the worst company. Better the devil you know and all that."

Conor smiled. "Yeah, actually I wouldn't mind one."

The three men entered Cartigan's and closed the door.

18.

Revelations

4th February 2018 (Sunday), 8th February 2018 (Thursday)
with memories of 3rd February 2018 (Saturday)

"A RE YOU THERE?"
        "Yes, child."

It was so faint as to hardly be audible, but it seemed so definite. The voice emanated behind her. Sienna's eyes rose suddenly to the wooden beamed ceiling and she slumped into a small pile on the floor...

"Ha! She fell right over! What? No, not you, ye thick, there's a little girl here outside me flat." A bald man in a grey fleece stood at the doorway to the chapel with a mobile held to his left ear, he was staring at the small Sienna-sized heap in the centre of the floor.

"Yeah, the little mental case was looking up at the ceiling asking if there was someone there... and I was coming in, so I says all heavenly-like 'yes, child' and the thick just passed out. Well, I don't know, do I? Maybe, she just came in to say her prayers. Here, maybe she's touched by an angel, the little special case..." The man loudly laughed.

He walked over to Sienna and placed his two fingers on her neck to check her pulse. "She's alive, anyway, I think she's that Farrell chap's daughter, another family of simple Jims. Yeah, he's the one with your one with the big baps for a wife. Anyway, getting back to it, I think it's all getting a little bit hot, get rid of…" The man in grey continued his conversation, ignoring the unconscious girl, who seemed to move ever so slightly. "I don't care where, but not a trace." Eventually, he hung up the phone and walked into his apartment, closing the door firmly behind him.

Sometime later, Sienna woke in the middle of the floor. The brownish dust that stuck to her skin felt chalky as she knocked it from her arms. There were small droplets of blood forming around a scrape on her elbow. She was somewhat disorientated as she slowly picked herself up. Gradually, she became aware that she was standing in the old chapel, but her memory of why was still hazy.

The sky outside was growing dark. It must be around 3.30 p.m. It was Sunday, she knew that. Why was she in this empty youth project? Then suddenly it hit her. The nun! She remembered the disembodied voice that had caused her lapse into unconsciousness. Sienna quickly scanned the chapel nave. She was quite alone. Still a little startled, and not wanting to tempt faith further, the teenager made her way to the exit. She must find out more.

***

It was early Thursday morning. Garda Paul Gibbons walked into the station at 7.45 a.m., a half drunken polystyrene cup of coffee in one hand and newspaper in the other. He walked the long corridor to his perfectly square office. It was a drab place, which suited his disposition. Two fluorescent lights perpetually buzzed, as the daylight struggled to make it through two slit windows in the rear wall. His desk was tidy, though stained with coffee spillages and covered in crumbs from yesterday's pre-made sandwiches. His computer, from the beginning of this millennium, wheezed to life, as if at any moment its digital lungs would finally give in. The monitor was covered with an old-fashioned anti-glare mesh that would more suit a fencer's face.

Gibbons shared this unhappy space with two lively lads fresh from the academy. One, a proud Limerick lad, whose father harboured a deep resentment towards Frank McCourt. The other from Roscommon, who hid his republicanism well, but found himself often conflicted when his colleagues spoke about those Shinner thugs in the canteen.

Gibbons liked their company, but as a well reared son, he felt that they were still yahoos. When he passed through the academy he wasn't half this immature. It seemed to him that recruits were coming out younger and younger. Of course, it is also true that he was getting older and older. The snob in him believed deeply that they weren't correctly trained. This assumption was wrong too. The curriculum had been severely expanded since his graduation.

Nonetheless, all they seemed to do was sit there, drink tea and talk about who they slept with after the last night out. Listening to them, Gibbons got the impression that there were a lot of people of easy virtue in the force. He sat at his desk, already feeling weary despite it being only the beginning of an overcast Thursday morning.

"How ya Paul?"

"Hi ya Paul?"

"Lads."

Gibbons began to sift through the paper. It seemed that "homeless gouger's" death was still on the front pages, with politicians accusing each other of incompetence. He recalled the stiffness of the young man's body when he went to check his pulse. How Quinlan stared to heaven when he began a prayer over the body. Stupid gouger, there were places he could have gone to get out of the cold. He didn't have to die there, alone.

"Paul, the Chief Inspector wants a word with you when you get a chance?" Quinlan hung off the door frame; she looked a little awkward.

"Where were you the other night? You missed the table quiz

and a dance with Garda Jackhammer," a Limerick voice asked from the other end of the office.

"Garda O'Rourke, can you please try not to come into work smelling of alcohol. Also, the Garda WhatsApp group is not to be used for pictures of your empty pint glasses and cross-eyed smiles, thanks," Quinlan tersely replied.

"Yes mam!" Garda O'Rourke immediately and earnestly answered.

"Thanks Aoife, I'll be with him in a bit." Paul Gibbons looked over at Quinlan and smiled; she had already gone. He turned back to his paper. As he perused the middle pages of the tabloid, he recognised a face. "There's that little posh toe rag from the flats, in his nice suit. Frank Cantwell, so that's his name. Wasn't he at the warehouse three weeks ago, yabbering with the auld ones about the centre being a terrible idea? Now here he is shouting for one? Two faced slug."

Paul went to the back of the paper and scanned the horses. As he had already done so several times that week, his mind went back to last Saturday morning when he and Quinlan had sat down for a pint. They both had come from a long shift standing over the body in that cold lane. While tired, they resolved to head to an early house to shake off the coldness and the feeling of recent death. A drink seemed like a good idea. Little did he realise it would lead to this present coldness between them. Sitting in a pub in Smithfield occupied by fish mongers, dockers and fruit and veg men; who else would drink at that time? Well there were, of course, a few grizzled, red-faced alcoholics at the bar. A lifetime spent on wooden counters had made them more bark than man. The two off-duty officers had found a small table beside a window. Sitting down in silence, they began watching the night slowly give way to morning, as the forklifts, heavily laden with pallets of fruit, entered and left the redbrick Edwardian market.

"Well that was a long night, fuck sake!" Quinlan lifted her pint and sipped it lightly as her eyes opened wide and stared directly at

Gibbons, who was chopping a beer mat against the table, waiting for his Guinness to settle.

"Yep."

"What's wrong with you? Usually, it's hard to shut you up from complaining about something." Quinlan set her pint down.

Gibbons looked up. "Do you think I'm hard on people? You know, like the folks around at Clementine, you know, do you think I'm a snob?"

"No and yes," she laughed.

He looked on with a firmly closed mouth and a look of confusion.

"No, you're not hard on people, you're actually very soft in your approach. It's what I like best about you. You don't seem to let the uniform get to you, like every other prick in the station, and yes, you are a snob." She giggled again. "Why do you ask?"

"Ah some auld lad in the pub last night said something about me talking about the junkie like he was an animal."

Quinlan tried to comfort the downcast guard. "Don't mind him, he probably was pissed. Besides, what would he know about it? None of them were in a hurry out of the pub when you told them that a dead man lay across the street, were they? Self righteous prick."

"I suppose. He looked like he was sincere enough about it."

"He was jarred. Anyway, I don't want to talk about last night. Any holidays planned?" Quinlan looked up at Gibbons.

"No, it's all about the overtime until the house is finished."

"You do have to live in between, Paul."

"Tell that to my builders." Gibbons took a large intake of stout. His palate had not adjusted to the bitterness quite yet and he let out a rather large gasp. "Guinness is a little rough here."

"I think you should go somewhere nice, like Rome or Northern Italy. I'd love to go there. See the Vatican and the Trevi Fountain. The food is meant to be lovely and flights are cheap this time of year."

"Yeah and who would I go with?" Gibbons realised how pathetic these words sounded immediately after he uttered them, but it was what he was thinking.

"Well, you could go with me?" She smiled at him. She didn't look like she was joking.

***

"Here Paul, what's the story with you and Quinlan?" Garda Harris, the clandestine Roscommon republican, fired the question over at Paul, rousing him from his memory of that conversation.

"I'd say he's riding her on the sly, am I right?" interjected O'Rourke.

"Lads, have you nothing better to be doing than annoying me?" an irritable Gibbons replied.

"Seemingly not. Why not, anyway, eh? She's gorgeous, lovely long shanks, narrow waist, auburn hair and lovely squishy, squashy titties!" The two junior officers broke down laughing.

"Lads! That's enough! Do not talk about Garda Quinlan that way! A barracks with over thirty-five offices and I get lumped in with you two fucking retards! One, who could be an undercover spy for some Limerick drugs gang, if he wasn't so fucking thick! The other, who actually had a desk covered in Vatican flags after the Pope's visit, right at the same time as we had the Prods from the PSNI down here for a cross border meeting. Way to not play into the stereotype, Harris, they probably thought your pen holder was made of semtex, thick!"

"I confiscated those flags as part of an investigation into illegal street dealing, Paul, everyone knows that," a now-serious Garda Harris retorted.

"Would you fuck off, Harris! I'm surprised the Super didn't put you on community liaison after that!" Gibbons replied.

"You're getting moody now, Paul, we must have touched a nerve. Come on, O'Rourke, we'll get some Monster Munch and wait till this prick calms down."

"She's already ruining ya, you used to be mad sound. Don't expect your usual Aero bar back from the vending machine." This comment from O'Rourke was meant to be more damaging than it sounded and the two left the office like a couple of sulky teenagers after a scolding. In truth, it kind of worked. Their immaturity made Gibbons reflect that he might have been too hard on them. "Squishy squashy titties, eejits!" He smiled to himself, and then thought, she really was well-busted.

"Where is that dopey Eeyore asshole? Quinlan, you told him I was looking for him?"

"Yes, Inspector."

"Well, go get him again."

Gibbons was already at the door to the inspector's large office, with the huge bright windows letting in the first bit of sunshine on to his cluttered desk. "Sorry about my lateness, sir, there were urgent matters of delegation that had to be attended to."

"I'm sure, who gets the biccies, was it?" The inspector was an unfortunate-looking man. His brown hair crowned a bald top, like a nest with one solitary fat egg. His ornithology was complete with a hawk nose and eagle slit eyes of blue. He stood as high as most average shoulders, but his foul temper and ability to use it added some more metaphoric inches. "I understand you were the two officers involved in the investigation/media circus that was the discovering of the late Mr Peter Williams' body?"

"That would be correct, Inspector." Quinlan looked well, Gibbons thought, her uniform sitting neatly tight to her body.

"Wunderbar, which one of you eejits told the press it was a suspected overdose?"

"Neither, sir," Quinlan replied.

"Neither? Why is it all over every paper and every news station that Mr Williams expired due to an expected crack cocaine overdose?!" The inspector began to sound somewhat incredulous. His Tyrone accent always made him sound that little bit angrier.

Gibbons looked worried and then stepped forward. This formality bemused the inspector. "That might have something to do with me, sir. I may have let it slip in a pub."

"*In* a pub?"

"Well, to a priest in a pub, sir."

"What the fuck am I dealing with here?! And was the priest working confession in this pub? Did he have a curtain over the snug and admit you one by one? What else did you tell him?"

"Nothing sir, I merely was trying to allay fears, sir, I realise now that I may have misspoke."

"Do you misspeak often, Gibbons?" the inspector angrily asked.

Gibbons thoughts went back to the pub with Quinlan.

***

"What?" Gibbons looked shocked behind his pint glass.

"Well, why not? Am I that bad company?"

"No, not at all, but you mean as friends?" Gibbons drank a large swallow of Guinness and nearly choked on it. He was trying now to look relaxed after his attempt at self water-boarding.

"Well, I don't know, I guess. You know, Paul, you're in your own world sometimes. We've spent every waking moment with each other for the last two years. I guess I'm kind of used to you, are you not used to me?" She smiled again, bringing her head down to her lager, barely sipping it from the table.

"Used to me? What does that mean?"

"Never mind, Paul, forget it." She took out her phone and started to scan through the messages.

Gibbons was still looking at her to see if this was an elaborate joke at his expense. It must be, it was such an odd way to ask someone out. "Do you want to go on holiday with me?" I mean, come on! Who says that to a guy? Fair play to her, though, she held it out to the last. "You're some bitch, Aoife." He started to laugh. "I almost believed you!" His North Tipperary accent served only to highlight his innocence. "Us two, some joke, eh, you dope, you had me!" He grinned and took a more relaxed sup of his pint.

Quinlan wasn't laughing now. She put her phone quickly into her pocket and took a drink. "Some joke, all right." Her voice was terse, not jovial. "Listen, Paul, I'm tired, I know I said I'd stay out but I'm just wrecked. Good morning and good luck." She rose from the table and walked out the door. It took maybe some twenty minutes for Paul to realise that he had just misspoken.

***

Once again, Gibbons snapped out of his memory. The inspector was still staring at him.

"Well, smartarse? Misspeak often? You're like that other thick with his fucking Vatican flags! I don't like the RUC, or whatever those cunts call themselves now, anymore than anyone else. Nonetheless, we looked like extras from 'The Quiet Man' for fuck's sake. The face on those three black hearts when they saw that table of Vatican flags."

"I believe he was carrying out an investigation, sir." Gibbons felt the need to stand up for his absent friend.

"Don't fucking lie for that idiot man-child, he robbed them for his family, Gibbons! We all fucking know it. The stupid prick muscled in on some Traveller street traders to get a few flags for his Roscommon mammy."

Gibbons was secretly delighted at this long digression; it was taking all the attention away from his accidental slip of the tongue to Fr Matthew.

Quinlan was smirking.

"Don't you fucking smirk at me, lass! You may think it's funny that this station has become a crèche but I don't!"

"No sir, sorry sir!" She stood to attention.

"The force is full of fags, whistle blowers and teenagers now," the inspector thundered.

"Sir, that's inappropriate! Homosexuals, sir, gay people prefer the term 'homosexuals'." Quinlan stared directly at the inspector; it unnerved him. He realised that he had gone too far. These were different times, there would be whistle blowing against him for these remarks. Who had given all these fuckers whistles anyway?

"Yes, sorry, I misspoke," the inspector conceded.

"It must be catching." Gibbons smiled at the inspector who stared but said nothing, knowing he had already compromised himself.

"Anyway, the two of you were wrong. The coroner's report is back, he didn't overdose. The stupid prick was poisoned. Rat poison mixed in with his usual fix."

"Sir, is it not possible that they simply spliced the crack without intent? These guys put everything into the mix. This could be just an accident."

"Usually, I would agree with you, Gibbons, but the coroner thinks otherwise. The quantity of anticoagulants was far too high. They're insistent that the chap was murdered. You two will be going back to Clementine Lane to canvass the area. Let's try to be a tiny bit subtler this time, Gibbons."

"Yes, sir!"

19.

We're Workin!

A WEEK HAD PASSED SINCE MR PETER WILLIAMS CONFIRMED HIS membership of the Choir Invisible. Tiny droplets of rain were hazing down from a dark, grey Friday morning sky. In five days it would be St Valentine's Day. The crèche staff were busy taking off the mildly damp tiny coats of the barely walking toddlers, while Phyllis was busy with paperwork. Everyone was busy. Everyone except Marion, who was standing by the window in the small crèche office, staring out at the rain, in boredom. Phyllis was adapting the newest policy required for their crèche. This policy was dreamt up by a civil service similarly as bored as Marion. It concerned itself with how the plates were to be washed in the crèche kitchen. Not too much soap, of course, and at a high enough temperature to kill all known organisms, as well as severely burn one's own hand. Water was to be equally dispersed over the entirety of the plate, to be scrubbed first vertically, up then down, then up again. Then the plate was to be scrubbed horizontally, left then right, and then left again, before a circular motion of scrubbing was to be applied in closing concentric circles. The plate was to be immediately dried (there was an additional page on drying methods) and placed in the appropriate cabinet (these were to be colour coded to insure ultimate hygiene).

This policy was the end result of a government-commissioned €20,000 report into crèche kitchen hygiene. It was incredibly important, according to the State. The policy was destined to join similar guidelines in the growing Magna Carta that was Phyllis's policy folder. Of course, this Magna Carta would never be read by any of the minimum-wage staff who worked in the crèche. They must have carried out their own research into plate washing, as they already knew most of the findings. Nonetheless, Phyllis must ensure that there were appropriate posters explaining these new revolutionary techniques, in case of an inspection. In different times, the infantile education signs on the walls were meant for the kids; now they were meant for the adults.

Marion did go through moments of boredom. She was not lazy, nor did routine fatigue her more than most, and while the grey sky wasn't helping, the problem lay elsewhere. The fact was she was an addict. Her addiction was shopping. It was of no importance what she bought or what she was shopping for, no matter how mundane. The process and healing power of the shop itself was enough to bring her back to full vitality.

Like many who have lived through hard lives in their youth, the fear of need never truly left Marion. It was a constant, ever-present anxiety deep within her, even if she was not cognizant of it. Her flat, which she shared with Mick, was full of unneeded goods, stockpiled in case the ghost of want ever visited again. The flat was small enough but Mick never opened his mouth; that would mean a terrible, terrible retribution. Marion needed her stockpile more than she needed Mick, and Mick knew this; to be fair, it did make a bit of sense.

Marion and Phyllis were volunteers for the local senior citizens service, as was Hope, though she was of age to be one herself. Marion was feeling the urge to shop and the small office seemed somewhat smaller. "You know the senior citizens have their bingo tonight? Hope was saying they don't even have the prizes bought, they'll be meeting at 5. What will they do?"

"Ah come on, Marion, you're only in the fucking door."

"Wha? I'm only saying they're at a loose end!" Marion looked wounded.

Phyllis knew where this was going. She also knew that not to concede would prompt a long day of mood swings; every addict gets snappy when their itch goes unscratched. "Fine, we'll go to the shops in a bit, just let me focus for a few minutes on this new shite and we'll go, just give me half hour until the place settles down."

Phyllis hated this level of nonsensical paperwork. It was patronising. She had worked in this crèche for nearly twenty years, she had learned at some point how to wash plates. She knew, too, that at some point an equally patronising inspector would come to the crèche and make her feel stupid. Their respective wages would have misled the casual observer as to their respective value to society.

Marion said nothing and continued to stare out the window at the hazy weather. Of course, this was a strategy too. As much as her voice could fill a room, her silence was equally all encompassing. Those who knew her, and Phyllis did, knew that one usually preceded an explosion of the other, making both effective techniques in control. "Fuck it, we'll go." Phyllis got up from the table.

Marion ran on ahead and hopped in Phyllis's hatchback. Her face muscles were letting her down, the smile impossible to repress.

Leanne shouted from one of the crèche windows, "Get us some cling film!" And they were off. As the small car slowly built pace along the wet lane, school children trudged on towards another boring day of school.

Marion's mood, now elated, began to move onto other subjects. "Mr Gallagher is organising the protest march for next Monday."

"I know, he has our Shane and Terry designing placards. I don't think Shane's heart is much interested in it." Phyllis was silent for a minute but then opened up a little more. "To be honest, he's gotten very distant. Sometimes we do be watching TV and I spy him looking like the world is on his shoulders, joker doesn't even have to get up in the morning."

"Maybe that's what's at him, Phyllis," Marion helpfully advised.

"Ah don't talk to me!"

The little car swished onto James Street, so named after the patron saint whose body sailed in a stone boat to Spain, after losing his head to Herod in Jerusalem. Well, that's the Galicians' story and they're sticking to it! The car turned towards the city centre.

"How's Sienna?"

"Another one keeping secrets from me. She went to the library, came back with a load of books and ran up to her room."

"That's good!"

"No, it's not, they're all on ghosts and morbid crap. Feck sake, I keep hearing from the neighbours that they see her peering into that stupid chapel like some kind of stalker. I could kill that addict for filling her head with nonsense. She's got more brains than any of us and that's what she spends her time on, reading about ghosts. And she won't say a word to me, like she was always a quiet one, but now she's turning into a newt."

"A mute, Phyllis," Marion pointed out.

"Is it? A mute then, I don't know what happened to her! I said to her, what's wrong with you? And do you know what she says to me? She says 'Why are you getting all up in arms about a drug centre? We should be helping them!' She's turnin' into a right little Bono pox bottle. I'm the sole fucking earner for a family and I volunteer out and about and now, just because I don't want a load of junkies needlin' beside me, I'm the devil incarnate! Get this, she even asked me on Sunday if she could see your man from the warehouse, yeah right, g'luck with that, love!"

Marion was only half listening, she was playing on her phone. "Teenage years are coming, Phyllis, she's been a little girl long enough, now it's the do-gooder phase. Be grateful it's not a do-badder phase!"

The car turned down the hill at Bridgefoot Street, where the Irish patriot Robert Emmet lost his head and most of his innards, taken by the neighbouring country, which was enraptured at the time by the humorous finesses and romances of Jane Austen. The car zipped towards the quays and towards the former farmer trading post of Stoneybatter, where the final destination of the supermarket lay.

"What are we getting for the auld ones, anyway?" Phyllis enquired while looking into her mirror.

"The usual, detergents, the seniors love their detergent."

"Those fuckers must have enough detergent to clean a hospital. Are they getting high off it? Stupid auld biddies, what kind of a prize is detergent?!" Phyllis had worked herself up thinking about Sienna and Shane and was now firing in all directions. Marion for her part returned to looking at her phone.

"Did you notice the guards were knocking on doors along the street this morning? Your pal was out there, Gibbons." Marion continued the conversation.

"It would be typical of the guards to knock on people's doors when most people are at work, wouldn't it? Look at this fucking cyclist, just bleedin' flies in front of me without even signalling. They think they own the fucking road, hippies! Yeah, fuck off!" Phyllis applied her middle finger to the side window as she overtook the cyclist and headed onto Queen Street, named after Charlotte of Mecklenburg-Strelitz, married to the man who managed to lose something as big as America, King George the 3rd.

Marion ignored the anger and continued, "I think they're investigating something, probably to do with that homeless chap's death."

"Thought that was an accident?"

"Why else would they be knocking on doors, Phyllis?"

"Well, I'm sure they'll catch him so," Phyllis said somewhat sarcastically, still a little annoyed over Gibbons' reticence to enter the warehouse several weeks ago.

They drove up Manor Street, named after the Manor of Grangegorman, where Thomas Stanley once lived. As a Royalist, he believed that kings should keep their heads in ideal circumstances.

"Fuckin' hipsters everywhere!" Phyllis fumed amidst the small over-priced cafés that sold every type of cereal, and gastro pubs that sold offcuts of meat that were considered worthy for consumption only by tenement dwellers of another age.

"Where did they get that name, anyway?" Marion sincerely asked.

"Because they're all skinny, malanky bastards with no hips, Marion!"

"Is it?"

Phyllis laughed at her naivety and her own mood lightened. They pulled into the shopping centre and parked. "So what if he was murdered then?" Phyllis struggled to free the shopping cart from the metal centipede.

"We could have a murderer just walking around Clementine. Maybe it's Terry, he has it in for those junkies, doesn't he?" Marion looked thoughtful.

"Firstly, so do you have it in for those junkies. Secondly, no, Terry has his own story and I doubt he thinks like you on the whole drug thing. Shane was telling me his brother was an addict," Phyllis replied as she finally freed the cart.

"I didn't know he had a brother! That's the thing about blow-ins, you never know what you're getting." The electric doors slid open and allowed the two women access to the florescent lit warehouse.

"Ah here, he moved into Clementine about twenty years ago and he was only from around the corner. Come on, Marion!"

Marion wasn't listening; she was evaluating two lemons, both of which entered the cart, both of which a crèche or a senior citizens' service would have little use for. "Jaysus, maybe it was that homeless guy who had your Sienna! Did you see him on the telly last Monday, your man McGlynn was interviewing him, he came off a right prick!"

"Yeah, he was shocking to his parents, the poor bastards, and then they have to see him wash his linen in public. Still though, he was in hospital, how could he kill anyone?" Phyllis pondered.

"Oh yeah, well, it proves what I was saying, there's nothing but bad news with those junkies!" Marion shouted across, she was now over at the bread, as an increasingly tired Phyllis pushed the cart.

***

"That's it, Terry and Shane, big letters, we will give them a fight if nothing else." Arthur smiled as both Terry and Shane painted onto a large piece of cardboard.

Phyllis was right, Shane's heart wasn't in it. For a start, he didn't really believe in his wife's cause. This had become increasingly true after his clandestine visit to Brendan on the previous Monday. Also, there was something infantile about all of this, an older man directing two middle-aged men to draw. In his own mind, the constant supportive utterance of their names, "well done Terry" and "well done Shane", had the effect of making them both sound like simpletons. Shane was a builder, he had provided for his family and raised them. Well, now he was the child. Nonetheless, he did not vocalise these thoughts to his wife; there was enough shame in his mind about being dependent on her, like the rest of the children. She wanted this protest, so he would help and that was it.

Arthur was sitting down in the upstairs balcony of the chapel, watching the two men work below him. The place was empty save for them. The youth project did not start till later.

"Do you honestly think this will achieve anything, Mr Gallagher?"

The old man looked at Shane wearily. "Probably not, the media will have their say and once they have said their piece the people in the real world scarcely matter. Just the same, we have to show them that we're people too and that we have pride in our area. The well-to-do are not the only ones whose views matter."

Terry said nothing, he just occupied his mind with painting the cards.

"What's the point if we're just going to be ignored again? Council, government, media, they never listen to anyone from this neck of the woods and they never will," Shane persisted.

"The point is, Shane, Hawkins is a greedy cunt. His places ruin people's lives, and they will ruin this area, and one way or another, we have to stop them. Do-gooders never pay attention to the lives they're messing with, the fine fragrance of their own shite occupies too much of their senses. It's for us to make sure our way of life is preserved, our homes kept safe and to protect ourselves from the ideas of the arrogant and non-affected." These words came from Terry's mouth, though his eyes did not lift from the canvas; he was hypnotised by it.

"Ehh... aside from the language, I would have to agree with Terry" Arthur added. "Are you ready for the television show tonight, Terry?" Arthur was eager to move the conversation on to something more positive, as unlikely as that was when one was preparing for a protest.

"As ready as I'll ever be. I'll have to watch the language though, your man McGlynn doesn't, does he?" The question was rhetorical, though all three had begun to hear stories of the reporter's candidacy. To most of the residents of Clementine Lane, McGlynn seemed to be badly reared. Most but not all; Marion thought he was a gentleman. "Thanks, Shane, for giving McGlynn my name."

"You're more than welcome, rather you than me any day. Going on the telly to say I am against junkies getting beds isn't exactly my bag just the same. I mean, lads, hold on a second, are we not the bad guys here? We're standing in the way of somewhere that houses, feeds, and rehabilitates the addicts. Are we not being a bunch of selfish mé féiners?" Shane stopped and looked at the other two.

The old man stood up and walked towards the balcony edge. "Mission statements aren't reality, Shane. What will be reality is ehhh… the place will be rougher to walk at night than it is already. We've no police, they don't give a fiddlers, ehh… the drug dealers will make a killing. The reality is the folk that place will house will have a mixture of psychological, social, familial or even criminal problems. Some are there to shorten prison sentences. Others are there only because it's warm. Neither may have any intention of rehabilitating. Who are we meant to trust with the keys to this dangerous asylum? A businessman with no interest in either their rehabilitation or our community? We may be cast as mé féiners, so what? That's exactly what we are, just like everyone else! Unlike others, though, we don't have much power, which is why we need to rally! Unlike others, we are expected to bear the brunt of these social problems alone. The place with the least resources dumped to deal with the severest of problems. A place considered a dump and, therefore, it doesn't matter if more problems are dumped into it. How many more times can they do this to us?! Let Dublin east deal with it for a change. Let the pious middle class, who see us all as scum anyway, get their ehh… damn hands dirty!"

Shane and Terry were both surprised in the sudden surge in Arthur's anger; he even said "damn." "Well said, Mr Gallagher! Well said!" Terry finally looked away from the sign.

Shane sighed and started to paint again.

***

Phyllis was watching a very contented Marion tucking into an éclair in the small bakery beside the supermarket. They were surrounded by shopping bags, which contained toilet paper, an assortment of fruit and veg, small cakes, minerals; everything but cling film and detergent. Neither had realised that they had omitted the items that were the purpose of their mission.

"We better be getting back to work, Marion."

"Nonsense, we're working all morning, Phyllis!"

Phyllis smirked to herself. Well, this was better than filling a policy on washing plates.

"I still think Terry could have done it for your man, there's an anger in him, Phyllis, or maybe IRA Hugh, cleaning the streets!" Marion said with a mouth full of éclair.

"If, and I mean if, he was murdered, Marion, then it was probably some no-name bastard over some personal crap between them that nobody else knows about or cares. Life isn't a movie."

20.

A Late Night Discussion

9th February 2018 (Friday)

THE SILVER SERPENT STREETLAMPS SLOWLY HISSED TO LIFE outside Cartigan's pub. It was once again Friday night, and it had been a long week full of reporters, interviews, political canvassing and Garda visits, which prompted suspicions among the locals. Nonetheless, the more things change, the more other things needed to stay the same, such as Friday night in Cartigan's. The laughter and shouting could be heard at a reasonable distance from the premises. The apartments on the street were mostly dark, their occupants off drinking in town or returning to family somewhere down the country. The morning's hazy rain had persisted throughout the day and the area was well and truly soaked. Shuffling along on the opposite side of the street, alongside the church, was a man with wild ginger hair. Here and there stumbling, here and there belching and half talking to himself, sluggishly uttering, "Sorry Taft… sorry."

This creature was caught somewhere between consciousness and sleep. He stopped and rested against the black railings, dimpled by thousands of tiny droplets of moisture. A goblin-green bottle of whiskey in one hand dinged clumsily off them. As he leaned heavily, his head, pulled by gravity down towards the pavement, hovered loosely on his neck. For the ginger headed man, it seemed, and was desirable that, at any moment he could vomit. Of course, it was Brendan; it would be insulting to continue pretence. A person introduced as a fervent alcoholic, who had a "road to Damascus" moment, only for the reader to see him belatedly and emotionally destroyed by a reporter's eagerness for a story, or maybe an author doing the same. Either way, the next scene was always obvious. Brendan was always going to fall off the wagon and rather lazily and predictably, he did…

Eventually, his legs could take him no further and he slumped at the closed doorway to the church. The church had closed sometime earlier; the wrong type tended to pray at 9 p.m. on a Friday night. Brendan sat in the exact same spot where Mr Peter Williams had expired a week before. Was there a divine connection between the two lost souls? No. The railings ended at the door and Brendan had no longer the ability to progress without them. Happenstance, nothing more.

For the time being he was still. His head fell back against the heavily varnished brown door, losing consciousness, his arms spread out exposing bare hands on the concrete. In this state, he had become a living, drunken, and slovenly crucifixion, lying prostate for everyone to see. One of dozens of similar crucifixions throughout the city that night. Each one filled passers-by with equal measures of disgust and pity. These profane passions also stirred self loathing for the observer's failure to act and a fear, the reason for that failure. After all, to a stranger, the unconscious man could be either the Christ or the unrepentant thief.

The night sky seemed to tip its yield and the rain began to fall into a steady torrent. It dripped heavily on to Brendan, not that it mattered; he was scarcely there. The unhappy scene was made more macabre by the noisy laughter emanating from Cartigan's. Some in there were strongly arguing the need to do more for the homeless and the addicts, and worst of all, the homeless addicts!

***

Elsewhere that Friday night, a more formal debate on that very theme was about to take place. In a warm studio, an audience was being roused to life by a mediocre comedian before the commencement of *Political Questions*, a late-night discussion programme.

Frank looked nervous. Unsurprising really; Frank was nervous. From the time he had been a young student protesting at the gall of the college shop selling chocolate made by an evil multinational, which exploited someone somewhere, as multinationals are wont to do, up until the recent local elections, Frank had believed it was his manifest destiny to lead. The people, rather awkwardly, decided otherwise and Frank had to satisfy himself with his property management committee. Even control of that drifted from him, populated as it was by other professionals, arguably of a higher caste, civil servants, architects, etc. They rather obnoxiously had opposing opinions to his own. It somewhat ruined the fun.

Now things had changed fast. He was staring from the wings onto the stage of a national talk show. Frank Cantwell was an expert now, on the community, no less, a community funnily enough he had largely ignored and now, when he opened his mouth tonight, he would still be largely ignoring them. To be fair, they did not vote for him to be their representative, so it seems fitting that he did not represent them. Nonetheless, he was nervous. He would be challenged tonight and his competency here was the only thing tethering him to a future in office. There was a lot to lose.

Somewhere in the distance, down a hall he could hear Terry Walsh sneeze, as he was speaking to the make-up lady, who applied too much foundation. "Ah choo! Sorry, sorry, I feel like Boy George. You know he's Irish?"

Frank shuddered.

***

Brendan was unconscious; he could not hear that there was a conversation taking place just up the street from where he lay. The parley took on agitated tones between the two hooded men, as they passed a package back and forth to one another. The street was otherwise deserted. Occasionally, a figure would come to the door of Cartigan's and a small flame would ignite, as they stood puffing away within the doorframe and out of the rain. At such moments, the two hooded men on Brendan's side of the street would lower their voices and stare awkwardly at the pub, waiting for the unwanted intrusion to return to the warmth and laughter inside.

A syrupy drool coagulated at the corner of Brendan's mouth as he dreamt on.

"You get rid of it! I'm already up to my neck in this!" The debate between the two hooded men continued.

***

"Mr. Cantwell, I presume?" The hand was produced first and caught Frank rather off guard as he played out various clever rebuttals, complete with audience applause in his head. "A famed community warrior, am I right? Well there's a pair of us in it." Hawkins smiled.

Frank knew Eamon Hawkins, as others did, from the TV. He was still trying to respond but Eamon had business to discuss and continued apace. "All joking aside, Frank, I think the two of us need to team up here. We both want the same thing. We need to drive the message home to the people on the other side of that camera that this centre is needed. Let me start it off, I'll go into detail on some of my own successes. I keep a load of case studies for this kind of thing. Get people onside to the good we're going to be doing. Then you can come in and talk about those in your community who are supportive of the service. You can talk about those guys out there who are being shouted down by the loudmouths. Does that sound like a plan?"

"To be honest, Eamon, there aren't many of those," Frank meekly replied, still remembering the cacophony of fuck offs he was subjected to, but two days before.

"It's group think, Mr Cantwell. There are people out there who agree, they just don't want to leave the swarm, human behaviour 101." Hawkins nodded knowingly.

"How are ye, Frank? Heard you got a rough time on the auld canvass, got to say nobody likes a Benedict Arnold though." Terry was now directly behind the two men, also looking out at the audience. He had not acknowledged Eamon, who, similarly, had not acknowledged him.

Frank felt increasingly uncomfortable. "People are entitled to change their minds, Terry. I think having someone die on the street outside your home gives one perspective."

"Is that why you were knocking on people's door wearing the red rose, Frank?" Terry replied, his eyes fixed on the stage.

McGlynn had joined the trio and was busy straightening his tie. "All right lads, Mr Walsh, Mr Clement Atlee, Mr Cuntface – sorry, sorry, Mr Hawkins."

"Charming as always, Donal, how was the 'fuck a pig' festival in Athlone?" Hawkins viciously smiled.

The presenter had entered the stage to general applause. "Ladies and gentlemen, welcome to *Political Questions*. On tonight's show we will be discussing two issues, the drug epidemic in our nation's capital and the ongoing homelessness crisis. These two issues tragically combined last week with the death of Mr Peter Williams and the ongoing dispute of the residential rehabilitative centre planned for Clementine Lane. Tonight's panel will consist of our own Donal McGlynn, who spoke to the residents of Clementine this week, Terry Walsh of the Clementine Lane Residential Association, Frank Cantwell, resident of McDonagh Street, where the remains of Mr Williams were found, and Eamon Hawkins of the Rebuild Foundation. Let's bring them out."

The four men stepped into the light.

***

The argument continued on the darkened McDonagh Street.

"Hold on, hold on, I'll fucking ring him and see what he wants to do with it." One of the hooded men produced a mobile phone.

Brendan had been urinating in his unconscious state for some time. The fluid was pleasantly warming his inside leg. He moved slightly in his slumber. A bottle rolled from the relaxed grip of his left hand onto the road, and rattled empty.

Suddenly, the two hooded men looked down the street, hitherto not aware of Brendan's presence. "Ah fuck, what's this about?" They slowly walked down the street towards him, one with a phone to his ear awaiting a response. "He's fucking out of it. Jaysus, the whiff off him."

"Hold on my chum, I believe I have a solution to our little problem!" The hooded figure put away his phone and took the package, a small sealed Ziplock bag, from his similarly hooded colleague. First tapping lightly on Brendan's forehead, only for it to fall further backwards against the door, the hooded man smiled to himself. "You're really not there, are ya, red beard?" He took the Ziplock bag and placed it inside Brendan's pocket. "Fuck it, it's not our problem now, that dipso will probably take them tomorrow, job done. Fancy a pint?" The two men headed onto the main street. They were barred from Cartigan's, something to do with antisocial behaviour.

***

"That's plainly not true and you know it is! People like you say the 'silent majority' when they know for a fact that what they're saying has no popular support. Can I ask you if you ever stopped to ask why it has no popular support? Even better, let's ask the audience, how would any of you feel about one of these centres opening up beside you?"

The audience was silent, more out of manners than agreement with Terry's argument.

"Also, just to add to that, is anyone here even asking if this company is fit to run such a centre? Sure, your own journalist here—" Terry gestured towards McGlynn, "—found all sort of irregularities and shabby treatment of the clients in other centres run by this man."

McGlynn looked at the floor. He was unwilling to endorse this point; visions of the tractors and of smiling gap-tooth farmers flashed into his mind.

"I would ask the gentleman to be careful of what he is implying. The report was rubbished a long time ago." Hawkins leaned in to emphasis his point and also to intimidate.

Terry stopped. He acutely felt the desire to talk about his brother Gerard, but the country did not need to know about him and he did not want them to know.

"I think Terry is missing the point. Yes, there are those who don't want this and I think we can all understand their reasons, but right now we have a government blissfully indifferent to people who, often through no fault of their own, have ended up in addiction. We have a government not willing to house these people. We have a government not willing to house those who work. That is where we are; the homeless crisis is not just their problem, it's each and every one of you at home's problem as well. They won't house you either. Let's stop defining each other as different, addict/non addict, homeless/renting. We all have one thing in common: an indifferent, uncaring government who will only protect the wealthy!"

The audience greedily applauded Frank's speech. His comments about the government were largely true, though they were somewhat beside the point of the discussion. Remembering his leader's words "remind them about their own mortgages,"

Frank was pleased. He held the adulation and endorsement of the audience. It felt nice.

***

Brendan awoke to a singular dropping of water from the arch of the doorway. Not quite lucid but more aware than he had hitherto been. He could hear talking down the street.

"Are you awkward with me? Every time it's just the two of us you're rigidly formal."

"No, ehh no, sure why would I be?" Gibbons had been awkward to Quinlan since that Saturday morning. In fact, he had been positively rigidly formal.

"Look, it was just a thought, I get it, you may not want to mix work with your personal life. Maybe you don't see me that way. Maybe you don't see women that way," Quinlan continued.

Gibbons eyes flashed open. "No, no, I'm not a gay, honest." He really wanted this conversation to end.

"So it's just me then?"

"No, no I…" How could he tell this streetwise Dublin Garda that he was nervous, or more accurately frightened. It all seemed so easy for her. Gibbons was at sea with this kind of thing. He always had been. When the other teenagers at school bragged about what they had done and with whom, he smiled and nodded, but he never knew how to broach the matter of the opposite sex himself. They were equally unsure of him, to be fair. It all seemed so confusing and intimidating. In his own mind he always assumed he would be married one day and that thought comforted him. Like many he thought it would just happen naturally, without effort, thought or prompting. Sadly, like many this was a dangerous route that could, ultimately, lead to loneliness. As with everything, love needed work and active engagement. Though something had awoken in him since that morning in Smithfield and she was occupying more and more of his thoughts. Still though, he hadn't a clue as to what to do and this conversation was far past his comfort zone. "I... I, oh fuck, not another one!"

Quinlan followed Gibbons' line of sight right to the now semi-conscious Brendan.

"You! Gouger!" This time Brendan was in no position to retort and simply looked hazily at the tall dark-haired guard towering over him. "He's after taking something. Do you know this fucker was actually on the news the other night? They make patron saints out of failed scumbags!" Gibbons fumed.

Quinlan simply stared at Brendan. Her mind was elsewhere but she was professional enough to always be able to give a judgemental look, at a moment's notice.

"Wha?" Brendan muttered, somewhat confused.

"He definitely took something, we should check him." Gibbons was already seizing the barely conscious Brendan.

"We don't have a warrant." Quinlan was briefly coming to her senses.

"Fuck it, the bastard could be dead in the morning, we best check him." Despite his harsh language, there was a note of genuine concern in Gibbons' voice. He was not long rooting through Brendan's jacket when he pulled out the Ziplock bag. "Janey Mac, Aoife! There must be 50 grams here!"

"He's not been using, Gibbons, that man's pissed."

"How can you be sure with all this crack?"

"I knew me auldfella, Paul," Quinlan said with a stern stare.

"Well, we better call it in. I knew this fucker was a gouger, I knew it! I hope you'll be a bit more talkative at the station, we're going to have a late-night discussion, you and I." Gibbons grimaced.

***

Donal began his own well-rehearsed speech. "Well I definitely felt there was a lot of anger to the proposal in its current form. The residents I spoke to, rather eruditely I may add, made the point that as an area they have more than their fair share of these kind of social services. They feel that both the national government and, indeed, local government have given up on them. From my own observation it has brought them to a state of indifference to the political system. A lot of people understand the issue of addiction, and indeed, homelessness on a personal dimension. They understand that a lot of addicts have reached a point of anomie and that their presence can have a destabilising impact on the local community. In fact, the people I talked to..."

Hawkins interrupted McGlynn before he could finish. "They understand that a lot of addicts have reached a point of anomie? Really? Donal, I don't think the majority of the residents of Clementine Lane have reached the dizzying heights of your sociology degree!"

A healthy majority of the audience laughed at this rather patronising putdown.

Hawkins continued, "I've been helping people in addiction recover for some time now and I have had to battle time and again local residents who just don't want to have addicts near them. Its NIMBYism, their fears are understandable if unfounded, but that's what it is. Someone has to help these people, and these people need somewhere to go."

The audience applauded again. Their own personal morality reassured, it was clear by now they had picked a side. The less complicated one, the one that made them feel like good people. Donal disengaged during the applause, fantasising as he was of rooting Eamon Hawkins continuously in the testicles while an attractive brunette fed him cake.

"Okay, we have the Minister on the line. Minister, your thoughts on the discussion tonight?" The presenter placed his finger to his ear as though the Minister was solely talking to him.

"The government has done much more than the previous

administration for people in this type of dire need. Of course, we need to do more, and through our national drug strategy that is what we are trying to achieve. I think Mr Cantwell is being disingenuous about the Williams case and has an eye to his own political future. You can be assured that this government is doing everything it can for the less fortunate. We are a caring party, a party who brought in gay marriage, an inclusive party," the minister rather disingenuously said with an eye to her own political future.

"Thank you for ringing in, Minister. While we have you, would you like to make a comment on the recent scandal of your cabinet colleague, Adam Loughlin, regarding his public expenses?" the presenter queried.

"Minister Loughlin is more than capable to speak for himself on that matter and I certainly will not be joining any witch hunt."

"Ok, well, thank you again, Minister. We've time for one more question from the audience, yes, you in the back?"

A young suited lady stood up.

"I think it's disgraceful that in this day and age, when we as a country have come so far, that we still have narrow minded people like this Mr Walsh and his type, impeding people's recovery. This is Ireland in the 21st century. I think I speak for most when I say we have moved on as a society of neglect and judgement. Can I ask this man, what if it was one of his family in addiction? Your brother or son who needed Mr Hawkins' help? I'm sick to death of hearing about selfish locals impeding the progress of our country. I journey into town from Raheny each morning and you can see these poor unfortunates everywhere. They need somewhere to go. They're from the inner city. They should be housed in their local area."

Terry was still reflecting on if he should say something about his own brother, while the audience applauded, and the young lady sat down. Perhaps he should have pointed out that this young lady lived nowhere near such a centre, and had no idea of the problems it potentially could bring, but time was up and the presenter had already begun his acknowledgements. The debate had been framed and lost. It was their problem and theirs alone; it was a parochial affair.

21.

Super Sunday

11th February 2018 (Sunday)

IT WAS SUNDAY THE 11TH OF FEBRUARY, NEARING 3 P.M. THE clouded sky was bright, though showers still peppered McDonagh Street. Two red coloured teams from northern England were dividing the erstwhile close community of Clementine Lane, in Cartigan's pub. It was Super Sunday. Defined as "Super" Sunday by English sport channels to differentiate from "regular" Sundays. Regular Sundays, i.e. those Sundays in June and July, which did not have a Premier League match on and were largely reviled by those not on holidays for the same. The pub was gradually beginning to fill up. A projector canvas was being slowly stretched down over the back of the bar by Vincent Cartigan, as the pub, united in colour, separated into two.

"There's the lads now, wet auld day there now, still a bit chilly too, am I right, Terry, am I right?"

"You're bang on as usual, Vinnie," Terry replied as he sat beside Shane on two small stools in the centre of the bar, which for comfort's sake necessitated both men to hunch and lean on their elbows on the small circular table in front of them. Terry's Man. Utd. jersey revealed with stark honesty his unfortunate beer belly, while Shane's jersey for the same team, but from a different year, allowed his densely freckled arms to breathe. Both men gasped heavily after their synchronised first long intake of Guinness.

"So that was me, up on the national broadcaster. Like I've been on the radio before, you know, giving out about those fucking cyclists, never thought I'd be on a politics show." Terry seemed proud.

"Fair play, it isn't my cause, but it takes balls to go on telly and stand your ground." Shane, as he spoke, stared on at the screen that had just turned blue as the projector searched for the appropriate signal.

Terry leaned in. "If I was honest, I was fucking bricking it. Here, your man Donal what's his face is some foul-mouthed bastard, all the same. After the show, he goes to me, 'nail that prick to the wall, Hawkins is fucking dirt, he'll fuck you and your area if there's a cent in it for him.' I was like 'yeah well no need to worry about me, Mr McGlynn, I know how to handle meself,' and he just stares at me and says 'I thought that and the fucker climbed up on top of, me, put me in farmer's wellies and rode me like a donkey,' then he just walked off. I was like 'bleedin hell, relax!' "

"He comes off a little intense all right." Shane stared on; the projector screen had flickered on into a TV studio where the commentators were busy planning the unplannable.

The door opened behind them. "All right, lads, are you ready for yet another pasting this season? This time from the Mersey Red, it must be getting old for yous now?" Confidently, Mick sauntered in. He slowly, if exaggeratedly, sat down at one of the long couches that made up the side wall of Cartigan's. Marion, wearing prescription sunglasses despite the dimness of the pub, walked past her partner and straight to the bar.

"Sure Mick, you've had years of being pasted and it never hurt your confidence, ye poor little lamb." Shane was smiling. In a way he was glad they were off the subject of the residential rehabilitative centre. He already felt that they discussed the bloody thing far too much, and was hoping and, indeed, praying, for this momentary issue to pass.

Mick was, of course, adorned in his 1980s Liverpool jersey, complete with curry stain from dinner the night before when he had also been wearing it.

"Give us a G and T and Guinness, Vinnie, thanks!" Marion placed her money on the counter.

"There you are, and the Guinness is settling, thanks, Marion! How's the kids?"

"Annoying and going nowhere, thanks, Vinnie." Marion had no interest in soccer but Leanne and Hope said they would join them. She was still texting Phyllis, as she brought her G and T expertly in one hand to the table. The players entered the field and peeled off to their respective halves.

"United! United! United!" Shouts from the back of the pub from three young Dubliners, affecting English accents, much to the annoyance of Hugh, who was at his usual spot at the bar.

"For what died the sons of Roisin, Vinnie? Was it twenty-something Dubs pretending to be British hooligans?" Hugh drearily asked.

"It's terrible, terrible, terrible, so it is, Hugh, do you know who I blame? The Government." Vinnie started pouring another pint. His glasses slid down his nose, forcing him to reposition them with his first finger, while looking at the screen.

Fr Matthew and Arthur had entered the pub and sat a table up from Mick and Marion. Arthur was a lifelong United man, which was a considerable statement, as he had been around a considerable amount of time. The priest had no interest in sport, but came along as he liked their chats and wished to be seen as an everyday sort, as part of his enduring mission to save the soul of the community, which of course was prefaced first with saving church attendance.

"I knew he was a rat, Father. God forgive me but nothing ever good came from Labour!"

"Corish housing, Arthur? They put a lot of folks who couldn't afford it in homes."

"Fianna Fáil would have done that! Did we not build enough? Wasn't that the problem, too many ghost estates? Now apparently the problem is not enough housing. How did that happen?" Arthur asked questioningly.

"I believe that was one of your lot's policies, Arthur, something about fire-selling housing stock to repay massive debt, caused by covering the losses of what are essentially gamblers, if I am not mistaken," the priest dryly replied.

Liverpool tipped the ball and the game began, to claps around the bar and shouts of "C'mon lads!"

"Look, we are, eh… where we are, no point in going over old ground, but the cheek of him! Pretending to unite us all for once, the apartment dwellers of McDonagh Street and the folk of Clementine Lane, to deal with a common enemy, and as soon as he gets the whiff of a vote he jumps ship and makes us look like we are divided when… when… eh…. we are not!" Arthur lifted his glass with a mild tremor. He placed it back down and waited for the tremor to pass.

"How can you be so certain? With all your organising, did you once ask anyone who lived in those apartments how they felt about anything? Fact is, Arthur, you're jumping the gun. There could be more like him." The priest observed Arthur's embarrassment over his Parkinson's and felt sorry for him.

"Whose side are you on anyway?" Arthur fumed.

"God's," the priest tersely answered.

Arthur said nothing. He felt momentarily ashamed. He was not raised to be so hostile, and to be reminded by a man of God of his lack of charity slightly hurt him. The ball was kicked out of play. Man. Utd. had first throw in.

The bar door opened again. Conor hesitantly entered. He had just returned from one of his now-daily trips to Stillorgan. His boss rang him on Friday, and was clear that this could not continue. In fairness to Conor, he agreed and quit; in fairness, to many others in similar situations quitting was not so readily an option.

Today his father, who was naturally playful, had spent his morning helping Conor's mother with the delph washing. Yes, they could afford a dishwasher, but she never felt such devices removed all the food, and though they were well heeled they never shied from work either. His father was on drying duty, and as he dried each plate, while in deep conversation with his wife, he replaced it back in the sink for his wife, otherwise distracted by his conversation, to wash it again. The man had done this several times, all the while winking at Conor, who sat at the table trying to hold in his laughter. After Conor's mother had cleaned enough delph to feed a party of nine when there was only three, she gradually became wise to the game her terminally ill husband was playing on her, much to the combined laughter of Conor and his father. "I'm not dead yet, Eileen," he wryly smiled.

It is tragic that this man who has been mentioned rather affectionately several times in this story has not been given a name. Perhaps it is better that way. There is an unusual and frightening power to a name. His story will conclude without surprise and a name could serve to draw the reader to make comparisons with their own life. Sadly, this part of the story is far too common and relatable anyway. Let us therefore proceed without a name. It was a beautiful morning which the family had together and that is probably the more important thing.

Conor stood awkwardly at the door. He wasn't sure why he had come. Yes, he had enjoyed Mick and Terry's company the previous time, but had they enjoyed his? Or was he still simply a fish out of water and alone in a place that he could never truly be a part of? His friends were still only in digital form. Promising him a night out when time was available. Of course, time is always available; he simply was not prioritised.

"Conor! Over here!" Terry beckoned with a large smile.

"Don't mind that shite, over this way in the winners' enclosure, Conor!" Mick waved to the left of the bar.

Marion and Shane, the mutual drinking partners of these two inviters, had no idea why this chap mattered so much.

Man. Utd. streamed up the right side. Their centre half took a shot from outside of the box, it was always going nowhere but the red devil side of the bar "oohed" anyway, as if destiny itself had been robbed. Conor, on the other hand, was now trying to figure out a new conundrum, erstwhile only a rugby fan. He now had to pick a team. Marion's slightly moody face intimidated him; he chose Manchester and sat with Terry and Shane.

"There's more room over here, Mick, sorry!" Conor shouted over to the disappointed Liverpool fan and his cross-looking wife.

"You're dead to me, Conor, dead to me," Mick said with a smile.

Terry introduced Conor to Shane. "I wish I could grow hair like you but sadly I was born a ginger prick, and I'll die a ginger prick, so this thing is staying shaved," Shane said pointing to his head and trying to be friendly.

Liverpool were in the box, a quick slip of the foot and Man. U's sole remaining defender was defeated and abandoned, bang! Liverpool 1 – 0 Man. Utd. One half of the pub erupted in loud cheers, while there was collective "ah for fuck sake" emanating from the other. Mick knocked over Marion's bottle of tonic when he leapt off the long sofa. He was now being berated by his loving purple-haired partner.

"Vinnie, something similar please, good lad. I wonder, will this generation ever watch a good game of Hurling?" The last game of Hurling Hugh had seen was the 2009 All Ireland Final between Tipperary and Kilkenny. Even for that match he had no idea where the sliotar was travelling to. His myopia was somewhat profound and, to be fair, the ball was small and moving at pace. Despite his blindness, he had not missed much in the nine intervening years; six of these contests were fought between these same two teams. Advertisements may say the skill must be something in the water, but a more accurate government report into the high amounts of incest in Kilkenny and Tipperary would suggest it's more likely in the blood.

"They don't know their culture, do they, Hugh? Eh? Am I right?" Vincent Cartigan pulled hard on the Guinness tap.

Man. Utd. had got Liverpool by a long ball counter, there was no one in between, a clean run and... GOAL! Liverpool 1 – 1 Man. Utd. After the immediate roar, the Man. Utd. fans relaxed into a disparaging song about council house conditions in Liverpool. These were Irish men, living in Irish council houses, the Lockout's solidarity with Liverpool a forgotten cause. The ever so slightly different shade of red surmounted all commonalities. The Irish love for English soccer was indeed an odd thing. It couldn't be geographically defined, as both teams were foreign; there was no ideological difference either. It wasn't even the more unlikeable distinction of race, as both teams were equally cosmopolitan in complexion. The European Wars of religion made more sense.

The half time whistle blew and the commentators were silenced, as Vinnie Cartigan muted the projection for the interval. There was a loud murmur in the pub as conversation regained control.

Hope was awkwardly stepping across Mick to sit beside a now smiling Marion. Leanne was finishing a cigarette at the door. "Hello Mick, Hello Marion. How is the game?" Hope politely enquired.

"Ah it's grand, Hope, grand. Hold on a sec, Shane ye thick, I saw that!" Mick answered, somewhat distracted by Shane who was waving his middle finger singing "you scouse bastard! You scouse bastard!" Something about watching soccer in the pub always seemed to make Shane drunk faster.

"Don't mind him, Hope, that fucking retard reverts to his twelve-year-old self at these games, not that there is much difference. How's things with ye?"

"Very well, Marion, thank you, I was in town earlier and I got myself these beautiful gloves…" Hope began to root through her bag, looking for her new purchase.

Conor made his way back from the toilet, moving like a snake between the now jostling crowds at the bar.

"So go easy on him, he's in a bad place, poor lad, the auld fella seemed like a good sort." Terry was in quiet conversation with Shane.

"There you are now, just when I think I have you figured out it turns you're not an aggressive simpleton." Shane was smiling.

"Who says I'm not an aggressive simpleton? I'll fucking batter 'em!" Terry said laughing.

Conor re-joined the table, oblivious that he was its topic moments before his return.

"So what do you do?" Shane asked, before swallowing a large mouthful of stout.

"I was a data analysist for a software firm near Spencer's Dock," Conor replied, while absent-mindedly looking at his phone.

The players returned to the field, now peeling off in the opposite direction. Vinnie Cartigan began searching for the remote to knock the sound back on.

"Was?" Shane looked up.

"I am currently unemployed, I left my job on Friday, I couldn't go visit my da as much as I liked, so I just said 'fuck it,' to be honest." Conor was trying to affect a Dublin accent he didn't naturally have.

"You just packed in a perfectly good job because you wanted to visit your da?" Shane sounded incredulous.

"C'mon Pool!" The game was back on and the sound restored.

Conor felt uncomfortable, then anger surged through him. "My da is dying, so fuck them and fuck their job. I am sick to fucking death of carrying halfwits around on my back and getting no recognition and no fucking space. Do you know what he told me on Friday? 'You let yourself down, you know that, don't you,

Conor, you let yourself down.' Like I'm older, more experienced and work harder than the little shit and just because he was able to get by with some buzzwords and a fancier degree, I'm answering to him. No, fuck them!"

Shane thought for a moment, his own situation never far from his mind. Eventually, he lifted his pint. "You're right, you know, fuck them!"

"Ye jammy bastard!" The younger Man. Utd. fans across the room from the priest and the old man voiced their disdain at an apparent foul not apparently given.

"Where will it all end, eh? Do you know, Father, I was watching the telly last night and it was some talent show and this heavy, bunter, dark skinned girl came on the stage and started to sing. Slowly at first, like a jazz piece but low and behold, in came the drums and she stripped down to her underwear and everyone was applauding! I didn't know where to look!" Arthur took a small sip of his drink.

"What show was this, Arthur?" The priest's curiosity was aroused.

"Henry Street, there's a great little bag shop there," Hope answered as she showed off her new gloves.

"The tram goes to Jervis Street from the hospital next time you're going in, save your feet the walk." Leanne interrupted Hope with pointless information.

"Yes, I know." Hope politely smiled, accustomed as she had become to these frequent moments of "advice." "Anyway, I went in to have a look and treat myself but I wasn't that keen on their bags and there they were."

Mick wished he was on Terry's table. They may be Man. Utd. fans but at least they weren't auld ones prattling on about the same pair of gloves for twenty minutes.

"He's through, he's fucking through, c'mon! C'mon ye bastard! YESSSSSSSS!" Terry was roaring, as was half those assembled. Liverpool 1 – 2 Man. Utd. Mick was beginning to wish he had never come to the pub.

"There she is! The woman who would launch a thousand ships! All to get away from her! Howya, me darling?" Shane was drunk and brave.

"There is my former breadwinner, spending me money on booze, but sure look he doesn't have to be up in the morning. Sure isn't life grand for him," Phyllis answered with narrow eyes as she made her way to Marion's table.

Shane went quiet and turned to face the game. It is amazing how two quick sentences can precipitate a fight. Whether it is one person's crudeness or another's sharp honesty, moods change quickly, arguments can create quickly, 24-hour days can be ruined in 15 seconds.

Phyllis sat down beside Leanne, with a bottle containing blue alcohol that had been sweetened for those who didn't like drink but loved its effects. "How long has my prick of a husband been here?"

"Ah sure, don't mind him love, boys and their games." Leanne made little of what was sure to be an argument sooner or later, between Shane and Phyllis, but the venue for that exchange would at least be behind closed doors and Leanne wouldn't have to hear it. Of course, Sienna and Joe would have front row seats. Perhaps, if Phyllis was allowed to blow off a little steam now, her mood would lift and the pre-booked altercation could be avoided. A friend would have allowed her to do that, but Leanne was not a friend. Leanne was a drinking partner; her goal was to have a laugh in the pub and that was it. The welfare of Phyllis's marriage was not her concern, nor did she want it to be her concern. Phyllis was only there to add to Leanne's moment of banter, nothing more. Her emotional baggage was exactly that, her own. Marion, an actual friend, was sitting too far away and the noise of the concluding moments of the game was building. The later fight would go ahead unabated. The current contest, however, was over as the whistle blew two short bursts.

"What a fucking joke!" Mick turned away from the screen and towards the ladies who now could, finally, collectively converse.

"What was that you were saying, you scouse prick?" Terry was shouting from the centre table, as Shane awkwardly looked into his pint. Conner laughed as Mick showed his middle finger to the table. In part he was relieved, he had found it hard to comment like the other two on a sport that he knew nothing about.

"Now that you are here, Phyllis, I want to tell you all something. I saw it on Friday," Hope began as the noise of the TV was silenced.

"Whatever, you fat prick!" Mick dejectedly retorted to Terry as he was celebrating with Conor.

"Mick! Don't be using that language around us!" Marion scolded quickly and sternly and made Mick momentarily forget about the recent loss. Eventually, thinking it was better to talk to former IRA Volunteer Hugh at the bar, he politely excused himself and headed over.

Hope continued, "I was out on my way back from the shop when I saw two police arresting a homeless man, just at the church."

"Sadly, that happens all the time, Hope," Phyllis absently said.

"Well hang on now, I was walking the other side of the street and it was that tall policeman, who came in here the night the other homeless man died."

"Gibbons, that fucking eejit." Phyllis' mood was very much set for the day.

"Gibbons, is it? He and a policewoman were arresting a homeless man, who had very deep, red hair. The man could barely stand. He was clearly very drunk, but I immediately thought about the man who was talking to your daughter. You said he was homeless, alcoholic with red hair?" Hope asked.

Phyllis picked up. "He was being arrested for what?"

"I do not know." The glamorous lady from Nigeria shook her head.

"I told you! Didn't I tell you?" Marion immediately interrupted. "That Williams fella didn't die of an overdose! He was poisoned with drugs! I'm only saying. Think about it, your man could have given Williams poisoned stuff before he collapsed in the warehouse. He wouldn't have to be there for your man Williams to take it! I knew he was fucking trouble. Oh and your poor Sienna, alone with him, oh mercy, what could have happened, Phyllis?"

Phyllis went quiet. She never countenanced that the dead addict had died by anything but his own misadventure, but it was possible what Marion was saying was true, it could have happened exactly so. To her, these junkies attacked each other all the time. This Brendan could have been a rival dealer or anything.

"They were canvassing us the other day, Phyllis. They're treating the death as suspicious, why else would they be asking all those bleedin questions?" Marion persisted.

"Oh Heaven above us! Your poor Sienna!" Leanne, like Marion, hated to be left out of a conversation for too long; she was entirely disingenuous. Enjoying the drama, she continued, "And she was with him for the night in that horror show of a warehouse, oh Phyllis! That poor girl, she could have been raped!" Leanne didn't really believe this, she had seen the catatonic state of Brendan as he left the warehouse; still though, the pot needed another stir.

Phyllis just stared at them. A shiver crept along the nape of her neck.

"You needn't be so snide anyway, Phyllis, I was the only one who could see our daughter was worried about that poor wreck of a man." Shane was now drunkenly hovering above the table, oblivious to its discussion. "I brought her to the hospital so she could see he was all right. I may not have a job but I am doing the best for our kids! They can't be brought up to hate 'down and outs' like the way you go on. What the fuck happened to you anyway? You used give a shit about people." This was indeed unfortunate timing.

Phyllis looked up straight into Shane's eyes with an unremitting fury. "You wha?! You brought my daughter in to see that murdering, junkie bastard?!"

Shane looked confused and drunkenly half smirked, "murdering?… Jesus, Phyllis, what are you on…"

Poor Shane never had a chance. Phyllis was on her feet before he could finish that sentence and punched him with the full force of her minute, if relatively powerful arm, in full view of all present. Shane fell straight over the small stool behind him. Conor's eyes could not have been wider, Marion gasped, Leanne's brain recorded all for regurgitation and analysis on the flat balconies later. Vinnie Cartigan missed the showstopper, engaged as he was asking a rather unsure Fr Matthew how the kids were. Terry quickly moved his stool out of Phyllis's way, as she marched out of the pub and into the still drizzling evening.

22.

The First Station

10th February 2018 (Saturday)

BRENDAN WAS AWAKE. HIS HEAD WAS SPINNING. HE WAS, OF course, somewhat accustomed to that feeling. The small fluorescent lit room began to come slowly into focus, blurred at first, but more defined as the seconds ticked on. Where was he? He felt the cool, flat, rubber mattress on the side of his head. Moving slightly, he could feel the wetness of where he had previously been drooling. Eventually, he placed his hand on the magnolia painted and heavily engraved cavity block wall and pushed himself into a sitting position. Holding his head and looking down at the black painted floor, he tried to remember why he was here, clearly now in a cell. In the background, he began to hear shouting coming from the hallway beyond his door. One voice was dominant.

"Garda give us a cig will ye?! Garda?! Ah come on, ye geebag, just give us a cig."

A gruff Mayo accent answered, "Quiet in number 3 or I'll put the fuckin hose on ya!"

"Ah just give us a cig please!" The call became increasingly pathetic, as it did desperate.

In another cell, Brendan could hear a somewhat more refined voice.

"Officer, I'm sober now, can I please go home? I am very

sorry. It was at an office party that I guess should have wrapped up a lot sooner than it did." An awkward laugh followed, then a slightly more worried tone. "Officer? Officer?"

The harsh Mayo accent boomed again through the hallway. "It is, somewhat unsurprisingly, Mr Davenport, a criminal offence to be over eight times the legal limit. It's also a fucking criminal offence to hit someone while over the fucking limit. You had so much alcohol in you that your bloody car exhaust couldn't pass a breathalyzer!"

Silence filled the hall. Eventually the first prisoner resumed. "Ah go on guard, give us a cig please, please!"

Brendan's memory was hitting a blank, though he could see that tall culchie Garda from the warehouse in his mind's eye. "Nah, I'm just remembering him from before, it couldn't be him." He looked around his cell. It was slightly warmer than the warehouse, no draught here. It was dryer than the church doorway too but it certainly was not the match of his warm hospital bed. God what he'd give to be back there! Nearly dying seemed a reasonable price, all things considered.

He thought again about that interview. "Prick of a reporter. It is for them bottom feeders to sensationalise the complicated. Making monosyllable worded sentences for their readers to open mouth read. If journalists were so fucking honest, they'd be researchers. No, for them it has to be villains and heroes, no shade, no context, nothing that would make it muddier for the reader or the viewer and their narrative agenda. My life, anyone's life, is far more complicated than that insincere bastard insinuated. I had hard parents, with too much fucking expectations, they didn't live in the real world. A college education is no great distinction in this day and age. A difficult past... What the fuck would that McGlynn fucker know about my life anyway?" His mind spoke these thoughts, but it did not truly believe them. There was, as before, an ever-present guilt. The sadness of his past had not left him; truthfully, it had not been asked to. Somewhere within him, he felt Freddie's ghost again, a memory still fighting to resurface. Somewhere, he missed his parents, utterly and completely.

"Officer, I would like my phone call, if that's okay?" The nervous refined voice in cell 1 spoke again. This time a sense of urgency pervaded every word, as a new memory, previously forgotten, was entering his mind. That girl, in the drying up of his binge, his memory of her evaporated. The headlights simply flashed on the back of her coat. Her eyes turned and opened large in horror then bang! Over the glass that protected the inebriated driver. Must keep driving, he thought.

"And tell me boy, who the fuck will want to talk to you at 4.30 on a Saturday morning? I hear solicitors love to hear about drunk hit and runs in the middle of their fuckin sleep!" There was silence again in the hallway.

Brendan got up from his bunk and walked over to his toilet. He unzipped his fly and urinated for at least a minute. He applied pressure on his urination as if he had somewhere to be. Of course, he did not. Maybe he did it out of boredom, or perhaps standing up was causing too many problems for him. No sooner had the last droplets echoed in the water than he violently threw up into the bowl. The mixture of regurgitated whiskey and saliva congealed into his thick red beard, glistening like vile greenish pearls. He continually spat into the stainless steel toilet. His heart burned and his stomach lurched as he heaved again, a little more, mixed with the tail end of a sandwich bought for him by a well meaning sort, who did not want to feed a habit. One final retch, nothing more to give, a small foul-smelling belch followed. His eyes watered as he once again began the process of spitting into the bowl, though, strangely, he felt better.

A metal lock turned behind him and he looked around to see two brown eyes with heavy dark eyebrows, peering through a spy hole. "Are you all right in there?"

Brendan nodded and rose from the toilet, using his hands against the wall to bring himself up. The spy hole slammed shut and the lock turned again. He returned to the cool rubber mattress and tried to sleep on his side. The effort was futile. His stomach ached from the unwelcome rewind of ingestion and his mind raced. It was still coursing through the many picture frames of the past, trying in vain to remember the events that brought him to his current situation. Eventually, he reconciled that he was simply lifted for being drunk and homeless. "It's getting like the Philippines. A man can't even carve a career out of being homeless anymore without being arrested for some lazy guard's numbers."

Forty minutes passed. Periodically, the buzzing noise of the fluorescent bulb was broken by the moaning in cell 3. "For fuck's sake will ye let me out, I didn't do nothin, fuckin pack of wankers!"

The tedium was okay for Brendan, he was used to tedium. He seldom had much to do anyway. However, the voice in cell 3 was grating and he felt that he would use the occasion to explore his cell. He moved to the cell wall and ran his finger along the engravings of past incumbents.

There were the usual collections of names, marking supposed notoriety for posterity. "Damo was here 06" and "Freddie says fuck the pigs". "Is that you, Taft? Were you here?" he thought to himself. Of course, there were the engravings in support of the narcotics culture, "lovin the weed" and "give me Columbian A". The latter must have had a long stay. "Columbian" was not easy to engrave, thought Brendan. Naturally, there were the messages approving counterculture in general, often written in Afro American slang, "thug life" and "propa gangsta". Brendan despaired at these, when he thought of all the wonderful psychopaths, murderers, thieves and blackmailers that Ireland had given America over the past two centuries. He found it disappointing that these Irish criminals would opt to adopt another culture, when their own could be so wonderfully malign when it wanted to. Had they not heard of the Dead Rabbits Gang? Mickey Spillane? Jimmy "The Gent" Burke or even Whitey Bulger? There were great movies about all of them! It just seemed wrong. Half the African American gangsters these men idolised would look at them with distrust, maybe even disgust, and perhaps for good reason.

Moving on, then there were the charming engravings that had been added to by different people over time. Messages that started off so simply. Brendan already had identified his favourite of these. It read, "I rode your ma in here". Just below it in different script read "da your drunk, go home". Finally, there were those of political bent. "Up the RA!" Brendan felt this abbreviation of an abbreviation wasn't helpful. There were many republican armies; hell, even "IRA" could have doubt cast upon it, on whether it was the Irish Republican Army or the Indian Republican Army, but given the geographic context perhaps this criticism was unfair. "Sands 82", that was an odd one, more informed than most; it related to the courageous death of one Bobby Sands, who died on hunger strike when not afforded the rights of a political prisoner. "What could this engraver have in common with that man?" Brendan thought to himself. "One who died for political recognition in the context of war, the other incarcerated for keying a car outside the Four Courts?"

Brendan had exhausted the wall of its hidden gems, and once again returned to his flat, black mat. He looked at his runners and saw that they were sans laces now, which prompted him to wonder how any of these scribes found the materials to engrave anything at all. He laid his head back against the wall and closed his eyes.

"Here bud, what's the story with ye?" a voice from behind the wall whispered, rather loudly.

Brendan was tired and to be honest did not want the intrusion. He was a solitary sort. Nonetheless, he was also raised with manners. His head nodded forward and slowly he uttered, "How's it going?" Speaking was not easy for him.

"What'd you do?" the voice from cell 3 asked.

"Drunk and disorderly, I think they'll call it, but to be fair I was really just drunk. I mean I am clearly disorderly in that I lack order, but I would have thought that the natural state of a homeless alcoholic." Speaking was becoming easier, it would seem.

"Ah sorry to hear that, bud, it's shit on the streets, shit, me mate's homeless too, poor bastard."

"Family trouble?" Brendan enquired.

"Nah, fucked on heroin, pal, could never hold anything down."

"What are you in for yourself?" Brendan asked, as he realised he had time for a story.

"Bit of a long one that, I come across as a bit of thick too."

"You don't have the time?"

"Point taken," the disembodied voice from cell 3 realised.

Brendan could hear the thump of head being placed against their shared wall. His neighbour misjudged the distance and would have a bump tomorrow for that, he thought.

"I was caught breaking into a house. A laptop, tablet and a wallet in hand almost at the window, the lights go on, there was this auld fella, fuckin ancient. He stares at me and then, just like that, just folds over. Just like that, turned on the light. Stares at me. Then drops to the floor face first. I made for the window, looked back, prick wasn't moving. Stupid old cunt. Back at the window, fuck it I'm out of here. Looked back, he was folded over on top of himself, like an arseways deck chair. I just couldn't leave him like that, so I rang an ambulance on his phone, I says 'they know now, I'm out of here,' but the fucking operator kept me on the phone getting me to move him into this position and that position, checking his breathing, loosening his collar, all this shit. Anyway, the next thing the ambulance arrives with a Garda. One of the fucking neighbours spotted me through the window and made their own little call. So I says bollix, I've been had!"

"I thought you said you didn't do anything there a while ago?" Brendan asked.

"I always say that to them fucking pigs, it's important you say it enough times and you might believe it for the next stage, the interview. Ah sure look I'm fucked either way. Fuck them. I just hope I didn't kill the old bastard."

"God I'm stuck with scumbags!" The thin refined voice in cell 1 spoke to himself, or possibly out of loneliness.

"Here, I didn't hit and run someone like you, ye posh cunt!" The shout came from cell 3.

Brendan felt the guard was unusually quiet.

"You don't know me, you're some scobie scum. I didn't know what was happening. She just came out of nowhere! She was wearing black clothing in the middle of the night. It was her fault!"

"Your memory coming back to you, ye murdering fuck? One rule for you and another for the rest of us is it?"

Brendan was silent in cell 2 during this exchange. He was acutely aware that their voices were high enough to provoke sanction from the on-duty guard and yet his silence continued.

"What I did was an accident! It was not my fault! Accidents happen. She should have been paying attention! You're a fucking burglar, who probably killed an old man. You're scum, I'm not, I'm a decent person! Not a leech on the state." The refined voice sounded worried.

Brendan spoke quietly through the wall to cell 3. "Maybe you should say nothing." It was far too late though, the immediate silence following the insult from cell 1 was charged. It was clear anger was arising from the third cell. Suddenly, it erupted.

"At least I stayed with him. Listen I know I'm a shit and I'm fucking sorry for it, I know I caused the old bastard to have a heart attack. It's my fucking fault! I shouldn't have broken in. You can't even admit you're a cunt, which makes you an even bigger prized cunt! You're an entitled drunk, at least I know what I am…" The voice started with anger but trembled at the finish. There were tear filled sighs coming from cell 3.

Eventually, silence returned to occupy the hall once more. Finally, it was broken by the Mayo Garda. "Well aren't you a fine trio just the same, eh? The eleventh station of the Cross, the innocent Christ is crucified between two criminals, one unrepentant and one seeking forgiveness. Lord have mercy on us all, eh?"

"Ah fuck," a low voice escaped cell 3, "this day gets worse and worse, ye stupid prick Damo! Say nothing, you're breaking your own rules!"

Brendan wondered was he the same Damo who visited his cell in 2006. Nah, too young, he thought.

Elsewhere in the station, Quinlan and Gibbons sat in front of a rather elated inspector.

"Ye did surprisingly well, aye ye did, I had my doubts, but that was some good work there."

Gibbons looked on in silence, somewhat pleased with himself. Quinlan was a little more uneasy. "Sir just because he had the contaminated drugs on his person may not mean he was directly responsible for Peter Williams' suspected murder."

"Careful with your phrasing, Quinlan, there is nothing 'suspected' about it. He was murdered. Pure and simple. I don't want any more undermining of this case. Anyway, why are you trying to snap failure from the jaws of victory, ye silly lass, eh?" the inspector patronised.

Quinlan stared on, visibly irritated by this now smiling older man, whom she believed moronic.

"You two got fucking lucky, lifting for possession only to find it was the same crack sliced with the same ratio of rat poison found in Williams' body. Very fucking lucky." The inspector moved the report from his desk and picked up a pen, which he then played with, carelessly, letting it flow through his left hand's fingers.

"The facts are, you have opportunity. Both men habituated around the same geographic area, more than likely in the same circles. Two homeless lacheycoes high or drunk or whatever. You have the murder weapon, a very specifically modified bag of crack. Traces of which were found in the victim's system. What you need is motive. So let's discuss approach. He's drying out at the moment?"

"Correct, sir, he should be more than sober at this point, he's been in that cell for close to seven and a half hours," Quinlan answered.

"Good, the fucker is still a bit groggy, now would be the time to sit him down. His head is pounding and he probably just wants to lie down, ideal conditions for honesty. The Yanks do it all the time with the mussies." Sleep deprivation was indeed a technique in torture utilised by the US security forces on would-be suspects of Islamic terrorism, or indeed any high risk security threat, although it would be wrong to assume that the inspector was aware of this outside of anything other than patriotic action films. The ones where some dark skinned lad got blown apart by a US Marine. The same marine would, subsequently, have a crisis of conscience over his actions. In such movies, only the invading American troops, who are honourable and fun, family orientated or kindly good-time boys, can suffer the emotion of guilt. Of course, in reality, soldiers get on with acts of violence no civilian would ever countenance. Professional indifference, it's endemic.

The inspector began to plan the next steps. "You'll need to be cute just the same. Considering his condition when you found him, he may only think he was simply lifted for being a drunk on the streets and brought here to dry him out. Don't start with the caution. Don't let him think we've found a connection. Start friendly and ask him about how long he has stayed in the area. Does he know people from the area, that sort of thing. The emphasis is on friendliness, but those questions will also serve as contextual evidence to hang the bastard later. Quinlan, perhaps you should lead with these questions. You can at least affect a smile."

Gibbons did not react to this comment. He grimly stared on at his shoes, parting his feet to peer under at his soles.

The inspector continued, "Then try to establish a connection with Peter Williams. Anything will do at first, we can delve into it later and pincer him then in further interviews. I want you both to emphasise that you are just at this stage trying to establish the facts, as he knows them. Try not to let him think you suspect him of anything. He may think we suspect someone else for the Williams death and be more candid. Then and only then, move onto the questions relating to the crack find. I'm hoping he's still too fucking hung-over to realise you caught him with the package. Remember, anything he says we can use. Encourage him to talk. He goes silent and we're fucked."

"Sir, we do have to advise him he can have legal counsel present."

"Aye, I know, Quinlan. I have been in this job a little longer than you I think. Old as I am, I can fucking work that out. Give him his rights, but finish by saying that this is only a preliminary interview, play it the fuck down! Don't have him up to 900! You got me?"

Garda Quinlan was troubled. "Sir, it seems objectionable to me to carry out an interview that may lead to a prosecution, without first informing the interviewee."

"Ah give it a fucking rest, will ya? Come on, let's get this job done and spare me the 'by the book' routine, it's not a fucking movie!" the inspector snarled.

Quinlan was unhappy about the dubious ethics of this approach. She was staring at Gibbons. He blankly stared back, then returned to looking at his shoes. Gibbons had realised that at some point he must have stood in dog shit, and discreetly placed his feet down on the floor, though truthfully, he could still smell it. He wondered could anyone else? He looked around again. They seemed preoccupied. Good.

The three officers walked towards the detention cells.

"There's the happy couple now, woo-tish!"

Gibbons stared with annoyance at Garda O'Rourke who was leaning against their office doorframe.

"O'Rourke, gobshite! Try and pretend that you have a fucking role here!"

O'Rourke had not seen the inspector following the otherwise awkward couple.

"Yes sir, of course, I was just on my way to…"

"Fuck off! Wee grovelling fuck. You know, I often think you're the lad from that *Departed* film, a little Limerick shite placed in the Garda to report back to the fucking gangs, only you're too thick to pick up on anything!" The inspector did like his American movies.

"Eh sorry sir." The young Garda disappeared down the hallway.

This was not questionable professionalism, it was straight out unprofessional. Nonetheless, Quinlan was smiling.

The trio had reached the holding cells. Gibbons stepped forward. "Cell number 2 please."

The Mayo guard moved to Brendan's cell and unlocked it, standing immediately to the side of the door. The guard was a portly, red-faced man with dark brown hair, too portly for active duty. Perhaps that was why he was the solitary sentry of the holding cells.

Gibbons walked into the cell and instructed the prisoner to stand up. "Brendan Freeman, a contaminated batch of crack cocaine was found on your person. The same substance was found in the bloodstream of Mr Peter Williams. It is believed said substance caused Mr Williams' death. I am here to question you in relation to the death and probable murder of Mr Peter Williams, on the night of the 2nd of February 2018."

The inspector put his head in his hands and said slowly to himself, "The fucking moron."

Quinlan looked impressed. She knew that Gibbons agreed

with her and felt that the prisoner should not be duped, as the inspector's strategy designed. The truth was, during the meeting Gibbons wasn't listening to the inspector, nor was he listening to Quinlan. During the meeting, Gibbons was wondering where was he when he stood in dog shit.

"You have the right to counsel. You do not have to say anything. But it may harm your defence if you do not mention, when questioned, something which you later rely on in court. Anything you do say may be given in evidence."

Brendan at first was in a daze. He had no idea why this same Garda from the warehouse was questioning him about the death of Peter Williams. He could hear, "Ah shit, sorry, mate," coming from the cell to the left of him and "Innocent? He's just another scumbag," coming from the cell to the right of him. All he could feel was his heart leap into his mouth and fear rise from his belly. He wanted to vomit again. He felt the tiredness lift from him as the frantic energy of worry zipped through his veins. This was not the Eleventh Station of the Cross but the First: Pilate Condemns Christ.

23.

Principled Folk

12th February 2018 (Monday)

IT WAS MONDAY MORNING AT THE COUNCIL BUILDINGS, A monument to the sacrilege of Dublin's Nordic origins. Created by an uncaring and unthinking rural elite (a concept developed by Terry), or the Council, as they were known to everyone else. The Council buildings were built sometime in the 1970s on one of the largest Viking sites in Europe. This prime location could have been Dublin's answer to the Forum in Rome, but forethought was rare and money rarer. Instead of a memorial to Dublin's past, the people were given a grey Brutalist monolith of the then Soviet Union's present. The constant rain from the weekend had not lifted. However, the wet and dreary clouds had provoked an array of beautiful multi-coloured umbrellas on the street below, as if the people of Dublin were trying to inspire the celestial realm. So far it was only drizzle, but it was promising to give more. A sapphire blue Rover drove under the Council buildings and into the car park, parking neatly between two yellow lines, funnily enough where King Sitric's head lay some ten metres below.

On the ground level, Frank, wearing a yellow and green tie against a navy suit, was arguing with Siobhan.

"It doesn't go! It looks like you're a snooker player!"

"Nonsense. Eccentricity and colour show independence of

mind, my dear, not that you would know," Frank dismissively retorted.

"What does that mean? If you want someone else to be your dogsbody, Frank, then I can resign. The promise of a parliamentary assistant job only really rings true if you get elected, and to be honest at the moment, I'm not that fucking sure of your chances!"

Frank realised he had gone too far. The fact was she was a volunteer and he needed her. Volunteers were scarce coming forward for mainstream parties these days. "You're right, I was ugly just now, forgive me?"

"Let's just get this over with."

Yes, he thought, I need her now. Contriteness is best. Keep her onside, then when I'm a TD, that's when I'll ditch her.

Siobhan was still not entirely sure as to why they were there. "In what capacity did you even get invited to this meeting?"

"Eamon felt it was necessary to have a representative of the local community there, who was in favour of the plan. I am Chairman of the McDonagh Street Property Management Company, Siobhan. I am a representative of sorts."

"Chair*person*, Frank, and let's be fair, you're only there to represent *him*. Independence of mind, indeed. And tell me, what of the other lot from Clementine Lane, will there be statue-touching grannies and 'howyas' fresh from the pub representing them?"

"They are unaware of today's proceedings, though I believe they have chosen their democratic right to protest outside today, by chance. I hope it stays fine for them, though looking at that sky I think there will be more than a few drowned rats." Frank's conversation with his leader some five days ago had been informative and reassuring. Informative in that he knew he had party support to develop his profile in the apartment-dwelling areas of the constituency. A constituency now made much larger, as he was now running as a TD, rather than a councillor.

Reassuring in that he no longer had to pretend to care for people he found otherwise so disagreeable.

The two walked into the large grey building and towards reception, where they were directed to the sixth floor. They entered a meeting room. A thin plaster wall partitioned it from the rest of the building, while the three remaining walls, consisting entirely of glass, provided impressive vistas over the city's southern, northern and eastern quarters.

Three men and one woman were sitting at a large Irish oak table, already making polite chit-chat about the inclement weather outside and the lamentable political affairs of the United States. Such topics of conversation were always comfortable. The United States was so far away, and seemingly so foreign, that nothing of their political situation could similarly happen in Ireland. Irish exceptionalism, just like French exceptionalism, German exceptionalism or any other form of national exceptionalism, tended to see another state's woes as impossible to be replicated on home soil. Surely, in America, they were talking about Russia in much the same fashion. Of course, media consensus had already assured that everyone in the room was likely to be on the same side of this particular debate. The media were useful to democracy in this way. They punished harmful deviation. One must be an idiot, mad, bigoted or all three to think otherwise. Indeed, this was an amenable way to start the meeting. "Stupid Americans", "Where will it all end? Eh?" "They're mad! They're mad!" Yes, it was reassuring to be smug at others' misfortune. Just like the Americans surely were to some other country before their present political problems started... There is no such thing as exceptionalism.

"Frank, lovely to see you and good of you to come! Let me make introductions." Eamon Hawkins rose from his seat and walked past Siobhan with his hand outstretched, towards a smiling Frank Cantwell. "This gentleman here is Mr Sean Collins of the planning department."

A tall, gaunt and grey-haired man with thick glasses clinging low to a hook nose, closest to Frank, stood up and said, "Nice to meet you."

Hawkins continued. "Ms Maire Boland of Senior Management."

A thin middle aged lady with blonde hair politely nodded on the opposite side of the table.

"And our Chief Executive, Mr Harry Griffith."

A purplish faced man with thin wispish light brown hair, still staring at documents on the table, briefly looked up and nodded, "Yeah, nice to meet you, Frank," and then returned to staring at the documents.

"Well, it's wonderful to be invited here today, to represent the folks back home." Frank beamed at the table. Three of the four politely smiled back. Frank sat at the table. Siobhan pulled a chair beside him, a little perturbed at the absence of an introduction.

"The Council has concerns about a few aspects of this proposed Centre, Mr Hawkins." Griffith was yet to look up from the documents on the table as he spoke.

"Harry, if this is about the residents in Clementine Lane, you know yourself they are a bunch of nay-sayers. How many times has this very Council built a rehabilitation centre or homeless shelter that the people of that very community need, only to meet a protest from a load of busybodies who love nothing better than to complain about progress. That is why Frank is here today, folks. He is the voice of the silent majority. He represents those people living in the area who want to see their community improved with this vital build. Frank is a man willing to say, 'actually, no, stop speaking for me, I have my own voice and I want to help these vulnerable people in addiction'." Frank nodded emphatically, as Eamon spoke for him.

***

Earlier that morning, in his small apartment on McDonagh Street, Frank Cantwell was waiting for his boiler to heat up for a shower. The pot belly former private company PR man, now self-PR man, was sitting in front of a laptop in his small living room. Draped around his shoulders was a rather garish silk Kimono dressing gown, decorated in monotone with a silver tiger on the back.

Sipping a heavily sugared tea, Frank was scanning a property website. The thought had occurred to him, after his stint on the national broadcaster and the plaudits he had received on the phone by Michael Norton immediately after same, that surely he was on a strong footing for membership of the 33rd Dáil. Of course, this was very much a case of counting chickens before eggs had hatched. Yet the applause he received on the *Political Questions* discussion show had knocked something loose in his mind. As often can happen, our most strongly held dreams can wipe away a lifetime of experience in matters of expectation, with just the smallest of encouragements. A studio of 150 people from all over Ireland was not equitable with a constituency vote of 8,500 from the very specific Dublin South West ward. Nonetheless, in his mind's eye he was soon to be a TD and that meant a significant improvement in finances. That also meant a necessary upgrade in accommodation. Particularly, considering that they were going to open yet another rehabilitation centre in the area. Mon Dieu, this place truly was going to the dogs!

The pursuit for a new home was thus far not going well. Frank was a Monaghan native, and despite his years in Dublin, he did not have a local's eye. A local may have understood that a moderate sized home with any proximity to the city and a reasonable price was a rare thing. The increasing focus on Dublin as a city state, at the expense of the rest of the Republic's development, had driven prices sky high in the capital. The present government's reticence to build public housing, combined with the recent waves of emigration, which took the people needed to build them, was not helping the situation. Frank, as a would-be legislator, probably should have known this kind of thing. It was something of a national issue. Nonetheless, his blindness to present problems of state was compounded by an understanding of class that was very much antiquated and absent of a perception of value.

To Frank, the best places to live in Dublin were, and always would be, the areas that had one or more Protestant churches. The same areas his father before him would have scorned as "West Brit" strongholds. His father's views were of course, over-simplifications, but they were of their time and geographic location. Most country folk did judge Dublin's leafy south-eastern suburbs with deep suspicions. Frank, a Dublin resident of some years, had no such excuse.

"Jeepers, who the fuck can afford these prices?" Frank's search began in the City's south quarter, Donnybrook, granted a charter by King John of England and famous for its annual fair's historic displays of violence and drunken revelry. Its history was somewhat not West British, housing as it did at one stage Padraig Pearse, Michael Collins, Eamon de Valera, right up to Shane McGowan. Frank did not know that, nor did he know that its main avenue, Morehampton Road, was not realistically a home for most present day politicians, wealthy though they may be. No, it was now home to dental surgeries, large private companies, embassies and the occasional state agency.

What about Blackrock? A town further south and east outside Dublin's city limits. Yes, there was value in its name. A Blackrock accent, that horrible mix of new American twang with nouveau riche money, was known throughout the country. Blackrock did sound like a good place for him. The prices on the other hand were less favourable. Yes, maybe he could afford some of the properties, but they were near social housing, so what was the point in moving? "Blackrock has gone downhill anyway, too much social housing and UCD students from the country lowering the tone," thought Frank, the Monaghan native.

Perhaps Dalkey, then? Dalkey, a coastal village near Dublin's Wicklow border, and Killiney, Ireland's Beverly Hills; hmm, on second thoughts, perhaps not. A casual eye ruled out Foxrock and Rathgar. "When is the government going to do something about housing prices for normal folk?" Frank thought as he got into the shower.

***

"Yes, yes, we know all that, I'm not bothered by what a load of revved-up locals shout on about. Part of our job, as unelected public servants, is to be beyond all that nonsense 'mé féiner' crap!" Eamon Hawkins did his best to smile at Mr Griffith's candidacy, but the truth was, he was failing. "What we are here today to discuss is the actual building specs."

Hawkins looked surprised at this statement.

Griffith continued. "Eamon, we received a report in the post on Friday comparing your centre with the national average for its type, and I have to tell you, you don't come up smelling of roses. For instance, the bedroom size for each service user is about a third smaller than most centres of this type. Eamon, you're stacking them in. I know you get paid by the State by the scalp but this is taking the piss!"

Hawkins stared on with deathly quiet, periodically drinking from a glass of water. There was mild tremor in his hand; his anger was getting harder to control.

"Canteen space is roughly half the size expected for this many service users. Lack of windows, to save on glass. Eamon, this is Third World stuff."

"Let's not exaggerate. Obviously, someone is trying to undermine what we are trying to do here, I suspect I know who." Hawkins' voice was low and swirling with contempt.

"Which brings me to the point, Eamon, you have someone who wants you fucked and worse. They have a bit of brains. If we approve you, we're in the firing line too. I could let you go ahead with this all day long, as far as I can see you're taking the bums off the streets. What the fuck do I care if their room is smaller than average? But someone has officially sent this to me, which now means me, Maire and Sean officially know. We proceed as is, Eamon, then in two maybe three months' time there'll be a fucking scalping job done on the national broadcaster and we're all fucked!"

The two other people sitting at the table, so far quiet, now nodded their heads in full agreement.

"The Council have already approved this planning permission, Harry. They're the ones responsible for it. Anyone comes knocking, they're the ones who approved it. Your job isn't to stand in the way of their decisions. Why, that would be undemocratic!" Hawkins was now pleading.

"Eamon, we know, and it is official that we know. We're public servants, the ones that are always here. Fuck the councillors, you think they won't throw us under a bus if some bloody reporter comes to their door with questions? Planning is denied until you come up with something better." Griffith looked steely eyed at Hawkins.

"You've done very well from me, Griffith. Each one in this room has done well off me! Not that the Revenue would know though…" Hawkins leaned in on the desk. Small orbs of phlegm spat from his mouth as he spoke these words. They landed happily on the table, unaware of their creator's anger.

Frank and Siobhan looked on in quiet shock.

"Careful, Eamon, let's not have to take back things we say in haste. You can always reapply," the older official soothingly replied.

Hawkins sighed heavily, then sat in silence, deep in thought. The room went quiet. The ticking of an office stationery shop clock seemed to emphasis each tock. Eventually, while rubbing his hands against his eyes, Hawkins spoke more to the room.

"Okay, Harry, I understand the problem, and I must apologise for that ridiculous outburst. I don't think I am getting enough sleep with all these media engagements since that poor addict's demise."

"Of course, Eamon, no harm done." Harry smiled across the table. "Yes, it was terrible sad", "that poor man", Maire and Sean dutifully nodded with great sympathy.

Hawkins smiled and continued. "Say I add a few more windows, and take out some partition walls, maybe lower capacity by four beds."

"Six beds," Griffith interjected.

"Six beds, then you can say you had a review of the plan and made some pertinent observations, which I acted on. You're covered, and I can continue on without redesigning the whole thing. Everyone is happy and we can continue to work well together, would that be okay?"

"I think we could be agreeable to that with a few little extras, you know yourself, Eamon." The three public servants smiled at Hawkins.

"Frank, we could say that you voiced some concerns as well, and give the old political career a shot in the arm, what do you think?" Eamon's temper was clearly improving as he smiled at the soon-to-be candidate.

"Well, it is important that these people have some dignity and I am glad to say that I was able to do my bit for them." Frank was elated; why, here he was influencing important policy at last!

"I'm sorry but those changes would still leave that centre ridiculously too small for any person to live." The room went quiet again and all eyes trained on Siobhan who, to be fair to her, was positively disgusted at the way this discussion had turned.

"And who are you?" Eamon smiled.

"My name is Siobhan Kearns. I am Frank's campaign manager."

"Was," thought Frank as he stared at her with unhidden revulsion. This was make or break time. Frank knew he had to quickly put this fire out. He smiled. "Ah Siobhan, we need to get this through, think of those people on the street now? We can't let some petty idiot with a grudge, who's just trying to have a go at Eamon here, undermine this great project. It was probably one of those scumbags who were quite pleased to tell us to 'fuck off' the other week, sure. They are basic low lives, against progressive politics, bottom of the barrel type. We can't let them intimidate us, when we are trying to do something positive for the community. Those people in addiction need us, Siobhan, they need us!" Frank almost believed himself; almost.

"It's wrong, Frank, and you know it."

"No Ms Kearns, it is confidential, is what it is, you have accidentally been given access to a private conversation and policy decision of the Council. The opinions voiced here are covered by Data Protection law. Just because the size of the build is a little smaller than average…"

"A little? You're building a fucking doll's house," Siobhan erupted.

"Let me finish," Hawkins growled. "A little below average does not mean it is against the law. However, you discussing the contents of this meeting with anyone outside this room, very much so is. So keep your fucking ill-informed opinions to yourself! Unless, of course, you wish to be sued and pay for an extension to the centre yourself?"

The room went quiet again though the trio of middle aged suited fates looked suitably gravely at Siobhan. She rose from her chair and stormed from the room.

"I have to apologise, everyone." Frank looked at the table.

"Quite all right, Frank", "Not to worry, self righteous types everywhere", "just another idealist, you do get them". Everyone in the room was once again of the same opinion; this time there was not even need for the media to deliver consensus.

A low chanting was heard from outside. The remaining five in the room got up and walked to the northern window. Below, the protest march had finally arrived at the Council buildings. Amateurish, roughly drawn banners and chants to old protest metres, kids standing around looking bored, people aiming camera phones, as the small crowd gathered around the steps below. "Here's the rentacrowd." "Well, they obviously don't have any jobs." "Selfish gang of mé-féiners the lot of them." "How can you be expected to do anything with this lot?" Yes, once again, beautiful consensus.

24.

Hard Facts

"INTERVIEW BEGINS AT 6.20 A.M., SATURDAY 10TH OF FEBRUARY. Brendan Freeman, you have been briefed on your rights?"

Brendan nodded. He was still processing his circumstances. The two officers stared grim-faced across the cheap chipboard table with the faux wood finish.

"Mr. Freeman, we will need you to answer in the affirmative for the purposes of the tape."

"Yes, yes."

"Thank you, interviewers present Garda Paul Gibbons and Garda Aoife Quinlan, with Inspector Daniel Roach in observance." It is no lie that Gibbons enjoyed interviewing, the formality, the assumed authority, the starkness of right against wrong. In a way, it soothed his ego; in this context he was always the lesser evil. Garda Paul Gibbons was a lonely man whose closest friends were two grown children with whom he shared an office; and Quinlan, of course, there was Aoife. This loneliness provoked questions of self worth. The answers to these questions were never spoken, but deeply implied in his mind. They were never favourable, but in an interview he was always the success, his doubt always momentarily exorcised.

It was his job to prove guilt as he saw it, and they were

always guilty, as he also saw it. This is not to say that Gibbons was an uncomplicated man and that he could not sympathise with whoever was the other side of the table. Sometimes he couldn't help it; a stupid child, a teenager whom he had watched grow in malevolence, due to an ever present malevolent home environment. No, guilt did not always mean evil but they must always be guilty. It was something of a lie, of course, they could not always be guilty, and to be fair, they frequently were not, but it allowed him to be focused and strong.

Gibbons' partner, Garda Quinlan, on any other occasion would have been happy to return home to her bed. She felt its need more than anyone, even Brendan, who was now wide awake. But her inspector's instructions prior to this interview troubled her. She felt it would be negligent to leave this "down and out" to what was, so temptingly, an open and shut case. She was entitled to go home but she stayed just the same; besides, overtime was always desired.

Inspector Roach sat at the back of the room, staring a hole right through Brendan's head.

"Mr Freeman, you are of no fixed abode?"

Brendan nodded.

"Again, Mr Freeman, please remember that we require audio answers for the purposes of the recording."

"Yes, sorry."

"Mr Freeman, you have recently been released from St James's Hospital, having been treated for pneumonia?"

"That's correct. I was there for two weeks. I also was suffering the effects of a kidney infection."

"Thank you, Mr Freeman, it would help this process along if you do feel free to offer any additional information where we may have missed something."

"May I have some water, my throat is feeling irritable."

Quinlan went to the water cooler in the corner of the room beside the inspector, and produced a cool plastic cup for Brendan.

"Thank you." It was funny that Brendan reverted to an almost childlike variant of himself, no rebellion, no sarcasm. The topic was too severe and he was smart enough to realise it. No, he had become Brendan Freeman, age 14, in English class, where a stern Mrs Grimes would scold him for talking to Freddie Taft.

"Before this hospital stay, you were briefly residing in a warehouse in Clementine Lane?"

"I had been there two weeks, probably a little less. I had noticed it was abandoned and the weather had turned nasty. I just wanted to get in out of the rain."

"I see." Gibbons looked at a notepad. "Did you know anyone from the area prior to your stay in the warehouse?"

"I had gone to school in the area, I knew some of the locals but I doubt they would have recognised me."

"Why did you pick the warehouse in Clementine Lane?"

"I was engaged with a drug rehabilitation clinic in the area. I noticed it was abandoned."

"So you have a drug addiction?" Gibbons looked at Brendan.

"I'm an alcoholic of some years."

"Why a drugs programme and not AA?"

"I was kicked out of AA for appearing on the premises under the influence. I also had taken to stealing their biscuits. It may seem small but I stole a lot of them. I love Mikado."

Quinlan had to repress her smile. Gibbons looked at her with a mild contempt and turned back to Brendan. "Well, we are not here to discuss biscuit theft."

Gibbons continued, "Have you ever taken drugs?"

"Yes."

"What type?"

"Grass, hash, benzos, coke."

Gibbons' eyebrow rose slightly. "Have you taken any of these substances in the last six weeks?"

"No. I took them socially when I was younger, I turned against them, I've seen their effects."

"But not the effects of alcohol, it would seem." Gibbons looked a little smug.

"No, suppose not."

"Have you illegally distributed banned substances for profit?"

"Am I a drug dealer? Are people usually so candid?" Brendan smirked.

"Answer the question."

"No."

There was an audible grunt from where the inspector was sitting. Quinlan now leaned in. "You said you knew the locals of the area from your school days? Did you know Mr Peter Williams?"

Brendan grimaced. He did. He also hated the man.

He had once awoken in the middle of the night to find Williams rifling through his pockets. Drunk though he was, he was aware enough to mount a defence and to push the thief off him, while demanding what was taken to be given back. This led to a brief altercation (more handbags at dawn than pistols). Pathetic though the confrontation had been, it had aroused enough attention to have the Garda summoned, by Vincent Cartigan. Fighting outside his pub could never be tolerated. Neither homeless man was aware of the squad car pulling up beside them as they limply threw arms at each other. Their names were taken, but it was late and the Garda did not want to have the bother of processing them, so he simply told them to fuck off in different directions. Still though, Brendan thought, there probably was a record of the incident somewhere.

"I know Peter, or rather I knew him. He is not a local though, just another person passing through."

"You people don't pass through though, do you? You squat!" Gibbons turned momentarily nasty.

"Fair point, well made." Brendan politely smiled.

Quinlan persisted. "How did you know the deceased Mr Williams?"

"I was involved in a public brawl with him."

A louder grunt came from the back of the room. The inspector felt that the net was about to drop.

"It was stupid. He tried to rob me when I was sleeping rough on McDonagh Street, before I found the warehouse on Clementine Lane. I demanded my money back, someone rang you lot. I was told to stay away from him, even though technically, he robbed me." Brendan was feeling confident; was this the strength of their case against him?

"You have no other connection with Mr Williams?"

"I knew him to see and I knew he was a drug peddling scrote." Brendan was serious in tone. He felt he was a different class of homeless person and expected to be treated as such. His confidence was growing.

Gibbons continued, "The coat we found you in tonight, that is your own?"

"Yes."

"Has it ever left your person?"

"In the hospital it was placed in a locker, but apart from that it is practically my bed. I'm something of a turtle." Brendan smiled at both of them. Quinlan looked down at the table.

Gibbons felt that they had danced around the point for long enough. "Can you explain to me why you were found with a dealer's quantity of crack cocaine on your person?"

Brendan froze. He had forgotten that one, big and unaccountable detail that Gibbons had levelled against him in his cell. "I have... I don't... I don't know where that came from? Even when I did take, I would... I would never take anything like crack." Back to being the 14-year-old in Mrs Grimes's class, it would seem.

"And yet you were found with 55 grams of crack cocaine in your pocket. Are you telling me you cannot account for same?"

Brendan shook his head in a slow "no" while staring rather blankly. Despite his tousled red hair and bushy rustic beard, or perhaps because of them, and their pathetic quality, he looked rather childlike.

Quinlan in her heart of hearts, believed him.

"For the tape, Mr. Freeman."

"No."

Gibbons did not.

"You say that you knew the deceased Peter Williams. You say you were reported as having an altercation with him over a minor incident, roughly five weeks before his death. You say you don't know where the crack, which was found in your coat pocket, came from. Is this an accurate account of your statement so far?" Gibbons stared at Brendan.

"Yes, yeah but like I really hardly knew him, I just knew he was a proxy for the dealers in the area. He tried initially to sell some of that shite to me, I wouldn't touch it."

Quinlan perked up; this was something new. "Mr Williams tried to sell crack cocaine to you? When did this occur?"

"Around two or three days before he tried to rob me." Brendan was beginning to feel his headache return.

Quinlan imploringly looked at Gibbons to end the interview.

Gibbons continued, "So you say the late Mr Williams was a drug dealer?"

"Undoubtedly," an increasingly worried Brendan replied.

"Mr Freeman, as it stands what we know from this interview is the following. You knew the deceased. You had a bad relationship with the deceased leading into the time period when he was murdered, involving a physical altercation that needed to be reported to the Garda. The two of you lived in the same small geographic location, in the weeks leading to Mr Williams' death. You have a history of drugs use. You were found with a dealer's quantity of tampered crack cocaine in your coat pocket, a coat that has not left your side, except for a visit to the hospital. The same mixture of crack cocaine and rat poison was found in the system of the deceased and was the cause of his death. These are the hard facts, Mr Freeman. I put it to you that you have reversed your role in this story. I put it to you that you were a dealer in the Clementine Lane area. You had a bad relationship with Mr Williams, possibly related to dealing in the same area, possibly over debt owed to you for services rendered. I put it to you that you deliberately mixed rat poison with a batch of crack that you sold or gave to Mr Williams, in an effort of petty vengeance."

Brendan just stared at Gibbons shaking his head in a silent and unheard "no" but Gibbons was now in his element.

"Mr Freeman, it would be advisable that you take this opportunity to accept the offer of legal aid. It would also be advisable that by time of next interview, you decide to admit, in full, your part in this story. It will be easier for you in the long run."

Brendan began to weep.

"We can provide you with some more water if you'd like?"

"No, no, thank you."

"Officer Quinlan and myself will now escort you back to your cell. Interview ends 6.57 a.m."

The cell door slammed shut on whimpering Brendan Freeman as Gibbons and Quinlan walked away. "That was a very neat little summation but the motive rings hollow, Paul. Who kills someone for not paying a few quid for a fix?"

"There is no morality with these people, Aoife, they're not in the room. He probably was high himself when he did it. I mean, look at the fucking state of him. Do you mean to tell me he's not still using? Do you not remember the way we found him in that warehouse? He's bit too young to be that fucked on alcohol alone, do you not think?" Gibbons was irritated. He thought he had gotten the measure of Brendan rather well and expected plaudits from his partner at the interview's end. Instead, all he could see was doubt in her face, which annoyed him, not least because it caused doubt over his own perceived success. He also did not want her to think less of him. This frustration was expressed as arrogance, yet there was nothing sure in his mind at this moment either.

"Of course it could be just drink. Alcohol is incredibly destructive, Paul. It can turn a young fella like him into a wrecked shell so easily. Besides, what if he is telling the truth about Williams, if he's a dealer himself? You might be right. Your original theory about it being a badly spliced batch could ring true. He took his own crap and it killed him, or maybe, someone who deals to him wanted him dead. All I'm saying is it's a weak case against Freeman. We have no motive."

"We have him with the murder weapon, Quinlan!" The inspector was walking behind, unbeknown to the two officers. His interjection was unfortunate timing, Gibbons was beginning to mull over what Quinlan was saying; after all she prefaced it with "you might be right."

"It won't be long before the media get wind of it, ye best have it tied down. There can't be any uncertainty with either of you. Uncertainty is contagious, and with the country looking in, we don't need to seem uncertain. You did well tonight, both of you, go home and sleep. There will be much to do and a little window of opportunity to do it in before the cameras show up." The inspector walked past both of them.

Brendan found his familiar black mat and lay on it. No sound came from either cell next to him, the compassionate burglar or the indifferent reckless driver. Both certain to face jail time too. What a difference an hour made. An hour ago, Brendan felt so sorry for the burglar, he could not countenance how anyone could be so calm when facing jail. Brendan was not naïve to the world. He had lived on the streets for a long time. He had heard plenty of cautionary tales about prison. The loneliness, the isolation, the rape, which made the loneliness desirable.

In many ways, Brendan could survive isolation. It had been his life for a long time up to now but, as he lay in his cell, it had not escaped him that he had been happier in the company of others, whether it was the mature for her years Sienna, his fellow patients in the hospital ward, or even his unlucky neighbour in cell 3. He had missed conversation. He had missed being listened to. "Where the fuck did that crack come from?" That thought echoed around his head. He could not yet remember his day yesterday, if he ever would. Could he have picked it up out of curiosity? Drunken Brendan was an odd monster, hell bent on destroying himself, but he had never been so reckless.

Somewhere in his mind still was the young boy who was quiet and studious in class, who was afraid to show an absence of manners, who was afraid of authority. That inner child was feeling deep shame. For all his years of shitting and pissing himself on the street, there was still a pride in him. While his theft of food from shops was a low, he never directly stole from people. He was as proud of that as he was ashamed of lifting cakes and biscuits in the local newsagent. This was all becoming too much. He had accepted that he would die soon; he believed it quite inevitable. That thought never troubled him.

This was different. Imagine what his parents would think when they saw him on the TV. Brendan Freeman, murderer of helpless fellow addict Peter Williams. Show them that clip of Peter eruditely arguing for better access to social housing. Show the clips of the locals reacting in horror when relating the young man's death. Then re-interview them, tell them that it was a lad who went to the local school. "Ah yeah, I remember Brendan, he seemed such a good lad, not a messer like the rest of them. You never know, do you? A murderer? A drug dealer? What can you say about that?" "I knew him all right, yeah, he was too quiet just the same, maybe the brain wasn't working right. You hear about these types, the quiet one, seems polite then turns out to be a ruthless psycho." "His mother was such a beautiful lady, the father is a good hardworking man too, it's them I feel sorry for, them and the deceased of course."

It's funny we have all seen those reports and never questioned their veracity. Brendan, in better days, had thought to himself, "God, they must have been some animals to do 'X', how could they sleep at night?" Now he would be that animal. He felt the eyes of everyone he ever loved, everyone who he ever spoke to, everyone, on him, what will they say? No one would speak up for a drunken homeless man. This was just another inevitable step in his descent. Once again, his thoughts drifted back to Freddie and that door marked "Taft" locked in his memory. He wondered, if his past had been different, would he be here now? Somewhere in the back of his mind, he wondered did the kind burglar in number 3 think less of him now. Somehow that mattered.

"So you're happy? Just like that? You didn't even think it was a murder a couple of days ago." Quinlan stared at Paul Gibbons, still searching for that fairness she, somewhat mistakenly, saw in him when he read Brendan Freeman his rights.

"Look, he's a fucking gouger. The night I came into the warehouse he was sweating bullets. Probably, because that very fucking day he gave that other fucking gouger his last party bag. Granted I don't know why he did it but we actually found the bag on him, what more do you need?" Gibbons' dark eyebrows lowered. The inspector had given him all the confidence he needed. It was that simple.

"He was sweating because his kidney was about to pack it in, Paul. There is more to this, and in that slow asshole Roach's eagerness for a win, we are going to sleep-walk into yet another Garda fuck up. When that happens, Paul, there will be no Roach. We were the arresting officers, we were the interviewers, and we will be the ones who sign the charge sheet, so you tell me, who he's going to point the finger at when the cameras come looking?" Quinlan imploringly asked.

"Look, we'll talk tomorrow, I'm shattered." Gibbons walked towards his car.

"Paul, you're too good a man to be so easily led."

That hurt, it hurt more than his conscience. Earlier that

morning, while waiting for Brendan to sober up, Paul Gibbons had resolved to ask Aoife Quinlan out; now, he could feel her disappointment staring into the small of his back. He got in his car, looked into his mirror, not entirely sure what to make of the man staring back him, and drove off.

25.

The Not Quite A Million Man March

12th February 2018 (Monday)

PERHAPS IT WAS THE SORE HEADS FROM THE PREVIOUS SUNDAY night or the rain in the sky, but not one of those who had gathered outside Clementine Lane Community Crèche was in great spirits. While the morning rain had begun to form into many puddles, most of the two dozen or so neighbours there were more mindful of the eggshells, which seemed as plentiful.

When Shane had come to, with the small crowd hovering over him, he still was somewhat unsure of what had happened. It did not take long for Marion to fill him in about the arrest of the murdering Brendan, while he compressed a frozen pack of cauliflower (a favourite of Vinnie Cartigan for his dinner; who knew? Maybe he would put a slice of plastic cheese over it like the French?) against his quickly swelling jaw. Once the story was related, Shane remained unconvinced. The man he saw in the hospital was a pathetic sort, but there was good in him. He was no murderer. In Shane's own mind, this was big mouthed auld ones with too little to do and too much to say. Everything that had been reported back to him seemed circumstantial. People were adding two and two and potentially getting sixty.

Of course, Shane was not to know that the combined assumptions of Leanne, Marion, Hope and Phyllis were actually correct. Not correct about Brendan's guilt, to be fair, but correct as to why Brendan was being lifted by Quinlan and Gibbons.

Either way, the crowd politely waited for Shane to leave the pub, which he duly did and stayed on Terry's sofa, on Terry's advice. With proper manners observed, they then felt free to discuss the punch, and more importantly, who was in the right. Of course, that was then and this was now, a rainy Monday morning. They were once again all together, awaiting the beginning of the protest, with Phyllis. She was not smiling; lots of eggshells. Shane was noticeable by his absence but, to be fair, he probably never had any intention of coming.

"Ah! Sure he'll probably be home tonight, you can forgive and forget then." Marion might be a bit of mouth, but she hated to think she played a part in the current fracas, no matter how accidental.

"I don't care if he ever comes back, God forgive me, he's a fucking waster, Marion." Phyllis had not cooled. Truthfully, her anger was not just at Shane. Her frustration was aimed at many mounting problems. Her increasing distance from her daughter, the strain of being the sole breadwinner with three other mouths to feed, and that persistent, if inaccurate thought, of an easier life if different options were chosen. This was simply the final straw that fell between the camel's two humps.

"Sure feck him, men are only good for one thing and even then technology has them beat, am I right, ladies?" Leanne coughed hard as she laughed. "I think we'd all be better off without them. Sure, you're doing all the work. Some provider, am I right, ladies?" Leanne continued.

In the pub on Sunday, she was unwilling to quell the increasingly imminent fight. Now she revelled in the sensationalism of it all. It's not that she hated men. Leanne's issue was a little more complicated. Boredom. She had enjoyed the further three beers she had while discussing Phyllis and Shane's marriage. As someone who never was married, it was clear she was an expert.

It is not unlikely that she envied the two of them, either. Their solidarity, the comfort they found in each other in better times, or even how they once were able to make each other laugh.

Marion, for her part, wanted to be a part of this union. Her own was lacking. Leanne had no union, good, bad, or indifferent. For her this was something to watch, as someone who is fascinated by a soap opera. Others' misfortune to liven her own life. It helped that she was a little jealous and it also helped that Phyllis was her boss. What fun!

"Ah here, shut it, Leanne, any man you've had in your life needed a forklift to lift the flab, to get his pecker at ya." Luckily though, Marion was still looking out for Phyllis, and that would not change.

The megaphone whistled sharply, provoking a hostile reaction from the crowd. Terry politely took it from Arthur and accordingly adjusted the volume.

"Eh thank you, now then, eh, can we stop the Chinese whispering! Oh wait, is that being racist?"

Terry sternly shook a "no."

"OK, well, first off, thank you all for coming out on this inclement day in Clementine Lane." Arthur chuckled to himself at this clumsy attempt at alliteration. The crowd were non-plussed. They weren't in great spirits, after all, and it was raining. "We've actually heard it through the grapevine that Mr Hawkins…" Booing from the crowd began. Somewhere in the background someone shouted, "fuckin wanker!" Remarkably it wasn't Terry.

"Yes, OK, OK, eh… well, Mr Hawkins will be in the Council building as part of some procedure in the planning. This is a real opportunity to get more involved and make your voices heard not just to Mr Hawkins, but to the Council itself!" Small applause greeted this call to war.

Donal McGlynn had been busy. Conducting comparative research in his free time, ensuring the Council was aware of its findings, ensuring the protestors were aware that the Council was aware, through an anonymous phone call to Arthur Gallagher. Of course, it was not that anonymous. McGlynn may have thought his fraudulent Kerry accent on the phone was convincing enough to con the old man, but that old man's bushy eyebrows were misleading. Arthur still had a keen mind. He had correctly deduced the anonymous caller's identity. It was this keen mind that was reading the crowd in front of him and figuring out that already it was a lost enterprise. These people were not motivated for this protest. There was no fire here. He took the megaphone from his mouth and guarded its all-hearing ear with his shaking left hand. "Terry, can you say something to get them moving? There's more life in Glasnevin Cemetery!"

Terry was only too happy to oblige. He had, once again, been practising his speech-making skills in the shower that morning.

"Hello folks." The crowd had begun to talk amongst themselves again. "Hello folks." Some in the crowd politely listened. Leanne was heard cackling in the back. Terry would need to try harder. "Folks!" There was an increasing murmur amongst the crowd. Suddenly he boomed. "Five score and two year ago, seven men signed a proclamation. This mountainous degree was the beginning of our stand to end the long centuries of our captivity to the neighbouring island. To be an equal nation. Yet, a hundred years on, and we the working class of Dublin, are still not free. We are still not equal. We were guaranteed the inaudible rights (*Terry's vocabulary was stretching a bit*) to prosperity, yet we are exiled from our native Dublin to the sticks, while those from the fucking sticks come to live in Dublin!"

The crowd began to quieten and turned to face Terry, who was growing in confidence. "Now as we are slowly pushed from our homes, to suburbs, those that are still here in the working-class areas of the city have the problems of society placed upon them. All this is done to protect the middle classes from the realities of urban life. Our government defied our proclamation. We are not equal. Our children will not be equal, either. They are the heirs of

242

the payment of promissory notes to those who would not have shared the profit, had their gamble won."

The crowd was now silent, even Leanne.

"What of the promissory note that was our proclamation? What of the promise of equality? Of freedom?!" The crowd actually clapped. "There is no money now for our areas. No money for the renovation of our flats. No money for new flats to be built for our children, who must now move away from their ancestral home. But we refuse to believe that our state's bank is empty! When they can refuse the money from the big companies! When they can cut income tax on the higher earners. We refuse to believe our state's bank, which we bought, cannot loan us equality, justice and fairness."

Arthur was beginning to think this speech was all becoming a little too familiar, but the crowd was still silent. He just could not quite place it.

"No, we are not free! When our voices don't matter to them, no more than any of our voices mattered to the British before them!" There was a loud applause. Some had even taken out their camera phones and were aiming them directly at Terry! Passers-by stopped and listened. "Now is the time to make your voices heard. Now is the time to say it to all those smug politicians. The rose wearers, the blue shirts, the green-blue shirts, the green-green shirts, and the commies, that we will not take any more. Now is the time to say stop dumping your society's problems on us!"

"Hear hear." "G'wan Terry, tell them to go fuck themselves." "Fair play, Terry."

Arthur was delighted at the eloquence of this speech; sure, Terry mispronounced a few words here and there, but how could he magic something so powerful out of thin air? Yet it seemed so familiar.

"There will be neither rest nor tran...tran...tranquillity in Dublin until there is equality for the working classes! In our attempt to make the Council hear us, let us not give them opportunity to once again cast us as thugs and scumbags. Do not drink from the cup of being an asshole, carry yourself with dignity. You are from Clementine Lane, you are Clementine Lane!" Terry was building his own momentum now and he could see the end in sight, and gradually, so could Arthur, who was coming closer to solving his conundrum.

"Jesus, he's very good, isn't he?" Marion was genuinely impressed, much to the annoyance of a nearby and jealous Mick.

"Ah, he loves to shite on."

"We cannot be satisfied by their insincerity. We cannot be satisfied with their indifference. They will try and further lead our area down into dil…dil…dilapidation and squalor. We cannot be satisfied with their snobbishness. No, No, NO! We cannot be satisfied until the people of this area are seen as equals to every other citizen. Till equality falls like a torrent down the waterfall of justice, like the rain that falls on you now. The value of a citizen is not in their wallet, but inherent to them!"

More applause, "Stick it to the bastards, Terry!"

"I say to you today, my friends, that even though we face difficulties today and there will be difficulties tomorrow…"

Hope had opened a bright yellow umbrella, which drew Arthur's attention to her in the crowd. Yes, maybe it was racist in a way but suddenly, he knew where he had heard something strikingly similar before…

Terry was just reaching the climax, "My FRIENDS… my friends, I… I HAVE A DREA…"

Immediately, Arthur stepped forward, spritely for a man of his years, and grabbed the speakerphone "Thank you so much Terry. Everyone, Terry Walsh!" The crowd did applaud although truthfully, they were somewhat confused. Terry had them in the palm of his hand and he almost had knocked the finishing blow. It did seem a little anti-climactic. Though had Terry finished that sentence, his whole speech to that point would have been lost to laughter, as the crowd would have finally realised they were being enthralled by a Terry Walsh, possessed by the spirit of a Reverend from Atlanta.

As it was, their mood had lifted and they, finally, had lit fire in their belly, as did Arthur. "We shall overcome, folks! We shall overcome! Sing it with me, as we walk down to the Council, altogether now." As if by magic, they began singing this often-used anthem of those who needed a prayer to St Jude. Slowly, the now larger group of thirty-seven souls began to form into columns of three abreast and began their march down the rainswept Clementine Lane. They held crudely written placards with "Not in my community" and "Playgrounds not drug centres." Some had tricolours, leftovers from national soccer games some months before. They were determined, but few.

As they left the shelter of Clementine Lane and turned onto McDonagh Street, Fr Matthew watched from his church door, smoke in hand. It was quieter at morning Mass than usual. His solid crowd of twelve had been halved. He imagined a nasty dose was doing the rounds and his flock forgot to mark their doors with sheep's blood. "I better head to the hospital and make sure none of the poor old biddies have flaked it," he thought to himself.

He himself had been late to the altar, having slept in. Where was Delores, anyway? She always woke him. The look on one of his parishioners, as she gently knocked on his apartment door to rouse him, and he fast asleep in his Dr Who PJs with a copy of William Shatner's "Tech Wars" split evenly over his snoring chest. The shame of it. Annoyingly, he had been trying unsuccessfully to read Joyce's *Finnegan's Wake* only the day before. Why hadn't she knocked on his door then?

Well, this was the reason of it all. The protest march. He could see his missing sheep singing loudly, with their placards, moving somewhat slower than the rest. They had given up their God to protest the housing and rehabilitation of the vulnerable?

He hated Hawkins, though he would never say it; nonetheless, protesting this type of work still troubled him. "Must not judge, Matthew, these people are expected to carry enough weight." His gaze met his sacristan who was now furiously waving at him.

"Come on Father! Get involved!"

"I'd rather not get involved in this, Delores. I don't think the Church would be too in favour of this movement."

"They weren't mad keen on the Rising either, Father, the Church can be a bit wrong at times." These were strong words for Delores. A stalwart Catholic at a time when each month seemed to bring another unpleasant or utterly evil story, she would still defend her faith, though increasingly less its institution. A helpful distinction, which helped her defend the easily defendable, the gospel, and drop the indefensible, the abuse.

Father Matthew felt like he was missing out on something. Too often he felt isolated in his gothic palace. He reasoned to himself that this was all part of his mission to ingratiate himself with his flock. He removed his collar and joined the march.

The march turned onto the main street, creating something of a nuisance for pedestrians trying to pass it. Umbrellas clashed and had to be pulled down, spilling their purpose on their hapless owners. A bald man in a grey fleece, flanked by two others coming the opposite way, stepped out into the wet street to avoid the procession. "Was I telling ya? I actually rang in to support the centre on that show. Your man Cantwell was beaming. I says, 'you're a great man Mr Cantwell for helping those poor unfortunates.' He lapped it up like cream, fucking simpleton, also he'd want to do something about his shirt and tie combos, fuckin prat." His two associates started laughing, as they returned to the path after passing the protest.

"Single-file everybody," Arthur called from the front, as the great march became something of an anorexic leviathan. Cars beeped their horns thinking it was some protest against the government. Probability would always have lent some support through the sheer number of cars passing by and, for every one person who voted for the present governing party, there were always several others who did not. Nonetheless, each beep of support emboldened their number, as they tried hard to chant above the traffic and the rain.

"Jaysus, he could have picked a better day for this shite, couldn't he?" Leanne hissed.

"You got the day off, didn't you? God help us if the funders cop I closed the crèche," Phyllis sharply retorted as the rain lashed against her face, slightly smudging her black mascara.

"Me fucking fag is falling apart, ah here." Leanne left the march and crossed the road back towards home. To the casual eye it seemed quite circumstantial; however, Leanne had planned to leave the march early as soon as she woke up and saw the dark clouds on the morning's canvas.

"She is some fecking wagon all the same." Marion saw an opportunity to undermine Leanne's earlier bad influence.

"Ah she's a real 'suit herself', fuck her anyway, she knows I can't dock her or she'll have me for closing the crèche." Phyllis was in agreement.

"She's a fucking waffler, Phyllis, always said it, and she's probably jealous of you and Shane," Marion persisted.

"She can be very crude, and exaggerate a lot, I must admit. I always thought your Shane was a gentleman," Hope chimed in. She was sensing what Marion was trying to achieve.

"Who'd be jealous of Shane, he's a gobdaw." Phyllis was still not having it. She was also becoming increasingly frustrated at people bumping into her as they pushed down the narrow path towards the Council.

"Leanne is right about fuck all!" Marion was trying to push it home.

"She's probably right about that lazy gobshite I'm stuck with, though." Phyllis's mind seemed set. No matter how hard Hope and Marion tried, the row would still come and maybe it had to now.

The group descended down Winetavern Street, a place once known as "Hell" due to the high amount of alcoholics, prostitutes and lawyers that lived there. As they wound down the street, two addicts under the influence of their affliction stared on.

"Here, what have you lot got against addicts?" one of them bellowed straight at Arthur, who looked a little shaken.

Terry stepped in and, with his hands raised in a manner that a culprit tries to appease the police, told the man to relax, which, as it almost inevitably would, further incensed him.

"Fuck off, don't tell me to relax, you posh cunts, looking down on me because I have a problem!" The addict was agitated.

Terry momentarily reflected, weren't they marching to protest against the posh cunts that looked down on them? "Listen, pal, we just believe the site could be better purposed as housing because no one can afford to live in the city," Terry lied, but not convincingly.

"Yeah, whatever, I know a rent-a-mob when I fucking see one." The addict returned to his now-sleeping companion. The march had moved on.

Finally, the small group had gathered below the Council building. The rain was flowing heavily above them, as people from the city centre coming from their offices looked on and read the signs, before sighing and moving on without comment. There was no media present. Donal knew that he had already flown too close to the wind. The only record made was the camera shots taken by Terry, which had to be strategically taken from the ground up, to suggest more volume in their small number. He would update the social media world later. They would similarly ignore this event even with these strategically taken photos.

The Council building, imposing in its size, served little more than to make the crowd look all the smaller. Somewhere in its upper floor Siobhan had just walked out of the meeting in a fury. Frank and Eamon were gathering at the window, smugly looking down.

The small crowd assembled on the soaked steps as Terry, now with megaphone in hand, was ready to give his speech. He was thinking something along the lines of Robert Emmet's oration in the dock, for this moment. He had been adapting the revolutionary's speech in his head as he marched down the street, and was currently wondering if it would be a step too far to suggest his epitaph not be written while a rehabilitation residential centre stood on Clementine Lane.

Arthur, already correctly second-guessing his companion's plans, was moving to take the megaphone from Terry's hand. "Thanks, Terry, sure I'll give 'em a bit of bluster." Terry looked a little disappointed. The protest went on and it finished without comment or response. It was people power, but people power is measured in heads, and not quite enough heads had shown up.

26.

The Tempest

"W̲HAT'S WRONG, SWEETIE?"
"He didn't do it, Da."

Shane Farrell may have had a reputation from his youth for being a capable man in a fight, but it was arguable if that was bravery. Courage is the quality to persevere in situations where your abilities and talents cannot aid you. If you're good at punching someone senseless, should a fight with fists be the measure of your bravery? Probably not. What Shane was truly frightened of was the oncoming war of words with his wife, Phyllis. He had just returned home, late into the Monday afternoon, as he was sure that she would not be there, engaged as she was with the protest. He had hoped to spend some hours preparing what he would say, acclimatising to what had become the waiting area of an arena, which before had been his home. As he sat in his sitting room, there was no comfort but a quite nervous energy. "Ave, Imperator, morituri te salutant."

It was this heightened state of anxiety that caused Shane to leap from his thoughts and indeed his chair when his eldest child entered the room.

"What are you doing here?"

Sienna started to cry.

"What's wrong, sweetie?"

"He didn't do it, Da."

"All right sweetie, come here." He hugged her tightly.

**

When Phyllis had arrived home from her fist fight with Shane the previous night, the knuckles on her left hand were grazed and bleeding. Her rotund nine-year-old was, crossly yet happily, staring at a talent show on the TV. Talent shows tend not to draw the talented Irish, cursed as the capable are on this island with an unhelpful modesty. Perhaps this was not a uniquely Irish disposition if one was to observe those who put themselves forward for election in most nations. Nonetheless, the tiny young man sat rather hilariously on the sofa that was five times too big for him, upright and with a scrutinising eye, staring at this latest crop of "talented" people. Sienna sat beside him but paid no heed to the oversized television. She was still engrossed in a book about ghostly manifestations in holy places.

Her mind was still buzzing with her experience of last Sunday. Whose mind would not? That voice, "yes, child," was it there? Was all this real or in her mind?

Both children became suddenly aware of the presence of their mother, who was clearly seething.

"What are you reading, Sienna? I want to know, now!"

Sienna was caught somewhat off guard but was innovative. "*The Shawshank Redemption*, it's for English, Ma."

"Yeah well, you could do with a bit of fucking work with your English, if your teacher is to be believed, anyway. With that foul mouth of yours! God forgive me, I don't know where you get it from!"

When Phyllis eventually met Mrs Grimes, Sienna's disappointed English teacher, she had torn strips off the authoritative and self convinced mentor. However, that was then. Then was a different place. Then, her daughter had just been kidnapped by a possible paedophile addict. Then, she was something to be protected, her offspring, an innocent. This arrogant, middle class bitch was not going to belittle her intelligent, talented little acrobat. Then, Sienna was at home feeling worried about Brendan's condition and bored by telly, but to her mother, she was traumatised. Then was then, but this was now, and now, Sienna was a co-conspirator with her father, trying to out-plot her mother. Now she was distant, which was hurtful; judging, which was unkind. Now was now, and, while mothers forgive and protect, they never, never forget.

Sienna just stared at her mother. Joe also turned and squinted at the matriarch, who seemed uncharacteristically hostile. This, of course, frightened him. He was a nine-year-old who depended on her. His survival instincts were attuned to her. Hostility was not an acceptable environment for a small rotund nine-year-old to be in, particularly when the hostile one was his chief protector, and he knew it. Phyllis briefly stared at him, momentarily cooling; he was her cute little angry asshole and she loved him. She loved both her children.

"Sienna, why did you go to see that man with your father?"

Sienna could not lie this time. The truth must have been outed and now must be owned. "Brendan was really nice to me, Ma, and there he was dying, I had to see if he was all right." Her eyes were reddening.

"That man is anything but nice, Christ, do you not know better than to befriend homeless addicts in warehouses?! Did we fucking manage to teach you anything?!" Phyllis started the fight as most parents of teenagers would, relying on a critique of her daughter's common sense.

"He actually listens to me! He didn't dismiss me when I told him I had a supernatural experience."

"Oh not this shite again, Sienna, you're a bit old for this nonsense. Marion told us the story in the crèche, it's some old folktale. There was no such nun, no girl with a birthmark. Mr Gallagher told her there is no historical truth to it. It's an urban legend that some deviant told you!"

"It is true! Anyway, you don't know him, you just judge people because they're homeless!" Sienna moved to take the moral high ground.

"He's a fucking murderer, did you know that?" A surprise attack that parried the attempt.

The two stood in front of each other in the squared circle of their living room.

Sienna began to cry, an emotional armour in other times and useful for manipulative purposes.

Phyllis stood with two hands anchored into her hips, an authoritative stance that fortunately covered the hand she had cut knocking Sienna's father senseless to the ground.

"Murderer? What are you talking about? You're losing it! He's just a lonely man who made mistakes. Christ, why do you have to make him out as some criminal?" The 14-year-old decided to ignore the previous charge and maintain her attempt of moral authority. An inexperienced move; clearly Phyllis had set this moment up for the finishing blow.

"No, Sienna, it isn't me demonising anybody, the guards lifted him for the murder of that other poor, homeless man they found dead at St Luke's. It looks like your pal gave him a bad batch of whatever drug he was taking!"

Sienna's face dropped. She went quiet as her mind processed this data. Of course, the time lost had granted victory to her mother.

It is strange how quickly instincts colour judgement on meeting someone. In totality, Sienna could not have spent more than a few hours in the presence of Brendan Freeman. Yet in her heart of hearts she knew that he was innocent and that there had been a mistake.

It had helped that in her time, she had known the guards to

have made many mistakes; not the ones her parents would have talked about, either. Not "so and so was decent skin, do you remember he found your phone on the pavement and gave it back. The guards are just looking for a fall guy" or "they were too harsh on him. Sure, his father was a bollox and he didn't have a chance. He'd always say 'hello'." No, in these instances, it was her parents who were wrong and would happily look the other way because someone was simply funny or polite, but they were not Garda mistakes. No, Sienna knew the real mistakes the Garda had made, the ones where they ignored the evidence that was in front of them. The dodgy dealings clearly happening on Mr Dempsey's floor in Clementine Lane Flats or when her friend Darren told one of them that he was being "hurt" by his da's mate only to be told "fuck off and stop messing." No, there were genuine Garda mistakes when evidence was ignored, though Sienna had no evidence now, just a feeling, like her parents, when they were wrong.

"Now that shut ya up, you don't know everything, do you?" Phyllis had mistaken silence for submission.

Sienna's thought process had been disturbed by her mother's triumphalism. It angered her. She stared at the most important woman in her life, not seeing her. The divine wind formed around her, and then she released. "You don't listen to me, you never have, you probably never will and you don't care. And you know what? I don't fucking care about you either! Why the fuck should I?"

To a mother where this statement was true, a lesser mother, it would have provoked a sharp slap across Sienna's face. It was not true in this case though, Phyllis did care, a lot, and these words stabbed right through her.

Sienna did not wait for her reaction. Perhaps this was cowardice; she was not expecting the slap, she knew her mother, she knew it was more likely that she had just made the woman cry. She knew her well. Black lines of mascara drew across her mother's cheeks, as she sighed deeply with her head in her hands. The upstairs bedroom door slammed shut. Joe was crying too. He may have looked like he had an attitude but he was an empathic and kind child. The two women he loved most were crying; he should cry too.

After a time, Phyllis regained her composure and comforted her youngest and she brought him up and got him ready for bed, as her eldest continued to read coldly, in the adjacent bed. The mother left the room without a word and went to her own bed, where she could cry in peace.

The next morning Phyllis left Sienna to stay in her bed, as she functionally told Joe to get ready. Not another word was spoken between them. Slowly, in the mother's mind, fatigue and emotional hurt were being replaced with anger and frustration. In a process familiar to all after a fight, the pain caused was someone else's fault and would have to be accordingly proportioned.

Phyllis was resentful. A narrative was already forming in her head. She was mother and bread winner. She was protector too. Her daughter, whom she raised, whom she nearly lost her life for through complications in a very difficult birth, now hated her. Why? Because she had sought to protect her from a "down and out" who was now in prison. While her husband, who contributed nothing to bills, delivered their precious little girl into his hands! That cowardly bastard did not even have the nerve to face her at home and probably stayed in the pub drinking and laughing at "his woman's" temper. Anger feeds anger. In her mind, the noble man who built homes for people, whom she loved, was turning into a sly lay-about, who cared for no one but himself and was flippant with the wellbeing of their children.

***

Sienna had related the previous night's fight to her father, who was now waiting on his own encounter.

"What are you at? How is that any way to talk to your mother? She is going to be going around with some head on her today. Imagine if she said that to you, 'I don't care about you, Sienna!' You need to apologise and fast. Your poor mother, she would do anything for you." Shane was quickly realising that his own forthcoming engagement with Phyllis had just become dauntingly harder. His wife's temper had just been super-charged and the vengeance she could not take on her daughter would surely be taken on him.

"She closed the crèche for that march and she's gone a while, she'll be back soon. You can see what she's like yourself, Da."

"Don't get cheeky! She's your mother and when she comes in the door, the first thing I want you to do is apologise to her." Shane was rather hopeful that this strategy might take some of the anger out of his spouse. Hope springs eternal.

"What happened to your jaw, Da?" Sienna was only now noticing the purplish swelling on the lower side of her father's face.

"I walked into a door." Shane smiled without meaning.

"What are we going to do to help Brendan?" Sienna looked imploringly into her father's eyes but this time Shane was not for deviation from his wife. Good deeds go punished.

"You must be joking! Your pal is on his own, Sienna. If he's innocent, he'll be found innocent, it's that simple." Shane tried to sound truthful but as a usually honest person, this lie was not sounding believable. In his own mind three words floated: "that chap's fucked."

Sienna was about to speak on the subject again when the door opened. A small cut hand was first visible, still hanging on to a key. The blonde geisha hair bowed as she struggled with a bag of shopping. Sienna stood beside the single sofa chair, where her father sat, both eyes transfixed on the new presence.

"Sienna, go to your room." The voice had finality to it and came with matching grim eyes and a perfectly horizontal lined mouth. The teenager was brave, but not that brave, and left the room without issue, and with her left Shane's strategy of an apology to placate some of what his wife was feeling.

"You found your way home eventually, good for you. Head throbbing?" Phyllis had not made eye contact with these words, and dropped her key into a small glass bowl by the phone as she placed the bag of shopping on the floor beside her. As angry as she was, there was still food in the bag for four people.

"My head is fine, jaw could be a little better though." Shane stood up and walked into the kitchen to make a cup of tea he had no desire for, but he felt the need to busy himself.

"Ah ye poor thing, me heart goes out to you, how was Terry's couch? Did he show you his 1916 medal collection? And his toy guns?"

"Funnily enough, no, he might have still been in shock at seeing his friend's wife punch him full force in front of a packed bar."

The two were moving about the kitchen cum sitting room in an awkward attempt to directly avoid the gaze of the other. Both seemingly busy to the untrained eye, preparing tea, fixing cushions; essentially, they were doing nothing at all. This was all a prelude to the fight. Like a bird's mating dance, this too was full of ritual, slow, as each antagonised the other. Neither wanted to be the first to fire the first direct broadside, but it was coming and coming soon.

"Are you calling me a knacker? Is that it?" Phyllis was the first to stop pretence. She now stood in the middle of the sitting room, hands once again on hips, her authoritative stance.

Shane turned around from the kitchen counter to face her. "You punched me! In front of all our neighbours, in front of all our friends, you actually punched me. What kind of behaviour do you call that?" Shane moved for the moral high ground.

"Don't you give me that! You brought our 14-year-old daughter to see a homeless alcoholic, who is probably now sitting in a station somewhere for murder. What kind of fucking thick does that?!" Once again, Phyllis correctly parried back.

"Well I didn't know he was going to get lifted, did I? I mean these days you've turned into one of those anxious grannies. Down with addicts! Down with the homeless! What'll be next? Down with the immigrants?! You're hanging around women that are at least 15 years older than you and they're fucking with your head. You were never like this."

"Fuck off, Shane, get off the cross, I take an interest in me children. Why do you think I do a job I hate *(this was not true)*, because I've two young children and an adult who refuses to take on his own fucking responsibilities."

Shane's eyes narrowed. "It's not my fault no one will hire me. I'm out there every fucking day being politely told to fuck off! Do you have any idea what that feels like? I'm in my 40s and I'm already redundant to the world."

"Ah piss off with the 'poor me' shit, Shane, I feel sorry for those who have to get up in the morning, not some…"

Upstairs, Sienna listened. She could feel anxiety, it was rising in her, she was only 14 and she had never heard such anger pouring from her parents.

"Let's be honest, Shane, you haven't said a fucking word to me in weeks. You've been in your own little world, while I struggle to feed you and our family. I can't cope with this life anymore. You're here for a free ride, you're doing nothing to support us." Phyllis was still trying to figure out if she meant these words.

"A free ride? Would you fuck off, I was the main earner in this house for years. Those auld ones, alco bitches every one of them, have turned you against me. They've turned you bitter. Although you were always a little resentful, if we told the truth, Phyllis. You always thought you could do a little better, didn't you? Big tits could have always done better than me. Why did you settle in the end, eh? Why did you stick with me?"

Sienna pressed her hands hard into her ears as she wished that her bedroom floor was just a little thicker. Both parties below struggled to justify themselves, to turn their opponent into the ultimate evil and them, the ultimate victim. Both jostled to be right and inevitably, were both wrong. The little girl upstairs, whom they had so quickly forgotten, was as quickly forgetting the happiness and the warmth of her family home.

"Maybe I fucking did have better options than you! That wouldn't have been too fucking hard, would it? Everybody else is getting a job, while you're still playing silly beggar in the house all fucking day. Probably making up bullshit that you're going looking for work, while you and that other lazy asshhole Mick laugh it up in Cartigan's, at stupid little Phyllis!"

"Piss off!" Shane dismissively uttered.

"No I won't, Shane, I could have done better, of course I could have, I was good looking, I wasn't like half the fuckin 'how yas' around here, but then I was pregnant. Pregnant with the same daughter you're now turning against me. A pregnancy that nearly took me fucking life and, God forgive me, I wish it fucking had! But I wasn't that lucky. Instead, it enslaved me to a do-gooder do-nothin and a… a newt daughter who hates me! What a fucking life, stuck with you two fuckers!"

Sienna heard every word, every single word. Tears rolled down her face.

Shane stood and looked out the window. Across the street two young teenagers were dragging a keenly determined Jack Russell, who had previously committed to emptying his bowels outside the Farrells' neighbours' door. "So I trapped you, did I? That's why you stayed, because you had no other choice. Well that's fucking lovely. We're at the bare bones of it now. Or was it our daughter that trapped you? Which one of us ruined your life, Phyllis?"

Somewhere in the back of her mind, she had realised she had gone too far. Perhaps Sienna had felt the same the night before, but anger feeds anger and she could not slow down now. "You both fucking trapped me! Made me your keeper, made me your fucking servant and you both treat me like I'm something just to be used. You're not the only one with self respect. You feel precious when they tell you're not good enough on the sites. Well, imagine when you're ignored by your own family."

This moment of melodrama brought the delicate potential for peace but it was fleeting, and unfortunately, Shane was still deeply angered by everything that had already been said. If he was astute and had sincerely asked "who ignored you?" it might have prompted a redirection. Phyllis might have spoken of her own loneliness, her own insecurity; who knows, they could have begun to comfort each other. But instead he stood stoically looking out the window, as his wife behind him became overcome by self pity mixed with the toxicity of anger. The fleeting moment had passed. Not seized.

"Get out, Shane! Get the fuck out! And this time don't come back. It's fucking over, Shane. FUCK OFF!" The sharp clear finality of that sentence suggested new territory. Never had she been so clear.

Shane was a little shocked but still found himself moving towards the door. The dictate was so direct. He thought as he left through the door, "fuck, it's over."

Sienna could hear her mother sobbing below, just as she had heard every word up to that point. There was no clarity to the teenager's own thoughts, only deep feeling. A feeling that danced through every nerve of her body; she was simply in pain.

27.

Time To Go

*12th February 2018 (Monday) to 13th February 2018
(Tuesday)*

SIENNA, SITTING ON HER BED, WATCHED HER ROTUND BROTHER
heavily snore. In and out, in and out, his small tummy rising
and gently lowering. It was the only time that his face did not
look so cantankerousness and cross. Indeed, he looked like an
angel. She would miss him.

Sienna was leaving.

A bag had been prepared containing what she felt she would
need for a life outside the home. It was hidden under the bed
before Joe had returned from school.

"What a fucking life, stuck with you two fuckers!" Her
mother's words replayed in her mind. Her eyes narrowed. It had
not occurred to Sienna that little under a month ago, she had
advised Brendan against this very action. Why would someone
leave their family? Things change quickly.

As she sat on her bed, staring across at the little heaving
mound that was her brother, she planned her next steps. Firstly,
she would break into that chapel, provoke the ghost again but
this time record it. Then she would show them! Her mother
would have to listen. A spark of resentment lit in Sienna. It
was no longer simply curiosity into the supernatural. No, now

it was much more important than that, it was about proving her mother wrong and establishing Sienna as a credible adult. Secondly, she would have to help Brendan; how this was to be achieved was unclear, but somehow, she knew he was innocent, almost like a memory. Then, a new life with her father? That too was unclear; the young teenager had thought about her future as much as a young teenager might have been expected to. Either way, something had to change.

Time to go.

Quietly, Sienna lifted her window, while glancing behind. Joe had not stirred.

Gracefully, she put one foot on the windowsill, then, grabbing it with both hands, she reversed rear first out the window. Sienna's planned descent via the drainpipe should pose little problem for the agile aerobics expert. As with before, she had grace, earned from years of practice and patience; if anything, this manoeuvre was a little easy, it seemed to Sienna... THUD!

The teenager had reached for the pipe and missed. She had fallen sharply. Her head had knocked the ground. There was no pain, just a small pile beside the backdoor. The pile was not visible to anyone, and it was no longer gracefully moving. Seemingly, there was no future to have to consider now.

Shit.

28.

I Dreamed A Dream

12th February 2018 (Monday)

H E HAD NO IDEA OF THE TIME. IT WAS FEBRUARY, AND FEBRUARY was consistently dark. The tiny slot for a window conveyed this message simply. It must have been Monday. He could remember Sunday perfectly, from morning to night. He remembered the casualness of the Garda outside his tiny cell, as they started another day. Their world had not changed; his had changed utterly. His last remaining neighbour, the drunk driver, was being moved to Mountjoy prison. His friend, the conscientious burglar, had been moved the previous evening.

Fully sober now, he spent that Sunday smelling the lingering taint of Saturday morning's vomiting. He even remembered his meal, provided for by the local chipper. There was a water leak in the station's kitchen. He could remember the portly Mayo guard commenting that it was his lucky day. In other times, he'd agree, a cheese quarter pounder and chips meal was a delightful dinner, but this Sunday he could not stomach it.

He remembered the evening too. The legal aid came and asked a barrage of questions, to which he could only provide half garbled answers. It was clear from the firmness of her tone that she did not believe him. However, he still felt that she would do her best. Her professionalism was coloured with a competitive streak that suggested she would not give in easily.

He found her very attractive. Knee high skirt blending into matching pin striped suit jacket with a purple blouse. Fair haired, shoulder length and well shampooed, deep green eyes with a small chin, a light bronzing achieved from expensive holidays rather than cheap bottles. She had a fit, slim body. For all the fear he was feeling and the important advice she was giving, his eyes were still transfixed and thinking on more base topics.

In his still hungover state, the polite pretence of hiding such obvious attraction slipped and she was visibly awkward. That embarrassed him now. Hands down she was the smartest person on the floor, there to defend him, and all he could think of was sleeping with her. For her part, she had become somewhat acquainted with leers but never became accustomed to them. An inevitable part of her work that had earned her friends' respect. Over empty wine glasses, they would call her clients "animals". This embarrassed her. She had represented the worst of people, this was true, but also the lost, the fearful and the mistakes. It was greyer and she knew it.

That consultation, though it felt more like an interrogation, left him feeling the acute hopelessness of his position. He could see past all of her professionalism to the truth. Unfortunately, she wore it clearly in her eyes. She was disappointed that she was given such a clear loss for her record. When she asked of people who could give character statements, such as his parents or siblings, it became clear that she was beginning to recall his face. That interview on the news. That homelessness guy who was estranged from his family? Fuck, he did not come off well in that piece. Public opinion already was introduced to Mr Freeman, and it was not a positive introduction. Back to the drawing board.

For his part, he could only think of Sienna. The legal aid immediately dismissed the suggestion. Unethical. Besides who would listen to a 14-year-old girl, as a character witness in a murder trial? Gloomily, he nodded in agreement. Indeed, the legal aid accurately assumed, the girl's parents would promptly drop any previous support or tacit engagement with him, when the severity of the case against him was made known. What he needed was someone who would support him, even if they thought he was a murderer. Did he know any such person? He thought again. The rehab workers he had mocked. The family he had abandoned. He had no friends. Tappers didn't; trust, like money, was not readily available on the streets. He thought, no one would help him now.

Gloomily, his large grey eyes begin to weep once more. In fairness to her, she did not insult his intelligence with platitudes and instead she provided a verbal slap. "Crying pathetically won't help you but I can, so, for the next time we meet, provide me a list of names and I'll try to reach out to their compassionate side."

He once again nodded gloomily.

The evening ended with the beginnings of backache from lying on that mattress and a surprise visit from the female guard. What was her name? Quinlan. She asked a few more questions in his cell, to which he reiterated what he had already told her. She stared at him but he could not read her thought process. She grimly left the room as she had entered it. Leaving him to the short-lived sleep that he had now just awoken from.

The only light entering the room emitted from the edges of the door frame, like it was a sacred portal. The window only presented a purple to the black of his cell. He knew it was night or at least early morning. It must be Monday. He was sweating profusely, as he had done in the warehouse the previous month. The darkness taunted his worn out and de-toxing senses. Red orbs flowed forwards and backwards with a syncopated rhythm, in front of his eyes, like plasma in the vein. The alcohol was finally near finished leaving his body.

Memory was setting up reels in the picture house of his mind. The film selection was devised to cause maximum pain. He could see Gibbons charging him, McGlynn questioning him with a shark's grin. Older memories were resurfacing. In his mind's eye a door was opening, a door marked "Taft". Eventually his consciousness left him and he believed he had escaped into sleep, but these dreaded thoughts were not done with him and they pursued into the hidden realm.

***

"This is a dipshit idea!" That half grin seemed especially obnoxious. Freddie Taft continued. "Bren Bren, this is a dipshit idea, what's the point? There's nothing in there but holy statues and rats."

"You not even a little curious if any of those old ghost stories about this place are true? You don't want to see a dead nun?" Brendan Freeman stood regarding the chapel.

"Dead nun me bollox. I try not to shit on me own doorstep. Bren Bren, remember just because it's quiet, doesn't mean you aren't being watched." Freddie pulled hard on a cigarette that he had curled within his left hand; furtively looking behind him, he blew out.

As the two teenagers entered the darkness of the alley that ran alongside the chapel, the gaze of the golden streetlamps of Clementine Lane and their protection went no further.

"Here, let's forget this for a lark and get that drunk outside the offy to go in for some cans. It's not too late." Freddie spoke as he moved to catch up with the determined Brendan.

To be fair to the drunk outside the local off-licence, his rate of one can out of every six that he purchased for underage drinkers was more than competitive. Admittedly, he did seem a little crazed, as he frequently shouted at passers-by that they were a "Dirty Finglas bastard." Finglas is a place in north Dublin, they are mostly nice people, most of them are even clean, and their legitimacy is less an issue in modern times.

Brendan was now at the back of the chapel and climbing the bins just below its rear windows. "I'm not spending another night just sitting around getting drunk in the lane, Freddie, who does that all the time?" It would seem fate had a sense of humour.

"Normal people, Bren Bren, normal people. Better question, who tries to break into a bleeding chapel on their Friday night? What do you think is going to be in there anyway? There are no such things as ghosts." Freddie was still on the ground, looking around for unwanted attention that could at any minute appear on the surrounding flat balconies.

Freeman had begun to peer through the window from left to right. Frequently, having to wipe the condensation from his breath off the glass. The darkness seemed quite impenetrable as the teenager leaned closer to the pane. As much as he focused, only rough outlines of unknown objects emerged from the blackness. He could hear a bored Freddie singing to himself below him. Good, at least he was distracted, there would be less talk of cans and drunks with biases against the north outer city. Brendan could focus on the real issue: was the chapel haunted? Did some apparition of a mortally wounded nun haunt its halls? His eyes were trained on the black, yet all he could see were orbs, little specks, here and there, nothing fixed, floating harmlessly in the dark. Dust caught in suspension. Brendan pressed in closer to the window; he could feel its coldness against the tip of his nose. Suddenly, his balance shifted, something had moved it! His face was sent forward at pace towards the window, walloping it hard. After cursing loudly at what no doubt would be a bruise, he looked down, and saw an apologetic Freddie staring up.

"What the fuck are you at?"

Freddie, who had accidentally moved the bin whilst singing and dancing to the Backstreet Boys seminal hit "I want it that way", gave an undertaking he would stay quiet and sat down on the cold ground.

The investigation continued, as the taller teenager once again attempted to break the code of the darkness and see past its invisible wall. He was a little more agitated now. Eventually, after further unsuccessful attempts to see through the black, he hopped down from the bins, declaring his effort a failure.

"Grand, now can we get cans?" an earnest Freddie enquired. "Or can I get cans and you can sit there and watch me drink said cans? I think you'll enjoy it, me drinking cans is a laugh riot for all the family."

Brendan ignored him and moved to the back door, which he immediately gave a hard shunt of his shoulder. The door held firm.

"What the fuck are you at? They'll call the guards on us, ye thick!" an incredulous Freddie whispered.

"I just want to get a look inside." Brendan shunted his shoulder against the door again. It gave way a little more, but still the lock held.

"Clementine Lane may be a playground for you, Bren Bren, but I live here, I have to stay here when you go home to your nice house. If one of the neighbours sees us, and tells me da, I'm fucked. You know what he's like! Come on will ya stop!" Freddie was now clearly pleading, but Brendan was singularly obsessed with opening the door.

He gave it one more shunt and it gave way, perhaps more due to its fatigue from years than to his less than powerful 17-year-old frame. The teenager paused looking into the darkness then, as if one in a trance, he walked into the chapel, leaving his friend at the doorframe begging for him to come back.

The chapel was not yet a youth project, but its time as an active chapel had passed; it had become a museum to the Order's past. Boxes upon boxes of black and white photos, records and diaries mixed with the Christian curios that live in such places. A calmer, less obsessed Brendan now absent-mindedly sifted through these various boxes, while a still-apprehensive Freddie had joined him in the main nave.

"Told you, it's just shite from when the nuns had it, why was it so important to get in here, anyway?"

"Just something to do." Brendan did not raise his eyes with this utterance.

The two teenagers waded through the boxes and looked around the chapel. The faint green light from their Nokia mobile phones was insufficient to really illuminate anything, and, as they distanced themselves from the door, they found themselves in increasingly darker territory.

"There's a whiff of old fanny in this place," Freddie muttered.

"And you would know?" Brendan replied as he awkwardly stepped over boxes.

"Let me tell you, son, I am a certified fanny expert in this locality. There isn't a young one on this lane that doesn't know Dr Fredrick James Taft."

"Yeah, their mothers probably tell them to keep an eye out for you when you are trying to cross the road. Bless." Brendan sniggered.

"Oh, their 'Mothers!' Posh prat," Freddie snidely replied.

While silence pervaded their surroundings, the atmosphere was charged. Forgotten instincts from a prehistoric time were beginning to fire; something was with them, they could feel it. They joked as normal, more to comfort each other than out of natural sincerity.

Ultimately, the teenagers could move no further into the chapel; several pews were stacked one upon the other, and it was too dark to be able to navigate between them. Freddie stood directly in the dark amber light of the stained glass windows, while Brendan was still in the shadows looking for a way past the pews.

"Tis no good, Bren Bren, time to head bac…" Freddie stopped speaking. He had heard steps. He knew that something had stepped into the chapel behind him. There was an awkward stillness. The teenager froze. Whatever was there must surely be regarding him.

Brendan had stopped searching in the dark, the abrupt silence from his friend alerting him to that other presence that was now with them. For a moment, nothing, an instant full of anticipation but empty of action.

Then the steps were heard again, but this time faster, and with increasing speed. They seemed to be moving at pace, heading in the direction of Taft. Freddie could feel the air quickly move towards him. He was afforded no chance to respond. They were almost upon him. He was caught by this unidentified other and he knew it.

Then, there it was, a heavy weight came down hard on Freddie's shoulder. To Brendan, who was still safely hidden in the darkness, it seemed to lift his friend from the ground directly up and then pull him back with an ugly, and terrifying, ferocity. All the teenager could do was yelp in terror as he was dragged backwards, stumbling over the boxes and curios he so delicately had avoided when he had first entered the chapel.

Brendan's grey eyes widened in horror. He quickly pursued this terrible apparition that now held his friend in its firm, unyielding, grasp. The teenager was wise enough to remain invisible in the darkened sides of the nave as he followed.

"Let me go!" Freddie struggled to scream.

The power that held him said nothing.

The back door of the chapel swung open and Freddie was thrown with an unmerciful force against the outside wall. Upon impact, he fell to his knees, and spat out a mouth of blood onto the pavement. He wheezed, unable to breathe, as the knock winded him. Still unable to see what monster was attacking him, a sharp blow came hard on Freddie's right cheek sending him straight to the ground.

Brendan had reached the backdoor, and was now watching from the dark, at this calculated deconstruction of his friend.

Tears were streaming from Freddie's face. The teenager was reduced to a mere child in seconds.

Then it spoke.

"I got a call from the neighbours that my darling child was

seen breaking into a fucking church of all places!"

Freddie said nothing and continued to cry.

His father, who stank of vodka, lifted him by the hair and smacked him as hard as before, again, across the right side of his face, this time sending him headfirst into some corrugated fencing.

"Who the fuck breaks into a church?" he roared into his son's face.

"I do."

"Who the fuck is that stupid?" he bellowed again.

"I am."

"Who has brought shame on this fucking family?!"

"I did."

Though Brendan had answered all of Mr Taft's questions, he had not made his voice heard. His friend, Freddie, who was no longer able to speak, simply stared at his father, who continued his deconstruction unabated.

Repeatedly, he threw the boy against the red brick wall and slapped him hard as he rebounded. Freddie had stopped making any noise at all.

"You're a disgrace!" Taft Senior bellowed, as the boy struggled in vain to rise to his feet, his hair thoroughly matted now in blood on his forehead. Freddie looked sorrowfully into the darkness of the chapel, as if one of the saintly statues would come alive and save him, or perhaps his friend, who had led him there in the first place. But no one came and the beating continued.

Eventually, the same balcony mouths who had summoned Mr Taft summoned a Garda car and an ambulance and both Tafts were taken away in different vehicles. Brendan waited for everyone to leave, then, unnoticed, he made his own way out of the chapel and home.

As this was a dream of a memory, Brendan knew several things at that moment. He knew that beating would leave the 17-year-old Freddie with a perforated ear drum and talking as if he had been savaged by a stroke. He knew that it would also knock the boy's left eye out of focus, which would leave him partially blinded. He knew that Freddie's father would, finally, answer for his crimes and go to jail. He knew that Freddie's mother would have to move them from the area and Brendan would not see his friend Freddie Taft again.

Brendan may have told Sienna that the opportunities for socialising in university were the cause of his downfall into addiction and alcoholism. That was a useful and sympathetic narrative. Brendan knew one more thing. It was a lie. After that night in the chapel, a new Brendan Freeman emerged, his wounds less visible than his friend's; but he was wounded, nonetheless. The living are far more dangerous than the dead.

***

He awoke with a start. It was still night in the station. He sat up on his mat. It was soggy with sweat. One nightmare had ended, yet another one still lay ahead. He began to speak to himself in a low muttering. "I'm sorry, Freddie, I'm sorry, Dad. I'm sorry, I'm sorry, I'm sorry, I won't let you down anymore."

It was Monday morning. In a few hours, a march would demonstrate outside the Council building, much to general ignorance. In a few hours, Frank would sign his soul over to Hawkins, and Hawkins, with some modification, would get his Centre passed. In a few hours, Phyllis and Shane would have their worst argument and Shane would leave their home, presumably for the last time, while their daughter lay in their backyard, with her eyes closed.

"In a few hours," Brendan muttered to himself, "in a few hours, I will end it."

29.

No Confidence

13th February 2018 (Tuesday)

"THE MAIN NEWS AGAIN. OPPOSITION PARTIES HAVE CALLED for a vote of no confidence in the government after it gave full support to Independent TD and Minister of Public Expenditure Adam Loughlin today despite yesterday's revelations of his extraordinary expenses claims at the Dáil's Public Accounts Committee. The Government is expected to lose the vote, as Fianna Fáil has stated that it will support the motion, thus ending the confidence and supply agreement. The State is now on an election footing. Joining us in the studio now is reporter Donal McGlynn. Donal, what do you think will be the main issues in this election?"

"Well, Nuala, housing is going to be a major bone of contention for this government. It will try to defend its performance by pointing out rising employment figures, but with the increases in rates of rents and housing prices, non-homeowners have now entered a situation where they are working but still barely surviving. The opposition parties will argue that there has been no coherent housing policy. They will point to the government's favouring of investors and vulture funds by their refusal to build public homes, thus keeping the price artificially high. We have already heard deputies stating that it is the preserve of government to build homes as they have done in previous generations, at such times of crisis, and I can see this being a major headache for Fine Gael going into this election."

"Donal, you recently covered the case of Clementine Lane, where a homeless man, Mr Peter Williams, died near the site of a proposed rehabilitation centre. What impact do you think that story will have on any political party's narrative at this time?"

"Excellent question, Nuala. The protests to the imposition of that centre are entirely local. If last Friday's *Political Questions* discussion show on this very station is anything to go on, then the court of public opinion has sided with Mr Eamon Hawkins's development plans. That said, the left will point out that such services are better run by the State and that private companies tend to cut corners in service provision to maximise profit. Now I stress, this will be 'their' narrative, not my own. Interestingly, Labour candidate Frank Cantwell for the Dublin South West Inner City ward has come out in favour of the development, putting himself and his party at odds with the rest of the centre left. I have heard many deputies speaking in the halls of the Dáil that it was rather shocking that a Labour candidate, not in government, would support private provision of what should be a state service. Even my sources within Fianna Fáil said that they will be attacking Labour over its support for the centre. The main opposition party has been, for some time, trying to position itself in the centre left and rebuild its ailing fortunes in the capital. They may try to gain a seat at Labour's expense with this issue."

Donal knew he had put the cat amongst the pigeons. He had a plan. Usually parties use people, but ultimately, the media can use parties.

"Well we'll leave it there, thanks, Donal."

"Thanks, Nuala."

The news continued in the background. Conor was focusing in on the back of a frozen lasagne packet. "Five minutes in an 800 watt microwave. How many minutes in a 900 watt then?" Conor

274

was still trying to work out this arithmetic, as if the additional seconds would radically change the contents of his dinner, when he could hear the buzzer. He immediately answered it.

"Hello neighbourino!"

Fuck, it was Frank. Conor was half hoping it was Mick or Terry, in the mood for a cheeky early pint. "How's it going, Frank?"

"Can I come up?" an annoyingly chirpy voice asked.

"Sure," came the somewhat jaded response.

Frank was surprisingly quick in reaching Conor's third floor apartment. "Hello there, Mr Maguire!" Frank did not wait to be invited in and though he knew Conor, he assumed a familiarity that Conor found presumptive and rude. "So, you've heard the news?"

"I assume you're on about the election?"

"You assume correctly, Mr Maguire!" Frank looked for a chair. He saw one, currently occupied by a hoody that Conor had meant to wash and his laptop. These items were quickly deposited on the unoccupied couch, further irritating Conor.

"You've given up on the black t-shirt and faded black jeans look, I see, Mr Copeland, these days?" Conor sneered at his smartly dressed guest.

"Prospective leaders have to look the part." Frank sat perfectly upright in the chair in his silver suit matching his hair, affecting an air of dignity.

"Prospective representatives, Frank." Conor coldly smiled. "Are you here to canvass my vote?" He moved to the couch and removed his hoody to sit down.

"Not at all, Conor, you are an upstanding member of the rugby classes, I know you're in the bag. I was wondering if you would be interested in canvassing with me? After all, you're a young, good-looking man. Smart, know what's good for the people of the area. Know the problems of the apartment folk." Frank placed his hand over his mouth as if someone could hear him. "Such as the 'Shinners' in the neighbouring lane. How did you describe them? Pissed and illiterate?"

This utterance, made without thought less than a month before in that very room, now made Conor cringe. It was strange, to be sure, but he had only been in Mick and Terry's company three times over the space of one week. That's all. One week, and yet he felt that he knew them for years. This Conor felt different from, and indeed ashamed of, the Conor from just a month before. "Yeah well, that was kind of a stupid thing to say, I was being a bit of ponce." The answer was to Frank's question, but truthfully, he was talking to himself.

"No you weren't, you've a wit, like all the young people today. You don't mince your words and you tell it like it is!"

"I told it like it wasn't." Conor started to rub his eyes, "Frank, I don't know if anyone told you, but my father recently got some very bad news and..."

"Oh, I know, he's dying. There are no secrets around here. I'm very sorry about that by the way, the big C, terrible business, your poor mother."

This pre-emptive interruption shocked Conor.

"Canvassing will take your mind off it, Conor. You see, I have a big team already," this was a lie, "and while I don't need canvassers..." So far, Frank had two college students sent by head office after Siobhan quit the previous evening for unspecified reasons. Frank had met them that morning. Both were depressingly young and inexperienced. Both were called "Tony", one with a "y", the other with an "i". Both had just read about Marx in their sociology degree and thought they had cracked society. One had the annoying habit of continually correcting Frank's grammar, no less than five times in their forty-minute meeting, while the other seemed to stare on in sheer terror. Frank had already berated both of them with such fury that he wasn't sure that either would turn up tomorrow.

The heated exchanged started when Toni with an "i"

commented on how wonderful it was to see an older man entering politics, unafraid about what people would say about his age. The split second of rage this prompted, and the enlargement of Frank's eyes, followed by the five-minute tirade, probably was enough to ensure that these two well-meaning volunteers would not be back. Hence Frank's visit to Conor. "Like, I have a lot at the moment, Conor, but even though I don't need any more, I said to myself 'I got to help my friend Conor, got to take his mind off things'."

Frank smiled and continued. "So here I am. Let's face it, you know the lingo of the young people around here, and you know how to put in a good word. I never forget my friends either, Conor, and you are currently unemployed. Hard times and all that now, but a bright future is on the horizon." Frank finished speaking, feeling assured that an affirmation was forthcoming, a grateful affirmation at that.

Conor looked at the brimming Frank. "Let me get this straight. You came to my apartment knowing that I have recently been told my da is dying of cancer. You came here with the intention of getting me to join your grubby little circus act. Trying to get the young hipster middle class vote, is it? Just so you can get a seat in the Dáil? You came here to use someone who deliberately left his job to spend more time with his father, just to get you a job for the next five years. Do I have that right, Frank?"

Frank stared wide eyed, not really comprehending that what he had done might be morally questionable. In fact, the only thought in his head was that this tone was neither affirmatory nor grateful.

Conor rose abruptly and went to the door, which he opened in one fluid motion. "Get out Frank, you're reprehensible, not representative."

***

"Hello, is this Siobhan Kearns?"

"Yes?"

"I was looking to arrange a meeting with Mr Cantwell?"

"Well, you'll have to ring him yourself because I don't work for him anymore."

There was silence for a moment on the line.

"I sense a little hostility, not an amicable separation?"

"Who is this?"

"My apologies, my name is Donal McGlynn. I work with…"

"Yes, I know who you are. Look, if you want an interview with Mr Cantwell you will have to ring him or his new PA, I have nothing to do…"

"No, no, maybe it is you I would like to talk to, are you free to meet?"

"Well, I don't see how I can help."

"I'll explain when we meet. Nealon's pub?"

"Fine."

"Perfect, I will see you then."

Siobhan hung up, confused.

***

"Aoife, this is time wasting." The two Gardaí stood at the turn onto Clementine Lane.

"Can you shut up complaining and help me? Do you want to have an innocent man's arrest on your conscience, or are you not the man I thought you were?" Quinlan sternly replied.

Gibbons thought for a minute. He liked that she thought him duty bound, even honourable, but this was time wasting. Freeman was guilty and that was it. Still though, she was right, they had a duty to pursue justice. Now to say that Gibbons would have thought this on his own would be misleading; nonetheless, he thought it now. He straightened his back and continued their canvass. She was an expert manipulator. "What are you hoping to find?"

"I don't have confidence in any of this, Paul. If someone asked me to swear in court that we have the right man, I don't think I could do it. I just want to ask the locals if they have heard of any rumours of dealing in the area."

"Jesus, Aoife, it's Clementine Lane, of course there are dealers in the area! Besides, not one of these 'locals' will talk to us, and you know it."

Aoife knew that Gibbons' pessimistic assessment was quite accurate, but she still had to try. "They may know something about this business, Paul, they might even be more willing to talk if they knew someone was arrested for it and they knew otherwise."

Gibbons looked at his watch. "Fuck it, it's dry anyway, we'll give it a go." They continued on walking into the lane.

***

It was near the end of lunch time. Two Fianna Fáil advisors sat in a café on South William Street, mulling over the day's events, while drinking two Americanos that were once simply called a coffee. Truth be told, they could be advisors to any party. The centre had become so squeezed that the similarities outweighed the differences. One, a suited professional, mid 30s, slim with tightly cut straight black hair. He was afflicted with the ridge of a broken nose, the result of a bike crash at the bottom of hill in Tuscany that had left his nose permanently scarred and a visible reminder to be cautious. The other, a member of what was once the vanguard, but now the rear guard, in his 60s, dark grey hair, sporting dark framed glasses that admittedly made him look like a member of McCarthy's red scare committee. These glasses hung below very bushy eyebrows on a purple pallor face that did more than suggest a fondness for whiskey.

Their names would usually not be important. In fact, in day to day life, despite their massive influence, their names would not be generally known; maybe that's the point. While this may be true in reality, it would doubtless be harsh on the reader to proceed without christening them, but to be fair to the author, he has no intention of putting much effort into the task. Therefore, our young 30-something will be called "John", while his elder counterpart shall be called "Paddy".

"Inside sources? Who? Us? What a spoofer. Why do you think he did it?" John was collecting rocket leaves and shredded carrot onto his fork.

"Jaysus, fuck knows and fuck cares, John. I'd say there's probably some animosity there between him and Labour, or your man Hawkins, or maybe he just plain doesn't like that fat thick Cantwell. The point is, he has done it." Paddy pouted while he chewed his sandwich in such a way that it opened up the evolutionary debate suggesting our progenitors were not apes but cows.

"He'll get a wrap on the knuckles I'd say, bold boy," John continued.

"He might, but if we all bite, which I suspect we all will, then he can simply say he was recording the mood, even if he did set it," Paddy replied.

"So is that what you're going to advise the boss?" The younger man drank a small measure of his Americano.

"That's what we'll tell him. John, we've been given an open goal. You heard it, 'my sources within Fianna Fáil said that they will be attacking Labour over its support for the centre'. Besides, he is right, the boss does want the party returning to the economic left in an effort to try and rebuild the grassroots. He'll probably be singing *the croppy boy* and waving the tricolour next week to try and shore up those arseholes that drifted to the Shinners. Long and the short of it is, we all missed the point on this. Labour are supporting private companies to do public work. The liberal vote is gone every way. Even the fucking conservatives are liberal these days. Nobody would dare challenge that accepted hegemony. So liberalism isn't enough anymore. Fine Gael, to be fair, have the right sewn up as tight as you like. Nobody is under any illusion where their bread is buttered. The boss is right, we need to move the party centre left. We're haemorrhaging to the Shinners, we can also pick up something from the Labour voters who find the IRA memory too distasteful."

John said nothing and continued to play with his salad.

Eventually Paddy continued. "Funny thing is if we were in power today, that centre would have already been built, when that junkie kicked the bucket. You have to seize the moment. It's not reactionary, it's democracy, it's listening to the needs of the people." Paddy wiped his lips with a napkin.

"That's bit cynical, don't you think?" The younger man seemed a little shocked.

"Tell me, son, did you ever believe in anything? I did. Do you know why I think this way now? Beliefs mean fuck all without votes. This is a job and it is straightforward, get the boss in power, that's what we're paid for, that's what we 'believe'."

"So how do we proceed?" John looked up as he was moving his red onions away from his salmon. He didn't want to have bad breath.

"Simple enough, Labour want to privatise what should be public health care services. Fianna Fáil is against privatisation of health care. Fianna Fáil believes in a strong State-run health service. Fianna Fáil believes in people before profit. Maybe scratch that last one. We need to make as much of this as we can. Housing will be the main issue of this election but our own bib has dirt on it there. Let's aim at this Cantwell chap, he's weak, inexperienced, looks like something of a metaphoric lightweight if not a real one. We might squeeze a candidate through and get back a Dublin seat. Then you should send a thank you letter to Mr McGlynn, foul mouthed toe rag though he is."

Outside the café, a cyclist on the path hit an old lady. She was knocked over, her shopping everywhere, while the cyclist, who was in the wrong, cursed her for springing out of nowhere. The two men stared onto the street, "Jesus, the poor auld one, I hope she's OK," then returned to their meal.

***

"Since when has Fianna Fáil gave a flying fuck about private provision of services? Isn't it their raison d'être? Fianna Fáil created the community sector for the exact reason of private provision of services over expensive public ones, you out-and-out thick! No, you fucking listen, nobody fucking said anything about election strategies for an election that hasn't even been called yet! Insider sources my fucking hole! It's your boy McGlynn having a poke at me again. Do I have to take your pathetic parochial fuck up of a broadcasting company to the High Courts? I want a fucking retraction, he is harming my business interests. How's it a matter of the public interest? Fine, fuck off but this won't be the end of it. You hear me there will be fucking hell to pa…" The phone hung up on Mr Eamon Hawkins before he could finish his threat; this did nothing to improve his mood.

Maire Hawkins, his well postured wife, entered the large sitting room with tea and sandwiches, which she set down on an American Oak coffee table. "Don't worry, Eamon, he won't get away with it. It's clear as day he's following an old grudge."

"Fucking media set the agenda, Maire."

The elegantly dressed lady moved and sat on the leather bound couch beside him. "Sure, you can just build a centre in another 'down and out' area."

"Build in another area? Do you realise the money this has already cost me both officially and non-officially? Some business expenditures you don't get money back from the tax man, Maire. Besides if this becomes some new hobby horse for the left, we're no longer the noble community-minded activists, we'll be portrayed as the East India Company. Don't you get it? He's changing the narrative. We'll be fucked."

"Eamon, I wish you'd watch your language, you're not with those knackers from the inner city now. Please talk like an actual decent human being and not one of your drug-addled pets," Maire scolded.

"In case you do not understand me, Maire, if he gets away with this and the parties bite, we're in the hole by quite a margin. That will mean cutbacks. No more filling the home with craft-made woollen scarves from Wicklow, silverware from Kildare, crystal from Tipperary, no more sly self-presents of jewellery, no more five holidays a year." Hawkins looked at her with eyes that were filling with a stinging malice.

"Oh we'll make do. You're overreacting, silly thing." Maire rose and left the room. The realisation had hit her, she liked her sly self-presents of jewellery. She was perfectly furious, but she hated to look stupid and instead would attack her husband later, on a seemingly unrelated incident.

Hawkins sat there lost in thought.

***

Brendan had taken to quietly humming to himself. It brought some comfort to him. He was innocent, yes, but he had no confidence that the court system would find him so. He had resolved the previous morning that death would be fine now. There was nothing to look forward to, there hadn't been for a very long time, if he was honest. He had hurt enough people, destroyed them even if he hadn't meant to; that was Brendan, a selfish destroyer. There would be no point in undergoing the media glare. The potential to see faces from his past staring disdainfully at him from the courtroom balconies. He would not subject himself to it.

Of course, there was a question of method, and being locked up in an empty cell with even his shoelaces removed, method did not seem obvious. So for once Brendan would think ahead, for once he would be opportune. "The next time they question me, I'll discreetly steal a pencil or pen, carry it in my underwear and once I'm in back in here, I'll loaf it through my eye. Nasty, certainly, but if I get it to the brain, this shite is finally over." A nasty plan indeed.

He sat on his mat, somewhat relieved. The realisation that this was all going to end soon brought some peace. Truth be told, the mixture of a sudden cessation of alcohol, the stress of what was facing him, and the dreams that these circumstances had provoked, had left Brendan quite mad.

He stuck his fingers underneath his mattress. It had become something of a habit for him since arriving in the station. The sensation was usually pleasurable. "Fuck!" He quickly withdrew his finger. A small droplet from its top oozed red. He lifted the mat, and there, shining beautifully, a past occupant's contraband. A happy little Stanley blade smiling brightly! "Hello Brendan! It's me, Stan!" This must have been the tool so expertly, sometimes philosophically, wielded by previous inmates to carve their legacy onto the cell wall. "Hooray," thought Brendan, feeling that despite its years of heavy graffiti-ing, it was still razor sharp. "I don't have to use the pencil plan after all." Hooray indeed, using the pencil plan would have been awful! Brendan could die today.

30.

The Cause of, and Solution to

13th February 2018 (Tuesday)

DONAL MCGLYNN WAS ALREADY IN NEALON'S PUB WHEN Siobhan entered. "Addiction, what a great industry! It's like an undertaker or a doctor, you don't have a choice, you gotta buy."

Siobhan sat down with her glass of white wine in front of the smiling McGlynn who was holding his neat whiskey in one hand. "Why did you ask me here, Mr McGlynn?"

"Please call me Donal, Mr McGlynn was a chemistry teacher I had in my Christian Brother school days. The similarity in names got me slagged more than I would have liked, but to be fair, I think I developed a fairly tough skin for it and most of those cunts went on to live rather unremarkable lives so…"

"Fine, Donal, why did you ask me here?"

Donal momentarily stopped smiling and looked around the busy Capel Street bar. Finally, his eyes trained on Siobhan, who was still staring at him. "First a question, my dear, why are you no longer in the employ of Mr Cantwell?"

"That would be a confidential matter," she quickly replied.

"Well okay, for what it's worth I am great with confidential matters, but that's fine. You are a party member who is probably untrusting of journalists, seems a reasonable position to me, so

let me take you into my confidence. I am not here for a story."
McGlynn sipped his whiskey and smiled with big eyes. "I am here
for vengeance. That may make me sound unhinged but fuck it,
I've a big house, I fuck frequently, and life is good, I can afford
to be vindictive."

Siobhan felt uncomfortable. "Are you drunk?"

"Not yet, but I will be. Let me continue, I know that the
Council received a rather damaging report, comparing the
proposed rehabilitation centre with other similar styled centres.
I know this, because, Siobhan, I sent it, din din dinnn!" Donal
tapped the table for dramatic effect.

Siobhan's brow raised a little.

"I also know, Siobhan, that you would have been at a meeting
with poor hapless Frankie, the Council top brass and Hawkins,
where this report was no doubt discussed, am I right so far?"

Siobhan took a large sip of wine but remained silent.

"That a girl, get it into you, I'm guessing that something was
agreed at that meeting that was rather unscrupulous as it resulted
in you walking away. The insinuation of a bribe, perhaps? Now
I'm not going to say you strike me as a conscientious person or
any of that shite because frankly, I don't know you and in the two
occasions we've met all I can say is that you know how to stand
up and sit down. What I do think though, is a volunteer who
was party to an act of corruption, with any brains at all, would
probably walk away. It wasn't Frank's personality that led to this
separation, was it, Siobhan? I've done my research. You were his
campaign manager before, for your sins."

"I left because the changes they were proposing to make
seemed minuscule. I left because Mr Hawkins had implied that
the officials had profited from knowing him. The whole thing
was sickening. It wasn't to save my skin, as you suggest. I do have
principles."

Donal sat his glass down on the table and leaned in. "Of
course you do, and that's swell, but the real question is do you

have ambition?"

"What's that supposed to mean?"

Donal looked a little exasperated. "Please feel free, Siobhan, to take the initiative and assume what I mean at any stage and this conversation may travel a little smoother. I am suggesting that it may be possible to move you into Frank's position. Do you want to be a TD, Siobhan? That is what I am asking you, do you want to be the ring master or the person who cleans up the elephant's shit?"

Siobhan's interest was beginning to peak, but she was still working it out in her mind, and instead played for time. "Showing your age there, Donal, that is a little outdated an analogy." Cheeky as this response was, for the first time since she arrived in Nealon's pub she was smiling.

Donal returned her smile. "The old circuses were the best, fuck animal rights, I want to see a bear in a tiny hat, not a load of fucking French queers dancing on a long rope."

"Mr McGlynn!" Siobhan was genuinely annoyed.

"You're right, mea culpa, mustn't be homophobic. Point is, Siobhan, today it went out on the airwaves that the opposition parties are lining up to attack Labour over its support for private companies performing State roles. Whether that was true this morning is anyone's guess, but it is true now. Your leader only wanted to make something of the Williams case to try and unseat the government. What he failed to realise is governments always unseat themselves. He has no further use for Cantwell and won't be too fond of getting it in the neck for some little junkie farm in the inner city. He'll be looking to drop his party's support for the project, looking for a way out. I suspect you have that way out for him."

"You want me to tell him about the meeting?" Siobhan looked a little unsure.

"I want you to look at this report." Donal took an A4 envelope from a leather satchel beside him. "It's the report from that meeting. I want you to give this report to your leader and tell him what happened at the meeting. If these changes are as marginal as you say, it'll mean that they have done a fudge on it. It will imply heavily that there were some shenanigans at that meeting. But more importantly, it will provide cover for your leader to drop support, as it clearly demonstrates that Hawkins' centre is nowhere near the acceptable standard. It will also provide the room needed to drop Frankie as a candidate, as he agreed to the new plan, which as we know is a grave, grave error in judgement. Allowing the auld head of the Connolly Bourgeois Brigade Michael Norton to remove himself from the whole business, hell, he even can have an internal workshop into what is the best form of provision for such services, and find out that it's better in State hands. Who knew?! Whatever, doesn't matter, the long and the short of it is he wants out, you get him out, he gives you Cantwell's job."

Siobhan sat there, her lips tightly pursed, thinking through what had just been said. Eventually a quizzical look came across her face. "If your plan was to settle some petty grudge with Frank, why did you originally want to meet him?"

Donal stared back a little wide eyed. "You're a little thick, aren't you, love? You'll make an excellent representative. My grudge isn't with that fat Monaghan moron. Had it been him still in the driving seat I would have simply blackmailed him, but with you it's cleaner. My grudge is with the fucking devil that is Eamon Hawkins. Your party joins the growing opposition and publicises that report, that centre is dumped. The Council will run a mile before there are insinuations of favours rendered for its original passing and Eamon is in the hole for whatever it's cost him thus far, with a reputation in tatters."

"Why do you hate him so much?" Siobhan asked.

"It's enough to say I don't like farms, Siobhan, and I don't like farmers. Are you in? Think of all the teeny tiny special interest groups you could help, while ignoring the unemployed."

Siobhan grimaced, but this mild provocative comment wasn't enough to spoil what was otherwise a highly profitable conversation. She took the report and put it into her handbag.

McGlynn smiled. "That a girl!"

***

As that moment of intrigue was taking place in a noted pub on the north side of the city over whiskey and wine, a different intrigue was occurring in a less noted pub on the south side, over two lagers, one largely flat due to its owner's excessive talking. Cartigan's was not busy that Tuesday. The local men had already spent enough of their wages on tomorrow's annual sacrifice to their partners. The dreaded St. Valentine's Day, named after the Italian saint whose remains reside (amongst other places) in Dublin's Whitefriar Street Carmelite Church. It is with stinging irony, that in life he became the patron saint of love for his willingness to pay the dowries of poor women and that now his feast day requires men to make great financial sacrifice, for fear of the harshest of punishments. Of course, this problem would mean little to the four men sitting in Cartigan's at this time. Fr Matthew, chaste for life if in body and not mind, sharing a short with Arthur, widowed some twenty years, Terry, chaste by choice, at least according to him, sitting across from Shane, who, well, neglecting Valentine's Day was the least of his worries.

"She's a fucking nut job, Terry, a fucking nut!"

"You're just angry, you don't mean it, relax, will ya."

"Relax about what? My wife has left me over bringing a kid to visit some chap in the hospital."

Terry looked dumbfounded, picked up his lager and took a large swallow. "Leaving a few details out there, Shane?"

"Ah fuck off, whose side are you on, anyway?"

"A smart man doesn't pick sides in domestics, Shane. Vinnie, something similar, drink up will ya, you're miles behind!"

"Is that right? A smart man, you must be a smart man, you never got married." Shane's eyes were only half opened. They had been that way before in Cartigan's, but this time, it was because he was miserable.

The bar had become deathly quiet. Fr Matthew broke the silence from across the room. "Shane, she loves you and you love her. Go and do the simplest thing and say 'I'm sorry'."

Vinnie broke his usual rule and served the two pints directly to Shane and Terry's table. He felt a need to be compassionate.

"It's not that simple, Father, breaking up isn't an event, it's a process. A silent, invisible process, that only catches you at the end. You think it was just an event but it wasn't. You were slowly drudging towards it all the while." He lifted his pint and finished it in one, moving the newly placed one in front of him.

"Bollox, absolute, fucking shite talk." Everyone was somewhat surprised to hear the usually reserved elder statesman of the bar use such foul language; Arthur seemed genuinely annoyed. "When I still had Doreen, we fought constantly. I didn't like it, I hate conflict, but she was moody. Some days happy and funny, other days melancholic, you could see it in her that a row was about to start. If the neighbours heard us, which I'm sure they often did, they would say there was going to be blood on the streets. But, but, Shane son, every night, no matter how bad, ehhh… one of us would turn to the other, in a bed of silence, and say 'I'm sorry' and that would be that. Breaking up is a process only if you are unwilling to think of the other person or listen to them. From what I can see, it wasn't just the homeless chap, that was the ending of it, what else did she say to you?"

Shane looked irritable. "Is there no privacy anymore? Shouting my love life across a pub seems to be the new national pastime."

Vinnie, pushing his glasses up his nose, looked at Shane. "Don't think you can have much of an expectation of privacy when your wife punches you out in a pub, don't think it's covered by the Data Protection Act, is it? Am I right? Am I right?" There was a mild chuckle in the quiet bar.

"She thinks I'm a fuckup because I haven't got work in a while. She thinks I'm spending all my time in here with you lot instead going to the sites, which if she walked in the door right now, would be pretty damning, to be fair. She doesn't seem to understand that things have changed, there's a greater expectation to have qualifications now. I just don't have them. It's not like before, when anyone could work on a site." Shane slowly rolled his pint in a clockwise motion and stared gloomily into it.

There was quiet in the room. After a period, Fr Matthew spoke again. "Would you not do a bit of training? There must be loads of courses out there for unemployed people."

"It's not that simple, Father, I was never school orientated, I'm a grafter not a student."

"More bollox." Arthur spoke again.

"Is he drunk?" Shane was somewhat surprised that this old man he knew all his life and never knew to swear was now increasingly enjoying the habit.

"I'm soberer and smarter than you, it would seem. To be a good student you need to be a grafter, they're not mutually exclusive concepts but complimentary. You don't want to go because you're scared, ehhh… of the classroom. I've seen it all too often around here. People smart enough to work the system, welfare, Revenue, worked out their odds and ends to a penny but say to them 'would you go get yourself a qualification?' 'Ehhh… no, I can't do that, I'm not book smart!' Absolute nonsense, nothing wrong with the brain, you've just got a phobia of formal education. You didn't even have Christian Brothers tanning your arse and you're still afraid. And I think that's the problem with this area, nobody going off to learn, too busy trying to screw the system, instead of trying to change it." Arthur took a sip of his pint.

"Even if I did, who says that would change anything in the short term? She hates me because I live off her now, like a parasite. If I turn into 'Shane the student', she'll think I've regressed further. I need a job now. I have two young children. Ah it's a bit more messed up than that, there isn't an easy fix. I don't think she ever wanted to live a life like this, I don't think she ever wanted to be stuck with two children and me. Fate got in the way." Shane returned to gloomily rolling his pint.

Fr Matthew felt that he had to speak now. His term was mentioned, it was his time. Faith was never a bad thing. "You mean kids got in the way and I've seen it, those couples who have kids and stick together, even though they have slowly grown to loathe each other. I have seen it in my old parishes but I haven't seen it once here. Do you know why, Shane? Because in my old parishes, 'faith' meant something different. It meant peer review because there was money in those parishes. There was a culture of propriety that is absent from any working class area in Dublin. Marriages stuck together out of hypocrisy, 'keeping up with the Jones', I believe they say. That doesn't happen here; for all the absent pews at mass, the faith the people have here is genuine. It's internalised, and to be fair, it's real, if a couple here fall out of love, then they separate and they don't give a damn what others think… and against theology as that is, there is something honest about it."

"A little patronising, Father?" Shane smirked but the priest continued.

"In the end, Shane, she stayed with you, not because of kids but because of you, and you're upset, not because of your kids, but because you love her, and that all there is to it." The priest's sermon had hit a chord with Shane, though he said nothing.

The door opened and the men dropped the conversation. Silence was once again popular in the bar. Hugh marched in with a paper under his arm.

"A pint please, Vinnie lad." Hugh was still two years younger than Vincent Cartigan.

"Government's fallen, good riddance. Am I right, Hugh?"

Vinnie peered above his glasses at the former Volunteer.

"That you are, Vinnie, blue shirt bastards with their pretend republic, it's 1919 or it's nothing. The army council are the only true inheritors of our democratic republic!"

"Would that be the army council that inherited its position from past members and never held a vote in their fucking lives?" Shane snarled.

"Jaysus, what's gotten into you, son? You're usually a bit more affable. Still at odds with the wife?" Hugh smiled. Shane stared; for a moment there was violence in his eyes and Hugh could feel it. "Relax will ye? I don't mean to offend! Calm down! Jesus, I walked into the Lonely fucking Hearts Club here," the single former Volunteer said while looking at the counter and at no one in particular.

"Well, welcome to the club then, Hugh." Terry snorted.

"A soldier can't truly settle down, Terry, especially a clandestine paramilitary soldier," Hugh stated loudly from the bar. "It would be too hard on the girl. What if I had kids and went to jail, or worse, what if the old enemy got me? No, I had to be fair to every lover. 'You only have Hugh for one night then I have to be gone!'"

"Jaysus, the man with the Milk Tray has put on a few pounds!" The rest of the bar laughed at Terry's rather straightforward put-down. Even Shane smiled.

"Laugh all you want, lads. It's called responsibility. Anyway, what's wrong with ya, Shane? It can't be that bad," Hugh continued while his pint settled.

"She left him because he doesn't have a job."

"Jesus, Terry, can you hold your fucking water, now the fucking army council knows and all!" Shane's rebuff was soaking with sarcasm.

"Is that it? Well, there's an obvious solution to that, isn't there?" The bar looked on in silence at Hugh. "C'mon, isn't it obvious?"

31.

Neither Here, Nor There

WHILE OTHERS ARE DRINKING AND CONSPIRING ON THAT Tuesday before Valentine's Day Brendan is finally ready. He is about to set himself free, a poetic nicety, but not a reality, the reality is he's about to make a bloody mess. He has slowly been guiding the blade vertically and lightly along his veins in preparation for the cut. Time is quickly coming to a close. We are nearing the end, we must be…

***

Downstairs in the little house at the beginning of Clementine Lane, Phyllis was dicing carrots, focusing on nothing in particular. She hadn't really said much since the previous evening. Her youngest, Joe, was watching cartoons in the front room, while discreetly sticking his hand into a packet of Skittles. The little boy's cross face was now made all the more pathetic by a pout; he missed his dad. Several elephants had entered the Farrell household and despite their obviousness, presumably due to their size, no one mentioned them. No one said a word. What was left of the family just mimicked what they would have usually done on a typical Tuesday evening, even if their hearts were not in it. No one had even noticed that Sienna was not at home. Indeed, some time had passed since her Icarus impression. Why, she could be dead for all they knew! She was not far away; her motionless body lay just the other side of the kitchen wall.

***

"Dee, da doo, da dee, da doo…" She could hear the humming before she could clearly see the large, if short, bulk meandering in small steps around the garden.

Her vision was blurred but it was slowly coming into focus.

"Dee, da doo, da dee, da doo…"

She could make out the black smock and veil, as the form lightly hummed to itself while deadheading her mother's flowers. Slowly, Sienna realised she was staring at a nun. The teenager began to move, though it did not come easy to her, as everything hummed and vibrated. She felt horribly sick.

"It hurts." She whimpered as she tried to rise but fell, flatly, on her bottom.

"Yeah, I imagine it would alright, chief. A fall from a two storey house, I'd imagine is just a bit sore."

"Who are you?"

"I thought you would have that all figured out, bright one like yourself." The nun continued with her back to Sienna, deadheading the plants in front of her.

"Sister Sheila?"

The nun turned round and stared directly at Sienna. She was portly, with a red face, most likely a woman in her 50s who did not deprive herself. Her right eye seemed larger than its left counterpart; it gave her countenance a mildly quizzical quality. "Your mother could do with spending more time in this garden, and less time in the pub. Dee, da doo, da dee, da doo…" She returned to deadheading the flowers.

"Am I dead?"

The portly nun stopped what she was doing. Momentarily she stood still, before moving to sit on a garden chair opposite Sienna. The furniture made no sound to suggest it was under any new pressure. She regarded the girl, and then looked away as if lost in thought.

"AM I DEAD?!" Sienna shouted, which woke the nun from her thoughts.

"Well, I hope not, I mean that would be a bit terrifying, wouldn't it? Me here, talking to a ghost. I mean, imagine? Jesus!" The nun shuddered. Sienna struggled to ascertain if she was being serious; no hint of irony emanated from the portly woman's face.

Sienna tried to rise to her feet, but once again, fell back on her bottom. She was confused. The world still hummed and vibrated around her.

The nun stared at her. "You probably shouldn't do that, chief."

Sienna crossly regarded this ample-framed apparition. She was frustrated by her own immobility.

The nun, sensing her frustration, tried to change the topic of her attention. "I would have thought you would be looking for answers to more insightful questions than 'am I dead?'."

Sienna thought about it; the nun was right, was this not the proof she was looking for? Or was this apparition the symptom of a worse scenario? Had the fall in fact killed the brittle teenager? Sienna grabbed her own wrist; it had a pulse, she was still of the living. This nun seemed solid too, if anything too solid, but there was something not quite right about her, or maybe that was the persistent buzzing.

Her own continued mortality assured, Sienna felt braver. Surely, there was an opportunity here. After all, was this not a direct line to the other world? Maybe the teenager could find out about others who were already members of the dearly departed, such as her beloved granny. She was a foul-mouthed senior who smelled like an ash tray and who forever lambasted the Polish lady in the local newsagents for never giving her the right brand of cigarettes.

To be fair to Sienna's grandmother, she did never get the right brand of cigarettes. To be fair to Lina, the Lithuanian and not Polish shopkeeper, who spoke two languages other than English, it was hard to understand the stroke-impaired octogenarian, who simply shouted "blue" when asked for her brand.

Or perhaps Sienna could make enquiries about Axl, her ill-fated Jack Russell, whose tiny stature served to inspire rather than deter a ferociousness equitable to an angered Bengali Tiger. The foul tempered pint-sized Cerberus finally met his match while chasing a 06 Toyota Corolla, he was lost in the chase and did not see the bin truck coming behind. It was a quick death, and for a tenner directly handed into the bin man's hand by her father, it was a quicker funeral.

No, the teenager thought, let's first hear this woman confirm it, let there be no more speculation. There could only be one first question.

"Are you a ghost?" she ventured.

"Well now, that's a bit personal, isn't it, chief? Never let them label you, that's what I think, they'll just box you in then." The nun produced a pack of cigarettes from under her habit. She offered one to the surprised teenager, who disdainfully refused. "Alright precious, no need to get your back up."

"You're her, aren't you? The nun?" Sienna pressed.

"What gave it away?" The nun took a long inhalation.

"Terry said you were in your 30s, attractive and small." Sienna looked accusingly at her, as if she were an imposter.

"Yeah, well, Terry sounds like a lonely man with an ecclesiastical fetish." The nun exhaled. She seemed a little put out. Her eyes narrowed. "I am attractive!"

"You don't sound like you're from Galway." Sienna continued her prosecution.

"Oh, and you would know what a Galway accent sounds like, do you?"

Sienna said nothing. She didn't.

The nun cleared her throat then attempted to spit on the ground, though nothing was produced. She stared at the unmarked ground. "Damning, that."

"You are nothing like the story. She seemed more ladylike."

The nun looked mildly incredulous. "Sorry to disappoint you, chief, propriety was not as common as you might think in a city knee deep in typhus, tenement squalor, and the biggest red light district in Europe. Anyway, I think focusing on my accent is rather missing the point."

"Was there anything about the story that was true? The snapdragon-marked girl, Emily? Jimmy Doolan and his horses? The mad granny?" Sienna earnestly asked.

"Well, I think the Rising happened," the nun glibly replied but upon observing the disappointment on her face spoke again. "Chief, you probably should leave the past where it is. Attractive heroic nuns aside, it does no good to dwell there." She smiled at the downcast teenager and continued. "Anyway, I can tell you one thing, the Emily in that story would not have been as hard on her mother, real or otherwise, as you are. Everybody thinks that they have a right to be listened to, but does anybody ever listen?"

"Why can't you just answer me?" A downcast Sienna fidgeted on the ground.

"Because I want you to focus on more important things, like getting your lazy-arsed mother to put down the bottle and deadhead her plants." The nun grinned.

Sienna gloomily nodded. "Why am I seeing you?"

"Severe brain damage or a life-threatening concussion, I would wager…"

"That's not funny."

"Oh, alright, precious!" The nun leaned in. "Time to forget about ghosts and start thinking about what you have living in front of you."

"Like who?" The teenager sulky asked; of course, with even a moment's honest reflection, the question would have

298

answered itself.

"Like your mother for a start, she works hard to feed you, you should stop being such a… such a teenager! It's important to remember that for everything you think you are owed, you in turn owe someone else. Responsibility is a two-way street, chief, and your mother does her best for you, maybe think of her sometimes."

Sienna said nothing but could feel a tinge of guilt.

"Then there's your friend Brendan. You know he is in trouble." The nun looked away before absently adding, "Trouble seems to follow that boy…" She stopped speaking for a moment, then thought better of what she was saying. "You're not stupid, Sienna. You know he is not responsible, you know exactly who the dealers are in the area; you always did, so if anyone killed that homeless chap with drugs, you know who. Finally, chief, do you remember what Brendan was like when you first met him? How long do you think he'll last in a prison cell? I'd say he's already thinking about doing himself a mischief, right this very moment." The nun looked knowingly at Sienna. "So my question is to you, were you planning on saying anything to help him?" She took another drag and stared at the young girl as she exhaled.

"How do I know they're the dealers responsible?"

"In real life, the drama is seldom the twist in the story; it's the thing that was obvious from the very beginning, always present but growing in intensity. You know who they are. Besides, chief, you are concussed. It's the perfect excuse for talking to dead nuns and making shite up about your neighbours. No one would hold it against you." The nun grinned.

"But why would anyone believe me?" Sienna thoughtfully looked at the nun.

"Chief, you know what happened. Just believe in yourself and the truth will out. Trust me." The nun was stubbing out her cigarette and wiped her nose with her left sleeve.

The teenager became momentarily incredulous. "How do I

know what happened? Are you telling me to lie?"

"I'm telling you what you already know. We were both there, Sienna, we both heard him. Just use your head, it's all in there." The nun pointed to her head.

Sienna looked hard. "We were both where? Look, it doesn't matter, they won't listen to me anyway. Nobody does."

"Now is the time to make them, chief, and hurry about it too, he doesn't have much time left. And when it's done, might be no harm to go see a doctor, give the old noggin a once over. Now hurry, think of Brendan, he needs you!"

The teenager pushed against the wall and brought herself to her feet. She rubbed both her eyes. The vibrations were beginning to stop.

"How do I know you are even real?"

The chair was empty. There was no one else in the garden.

Around this time Paul Gibbons and Aoife Quinlan were thinking about packing it in. Their day, as prophesied, had been a waste, a mixture of "I wouldn't know anything about that, Guard" and "sure there's loads of drugs in the area, and your lot do nothing but pick on the ordinary folk." The two officers were close to calling time on their canvass.

"This is pointless, honestly, Aoife, I'm tired of being abused by the great unwashed."

"That joke was not funny the first time you made it, Paul." Aoife never approved of Gibbons' attempt of class posturing. Though she did concede to herself that this mission of hers born out of a feeling was proving fruitless. "Look, one more house, just give me one more house," she pleaded with Gibbons, who was observably less enthused. He had recognised the Farrell door and remembered the hot-headed woman who berated him the month before. Still, he could not refuse Aoife, could he?

They knocked on the door. Gibbons' hand was barely off the door knocker when it opened. Phyllis Farrell stood there with expectation on her face, expectation for someone else. She eventually realised two uniformed officers were standing before her and raised her hand to her mouth in startled confusion. "What's he done?! Fuck, what's he done?! Has he done himself a mischief?"

"Who, Mrs Farrell?"

"Shane?"

Gibbons looked confused. He was about to ask what mischief Shane would be involved in when Quinlan spoke up. "We're not here about your husband, Mrs Farrell. We would like to have a little chat about anti-social behaviour in the area. Can we come in?"

Phyllis, relieved though she would never admit it, stood aside and allowed the two officers entry.

The two officers sat on the sofa in the living room after they were gestured to do so by Phyllis, who previously gestured an annoyed Joe off. Quinlan began in her most sympathetic voice. "Mrs Farrell."

"Phyllis," the matriarch of the house interjected.

"Phyllis, thank you. Phyllis, we understand with the recent death of Mr Williams that there is an increase in drug flow in this area and we are trying to identify its source. Would you have heard of, or seen, any explicit dealing in the area? Naturally, this is of course entirely confidential."

"Naturally, you lot are about as subtle as a Can Can line in a church. Even if I did know anything, if I said it to you, me life wouldn't be worth living!" Phyllis, for all her good community work in the area, did not want to put her own family at risk to become a stool pigeon for what she saw as a snobbish and ineffective force.

Gibbons looked knowingly at Quinlan, who could feel his annoying smugness and did not find it endearing.

Quinlan made to get off the sofa and was about to exchange a farewell pleasantry, while feeling the exact opposite, when there was a voice from behind her.

"I know where you can find the crack dealers, Garda."

Quinlan turned quickly to the teenager standing in the doorway. Gibbons turned too. His left eyebrow was near rubbing off the ceiling.

"I know who killed Peter Williams."

"Who's selling crack, Shauna?" Gibbons struggled to remember the girl's name.

"Sienna, my name is Sienna and I ain't saying another fucking word about it until you do exactly what I tell you."

The other three in the room just stared. If they weren't listening before, they were certainly listening now.

***

It was funny. Brendan had moved that blade up and down his arms so many times that it almost became a meditation. He had quite forgotten his purpose. A cell door slammed shut outside, awakening the grey-eyed cellmate to his surroundings. Realising where he was and what he was doing, he looked around and thought to himself, "Fuck it." With the gentlest application of pressure the crimson liquid began to flow down his left arm. It felt at first like a little pinch, then a little warm, then he felt nauseous; finally, he could feel the cool air entering his exposed vein.

He rolled up on his mat and was barely strong enough to repeat the process on his right arm but he did; fair play to him, too. It wasn't easy, though his cut this time was not as clinical and surgical as the first had been. His weakening strength required a quicker motion to ensure a deep enough cut. What a bloody mess. He slowly closed his eyes.

Time is moving on and a happy ending certainly cannot be presumed, that is not so in reality. No, life is neither here, nor there, good, nor bad.

Brendan began to lose consciousness. There is little else to trouble him now and perhaps that is his happy ending. We are nearing the end, we must be…

32.

End of the Line

"Sienna, my name is Sienna and I ain't saying another fucking word about it until you do exactly what I tell you." These words were delivered with a ferocity that commanded the attention of the three adults in the room and forced them to listen to the young, slight-framed teenage girl. "Brendan Freeman is in your custody and is, at this moment, trying to kill himself. You need to call an ambulance, now!" Sienna's tone held a sincerity and a finality about it that almost went unchallenged; almost.

Gibbons stared on in disbelief. "Ye wha? How did you know we picked up Freeman? I want you to explain everything to me right now."

"You don't have time, ring the ambulance!" Sienna was emphatic. Her mother looked on in utter confusion.

There was something about her earnestness that worried Quinlan. When she had visited Brendan in his cell two days before, she felt that he had drifted into a dark melancholy. "Did you recently speak to Mr Freeman, Sienna?"

"No, will ya just call an ambulance!"

"How do you know that he is attempting self-harm?" Quinlan believed her but could not understand how the girl would know such specific information.

"She doesn't, she is just some messer making nonsense up." Gibbons had enough of humouring this seemingly nonsensical conversation.

"Here watch it, you, my daughter isn't a liar!" Phyllis was beginning to remember why she didn't like the Tipperary guard, though truthfully, she was as confused as him.

Immediately, Quinlan spoke into her shoulder walkie talkie, requesting an ambulance for cell 2, back at the station. "He must have a mobile on him, Paul. It's the only way any of this makes sense. He must have sneaked a mobile into the cell and is currently contacting the little girl." Quinlan was unsure of her own thesis, but she felt a growing need to check on their prisoner.

This was the only logical assumption. It was entirely wrong but it was the only logical assumption. The truth was that this concussed 14-year-old standing in front of them had just received a pep talk from a nun, who at best had been dead this past 102 years and at worst never existed at all. Still though, probably best not to be too honest about that right now. Sienna had realised this too. Before she had entered the house, she had wondered how she could get them to comply with her request. On hearing Quinlan's logical explanation involving mobile phones, she realised that it was probably better to go with this narrative, dishonest as it was, for the greater good.

Gibbons was still not sure what was happening and he did not honestly believe that there was a mobile phone on Brendan either. He had searched him thoroughly himself. Nonetheless, he saw an opportunity to move back to the original topic of their visit. "Your ambulance is ordered, little girl, now tell us what you know about the crack dealing. All of it, do you have any mobile phone links with them too? Or are you the kingpin in the area? Is that why you know everything that we don't?" Gibbon's attempt at humour missed its mark with everybody in the room. No one even smiled. Still, it was now incumbent on Sienna to shed light on what she knew about the death of Mr Peter Williams.

***

Brendan could not see the light at the end of the tunnel. In fact, the opposite was true, his vision was growing darker, blurred. He was beginning to feel so very tired. The blood was spurting from his left arm and forming a torrent, which cascaded onto his cell floor. His right arm was also bleeding, but not in the sporadic spurt. He could hear a commotion outside his cell door. There were raised voices, the Mayo guard protesting loudly and another voice that sounded vaguely familiar, if distorted.

"Open the fucking cell!" the familiar voice thundered.

"All right, calm down, chap. I don't know who sent for you, but there is nothing in here but a homeless drunk drying up," the Mayo voice retorted, annoyed and somewhat shocked at this intrusion to his stint. The sound of key rattling in the lock came from behind his head and then nothing; Brendan had lapsed from the waking world. There were no nightmares now, just a relaxing quiet. We are at the end of the line now.

***

The two guards did not know what to make of what this girl was telling them. Yes, they had the addresses of the dealers' flats, what they usually wore to identify them, how they always travelled together and how they always unnerved her, often causing her to step into the street just to avoid them. But still no smoking gun, still nothing to give them cause for a warrant. Sienna could see their attention shifting. Sienna knew she was losing them.

"Is that it?" Gibbons looked like he was readying himself to leave.

The nun's voice echoed in the teenager's head; she had to make them listen. The teenager took a breath and stared directly at Gibbons. "No, that's not it.

"Those dealers were being blackmailed by Williams. He was spreading their shit for them and wanted a bigger cut in their takings, he threatened to go to you lot about the whole operation. So, they made a poisoned batch, cut him a bit as a first payment, which he took and died. They then must have planted the rest on Brendan, I don't know how, but I do know they were planning on getting rid of it. Their flat is probably caked in the crap."

Remarkably enough, everything Sienna had told the two police officers was true! Though she did not know that at the time; she wondered what the phrase "touched by an angel" meant and why it kept popping up in her memory. It's amazing what the brain can retain even when slightly unconscious on a chapel floor... unguarded phone conversations for example.

The two uniforms were surprised. It seemed too complex to be conjured in a 14-year-old teenager's imagination, and far too real to be hyperbole. Admittedly, Gibbons, for a moment, began to suspect her father's involvement in some form of drug ring. That would have provided the opportunity for Sienna to be party to this information, and yet it didn't ring true with his own impression of the man. Yes, he had only met Shane Farrell once and yes, in that encounter, her father was hyped up with worry, perhaps to the point of aggression, for the welfare of his daughter. None of that was at all surprising. What father wouldn't be so anxious when his daughter shared an abandoned warehouse with a homeless vagrant? There must be another connection.

"Can I ask you, Sienna, do you have any uncles or cousins living in the area?" To be fair, this comment was more than a little sexist. Surely, a woman could make every bit as ruthless and efficient a drug dealer as a man.

"Here, what's that got to do with anything?" Phyllis did not like the connections that Gibbons was beginning to make.

"I just want to know if there are other people in the area that can help verify your daughter's story, Mrs Farrell."

"Well I have one uncle, Harry, who lives in Tallaght with my aunt Anne. They have three boys, Sean, he's my age, Billy, he's 18 and Oscar, he's 19. They've a sister called Cassandra. She's 25 and has moved in with her fella in Clondalkin. Then there's me other uncle who lives in Ballyfermot, now he's on me da's side. His name is Phil and he's married to Deirdre, we call her Dee, they have five kids, their names and ages are…"

"Yes, yes okay, that's fine. Sienna, how do you know about the events you just described to us?" Gibbons could foresee a detailed demographic analysis of her entire family.

"Listen guard, I didn't knock on your door and ask you did you know any crack dealers in your area. You asked us. If you go to that flat you will find what you're looking for and you can ask them yourselves. Everyone knows everyone's business around here, they're just afraid to say it."

"If my daughter says it's true, then it is." Phyllis stood behind her girl, lightly grabbing her shoulders.

Sienna beamed at this unexpected maternal support.

Something in Phyllis was impressed by her daughter's selfless concern for Brendan; maybe she was wrong not to listen to her, she seemed so sure.

Quinlan spoke into her shoulder-mounted walkie talkie again. "Can I get an update on that ambulance?" Everyone fell silent in the sitting room. No one said a word.

"Yeah unit 3, your intel was spot on, the prisoner in cell 2 had self harmed, slashed both wrists. He was in a critical condition. The paramedics have moved him directly to James's Hospital."

Tears formed in Sienna's eyes. A simple whisper escaped her lips. "Brendan."

Phyllis was still not sure what to make of all this, but on seeing her daughter beginning to cry, she instinctively brought the teenager close to her chest and began to soothe her.

Quinlan, moved by the sadness in the girl's face, could feel guilt over her indiscretion. She turned and walked into the hallway, though truthfully, she was still very much in earshot. "What's his condition?"

"The amount of blood on that cell floor tells me he's gone, one paramedic looked very grim. The other in fairness to him was very active in trying to seal the wounds. God, he was some man, he seemed very committed, even emotional. But I just think we were too late."

"Thanks dispatch." When Quinlan returned to the room she could clearly see Sienna heaving with tears. Her mother was holding her tight. Gibbons also moved to soothe the girl.

"We don't know anything for certain yet. They've very good doctors in James's Hospital, it'll be okay, little girl." Gibbons was clumsy in his words, but sincere in his attempt.

"I'm not a little girl, my name is Sienna," she angrily replied without lifting her head from her mother's chest.

"Sorry, Sienna, you're right, I'm sorry. Mrs Farrell, if you like we can call you as soon as we get an update on Mr Freeman's condition. It's not strictly good practice, but I guess it is our fault that you know what you do now. Perhaps an allowance can be made," Gibbons said to the comforting matriarch.

Phyllis, for the first time, politely smiled at Gibbons and the two guards took their leave.

Outside and back in the lane, where life continued on without drama, Quinlan turned and ashamedly looked at Gibbons. "Thanks, Paul, I really fucked up just now, that poor girl, I'm such a clown." It was clear from her expression that she felt incredibly guilty.

Gibbons did not answer straight away, as he looked around the quiet lane of cottages. This moment of silence only added to the female guard's sense of shame. "I don't know how any of this has come about, Aoife. I don't understand how that girl knows what she does. I don't know how she knew about Freeman or about this flat full of crack dealers, but I know one thing, if that man has any chance of survival, it's because of your instincts. Which does not surprise me, you're not just good at your job, you're a good person. You wanted to be sure Freeman was not just a number on our arrest sheet. That doesn't surprise me, either. I just hope…" At this point Gibbons' voice quavered a little, as suddenly nerves took him. "I just hope I haven't fucked it up with you. If anything, I'm the clown." Now it was Gibbons' turn to stand in a charged, awkward silence.

"You haven't fucked anything up with me, Paul." Quinlan lightly touched the back of his hand, which she quickly removed on seeing Shane turn onto the lane and make straight for the Farrell house. That would all have to wait. Now the two Garda would have to approach a district court judge, swear an oath that they had reasonable cause for suspicion and try to persuade said judge to issue them with a warrant, solely on the confusing words of a solitary 14-year-old girl, all of which, if it backfired, would serve to antagonise their already excitable and antagonistic inspector.

As the two officers politely nodded to him and made their way back onto McDonagh Street, Shane stood, admittedly looking nervous, outside his home waiting on the door to open. Phyllis opened it, and before she could say a word Shane spoke pleadingly. "Wait before you say anything, I got a job, I got a job, Phyllis, it's not much, but it's a start. It's not much but I can be earning and I was thinking of doing a course in maths, get myself up to speed so I can get back to the sites."

Phyllis just stared at him. Shane took this as a look of disbelief and continued, "Look, we will have enough. I know you think all of this was a mistake, but I love you, Phyllis. I know I don't say it all the time because I'm a thick. Maybe our marriage was an accident, and maybe that's the point. Something this beautiful could not have been planned for!" Believe it or not, out of all the lines Shane had practised in the Cartigan's gent's toilet before coming home, that one was his favourite.

"I have two wonderful kids and it's all thanks to you. Any

happiness in my life, Phyllis, any happiness at all, always starts with you, you are the one who creates my happiness." Believe it or not, this was the second favourite line that Shane had practised in the Cartigan's gent's toilet.

Unbeknownst to Shane, and it is probably for the best that he did not know, all Phyllis really wanted to do from the moment she opened that door was hug her husband, which she now did with gusto. She had heard all that he said. The more practical aspects had not yet quite sunk in, though they would, and they would be welcomed. While he savoured her embrace, he could hear tearful sniffles emanating from behind her. Shane looked over Phyllis' shoulder and saw Sienna with her head in her hands. He walked past his wife and into the living room, sitting beside the red-eyed girl.

"Sienna love, what's wrong?"

She leaned into his shoulder and started to cry. Phyllis closed the door behind him and sat the other side of their daughter. Joe ran into the room, at first smiling (as best as his perpetually cross face could manage) on seeing his father, but upon seeing his sister, he too moved in. Together, the Farrell family held a crying Sienna. In her sadness, she did feel better for their combined warmth. Whatever else they were… they were a family again.

***

It was two days on from the Farrell family reunion.

"Well, you're alive anyway, despite your best efforts."

Brendan did not acknowledge this disembodied voice and stayed still in the bed. His eyes were barely open. He had not been awake that long and had little idea of where he was. He felt heavy, unable to move.

"I said you're alive, Bren Bren, ye thick! What are you going doing that for anyway?"

Brendan realised the voice was addressing him, though it

seemed a little slurred. Slowly, he turned his head to the man in a paramedic's uniform, looking down on him.

"There he is! What were you in for that had you doing yourself a mischief like that, anyhow? Fuck it, I thought you were meant to be the good one."

"Taft..." Brendan's voice was worn, near breaking.

The paramedic, sensing his need, walked over to the water cooler and filled a small plastic cup, which he leaned gently into Brendan's mouth. He took the smallest of sips; it was so very cold. The man's left eye did seem a little lower than his right and he wore a half grin, though he was completely bald now. "Why'd you do it, Brendan? Ya silly bugger! The guard said you were a homeless drunk these days. I didn't think you got the points for that in the Leaving Cert? Jesus, if it was an option, I would have went for that myself!"

Brendan felt so pathetic lying there, attached to numerous beeping machines, which kept him in existence. Looking up at this man that, if he was honest, he had always looked down on, he felt such shame.

"Taft... I'm sorry."

"Alright champ, relax, what happened wasn't your fault, well, not really. It was a bit but to be fair, it was probably me old man's a little bit more, considering he did all the batterin.'"

Freddie walked to the other side of the room and dragged a chair across to Brendan's bed. "For the most part, Brendan, you were a good friend, and we all make mistakes. In a weird way, if that night with the old cunt hadn't happened, I'd probably have ended up the homeless, drunk one." Freddie Taft looked aimlessly across Brendan's feet.

"I shouldn't have brought you there... I shouldn't have broken in... I should have done something," Brendan murmured quietly, so quietly that, for a moment, Freddie wondered if he was addressing him at all.

"It's a long time ago, Brendan, water under the bridge. I've a home in Lucan of all places, a wife, though I'm not sure if that's a plus, and a little boy. I have a good job, even if it means I have to deal with the bottom feeders like yourself." Freddie smiled at the highly bandaged man. "If anything, it sounds to me you need to take responsibility for yourself. How are Mr and Mrs Freeman? Where were they during your rockstar-like fall? Oh Jesus, they're not dead, are they?" Freddie, for a moment, thought he had just put his foot in it.

"No, well, I don't know, I haven't spoken to them in some time," Brendan listlessly replied.

"Well that seems like the first step, get some support, pal. No one can do this sort of thing on their own."

"What sort of thing?" Brendan's eyes opened a little.

"Get back on your feet, get a job, stop the drinking, you know, generally, stop making a cunt of yourself, you dopey prick." Again, Taft smiled.

A nurse walked into the room to dress Brendan's wounds. Freddie, sensing he was an intrusion (the nurse was bad at hiding it), rose to leave. "Besides, Bren Bren, you're fucking useless at this suicide lark, may as well give living another go."

Brendan smiled and slowly waved at his old friend, as the paramedic left the room.

Brendan sat in silence as the nurse turned on the small box television. She had been following the news throughout her rounds and now, as she was dressing Brendan's wounds, she wanted to catch the end of the bulletin. The ads were still on so she continued with her work without distraction.

"You know Freddie?" she asked, not raising her eyes, and continuing to stare directly at the wound.

"He's an old friend," Brendan weakly replied.

"He saved your life, that man. When you came in first, a couple of days ago, you were a right mess. How he was able to seal that wound in your left wrist so quickly I will never know. You may not feel like it now but you're going to live, Mr Freeman. Though if you were only marginally more accurate with the cut on your right arm and hit your mark, we certainly would not be having this conversation, Freddie or not."

Brendan was only half listening.

"Now you don't go undoing Freddie's handywork, all right?" The question was rhetorical, or at least it was treated as such by Brendan, who remained silent. The nurse continued. "Is there anyone we can call? Inform them that you are here?"

Brendan looked at her for a moment with his mouth slightly ajar. The news came back on and the nurse momentarily silenced him before he could speak.

In front of the camera was an unfamiliar reporter standing outside Clementine Lane Flats.

"The raid took place in the early hours of this morning. Large quantities of crack cocaine were found on the premises. Three men were arrested at the scene." An image of three men with their hands over their faces was beamed, one of them wearing a grey fleece. "A dusting of the flat complex found additional trace amounts of crack cocaine that was spliced with rat poison. The Garda have since confirmed that this same contaminated substance, in the exact specific ratios, was found in the system of Mr Peter Williams and was believed to be directly the cause of his death. According to intel received by Garda officers, operating in the area, Mr Williams was part of an ongoing drugs feud, with the suspects arrested today. It is likely that this substance was given to Mr Williams in a deliberate attempt to silence him and prevent him from exposing their operation. Though the Garda are yet to press charges, sources have indicated that one of the suspects has already confessed to their part in the murder of Mr Peter Williams and its subsequent cover up."

A vignette played of Quinlan and Gibbons' hostile non-PC-compliant superior congratulating his officers. In the same vignette, he heavily implied that it was his encouragement to pursue all avenues of investigation that led to the arrests.

"I guess… I'm off the hook," Brendan whispered to himself.

"I'm sorry?" The nurse looked at him, puzzled.

"I said yes, yes, I would like to give you someone's number, if you don't mind."

33.

The Ides of March

"INTO YOUR HANDS, FATHER OF MERCIES, WE COMMEND OUR brother in the sure and certain hope that, together with all who have died in Christ, he will rise with him on the last day. Eternal rest grant unto him, O Lord. And let perpetual light shine upon him. May he rest in peace."

It was a bright and sunny 15th of March in Mount Jerome Cemetery. A small gathering from Clementine Lane gathered over the open pit, with its bright green canvas lightly covering the beautifully varnished coffin that had just been lowered into it. Fr Matthew was busy haphazardly sprinkling holy water, splashing Sienna who stood beside her mother. She moved to wipe it from her face, prompting her mother to clip her on the ear for what she assumed was being disrespectful.

Phyllis smiled at her daughter. Truth be told, she was still feeling guilty that she hadn't noticed Sienna's concussion that Tuesday over a month ago. Still, the doctor was right, teenagers are resilient, and Sienna had made a complete recovery… Well, maybe her brain was one or two memories and the ability to do long division lighter; it was a bad knock after all .

There were a lot of tears and snivelling in the small assembly. He was young enough in the end, not old enough certainly for a soil bed. It was true that he was a well-loved man, which if he could see this combined outpouring of grief and he might, it would have made him very happy.

Terry, out of respect, had corralled the small group from the Lane to attend the service. It was a show of communal support. Phyllis even gave Marion and Hope time off to attend, though their connection to the man in the box was practically non-existent. Leanne was perturbed at her lack of an invite, but Phyllis was resolute she stay behind in the crèche. Still Terry felt it was important that there was good numbers present, even if they were somewhat contrived. The presence of Fr Matthew was also somewhat contrived, but a friendship had been struck and it was felt important he be there for the final committal.

Mick looked an odd shape in a suit. It was true that he hadn't worn one since his own father's funeral; come to think of it, it was probably the same suit. Marion had dyed her hair a deep crimson red, stating that purple was for auldones, though truth be told, this red was probably more for young ones, and subsequently she looked suitably aged.

Sophisticatedly attired in a black and white blouse that screamed 60s chic, Hope was the only one of the Clementine Lane contingent who was capable of following the rituals of the ceremony. The level of spiritualism of the others from the lane could be summed up by the phrase "share this post if you want God to bless you and your family".

Perhaps this was a harsh summation. The people of Clementine practised something of an odd mix that was entirely bespoke to them. They mixed Catholicism, with their tacit worship of Christ and Mary, with Voodoo, insofar as they treated saints not unlike Haitian Loas, particularly St Anthony who must be paid to find lost things, and they certainly were not unlike the Shinto faith in how they prayed to their grannies and granddads for advice and good fortune. Icons of dust-covered Sacred Hearts adorned their walls, and were shown the same reverence as discoloured plastic portraits of St Anthony and worn black and white photos of antecedents long since passed. To call them "Roman Catholic" was misleading; they were "Irish Orthodox", a belief more fluid and, perhaps, more compassionate.

It was this compassion that had brought them to the small ceremony. Not one of them ever met Raphael "Ray" Maguire but Terry and Mick organised them for the sake of his son, and their friend, Conor. A young man, standing by his mother, with his long hair tied in a ponytail. Eyes corroded red from tears he refused to release, following an ancient and outdated concept of masculinity. His digital friends had finally found their physical form too. Their indecision had meant that none of them visited Conor until after his father's demise. Things were just too busy at the moment and they had rents to pay. It wasn't their fault really. Life is harder on the young now. They are funnelled to only see their immediate reality, the next pay cheque to pay the next bill. There was simply no time for the altruism their parents invested in those around them. This reality will, of course, place pressure on them at some point in the future too. After all, not one of them could say that they made the time, and what happened to Conor would surely happen to each of them.

He politely greeted them after the church service and they made the mildest of jokes with him and shared the softest of memories of his father. It helped, though he did not know that at the time. In the future, when he would think back, he would then remember them. For now Conor was touched simply by the presence of this small group from Clementine Lane. He knew now that he had made a home. There are many dwellings that people call "home", but really the concept is reserved for the nods on the street, the annoying "stop to talks" when you are on your way somewhere, the sneaky midweek pints in pubs where people share a joke about the one who is absent. These minute and seemingly insignificant interactions are "home". The currency they are bought with isn't something as crass as money, but something more valuable, time. Conor may be in pain now but he had built himself a future, if only by accident. He would be all right in the end.

The small party moved towards the gates of the cemetery. Some among them pointed to plots where, on previous occasions, they had similarly watched a priest commit a fresh convert to the soil. Mick and Terry would follow the Maguires back to their home for drinks and sandwiches. The rest of the mourners from Clementine Lane had to return to work. For some this was a happier prospect than for others. Marion was complaining to Hope about her husband, Mick, "milking it", out of resentment of having to return to a noisy crèche. Phyllis was going to drop Sienna back to the school, but first she would have to make a minor detour, to drop Shane to Cartigan's. Truly it would be a happy ending for Shane, if not only had he restored his marriage, but also could maintain his frequent visits to the pub. Sadly, this isn't fantasy.

Phyllis drove her husband, her daughter and the two ladies back through the small warren of houses that made up the historic and beautiful Liberties. Above them, election posters climbed like ivy up every streetlight and power line. Posters with colourful acronyms and symbols, icons of the island of Ireland, flashy stars, green harps, black fists, and red roses. The car parked outside St Luke's Church, where Shane alighted and made his way across the road to Cartigan's pub. Outside the bar, half torn by local youths, and hanging somewhat loosely as if put up by two non-mechanically minded arts students, was a poster with a bright red rose reading "Votáil No 1. Siobhan Kearns – Labour Party, for a progressive future".

Shane entered the familiar lounge to a smiling Vinnie Cartigan.

"Beautiful out there, Shane, maybe it's a good omen, maybe we will get a good government next, am I right? Am I right?" Vinnie smiled, peering over his glasses.

Shane stepped behind the bar and took off his jacket, revealing a black short sleeved shirt, with "Cartigan's" neatly emblazoned in gold above the left breast. Vincent had never thought of a uniform before, but Hugh was right; now that he had staff, it was only fitting they would be suitably attired for the day's work ahead. "Sure look, Vinnie, as you often heard in here, we'll have something similar."

In shuffled Arthur, and sat at his usual spot. Fr Matthew would be along shortly after he had said his goodbyes to the Maguire family and tried yet again to encourage Conor to attend his Sunday mass. Strangely, Conor was not as hostile to the idea as he was before. Maybe he would be there, who knew?

"Give me a whiskey, Shane, I'm celebrating!"

"Sure enough, Arthur, I take it this is drug centre related?" Shane made it a habit of dropping drinks to the table, though Vinnie did not really approve of the practice in case it would become expected of him. Nonetheless, it made it easier for Shane to share a joke or a story with the customer, and it was a clever tactic. The locals were less likely to mock him for his new vocation, when treated so well.

"Ehhh... it is indeed, Shane, it is indeed, the planning has been rejected for the centre. Too small apparently, saw it on the news this morning. Some report was leaked and the whole thing has become something of a political football. Ehhh... knock on the telly there, you'll catch it on the 3 o'clock bulletin."

Shane picked up the remote controller and obliged the elder gentleman. Their timing was impeccable; stood in front of a Dáil Eireann was Donal McGlynn in a navy suit and with microphone in hand, trying vainly to hide the rising smirk on his face. "Labour Leader Michael Norton has condemned Mr Eamon Hawkins for the design of the rejected residential rehabilitation centre, amid rising calls from all the opposition parties that a committee be formed to investigate the previous centres built by the Rebuild charity, and to open a tribunal into the dealings of its former CEO with the Council. This scandal is gaining traction with the public who are outraged that people in rehabilitation would be housed in such subpar conditions. The embattled administration, in a bid to quell the controversy, promised that if re-elected it would…"

Shane knew that a good barman should avoid politics but a part of him couldn't help feeling a little sorry. "So where will those poor addicts go now?"

Arthur's response was terse. "Somewhere else."

Three doors down the street from Cartigan's pub, in a second-floor apartment, halfway through a large tub of triple chocolate ice cream, and sitting in a semi opened kimono that exposed a rather large belly, sat Frank Cantwell. There was a large glass of white wine on the coffee table in front of the telly. The sunlight reflecting through his blinds sparkled on the small white hairs that boldly protruded from his unshaven face. He was watching a recording of the *Political Questions* show, in which he appeared and so valiantly defended the rights of those in addiction. The applause he received from the crowd still pushed the grey hairs vertically up along his arms. What a difference a month made, one sole month; he had been on top of the world, and now it felt like there was no bottom.

Frank shuddered when he thought back to that conversation with head office. Norton didn't even have the courage to say it to his face. Instead, he was put onto one of his suited goons. It was a simple phone conversation from Frank's perspective, a request for more canvassers. After all, there was an election to fight. "I'm sorry to be the one to tell you this, Frank, but the party feels your proximity to that centre places you in an untenable position going forward. The party executive feels this is only the top end of an iceberg. It would be best for everyone if you moved aside and let someone untainted by this scandal step forward, for the good of the party. I know a committed party man such as you understands… Please, Frank stop crying, it serves no good for anyone, you should have known the Labour Party would never stand for corruption."

Of course, this last uncomfortably made plea went unheard, as Frank's crying broke into a high pitched barely recognisable tirade of curse words. Eventually the party representative was simply forced to hang up. There would be no move to Donnybrook, or Killiney; hell, not even Blackrock, with its students from the country.

There was a knock on Frank's door. He ignored it. It was persistent though and after a while he knew that it would be inevitable that he would have to rise to answer it. Cursing to himself he paused the show and rose to open the door to a fresh-faced young lady in her mid-twenties.

"Hi, my name's Donna, I just moved in here and I'm keen to get involved in the area. So I'm originally from Lucan, you'll be glad to know I'm Labour through and through just like yourself. I want to get involved in the local residents' association, you know, pull up the shirt sleeves and get involved. It must be tough for the people here to live in such dilapidation. I was looking at the flat complex around the corner and it certainly needs a lick of paint. Where's the Council when you need them, am I right? We need more activists in the area like ourselves. Anyway, my neighbour tells me you're head of the local residents' association for the block, so I guess you're the man to talk to! Sorry, I know I go on, my mother always says 'Donna, take a breath before you pass out!' So when's our next meeting?"

Frank belched, wearily he rubbed his right eye, and, in a strong Monaghan accent, said, "Fuck off!" before slamming the door and returning to his squalor. "Maybe my father was right," thought Frank lying on his couch, "maybe I should have stayed on the farm."

***

Eamon Hawkins hung up the phone. He slumped into his red

leather-back chair at his home office desk. His threats to sue the station had not been heeded this time. There would be no reassignment of Donal McGlynn to agriculture now. Quite the opposite, in fact. His story on the dealings of Mr Hawkins and his Rebuild charity were making the daily headlines. Made all the more impressive by the fact that there was a general election on! Donal McGlynn would have his choice of positions by the end of this affair; and Hawkins? Who would listen to that discredited slum landlord? He had no creditability; the charity sector was quick to close ranks and condemn his organisation. That same organisation, fighting for its very survival, was quick to remove Eamon from his CEO position. The former saviour of the marginalised now needed saving but was far too marginalised to get it from any quarter.

Eamon thought about leaving the country. This quagmire was not going away and all that business about a tribunal seemed unnecessarily messy. Those spineless weasels in the Council would not be long in selling him out, and of course, there would be the outcries for his head. While it was entirely unlikely that he would ever see the inside of a jail, tribunals were seldom about practically serving justice, they were more about creating a pale illustration of it. Still though, they were expensive, and the idea of being vilified for the next several years as the news coverage lurched from one shocking revelation to the next did not appeal to him. The fall from white knight to public pariah would be too much of a shock for his system.

Naturally, his wife would no doubt kick up terribly when he broached the subject of emigration, but still so what, she kicked up terribly a lot anyway. The real question was where to go? Extradition accords would have to be a consideration, just in case. He would have liked to head somewhere hot, but then Maire would more than likely complain; she always hated the heat.

While looking out at a chestnut tree that stood beautiful and radiant in the March sun, he could see an envelope on the periphery of his vision. It was unsealed and simply read "Eamon" in his wife's handwriting, placed on the side of his desk, so as to not be immediately obvious. He picked it up and opened it.

Dear Eamon,

It is with great sadness that I write these words. Tears are dripping down my cheeks in such terrible torrents that they flood my vision, my love for you is still so very strong. Yet I know I have to, I know I must do what is right for our children. We cannot hope for them to have a future while linked with the name "Hawkins". The tenacity of the media will see them hounded, as they are now hounding you. I must do what is right for them and boldly continue on, without you. I know these words will be devastating to you and it fills me with a deep shame that I now must leave you at this the moment of your greatest need, but I also know that in the fullness of time, you will realise that what I have done is actually brave, for our children.

I have moved to my sister's place in Waterford. Please don't try to contact me. The pain would be too great for both of us.

Maire

Eamon's eyebrow raised more than a little reading these words. Several thoughts entered his mind. One: if she had been crying so much, then truly it was remarkable that the paper she had written this note on was completely unstained. Two: their two sons were aged 29 and 31. Were these the children she was referring to? Surely there wouldn't be a custody case! And three: for 34 years of marriage, it did not seem unreasonable to him that his separation letter should be a little longer than a paragraph. As Eamon pondered these thoughts, he picked up a frame on his desk. In it, he stared at a black and white photo of a lady; she had a curious birthmark over her eye in the shape of a snapdragon flower that aimed towards her nose. He made one further realisation. "Well, Gran, all things considered, it's not all bad news."

Epilogue

P RE-EMPTIVE, ROUGHLY COLOURED ST PATRICK'S DAY PICTURES littered the walls of the youth project in the small convent chapel. It was closed now, as evening time had come and relative darkness had descended on the lane. Outside, nestled warmly on his ledge, the crow sat thinking it was time to return to Picardy. His breed was not known to be migratory. The little French crow was just the restless traveller type. Enough time had passed and he had begun to miss home. Besides it was well into March and this island had warmed little since winter. "Baise ça!" thought the crow. It would at least be warmer back home. Thinking there was no time like the present, he spread his wings and hopped once, then twice, before finally, once more off the ledge and into flight.

The little bird flew low over the lane, spying a little scrawny female talking with her three friends and a little boy, who looked at the bird as if he might throw a rock at him. Sienna and her mother had spent that day shopping. Though truthfully, her mother seemed to enjoy it more. The shopping, that is. For Sienna, it was a chance to chat; and to be fair to her mother, she listened. Sienna felt so much lighter than she had in some time. It had been a week since she visited Brendan, and he seemed in high spirits. His father seemed nice as well. Maybe they were both wrong about their parents.

Untrusting of that cross-looking boy, the crow rose suddenly. He climbed to the height of the flats. On the balconies below, he could hear shouts, calling people in for their dinner. There were also the mutterings of one Hugh Dempsey, telling Leanne that he had no idea that the thugs three doors up were drug dealers and it was lucky for them that he didn't. After all, he knew "people". Leanne of course, was not to know that the people Hugh "knew" were the drug dealers three doors up, and instead nodded with an impressed expression.

The crow flew on over the little cottages that formed the mouth of the lane. Phyllis was just locking her front door, while Marion stood waiting for her with crossed arms, complaining about the cold. It really wasn't that cold. They were heading out to meet Hope for a quiet drink around the corner. Phyllis was feeling a little guilty. Having met Brendan and his family, she had begun to regret the harshness of her words and her assumptions.

"They're not all bad, Marion," she said mid conversation, as she turned from the door to which Marion replied...

"No, just most of them."

The little crow cut across the houses and was now gliding over Cartigan's pub. Shane was beginning his shift. Fr Matthew and Arthur had just arrived there, having been joined by Delores. She enjoyed the efforts of cajoling that Fr Matthew employed to get her there, but truthfully, she had her coat half on when he first invited her. Terry and Mick were waiting at their usual table; Conor said he would join them later. They were half engaged in idle talk about what a lovely service the day before had been. Mick was eying the gambling machine in the corner and thinking about a game before Marion arrived.

The bird flew on and was now passing over the Liffey, as employees were leaving the city in their droves, only to return later that night as customers. Flying along the quays, he could see two brightly coloured humans lifting metal. Quinlan and Gibbons were assembling barricades for tomorrow's St Patrick's Day parade. Rather pedestrian stuff, compared to their experiences from just a few weeks ago. Nonetheless, someone had to do it and it might as well be them. Besides, why should they expect a promotion? They did receive more than a little help. They were happy, for what it was worth. Appropriately enough, their first date fell on St Valentine's Day. It was a clumsy affair, and more than a little awkward. That was just Paul Gibbons, but then that is broadly why she liked him in the first place. It was early days for these two, but so far, so good.

The crow was approaching Irishtown. He was not far from the Irish Sea, and above the home, for the last few years at least, of the Freeman family. Brendan Freeman was eating dinner with his folks. Things were getting better but things would move at a slow pace. There was warmth in the room and they were talking, even mildly teasing. From the crow's perspective all seemed well, as he turned and continued on his trajectory towards France.

Of course, the view of a crow, so loftily held in the sky, should be taken with as little worth as the little understanding he afforded it. Back down on the earth, as grim as it could be, things were a little different. The truth was, the family had a lot of history to deal with and Brendan had far more than a few problems that would not just simply vanish. In the future, there would be arguments, there would be relapses and it would be hard for all concerned. Though it would be a lot easier than it was, for everyone had, finally, understood the value of everyone else.

This is not a happy ending. Unfortunately, life doesn't have those; or bad ones either, only indifferent ones. Life is a process, with good and with bad. At the very least though, the recovery could begin and they had each other. While everything now was rosy, even picturesque, there would be difficulties in the future. Sienna would still have to cope with her anxiety but at least now she would have a mother who would listen to her. Shane would become a little too accustomed to his barman job and delay his pursuit of a qualification. Academics are intimidating to those not used to them. Conor would undergo a long bereavement process and even right now, in a pub somewhere, they are discussing what will become of the Clementine Lane warehouse.

Perhaps, something worse? None of these issues have fantastical and concise solutions. They, too, are the processes of life, but the small inner-city community of Clementine Lane was somewhat closer for their experiences. They would face these problems together.

Post Script

"IT'S A FUCKING DISGRACE!"
The agitated small group of twenty-three neighbours sat in silent agreement.

"We're always a dumping ground for these Council arseholes!" Terry continued.

A year had been and gone since the last controversial proposal, but the new planning was equally as disagreeable. The residents' committee fumed at the proposal. Their anger continued right until 10 o'clock, when it was agreed that they would retire to Cartigan's pub to fume some more. As the last light was turned off in the chapel, darkness reclaimed the stage. There, after a few moments of charged silence, the balcony planks gradually creaked as slow steps moved towards the spiral staircase. A form scarcely distinguishable from the darkness made their way down the stairs. The portly, unseen twenty-fourth had not entered with the group, the group were not aware that they were there. But there they were.

Glossary

Bodhrán	Small Irish drum played with the hand
Culchie	Derisory term meaning country folk, not dissimilar to a "redneck"
Da	Daddy or Father
Dáil	Irish Parliament's lower house
Garda (Gardaí)	Irish Police Officer (plural), colloquially referred to as "guards"
Glendalough	Area in Wicklow renowned for its monastery and natural beauty
Gluaisteáin	Irish term for "Car"
Gouger	Someone who is not to be trusted
Knacker	Derogatory term meaning someone from the Traveller Community
Lacheycoes	Cowboy, carefree, somewhat reckless
Ma	Mammy or Mother
Mé Féiner	Irish for "Me, Myself" – Derisory term meaning someone who is quite selfish
Messer	Someone who messes things up, someone who does not take things seriously
NIMBYism	"Not In My Back Yard" – Derisory term meaning that people protest a social facility placement in the area only because they do not want it located near them
Scobie	Derisory term meaning working class not too dissimilar to the English "Chav"
Scutters	Diarrhoea
Seanbhean	Irish for "Old woman"
Spoofer	Derisory term meaning someone who tells lies to make themselves sound important
TD (Teachta Dáil)	Member of the Irish parliament's lower house
Waffler	Derisory term meaning someone who tells lies to make themselves sound important

Political References

Fáilers	Member of the Fianna Fáil Political Party
Blueshirts	Derogatory term for a member of the Fine Gael Political Party
Shinners	Member of the Sinn Féin Political Party
Trots	A member of a left-wing political party that follows the philosophy of Leon Trotsky

About the Author

Dublin native Eoghan Brunkard has worked on various inner city community development projects for the past 11 years. Qualified in social policy and research, Eoghan started his career providing enterprise and training advice to people in long term unemployment. From there he has supervised a labour activation scheme and several community led youth services. As a qualified social researcher, he has also worked on several policy papers and research projects for civil right advocacy bodies. When not walking with his unfortunate fiancée, Eoghan enjoys reading and writing novels that are critical of civil servants, as he is not a civil servant, and is somewhat jealous.

Eoghan's official motivation for writing this novel was to create a hopefully humorous parable for the importance of community in an increasingly isolating and individualising world. Eoghan's unofficial motivation was money and plaudits…

To contact the author email
Clementinelanepublishing@gmail.com

Printed in Great Britain
by Amazon